Margaret Thornton was born in Blackpool and has lived there all her life. She is a qualified teacher but has retired in order to concentrate on her writing. She has two children and five grandchildren. Her previous Blackpool sagas, *It's a Lovely Day Tomorrow*, *A Pair of Sparkling Eyes*, *How Happy We Shall Be*, *There's a Silver Lining*, *Forgive Our Foolish Ways*, *A Stick of Blackpool Rock*, *Wish Upon a Star* and *The Sound of her Laughter*, are also available from Headline and have been highly praised:

'A great read' *Best*

'A rollercoaster of emotions' *Newcastle upon Tyne Evening Chronicle*

'A delightful book; full of humour and warmth against an authentic war-time Blackpool when Pablo's sold ice-cream and troops from abroad drilled on the promenade' *Lancashire Mag*

'A Blackpool saga filled with heartache and happiness' *Western Morning News*

'Smashing' *Lancashire Evening Telegraph*

Looking At The Moon

Margaret Thornton

HEADLINE

First published in 1999
by HEADLINE BOOK PUBLISHING

First published in paperback in 2000
by HEADLINE BOOK PUBLISHING

10 9 8 7 6 5 4 3 2 1

ISBN 0 7472 6043 5

Typeset by Avon Dataset Ltd, Bidford-on-Avon, Warks

Printed and bound in Great Britain by
Mackays of Chatham, Chatham, Kent

HEADLINE BOOK PUBLISHING
A division of the Hodder Headline Group
338 Euston Road
London NW1 3BH

www.headline.co.uk
www.hodderheadline.com

For all my friends at Springfield Methodist Church, Bispham Townswomen's Guild, the Federation Choir, and Blackpool Writer's Circle.

My thanks to Patricia Butterworth, of the Writer's Circle, for her information about the Women's Land Army and her loan of WLA magazines.

Thanks, also, to my agent, Darley Anderson, and my new editor at Headline, Andi Sisodia.

And my love and thanks, once again, to my husband, John, for all his patience, encouragement and support.

Chapter 1

'Has the doctor nearly finished, miss? It's urgent, you see. It's my little brother, our Tony . . .'

Abigail Winters, hearing the anxious voice, looked up from the appointments book into the worried face of a young woman; aged seventeen or so, she guessed, a couple of years younger than herself.

Abigail smiled politely, in the way she had been instructed by her mother, but not too effusively. It was not 'the thing' to get too closely involved with patients, her mother had always maintained. That was what they were when all was said and done; patients of Dr Winters', Abigail's father, entitled to courtesy – after all, they were paying for his services – but not friendship. But from the look of the young woman on the other side of the polished mahogany table Abigail guessed that her mother would scarcely consider this one to be deserving of a polite smile. Her cotton dress was decidedly shabby and she was not even wearing a hat.

Abigail did remove the smile from her face, but only because the young woman seemed so distressed. Her big blue eyes were misted over with unshed tears. 'Dr Winters has almost finished,' Abigail told her. 'There's just one more patient for him to see.' She nodded towards the middle-aged lady in the far corner of the room. 'And then I'll give him your message. Your brother, you said? If you could just give me the details, please . . . Your name and address and what is wrong with the little boy . . .'

'I've already told you, it's our Tony.' The girl sounded irritated now as well as distressed. 'Tony Miller – that's his name – and me dad's Harold Miller. He's one of Dr Winters' patients. Me mam's dead worried about him; he's wheezing like mad an' he

1

can't get his breath. Go and ask him to come now, this minute, can't you, miss? It's an emergency, I've told you.'

'Very well, I'll see what I can do,' said Abigail, although she doubted that her father would be able to leave until he had finished his surgery. Mrs Peacock, his one remaining patient, a wealthy woman with an authoritative manner – as many of his clients were – would take a very dim view of it if he were to do so.

A bell sounded in the consulting room as Abigail rose, signalling that the doctor was ready for the next patient. 'Just a moment, Mrs Peacock.' She smiled vaguely in the direction of the woman, who had already risen to her feet. 'I just have to consult with my father.'

'If you think I'm going to cancel my appointment for the likes of that one then you can think again,' said Mrs Peacock, who had obviously been listening to the conversation. Indeed, it would have been impossible for her not to have heard the voice of the young woman, shrill at times with worry. 'It's far more important for me to see the doctor, right now. I won't wait. It's my heart, as you well know.'

'Very well, Mrs Peacock.' Abigail hastily retreated towards the surgery at the back of the house. If the truth were told she did not have any idea what was wrong with the woman, or with any of the patients. Her father, mainly at her mother's insistence, did not allow her to see any of the patients' records. She was there merely to book appointments, answer the telephone, keep the waiting room tidy ... and smile politely.

She knocked at the door, entering at her father's 'Come in.'

'Oh, I was expecting Mrs Peacock,' he said with a slight frown.

'There's an emergency, Father. There's a young woman here; she's very upset. She says can you come at once to see her brother ... Tony Miller. Apparently her father is a patient of yours.'

Dr Winters nodded. 'Oh yes, I know the family. Harold Miller, decent sort of chap, one of my panel patients. What's wrong with the boy? Did she say?'

'He's wheezing; can't get his breath.'

2

'Hmm . . . Could be whooping cough. There's a lot of it about. Tell her I'll be round as soon as possible. After I've seen Mrs Peacock, that is. You can send her in now, Abigail. Thank you.'

'Well, is he coming or isn't he?' the girl demanded as Abigail re-entered the room.

'Yes . . . just as soon as he's seen this lady.' Abigail nodded towards Mrs Peacock who was by now tapping her foot with impatience. 'You can go in now, Mrs Peacock.'

'And about time too!' The woman departed in a huff.

'If our Tony dies it'll be all your fault. I told you we wanted the doctor right away, never mind her.' The girl jerked her thumb in the direction of the door, then, to Abigail's consternation she burst into tears.

'Oh, come on now; it can't be as bad as that,' said Abigail. 'A few minutes won't make much difference, surely. My father says it sounds like whooping cough.'

'How would he know? He hasn't seen him, has he?' The girl looked at Abigail curiously. 'Your father, you said? Dr Winters, he's your dad?'

'Yes, that's right. Try not to worry, Miss . . . er, Miller. Tell your mother he'll be with you in less than half an hour. If you could just give me your address, please . . . It will be in the records, but it will save time if you tell me now.'

The girl gave the name of a street which led off Central Drive, about a mile or so from Whitegate Drive where Dr Winters' house and surgery were situated – a much less salubrious area than this tree-lined, prosperous part of Blackpool, an area which Abigail had never visited although she knew roughly where it was.

'He'd better 'urry up, that's all. Me mam's nearly out of her mind with worry. Not that you'd care . . .' Miss Miller almost ran out of the waiting room, angrily brushing the tears from her eyes as she went.

Abigail felt truly sorry for her. She wished she could have done more to help. Miss Miller was a pretty girl, blue-eyed and fair-haired and, despite the tears she had shed, there seemed to be an underlying toughness about her; a resilience and a self-reliance which Abigail knew that

3

she, with her sheltered upbringing, sadly lacked. As she tidied the magazines in the waiting room and threw out the wilting roses in the cut-glass vase she found herself, to her surprise, envying the girl she had just encountered. No, perhaps envying was too strong a word. How could she be envious of someone who was obviously so far below her on the social scale? Or so her mother would say. Or of someone who was so deeply troubled?

Abigail had no real worries. Her parents, particularly her mother, did their utmost to shield her from anything that might distress her unduly. There was the war, of course, which had been going on now for almost two years, but there was little that anyone could do about that. Except to do one's own little bit towards the War Effort and to go to church each Sunday and say one's prayers. Her mother was frequently involved in fund-raising events organised by the Church and the various committees on which she served. Abigail was encouraged to do likewise and in her spare time, of which she had an abundance, she knitted socks and mufflers for the gallant servicemen who were fighting to save their beloved country. It was a nice, genteel sort of thing for a girl of Abigail's class and upbringing to do.

But it was not enough. In her heart Abigail knew she was doing nothing of any significance – and also that she had no one about whom she could be really said to care. That was what had struck her so forcibly about that girl, Miss Miller: her heartfelt concern for her little brother . . . and that was what she had envied. How she wished there was someone about whom she could really care so much that she was moved to tears – a brother, maybe, in the army – but to her constant regret she was an only child. Or a boyfriend . . . Abigail found herself smiling grimly at that thought. There was little likelihood of that, the way her mother guarded her like a gaoler.

Some might think she was fortunate, Abigail supposed. If there was no one for her to worry about then there was no fear of her getting hurt. She cared about her parents, at least she honoured and respected them . . . but did that amount to loving them? She very much doubted it. She did not, for instance, regard them with the same fondness that she felt for her Aunt Bertha. If it wasn't for her aunt she felt she would go mad at times with the monotony, the sameness of her life.

Mrs Peacock swept out of the consulting room, along the passage and through the front door without so much as a glance in Abigail's direction. Dr Winters followed hard on her heels.

'Oh dear, I fear the lady's feathers were somewhat ruffled.' His beetling brows were drawn together in a frown, but Abigail detected a glint of amusement in the grey eyes, behind the rimless spectacles. Her father did possess a faint sense of humour, which was more than could be said for her mother. 'That's rather good, isn't it, Abbie, come to think of it?' He gave a dry chuckle. 'Peacock . . . feathers . . .'

Abigail smiled. Yes, she did feel a certain fondness for her father, although displays of affection had never been encouraged. She could not remember ever being cuddled or fussed over by either of her parents. 'Yes, very amusing, Father,' she replied, 'although the lady was not amused, was she?'

'Yes, well, Esme Peacock imagines more than half of what's wrong with her. She's as fit as a racehorse. But her little trips to the surgery keep her happy, and she doesn't mind what she pays. If you could slip round later, Abbie, with her pills, I would be obliged to you. She appreciates these little courtesies.'

As did most of Dr Winters' wealthy patients; and this was another of Abigail's meaningless – to her eyes – little jobs. Acting as messenger girl, taking out the various pills and potions, some of which were made up in her father's rather limited dispensary and some at the chemist's shop on the Drive, to the superior residences on and around Whitegate Drive and the Raikes Estate.

'You haven't forgotten the Miller child, have you, Father?' Abigail reminded him now.

'No, indeed. In fact I'm on my way right now.' He reached to the hallstand for his bowler hat and his light raincoat, although it was a mild summer evening. 'I have a bottle already made up in here.' He pointed to his black bag. 'I'm pretty sure it will turn out to be whooping cough, but I know Mrs Miller will be

5

worried. Nice little woman; she looks after them all very well, considering . . .'

'Considering what, Father?'

'Well . . . that there are so many of them. A big family. A lot of children.'

'How many?'

'Oh . . . five, six. I'm not quite sure. The girl that came here, she would be the eldest, I dare say. Anyway, I'd better be on my way. Tell your mother—'

'Tell me what?' Eva Winters appeared through the door of the sitting room, which was on the opposite side of the passage from the waiting room. She frowned when she saw her husband in his outdoor clothes. 'Oh, Cedric, you're not going out, surely? Bertha's cooking something special this evening. She managed to get some mutton chops. I was just going to see how she's getting on.'

Eva was not dressed for culinary chores, however, and Abigail knew that her mother would have no intention of doing any. Her pale blue silky rayon dress was one of her best afternoon frocks; she had recently returned from her weekly whist drive held by the Mothers' Union, ostensibly for the War Effort, but in fact an excuse for a get-together and a gossip. The blue of the material exactly matched the blue of her eyes. They looked a more icy blue than usual at the moment, expressing her annoyance, as they often did.

'I'm sorry, my dear, but I really must go. I'll try not to be long, but it is an emergency. I'll take the car as this patient lives in the Central Drive area.'

'Central Drive?' Eva Winters raised her eyebrows and her tone was scornful. 'Oh, Cedric, really! You surely can't mean it's one of those wretched panel patients? Honestly, some folk have no consideration, calling you out right on a mealtime. Of course I don't suppose civilised mealtimes mean much to them, people like that.'

'It's a respectable family, Eva.' There was a distinct frostiness in the doctor's tone. 'A hard-working father and a mother who does her best. They deserve my attention as much as the folk round here do. More, if I'm honest,' he added in an undertone. 'Anyway, I'll be home as soon as I can. Tell Bertha

6

to put my dinner in the oven if I'm not back.'

'Wasting our petrol allowance on panel patients,' Eva Winters muttered as her husband closed the door behind him. 'Whatever are things coming to?'

'You did tell him to be quick, Mother,' said Abigail, with unusual daring. It was very rarely that she challenged her mother. As a little girl she had never been allowed to 'give cheek', as her mother called it, or, indeed, to express any opinions of her own. Even now, at nineteen years of age, Abigail was regarded by her mother as little more than a child.

'Don't answer back,' Eva replied now, automatically. 'I wasn't asking for your opinion. Go and tidy the waiting room. That's what you're supposed to be doing, not standing here arguing with me. Then you can help your Aunt Bertha to set the table.'

'It is tidy, Mother. I've already done it.' Abigail was aware of the stubborn edge to her voice, but she didn't much care. She was feeling unusually defiant.

Eva glared at her before poking her face round the waiting-room door. 'Tidy? You call that tidy? Just look at the state of those cushions and chairback covers. Get them straightened, then run a duster over that table top. I could write my name in the dust. And be quick about it, too. I don't suppose Bertha's even started on the table. Dreadfully slow she is sometimes. I'll have to go and see . . . Really, it's too bad of your father. I was looking forward to that bit of mutton. If we wait for him it'll be ruined . . .' She was still grumbling away to herself as she went off to the kitchen.

If she thinks Aunt Bertha is slow then why doesn't she get her pinny on and help? thought Abigail. But never had she seen her mother in an apron of any sort; she would certainly never be seen in the floral wrap-around sort of pinafore that Bertha wore when she was in the kitchen, which was a goodly part of each day. No, all that Eva could do was offer advice, criticism and – occasionally – praise. The praise should, in truth, be more fulsome and given much more readily because Bertha was an excellent cook. Abbie, from odd snippets of information she had gleaned over the years, knew that her aunt at one time had been 'in service' in one of the big houses near the Lancashire

Yorkshire border, but she had left under a cloud. Just what sort of a cloud the girl had no idea. Her mother had always believed 'little pigs had big ears' and 'children should be seen and not heard', truisms she had trotted out time and again when Abbie was growing up. All Abbie knew was that her aunt – not really a true aunt, but a sort of second cousin of her mother – was the only person in this household or, indeed, anywhere, to whom she could talk with anything like freedom.

There was a delicious smell of cooking meat when Abbie, after retidying the already spick-and-span waiting room, entered the kitchen. Her aunt was prodding the cabbage, which was boiling on top of the stove, providing another, less appetising aroma. Abbie detested cabbage, but one was always being told 'Don't you know there's a war on?', and she knew she would have to eat every last scrap from her plate.

Aunt Bertha turned round and smiled. 'That's doing nicely. I'd best turn it down, though, or your mother'll say it's gone all mushy.'

'If it wasn't too soft it would be too hard,' Abbie observed. 'I don't know how you put up with her complaining, Aunt Bertha.' Bertha looked at her sharply. It was not often that the young woman openly criticised her mother.

'I try to please, Abigail. You know that. I've got a good home here, far better than a lot of women in my position have, and I'm very grateful.' What position? Abbie wanted to ask, but she didn't. Her aunt hurried on to say, 'The meat's done to a turn, thank goodness. They were a wee bit fatty, them mutton chops, but I've cut most of it off and I've been cooking 'em slowly in the oven with an onion. Would you believe, the greengrocer let me have a couple of onions as well as the carrots and cabbage, so it should be a nice dinner tonight.'

'It always is, Aunt Bertha.'

'Thank you, dear. It's good of you to say so.' Her aunt wiped the beads of perspiration from her brow and shoved back a hairpin that was escaping from her bun of iron-grey hair. 'If you could just . . . the potatoes, perhaps you could start to mash them . . .' She looked red-faced and flustered, and Abbie realised she had been standing there passing idle comments instead of helping.

'Oh, sorry, Auntie. Of course I'll do the potatoes, then I'll set the table.'

'Oh Lor . . . there's that an' all not started of yet. I don't know, love. I'm not so organised these days as I used to be. I don't know what's up with me, and that's a fact.'

You're getting older, Aunt Bertha, thought Abbie. And Mother is working you into the ground. She guessed that her aunt must be sixty or thereabouts, some ten years older than her mother and father, although Abbie was not sure how old they were either. Certainly not all that young to be her parents. 'You're tired with looking after us all, Auntie,' was what she said. 'And I'm not surprised. Now, do you want these potatoes turning out into a dish? Or shall I leave them in the pan?'

'Oh, a dish, I reckon. It'd be easier to put it all out on the plates, but your mother likes to have everything nice and served correctly. I'll see to it, love, if you could just set the table now . . .'

The house was not built in the most convenient manner. The kitchen opened off the small parlour, Bertha's private domain, where she spent most of her free time – such as it was – especially when Cedric and Eva had visitors and she knew she would not be welcome to sit with them. Bertha was a member of the family only as and when it suited Eva. You had to pass through the little parlour and into the passage to get to the dining room, and this was where Abbie went now.

She spread out one of the white damask tablecloths, laundered and starched to a pristine condition each Monday by her aunt, on top of the maroon chenille cover which always adorned the table. Then she put out the heavy silver cutlery, wooden table mats, rolled napkins in their silver rings, cruet and cut-glass tumblers for the water which they always drank with their meal, making sure that everything was aligned with mathematical precision. Her mother liked it that way and her Aunt Bertha, too, had instructed her that was the way the gentry – the class of people she had once worked for – insisted things should be. Abbie's father enjoyed a morsel of sauce or tomato ketchup with his meal at times, but that was placed discreetly on the sideboard, certainly never on the table. To put a jar or bottle with a label on to the table was 'common' according to Eva.

Her father wouldn't be here, though, this evening. Abbie had laid a place for him, but there would most likely be only the three of them. Bertha was allowed to dine with the family when there was no one else – or at least no one of any importance – present.

The three women had eaten their first course, and delicious it was, too – even Eva said so – and had almost finished the apple pie and custard before Dr Winters came back. His face was grim as he sat down, spreading his napkin on his knee, but Eva did not ask him about his patient.

'It's too bad of you, Cedric,' she grumbled. 'We've almost finished, and that mutton was really quite tasty, considering . . .'

'Considering what, Mother?' asked Abbie. She was surprised at how rebellious she was feeling tonight.

'Considering there's a war on, you stupid girl!' Eva snapped. 'We all have to learn to economise. I would have preferred a nice leg of lamb, I must admit, but times are hard for all of us. And don't answer back! That's twice I've had to tell you about giving cheek. You're getting above yourself just lately, Abigail.' She turned to her husband. 'Don't blame me if your dinner's ruined, Cedric. It's most likely burned to a cinder. Go and fetch it, would you, Bertha?'

'It'll be fine, Eva,' replied Cedric wearily. 'I haven't much appetite, anyway.'

'How was the little boy, Father?' asked Abbie.

'Really, Abigail, not at the dinner table,' her mother retorted. 'You know we never discuss your father's patients at mealtimes. I certainly don't want to hear all the gory details.'

Do you ever? thought Abbie. Eva took little interest in her husband's work at any time, although she could show a normal curiosity when it was her own affluent friends or acquaintances who were involved. Cedric, however, like any reputable doctor, was very circumspect when talking of his patients.

He ignored his wife now, speaking solely to Abbie. 'I'm afraid I may have been rather too late, my dear,' he said sadly.

'You mean . . . the little boy has died?'

'No . . . no, he has not died, but it turned out to be more than whooping cough. I'm afraid little Tony has diphtheria. That's why I have been so long. I had to arrange for an ambulance to get the poor little lad into the sanatorium.'

'Good gracious, that's dreadful, Father,' said Abbie. 'I'm so sorry. That girl, she kept urging me to be quick. I feel so responsible.'

'It wouldn't have made any difference, Abigail. I'm afraid they'd left it far too late before they called me. Anyway, I've done all I can.'

'Of course you have, Cedric.' Eva sounded a little less belligerent now. Diphtheria was a killer, everyone knew that. 'Whatever happens to the child it can't be your fault. This sort of family; they are so feckless. Hordes of children and they can't look after them properly. Why didn't the mother call you earlier if she knew the child was so ill?'

'It all comes down to finance, Eva.' Cedric's glance was frosty. 'They can't afford the doctor. They haven't enough money. It's as simple as that.'

'But I thought the father was one of your panel patients?' Panel patients were those who had free medical treatment, under a government scheme.

'So he is. But that doesn't include his wife and family . . . as you well know. Anyway, Mrs Miller won't have to worry about a fee this time. There won't be one.' He glared at his wife as if daring her to say anything. She didn't. Eva knew when it was expedient to be silent.

'But what about the hospital fees?' asked Abbie.

'We'll come to some arrangement.' Dr Winter shook his head dismissively before starting to eat his meal, but it was obvious he was not enjoying it.

Eva was not silent for long, and when she spoke again it was about a very different matter. She could very quickly clear her mind of any unpleasantness. 'Abigail, I would like you to come with me tomorrow afternoon to a function that is being held in town, in the lounge of R. H. O. Hills.' This was Blackpool's leading department store. 'It's for the "Spare a trinket" fund and I think it should be quite a nice occasion. I

11

feel I should be there, so you can come with me.'

'Spare a trinket? What does that mean?' asked Abbie.

'Well, it speaks for itself, doesn't it? They are asking you to spare a trinket – a brooch or bracelet, or a little piece of silver or china – and they are to be auctioned to raise money for a Benevolent Fund. I believe it's for the ATS this time, to provide some extra comforts for the women.' The ATS was the women's branch of the army, the Auxiliary Training Service. 'Anyway, it doesn't matter what it's for, does it? We all have to do our bit and it's organised by the Duchess of Northumberland so it must be a very worthwhile cause. And it's being opened by the Earl of Derby.' Eva nodded as if that august personage was an acquaintance of hers.

'Very well, Mother, I'll come,' said Abigail. She knew she had no choice.

The lounge of R. H. O. Hills was crowded, in the main with women, although there were a few elderly men here and there. Well-dressed, obviously well-heeled women. Fox furs and fur capes abounded even though the July afternoon was quite warm. Eva was wearing her fox fur stole over the blue marocain dress, and a tiny forward-tilted hat in a darker shade of blue, with an eye-veil, completed her outfit. Abigail, at her side, in a green and white cotton dress with an all-over pattern of daisies, and a green wide-brimmed felt hat of the type she had worn when she was at private school, felt like an overgrown school-girl. She was always aware of her height and of her tendency towards plumpness when she was next to her slim and elegant mother.

Abbie, at five foot seven or thereabouts, was a few inches taller than Eva. She guessed she had inherited her tallness and her build from her father. Her dark hair, too, although her father's was now almost white. She had no idea where her brown eyes had come from; Aunt Bertha said they must be a throwback. She had found herself wishing, as she'd looked at herself in the mirror earlier that afternoon, that she looked more like that girl Miss Miller (she didn't know her first name); small, blonde and blue-eyed, instead of brown-haired, brown-eyed and buxom. Aunt Bertha always said she was bonny, but

12

Abbie thought of herself as fat. She did spare a thought, though, for Miss Miller's brother, hoping there had been some improvement in the little boy's condition by now.

There was a display of gifts given by Her Majesty the Queen and other members of the Royal Family. The Queen had donated a china vase shaped like a shell and there were other items of silverware, ivory, tortoiseshell and china, all very fine and costly, but not, apparently, to be auctioned that day. The ladies of Blackpool and the Fylde had been generous, too. There were a number of glittering brooches and necklaces, though none of them, Abbie guessed, would consist of real diamonds, rubies or emeralds; quite fair imitations, though. There were silver-topped scent bottles and hair tidies, dressing-table sets, cut-glass bowls, china figurines, brass candlesticks, photograph frames . . . The whole resembled a very superior bric-à-brac stall at a church bazaar.

Abbie had been undecided what she should donate. Whatever she chose she felt it would be considered wrong. She would not dare to part with any of the gifts her parents had given her. She had to admit they had never been ungenerous with regard to material possessions, but she would have preferred them to show their love for her in a more human way. And she would not give away any of Aunt Bertha's well-chosen little presents. On the other hand, if she gave something of too little value her mother would accuse her of being mean. In the end she had opted for a leatherette writing case which had been a present from her Aunt Edith. She had another, far superior, one which her parents had given her, and as Edith was a not very favourite sister of her mother the choice had gone unquestioned. Eva had donated a silver candlestick which Abbie had always considered quite hideous, and she guessed her mother thought so, too.

Eva seemed far more concerned about what she should buy, her eyes scanning the various items with an avaricious gleam. Finally she decided to bid for, and was successful in acquiring, a china shepherdess by Royal Worcester. Abbie gasped inwardly at the price her mother paid for it. What was it she had said, only yesterday? 'We all have to learn to economise'? There was little evidence of that with Eva, or with any of the women

13

present at R. H. O. Hills that afternoon.

'It's all in a good cause,' remarked Eva, smiling complacently at her daughter now she had got what she wanted. 'What about you, dear? What are you going to buy? There must be something you would like.'

Abbie did have some money of her own to spend; poverty was not one of her problems. Her father paid her quite well for the assistance she gave him. There was nothing, however, amongst the splendid array of objects that she had set her heart on in the way her mother had desired that piece of china. 'Oh, I don't know, Mother,' she said. 'There's nothing I need, is there?'

'Nonsense!' retorted Eva. 'You must buy something or it will look very mean. What about that brooch shaped like a treble clef? I saw you looking at it.'

'Yes, that's quite pretty, but I feel rather nervous of shouting out in front of all these people.'

'Nonsense!' said Eva again. But it was Eva who, in the end, did the bidding for her. Abbie was pleased with the diamanté brooch she ultimately secured. The symbol it displayed would be an indication of her interest in music, and it should look very nice on her tweed coat or on a dark dress. The dresses she wore were almost always of a dark hue, the most suitable wear, her mother insisted, for a doctor's receptionist.

On the whole it was a very pleasant afternoon, although Eva was inclined to ignore their real reason for being there: to raise money for the Benevolent Fund of the ATS. The chief Commander of the East Lancashire Regiment, a woman whose age was difficult to define – brusque, efficient and somewhat manly in appearance, though it could have been the uniform that made her seem so – gave a stirring talk in which Eva appeared to be taking very little interest. The woman said how much the girls had already benefited from the scheme, especially those who were convalescing, for one reason or another, in army hospitals.

'We are honest to goodness soldiers and proud of it,' she proclaimed in her strident tones, 'but we are still women when all is said and done.' Funny to hear women spoken of as soldiers, thought Abbie, but here was a person who obviously thought that women were the equal of men any day. Another hundred thousand auxiliaries were needed, she said, and there would be the same chance of promotion, should they prove worthy, for all of them.

Girls such as me, thought Abbie, glancing down at her rather large feet encased in sturdy brown sandals and her thickset body, so unfashionably clad in the green and white summery cotton. How much more suited her stature would be to a uniform such as this woman was wearing. But whatever was she thinking of? Abigail Winters in the ATS – or the WAAF or WRNS for that matter? Her mother would throw a fit at the very idea.

She was determined to mention the matter, however, as soon as they arrived home. Not that she was seriously considering joining the ATS. She was only nineteen, under the age of consent, and she knew her parents would scotch the idea right away. She had no desire, if she were honest with herself, to join any of the women's services. The Commander had been very persuasive, but Abbie found herself quaking at the thought. And that reaction, she knew, was the fault of her parents. They had always overprotected her and, at least as far as her mother was concerned, repressed and overruled her to the extent that she was now afraid of branching out on her own. No, maybe not the ATS, but she knew she had to do something; something that was worthwhile to the War Effort, other than arranging flowers and running piddling little errands for her father.

Some of the girls she knew, acquaintances rather than friends – Abbie did not have any close friends – had gone to work at the Vickers-Armstrong aircraft factory. Surely her mother could not object to her doing that. It would not involve living away from home. The factory was not all that far away, at Squires Gate, with one of the branches of it on the upper floors of the Talbot Road bus station. She would be able to travel there easily each day.

'What a ridiculous idea!' scoffed her mother when she plucked up courage to suggest it. 'War work is not for girls such as you, Abigail. Besides, you have a job here with your father.'

'Hardly one of national importance, Mother; running errands and tidying the waiting room.'

'Whatever is the matter with you, Abigail? You seem so dissatisfied lately, and so contrary. What you do here is very useful. Whatever would your father do if you were to walk out on him? Not that there's any likelihood of that. You're staying here, my girl.'

'You could do my job, Mother, quite easily.'

'What! What on earth are thinking about? Don't you realise I've a home to run and meetings to attend and all sorts of fund-raising functions to arrange? I don't want to hear any more of this nonsense. Now – off you go and see if your Aunt Bertha wants any help in the kitchen.'

Abigail stood her ground. 'Girls of my age are doing all sorts of jobs now, jobs that men used to do before the war started, before they were called up. That woman said so this afternoon. You heard her, Mother.' She knew full well that her mother had not been listening.

Eva gave an exasperated tut. 'That woman! More like a carthorse than a woman!'

'Girls of my age are joining the ATS,' Abbie went on boldly. 'They need thousands and thousands more recruits.' A spark of devilment arose in her such as she had not experienced before. She knew her mother would be furious, and she didn't really mean what she was saying, but she might as well be hanged for a sheep as a lamb, as the saying went. She looked her mother straight in the eyes. 'I might even join up . . .'

She got no further. 'What!' Eva's bellow could have been heard out in the drive.

'. . . myself,' Abbie added in a more subdued tone.

'Never in a thousand years! I've never heard such ridiculous nonsense! Just wait till your father hears what you've been saying.' Eva's outburst had coincided with the sound of the front door opening and Dr Winters now entered the sitting room. 'Cedric, you're just in time. You've never heard such nonsense as your daughter's been talking. Wait till you hear. She's actually suggesting that—'

'Not now, Eva, please.' The doctor raised an admonitory hand before flopping down, in an unusually undignified manner, in an armchair. His face looked drawn and there was a defeated look in his eyes. 'I've just come from the sanatorium. I'm afraid little Tony Miller has died.'

Chapter 2

The sad news about the little boy drove all thoughts of rebellion from Abbie's mind, for the moment at least. She felt unusually disturbed by the news, considering she had not even known the child; but she kept thinking about that young woman whose name she still did not know, and how grieved she would be at her little brother's death. And the parents, too; how dreadful it must be to lose a child, to see him safely through babyhood, to watch him starting school, and then to have him snatched away from you at the age of six, which was how old Tony Miller had been.

Abbie's mother, however, did not seem to see it this way, although she may well have done so if it were her own child or one of her close friends', from her own class.

'I really can't understand why you are getting so worked up about it, Cedric,' she told her husband. 'Yes, it is very sad, I admit, but . . . well, that sort of family. It can't be the same for them as it would be for such as us. They have so many children. It stands to reason that they can't rear them all.'

'We're not living in the Dark Ages, Eva.' Dr Winters looked quite angry as well as distressed. 'We are nearly halfway through the twentieth century and children don't die in infancy so frequently as they used to. Forty years ago it was quite common to lose a child – often before its first birthday, but we've progressed somewhat since then, thank God. But not, it seems, as far as diphtheria is concerned.' He shook his head sadly. 'Immunisation helps, but in this case it didn't.'

'I don't suppose the woman had even bothered to have him done,' observed Eva complacently. She appeared more concerned with positioning the china figurine she had acquired that afternoon, moving it to the right of the carriage clock – the third spot it had been in since she brought it home an hour ago – than in the plight of one of her husband's less desirable patients.

'Then that is where you are wrong,' replied her husband. Abbie had seldom seen her father so worked up about anything. 'Mrs Miller is a very conscientious mother. I can tell that from the little I know of her, although I have told you before, they didn't call on me very much. They couldn't afford to. But I find your attitude extremely callous, Eva. You seem to be suggesting that parents with large families love their children less. I have certainly never found it to be so, at least in the households I have visited.'

'Which does not amount to very many, Cedric,' Eva replied with an arch little smile. 'You know as well as I do that most of your clientele is in this area. Anyway, how many times have you told me that doctors should not get emotionally involved with their patients? It seems to me that you are doing just that, and for the life of me I can't understand why. I told you yesterday, whatever happened to the child you could not be held responsible.'

'I know that and I think the Millers know it, too, but I can't help the way I feel for them. I care, Eva. Yes . . . maybe more than I usually do, maybe more than it is wise to, but . . .' He gave a slight shrug. 'That's the way it is.' He looked unsmilingly at his wife, almost, Abbie thought, as though he were seeing her, assessing her, for the first time, and not really liking what he saw. Both her parents seemed to have forgotten her existence. She had never known her father to reprimand her mother before when she, Abbie, was present.

'Maybe I am waking up to reality,' he went on, 'realising that there are others – thousands of others, here, in this town – who are not in the comfortable position that we are.' He glanced round, his eyes taking in the deep-piled green carpet, the matching velvet curtains, the occasional tables, the cut glass and silverware, his eyes finally resting on the new china figure. His eyes narrowed and he frowned slightly as he looked back again at Eva.

'Do you realise, Eva, that there are women, any number of them, who are suffering from all kinds of ailments – anaemia, backaches, headaches, rheumatism, prolapsed wombs . . .'

Eva gave a shudder of distaste. 'Really, Cedric, must you? And don't forget . . .' She cast a wary glance in Abbie's direction.

But Cedric continued as though he had not heard. '. . . varicose veins, decaying teeth, all manner of problems? Married women, most of them, worn out with looking after their families. And yet they never see a doctor. And do you know why?'

'Yes, yes, I know why,' Eva answered irritably. 'You keep telling me. Because they can't afford it.'

'Quite. They are still not entitled to free treatment even though their husbands are. It's a disgrace.'

'Hardly your fault, though, Cedric,' Eva replied. She was looking rather ill at ease. Abbie, too, was surprised. She was not used to hearing her father speak so vehemently. Always, before, he had taken a matter-of-fact attitude towards his patients, not uncaring, but certainly unemotional.

'No, as you say, Eva, not my fault. The fault of the government, if anybody's. Lloyd George's scheme didn't go nearly far enough.'

'But that's ages ago, Cedric. Before the last war, wasn't it?'

'Yes, and we haven't progressed much since then, at least not as far as these poor women are concerned.'

'God helps those who help themselves. That's what I always say.' Eva's eyes were still on the precious piece of china, so she missed the look of sadness that her husband cast at her.

'Many of them try to help themselves,' he replied. 'They try all kinds of remedies, Eva, many of them old wives' cures, but they are all they can afford. Camphorated oil, goose grease, brimstone and treacle to clear the bowels . . .'

'Cedric, please!'

'. . . but what they really need is free medical treatment from qualified persons, general practitioners such as me.'

'Good heavens, Cedric; you're beginning to sound like a socialist!'

'Then maybe I am, if socialism means caring about what happens to people. But changes are on the way. I've heard rumours that the government has great plans in mind for the future, but at the moment it is more concerned with winning the war.'

21

'Huh! Losing it more like.' Eva's tone was sarcastic and her husband turned on her.

'Don't talk like that! It's bad for morale. You know what we've been told. There is no possibility of defeat. None whatsoever.' His eyes strayed again to the china figurine. 'Anyway, you don't appear to be doing too badly, war or no war. There's not much that you go short of, even luxuries. That's new, isn't it?' He nodded pointedly in the direction of the mantelpiece.

'I paid a generous sum for that – very generous – towards the ATS Benevolent Fund,' Eva retorted. 'Besides, one has to try to cheer oneself up. The war news is very grim, despite what you say about no possibility of defeat.'

'Yes . . . I know.' Cedric gave a sigh. 'But we must not let ourselves resort to defeatist talk. Besides, we've been very fortunate here in Blackpool. Apart from those bombs on Seed Street last September we've escaped more or less scot free. People still have their problems, though, human problems, even in the midst of the war. Like the Millers. Eva . . .' He looked imploringly towards her. 'I do wish you would try to be a little more charitable towards people who are less fortunate. Try to put yourself in their position.'

'Charitable! Of course I'm charitable. I work for any amount of charities, the committees I am on . . .'

'Perhaps on a more . . . personal level, my dear?' Cedric's tone was much gentler now. 'I have a plan in mind that I would like to discuss with you. And Abigail as well.' He turned to his daughter for the first time. 'It's the Miller child dying that has forced me to think about it seriously, although I have had it in mind for some time.'

'Think about what?' Eva's voice was guarded.

'About starting a clinic – one day a week was what I had in mind to start with – for the wives and families of my panel patients.'

'But how would that be any different from the ordinary surgery?' asked Eva. 'They can come to the surgery, with or without an appointment, so what difference will it make? Anyway, as you've already told me, they can't afford it.'

'The difference, Eva, is that this clinic will be free.'

22

'Free? How can it be free? When people come to see the doctor they know they have to pay. Except for those panel patients, of course. Are you trying to say that you would treat these people for nothing?'

'Yes, why not? I can afford it. We can afford it, Eva. What does it amount to? A few rolls of bandage, a few bottles of medicine or pills and a little of my time. Not very much to me, but it would make a world of difference to some of these poor people.'

'It's a ridiculous idea, Cedric,' said Eva dismissively. 'Free medicine . . . and treatment? You wouldn't be allowed to do it. If the authorities heard about it they wouldn't like it. They would soon put a stop to it.'

'I very much doubt it. I won't be the first doctor who has waived a fee when the patient couldn't afford it, and this will be very little different from that. Maybe I will have to charge a nominal fee – very nominal – but these women must be encouraged to come, to seek advice instead of trying to cure themselves.'

'But there are clinics already for mothers and babies,' Eva protested. 'For women who are . . . you know what I mean.' She cast a wary glance in Abbie's direction.

'Pregnant women? Is that what you mean?' Dr Winters gave a dry smile. 'I shouldn't worry too much about Abigail. She's a big girl now, aren't you, my dear? I expect she can tell when a woman is expecting a baby. She has seen them coming into my surgery, haven't you, Abbie?'

'Er . . . yes, Father,' mumbled Abbie, amazed at the things her father was saying this afternoon. She had never heard the like. Indeed, she had seen pregnant women coming into the surgery, wearing heavy coats even on warm days, to disguise their bulges, as though they were something that must be kept secret.

It was still a complete mystery to Abigail how the baby got there in the first place. She knew it grew inside the woman's stomach, or, more correctly, the 'womb'. That was the word she had heard whispered when she was at school, by more knowing girls, and she had a vague idea that it was something to do with a man and a woman lying down together when they got married.

You couldn't have a baby unless you were married, at least you were not supposed to, and that was another mystery to her. She knew of a girl – at church, of all places! – who had done just that. Her mother and her whist drive cronies had whispered about it, but had stopped talking abruptly when Abbie appeared. How this girl – who had been sent away to live with an aunt in the country – had managed this feat without a husband Abbie did not know. Abbie had been a shy sort of girl at school, not given to giggling in corners about 'rude' things as some of the girls did.

'Yes, there are clinics of a sort,' her father was saying now, 'but for one reason or another some women are suspicious of them, and I must admit that some of them are not well run. Women resent what they consider to be outside interference, but I am sure those same women would come to see a doctor if there was one available where they did not have to pay. In a few years' time free treatment will be taken for granted – you'll see – so all I am doing is trying to speed things up a bit, in my own small way. And ... I would like Abigail to help me, in the surgery.'

'What! What on earth are you saying?' The cry came from Eva, not from Abbie. Abbie was still bemused at the surprising things her father was proposing. Help him? What did he mean? Did he mean for her actually to go into the surgery? Had she really heard him say that?

This was what her mother asked now, in tones of disbelief. 'Am I hearing you correctly, Cedric? Did you actually mean that Abigail is to go into the surgery, to assist with the *ailments* of ... these people? No, most certainly not! It's out of the question. Abigail is not a nurse nor would I ever want her to be. I only agreed to let her help you when she left school on the condition that she did not do anything ...' Eva paused, searching for a word.

'Unpleasant? Distasteful? Is that what you are trying to say?' asked Dr Winters, his bushy eyebrows raised as he looked keenly at his wife. 'Yes, Eva; things that doctors have to deal with are often far from pleasant, but you don't need to worry. I would not expect Abigail to deal with anything too nasty. No, what I had in mind was for her to help me in the dispensary. I do all

24

that myself at the moment, as you know. And to sort out the patients' record cards for me . . . another thing you have tried to shield her from,' he added pointedly.

'Time enough for Abigail to know about such things when she really has to,' replied Eva. 'It is not necessary to fill a young girl's head with gruesome details.'

'She's old enough now to know a little more of what goes on,' said Dr Winters, quite curtly. 'And there are times when an extra pair of hands would be useful to me in the surgery. To help with bandaging, or treating boils . . .' he ignored Eva's sharp indrawn breath, '. . . or with a nervous child, or a woman who is rather embarrassed. Some are, you know, even amongst the, er, lower orders.' Abbie noted his faint sarcasm and smiled to herself.

'But I think it is time we heard what Abigail has to say about it all. We have been talking about her as though she is not really here. What do you think about my suggestions, my dear? Would you be willing to help a little more?'

'More than willing, Father,' she replied eagerly. 'I would love to help in the dispensary. You could leave that to me entirely, once you have shown me what to do. And I don't mind helping in the surgery either. I'm not worried about . . . unpleasant things.' She did not look at her mother, addressing her remarks solely to the doctor.

If she were honest she was a little apprehensive. She had never had any desire to be a nurse, and she was a little squeamish at the idea of bleeding wounds or . . . boils, her father had mentioned. Lancing them, she supposed he meant, and she felt herself almost turning green at the thought. But it was what she had wanted, wasn't it? To feel she was doing something more worthwhile, although it still did not amount to much compared with what that ATS woman had been talking about this afternoon, enlisting in one of the services, or helping to make aeroplanes or tanks.

'It seems to me you have got it all cut and dried between you,' said Eva with a slight sniff. 'So it doesn't really matter what I think about it, though I still believe it's a ridiculous idea, pandering to these . . . impoverished people. The more you give to people like that the more they will want. Still . . .' she gave a condescending smile, 'I suppose it's better than Abigail joining the ATS, which is what she was talking about earlier.'

'You were?' Abbie's father looked at her with something akin to admiration.

'Not exactly, Father,' replied Abbie. She couldn't admit she had only said it to annoy her mother, something she was wanting to do more and more just recently. 'But the woman who spoke to us made me realise I was doing nothing useful. I was thinking I might volunteer to work at the aircraft factory, but now you've suggested I should help you . . .'

'It might be better if you worked here for the moment,' said her father. 'But the longer this war goes on, who knows what any of us might end up doing?'

'And who, may I ask, is going to be doing the rest of Abigail's work?' enquired Eva. 'Answering the phone and looking after the waiting room? It won't take care of itself, you know. And I like there to be somebody there most of the time.'

'I thought you could do that, my dear,' said Cedric, smiling brightly at his wife. He hurried on, not waiting for her reply. 'We can't expect Bertha to do any more. She's run off her feet already with the cooking and cleaning and the shopping. And please don't tell me you are too busy with your committees and your fund-raising. All that could be fitted in quite nicely around your work here. You are always telling me how we all have to "do our bit", are you not?

'And there is just one more thing you could do for me, Eva, if you would. The Miller family – I feel so concerned about them, and the mother works so hard looking after them all. I wondered if you could sort out a few clothes for them? Dresses and cardigans, all that sort of thing – you will know what would be useful. I know you've kept nearly everything, haven't you, from the time when Abigail was little, and, as it happens, nearly all the Miller children seem to be girls. There was poor little Tony, of course, the one who has just died, and there is one other boy, but I believe there are three more girls as well as the grown-up daughter who came here. And then Abbie can take them round for me, if she doesn't mind?'

'Yes, Father; of course,' replied Abbie.

Eva gave a brief nod, but said nothing at all. She knew when it was advisable to be silent, and she knew, too, when she had lost.

Abbie had suggested to her father that it might not be such a good idea to call on the Miller family during the next few days. That it would be better to wait until the next week, at least, as by that time the little boy's funeral would be over and the household settled down again to more normal living, if that were possible. Dr Winters had been of the same opinion, so it was some ten days later that Abbie set off, one warm July evening, for the little street which led off Central Drive. She was carrying a large holdall which contained a selection of clothes – skirts, jumpers, a dress or two, socks and underwear – all washed and pressed and neatly folded, which her mother had sorted out. It was Aunt Bertha, however, who had done all the washing and pressing; not that they had been dirty, just smelling a little musty and moth-bally with years of non-use.

Her mother had said very little about the clothes or Abbie's visit to the Miller household, or, indeed, about anything recently, performing her various duties in the house with a closed expression on her face. Maybe she was more communicative when she was with her friends outside of the house, but the sense of silent disapproval emanating from her in the home was almost palpable. Abbie felt that it boded ill and that before long somebody would have to suffer the backlash of her mother's resentment. Most likely her, Abbie.

She could not, in all honesty, see why her mother should be so resentful. After all, it was very little she was being asked to do: answer the door and the phone, look after the appointments book and see to the patients' queries. She guessed that her mother did not like taking orders in any shape or form and that she was piqued that her husband should have reproved her, however gently, in front of their daughter.

As for Abbie, she was enjoying her new work; being more closely involved with the patients was giving her a sense of purpose she had lacked before. She now wore a white coat-overall on top of her dark dress, which made her look, and feel, much more efficient. She was finding the work in the dispensary extremely interesting. She had had little idea, until now, of the various medicines her father prescribed. She was surprised to find, however, that for many disorders he prescribed the same remedy: ordinary aspirin. Abbie knew the patients could have bought the same thing, possibly more cheaply, over the chemist's counter, but she also knew that the more affluent patients felt that if they were paying more then it must be better and they regarded the doctor's prognostications almost as holy writ. To many people, indeed, the doctor was on a par with God.

Abbie learned, too, about the prescribing of medicine known as placebos for the many patients with imaginary ailments. Mrs Peacock was a case in point.

'But . . . is it honest, Father,' Abbie had asked, somewhat perplexed – she had always believed her father to be scrupulously honest in all his dealings – 'to expect people to pay for something that is worthless?'

'Not so, my dear,' he had replied. 'Not worthless. These medicines – coloured water, sugar-coated pills or whatever – are of considerable worth to the people involved. They believe in them, you see, like they believe in me. The medicines may have no physical effect, but the psychological effect is tremendous. You look dubious, but I can assure you it is true. I am only doing what all good doctors do, Abigail, trying to look after the mental state of my patients as well as the physical.'

There was a lot that Abbie was learning, not only about the practice, but about her father, too. She guessed that by starting the clinic, which was still just getting off the ground, he was attempting to redress the balance, to make amends for the sizeable fees he received from his wealthy patients by giving free, or almost free, treatment to the needy. She had felt closer to him this last week or so and was surprised at the things she was discovering. He was a good man – she had never doubted that – but she was realising how, in the past, he had allowed himself to be influenced, to a degree, by the superior attitude of his wife. Somehow, the death of Tony Miller had brought about a change in his way of thinking. Now he was acting, more and more, in the way his conscience told him was right. And her mother did not like this change of attitude.

Eva Winters was a person who wanted always to be in complete control, not only of her own life, but that of her husband, her daughter, her long-suffering cousin, anyone, indeed, who would kowtow to her. Now her authority was being opposed and Abbie knew that this would lead, sooner or later, to trouble. In spite of their recent closeness Abbie still remained, to a great extent, in awe of her father. Years and years of being subjugated to her parents' control could not easily be swept aside by his comparative friendliness during the last couple of weeks. But she knew her mother was jealous of their developing companionship.

Abbie was more than a little apprehensive as she approached the Millers' home. Would they regard her visit as an intrusion upon their grief, as interference, or as charity they were too proud to accept? Would the oldest girl still be holding her, Abbie, responsible for her little brother's death? Abbie could not forget the way the young woman had berated her, nor the frantic anxiety and fear in the girl's eyes. Or would she be received with courtesy and friendliness? Her father seemed to think that would be the case.

The street was not difficult to find, one of a number of rows of small terraced houses leading off Central Drive in the area known as Revoe. This street consisted, in the main, of well-cared-for little houses although there were, here and there, ones that were shabby with peeling paintwork, dirty windows and unwashed doorsteps. But these neglected houses only served to show up the cleanliness of their neighbours. The Miller home was one of several where not only had the doorstep and windowsill been washed and donkey-stoned, but the paving flags at the front of the house swilled down as well.

Abbie had passed a few children playing in the street with skipping ropes or whips and tops, and further along she could see a small group chalking on the flagstones in readiness for a game of hopscotch. She felt slightly envious. On Whitegate Drive, of course, where she lived, you could not play out in the street, it being one of the busy main thoroughfares leading out of the town, but children had played in the streets leading off it. Not Abbie, though. Such behaviour would not have been proper for a well-bred little girl.

She knocked on the door and it was opened in a few moments by the very girl she had, of all people, not wanted to see.

'Yes?' said the girl enquiringly, a half-smile of welcome on her face, which soon disappeared when she recognised the visitor. 'Oh . . . it's you. What do you want?'

'I've come . . . my father has asked me to come,' faltered Abigail. 'I've brought some clothes. My mother thought . . . I mean, we all thought . . . you might find them . . . useful.'

The girl continued to stare at her, her eyes narrowed, a look of dislike, if not hatred, on her pretty face.

'Who is it, Doreen?' A little woman, no bigger than the girl on the doorstep, appeared from a room at the back of the house.

'It's the doctor's daughter,' said Doreen curtly.

'Oh . . . oh, how do you do, miss?' The woman – Mrs Miller, Abbie assumed – quickly wiped her hands on her floral apron as she hurried down the short passage. 'I'm very pleased to meet you, Miss . . . Winters, isn't it? Do come in, miss.' She turned briefly to her daughter. 'How rude of you, Doreen, not to have asked the lady to come in. Whatever were you thinking of?'

'Why should I? Coming here like Lady Muck . . . and she couldn't even get her dad to come and look at our Tony.' She gave Abbie another baleful glance before turning on her heel and flouncing up the flight of stairs directly inside the front door.

'Doreen! How very rude!' Mrs Miller sounded shocked as well as angry. 'You haven't been brought up to behave like that. Come down here at once.' There was the sound of a door slamming upstairs and Mrs Miller turned in embarrassment to Abbie. 'Oh dear . . . I can't understand what's got into her, behaving like this. Well, I suppose I can, really. It's our Tony; she's been that upset. But whatever must you think of her, miss?'

'It's all right,' said Abbie, feeling very uncomfortable. 'I think I can understand how she must feel.' Rather belatedly she held out her hand. 'How do you do, Mrs Miller? I've called round to bring you a few clothes. We thought you might be able to make use of them for your girls. My father said he thought you had a few daughters?'

'Yes . . . yes, we have.' The woman seemed flustered by the act of shaking hands, and after touching Abbie's hand briefly she quickly pulled her own away. 'Do come in, Miss Winters. It's real kind of you to call, to think about us. The clothes will be ever so useful. Thank you very much. The girls are growing so fast . . .'

She led the way into a sizeable living room; not large compared with the rooms in Abbie's own home, but quite commodious considering the smallness of the house. A man was sitting in an armchair reading a newspaper and he looked up curiously as the two women entered the room.

'Harold, this is Miss Winters – you know, the doctor's daughter,' said his wife. 'She's brought some clothes for the girls. Isn't that kind of her?'

The man rose to his feet, holding out his hand. 'How d'you do, miss? I've seen you at the doctor's, haven't I? You look after the books an' all that, don't you?'

'How do you do, Mr Miller? Yes, that's right. I help my father. I remember seeing you there.' She didn't, but it would have been impolite to say she didn't remember him. He did not seem overawed, as his wife had been, by shaking hands and he welcomed her very courteously now.

'Very kind of you to come, Miss Winters. Do sit down, if you can find a chair. You have to take us as you find us here, but you're very welcome. Go and make the lady a cup of tea, Janey, there's a good lass.'

One of the two girls who were sitting at the large table with books propped up in front of them – their homework, Abbie assumed – smiled shyly at her before disappearing through the door that led to the kitchen. Mrs Miller hastily removed a pile of clothes from the other armchair and placed it on the corner of the table. 'I've just finished ironing this lot and I was starting to put it on the maiden when you arrived.' She picked up the clothes horse, which stood at the side of the fireplace, half filled with towels and undergarments, and moved it to the back of the room. 'You must excuse me. I'm afraid the place is very untidy.'

'I don't think it looks untidy at all,' said Abbie, smiling reassuringly at the little woman. Already she felt that she liked her. 'I think it all looks very cosy . . . and friendly.' She sat down in the chair. 'Thank you; I will sit down for a few minutes,

31

but you shouldn't have bothered about a cup of tea.'

'No trouble, Miss Winters,' said Mr Miller. 'It's the least we can do, after all your father's done for us ... or tried to do,' he added, a pained expression coming into his eyes. 'I know he did his best.'

Abbie guessed that he was normally a cheerful man. His rosy, healthy-looking face and the candid expression in his bright blue eyes made you feel he was not only trustworthy, but trusting. She knew he must have placed his trust in her father and she was only sorry that the doctor had not been able to work a miracle for them. It seemed that the eldest girl, Doreen, might be the only member of the family who was bearing a grudge. She wondered why such a fit man as Mr Miller appeared to be should have needed to visit the doctor. Only recently had she been allowed to see the record cards, but she had not yet perused his. His next remark answered her query.

'Your dad's done his best for me an' all, miss. I have trouble with me old back, y'know, working in the building trade. It gives me gyp at times, that and an old war wound, but the doctor's got healing hands all right, and his pills work wonders. Can't afford to take time off, y'see, miss.'

'No, of course not,' replied Abbie. She knew instinctively that this man was not a malingerer, as people with 'a bad back' so often were, and her father had already said how hard he worked, both he and his wife.

'My name is Abigail,' she said now. 'I do wish you would call me that. Or Abbie; that's what I prefer. That's what some people call me.' Not many, though: her Aunt Bertha, her father now and again when he was in a friendly mood, her mother, never. To Eva and her friends she was always Abigail, an old-fashioned, serious sort of name, the girl often thought. Abbie was not sure why she had invited such intimacy now – her mother would consider it most improper – but she thought it was because she felt quite at home here, in spite of the attitude of the eldest daughter, who had still not put in a reappearance.

She had been speaking the truth in telling Mrs Miller that the room looked cosy. And it was not untidy, no more than you might expect the living room of such a large family to be. As well as the clothes airing on the maiden there was also an assortment of pillow cases, towels, shirts and underwear on the pull-up clothes airer drawn up to the ceiling by ropes. (There was a similar contraption in Abbie's home, but there it was in the brick-built wash house which also contained a fireplace.) All the garments were very clean, 'dolly-blued' to a pristine whiteness, although some of the shirts and underwear had been carefully patched and darned. A small fire, in spite of the July warmth, was burning in the grate, and Abbie supposed this was where Mrs Miller did most of her cooking and baking, in the fireside ovens, although the sound of a kettle whistling in the next room told her there was probably a gas stove, as well, in the kitchen.

There was a rag rug made of a myriad small pieces of material of all colours and textures on the hearth – her Aunt Bertha had a similar one in her little parlour – and highly polished brass candlesticks, a pottery jar of coloured spills, and a couple of Coronation mugs on the mantelpiece. The red plush curtains, though faded, gave the room a cheerful aspect and the collection of family photographs on the oak sideboard – the largest piece of furniture in the room – indicated that this was a happy close-knit family. Abbie noticed there was also a statue of the Virgin Mary in a bright blue gown on the sideboard and one or two religious pictures elsewhere in the room. The Millers were obviously Catholics and Abbie guessed that this was why they had such a large family. She knew that Catholics often had a lot of children, but why this should be so was just as much a mystery to her as everything else surrounding the perplexing subject of marriage and babies.

'Oh . . . I don't know about that, miss,' Mrs Miller was saying now, in answer to her invitation to call her Abbie. 'I don't know as how it would be right, you being the doctor's daughter an' everything.' She looked a little confused and was clearly relieved when the girl called Janey came from the kitchen with the tea tray, holding mugs of tea for the three adults.

'Now, we'd best look at these lovely clothes the lady has brought,' said Mrs Miller, beaming at the two girls as she drew out the garments from the bag, exclaiming delightedly at each one. 'Oh look, our Janey; you'll look a real bobby-dazzler in this nice red dress!' One of the rare occasions, Abbie recalled, when her mother had bought her something bright and pretty. 'And this skirt and jumper are just about your size, our Peggy.' She held the garments in front of the smaller of the two girls. Abbie made a guess that they were about twelve and thirteen, one small and fair, like her mother and the absent Doreen, and her sister sturdier and dark-haired, more like her father. Polite, seemingly friendly girls, both of them, though somewhat subdued at the moment. Abbie suspected that their little brother's death had spread a miasma of sadness over this normally happy household.

'Socks – those will be ever so useful, the amount these two go through. Liberty bodices, vests . . . and here's another nice jumper. Dark blue, that'd even do for our Billy.' Mrs Miller explained that besides these two girls there was another older girl, Vera, aged sixteen, 'a couple of years younger than our Doreen,' who was round at a friend's house, and Billy, aged fourteen, who had also gone to see one of his mates.

'Then there was our Tony, God rest his soul,' said Mrs Miller. 'Peggy and Janey . . .' She cast an anxious look in the direction of the two girls. 'Would you go upstairs and finish your homework up there, there's good girls? I want to have a little chat with Miss Winters here.' Abbie knew that the woman wanted to talk about her little son, Tony. She had heard from her Aunt Bertha and from odd remarks her father had made that talking about a lost loved one often helped to ease the pain.

'Yes . . . I was so sorry about your little boy,' said Abbie, when the girls had gone. 'I was sorry that my father was too late to help very much. I think your daughter – Doreen, is it? – still blames him. Or me. He was taking surgery, you see, and couldn't come immediately.'

'Yes, she's taken it badly, our Doreen,' said Mrs Miller. 'We all have, of course, but her more than the rest of the kids. They were very close, y'see, miss, with her being the eldest and him the baby, like. She looked after him a lot when he was little. I was quite poorly, y'see, after he was born. Then I started with bronchitis; can't get me breath sometimes . . . Anyroad, like I was saying, she's taken it real bad, but there's no excuse for her being so rude to you. It weren't your fault. I shall give her a piece of my mind, I can tell you.'

34

'Please don't be hard on her,' said Abbie. 'I understood how she felt . . . at least I tried to. I haven't any brothers or sisters; I wish I had.'

'I just thank the Lord we had him as long as we did,' said Mrs Miller. 'I think I always knew we wouldn't have him all that long. He was always a sickly sort of child, wasn't he, Harold?'

'Aye, it was one thing after another,' replied her husband. 'Chicken pox, measles, mumps, he had the lot. And he never seemed to pull round like the others did. We've had the doctor – your dad – now and again when we felt we could afford it, but mostly the wife has tried to care for him herself. And she's been a grand little nurse to all of 'em, has my Nancy.' He smiled affectionately at her. 'None better.'

'I've only tried me best, Harold,' his wife replied, flushing a little at the praise. 'What any good mother would have done. I can't help blaming meself, though, over his last illness. I just thought it were his chest again. He inherited my weakness, y'see. So I rubbed him with Vick – I'm a great believer in Vick, Miss Winters – but he only got worse and worse . . . We should have done summat sooner, Harold. I'll never forgive meself.' She turned an agonised face towards her husband.

'Now, now, Nan,' he said, getting up and taking hold of her hand. 'We've gone over all this, time and time again. The doctor told us afterwards, didn't he, that he wouldn't have been able to fight off the diphtheria, not with the weak constitution he had. We did what we could, and so did Miss Winters' father. Don't go upsetting yerself now, not in front of . . . Abbie here.'

'Sorry . . .' Nancy Miller dried her eyes. 'I must try to get a grip of meself. But it comes over me sometimes.'

'Of course,' replied Abbie. 'It's sure to. It's . . . less than a fortnight, isn't it? Did you say you had bronchitis, Mrs Miller?' she asked, in an attempt to change the subject.

The woman nodded. 'All me life. But sometimes it's worse than others.'

'I'm sure my father could do something to help,' said Abbie. 'He's starting a clinic to help . . . people like you, the families of his panel patients.' She was careful not to say 'people who can't afford it'.

'You mean . . . free?'

'Well, more or less. I think so. Why don't you come along?'

'Yes, maybe I will . . . if I'm badly again. Yes, thank you, miss.'

'Abbie . . .' Abbie smiled at her,

'Sorry . . . Abbie.'

Abbie thought again of the girl upstairs. 'I've a feeling I've seen Doreen somewhere before,' she said. It had, in fact, been puzzling her ever since she had encountered the young woman in the waiting room.

'You may well have done,' replied Mrs Miller. 'She works on Whitegate Drive now, at Harding's Grocers. You might've seen her there.'

'Of course,' said Abbie, suddenly remembering. The girl had looked different without her overall; besides, Abbie did not often go into the shop, Aunt Bertha being largely responsible for the shopping. 'That's where I've seen her. Has she worked there long?'

'Only a month or two, since their young man assistant joined up. She worked at Redmans in Blackpool before that. But I don't think she's settled there. She's been talking about joining up, the ATS or something like that, hasn't she, Harold?'

'Aye, she has. But she hasn't mentioned it lately, not since . . . our Tony. That's taken the wind out of all our sails. I reckon she'll stay put for a bit now. But she's a plucky lass, our Doreen.'

'And wouldn't you mind her joining up?' ventured Abbie.

'Not a bit of it,' replied Harold Miller. 'Why should we? We'd be proud of her, wouldn't we, Nancy?'

Nancy Miller nodded, her eyes suddenly filling with tears again.

Chapter 3

'D'you know, I felt right sorry for that girl,' said Harold Miller to his wife, after Abbie had departed. 'I know she might've been born with a silver spoon in her mouth, an' all that, but did you see the look on her face when she said about her having no brothers or sisters? She looked . . . I dunno . . . real pained, as though summat were hurting real bad.'

'Yes, I noticed,' replied his wife. 'I dare say it was partly that, her wishing she wasn't an only child, like, but I think it was something else as well. I think she really was sorry about our little Tony, it wasn't just something she was saying to be polite. I thought she was a real nice lass, no edge to her at all.'

'Not a bit like her mam,' replied Harold. 'Different kettle of fish altogether, the doctor's missus. I've only clapped eyes on her once or twice, mind, but that were enough for me. Looks as though she's got a poker stuck up her bum.'

'Harold, honestly!' Nancy Miller smiled, in spite of herself, then she cracked out laughing, the first time she had laughed since Tony died. It wasn't like her husband to be so coarse, not in front of her or the children at any rate, although working on a building site she knew he was no stranger to lewd remarks. But she guessed he was trying deliberately, now, to jolly her along a bit, and she knew she couldn't go around with a miserable face for ever. She had the rest of the children to consider, and they would like their mother to be the smiling, cheerful person she had been before. 'What a thing to say!' She shook her head reprovingly at him. 'I can't say I've ever seen the doctor's wife. What does she look like then? Apart from . . . what you've just said.' She smiled again. 'Doesn't she look like . . . Abbie at all?'

'Not a bit of it. You'd never guess they were mother and

37

daughter. No, the doctor's wife's not very tall and quite slim. I dare say she'd be quite a good-looking woman – in a snooty sort of way, y'know what I mean – if only she'd smile. But she's a real frosty-faced . . . lady. Not young, mind. Fifty if she's a day, I'll be bound.'

'Quite old then, to be Abbie's mother, I mean. Nice of her to ask us to call her Abbie, wasn't it? I didn't feel as how I ought to, really, but the lass might've been hurt if we hadn't tried. I don't think she's much different in age to our Doreen, do you? Looks older though. With her being so . . . big, I suppose.'

'That's a polite way of putting it.' Harold smiled. 'Yes, she's a hefty lass all right. Wasn't on the front row, neither, when looks were given out, but she can't help that, poor girl.'

'Oh, I don't know so much, Harold. That's unkind. Didn't you notice her lovely brown eyes? And she looked real bonny when she smiled; her face sort of lit up. I reckon that girl doesn't smile all that often. I noticed her looking round at everything – the photos on t' sideboard and the pictures of our Lord an' all that. I thought at first she might be thinking how messy and untidy it all were, but, d'you know, I think she really liked it all. I felt she was glad to be here, that she felt sort of . . . comfortable with us. Does that sound daft, Harold?'

'No, not at all. I thought the same. She wasn't in any hurry to dash away, was she? No, I think you're right, Nan. That lass may not have all that much to smile about, in spite of her dad's big house on Whitegate Drive and her posh clothes. That frock she had on didn't come from Abingdon Street market, did it?'

'No, it 'ud cost a bob or two, that. But real old-fashioned, wasn't it? Our Doreen wouldn't be seen dead in a frock like that . . . Oh dear!' Nancy bit her lip, realising what she had just said. 'How dreadful of me! What a thing to say. I didn't mean—'

'Of course you didn't, lass,' replied her husband. 'Now don't go upsetting yerself again. It were just a figure of speech, I know that. We'll have to stop this business of watching our every word in case we say summat wrong. We'll just have to try and act natural, like, same as we did before . . .'

Before our little Tony was taken, Nancy finished off in her mind. Yes, Harold was right, that was what they had to do now; get back to normal life again, normal conversation. That was

38

what she had been trying to do, nattering on about that girl's frock, comparing it with the clothes Doreen wore. Second-hand, most of them, or run up on the old Singer machine from a two-bob remnant from the market – Doreen was clever with her fingers. Nothing posh or stylish, but Doreen liked bright colours and she always looked pretty. She had behaved very badly tonight, though, and Nancy felt ashamed of her.

'I could have murdered our Doreen,' she said now. 'There I go again – I don't mean that, of course – but I was real annoyed with her, Harold. Whatever must that nice girl have thought of her, storming upstairs like that, refusing to come down?'

'She didn't think anything, the doctor's lass; she said she understood. But I agree, our Doreen didn't behave very well. Speak of the devil. I can hear her coming down now. So you've decided to show your face, have you, lady?' Harold Miller raised his voice as Doreen put first her head round the door, then came into the room. 'And about time, an' all.'

Doreen's lips, lightly coloured with pink lipstick, her mother noticed, were set in a stubborn line before she spoke. 'She's gone than? You managed to get rid of her?'

'Get rid of her! Our Doreen, how dare you?' Nancy Miller sprang to her feet as though she were about to launch a physical attack upon her daughter. Not that she ever did, nor had she ever needed to. Doreen could be cheeky at times – what girl couldn't? – but usually one word from her father was enough to make her toe the line. Harold, also, was not one to use violence towards his family, not like some of the fellows in the street. But at this moment Nancy felt like striking out at her eldest daughter and she clenched her fists hard to stop herself. 'That young woman came here, out of the kindness of her heart, and what did she get from you? Nothing but rudeness and abuse. I felt ashamed.'

'Oh, come on, Mam; I wasn't all that rude,' Doreen mumbled. 'I only said what was true, that her dad never came until it was too late. And you know it, Mam. Our Tony didn't know any of us by the time he got here.'

'That wasn't the doctor's fault, nor that poor lass's fault neither.' Harold Miller spoke sternly. 'It was us that were to blame, not realising how bad ... Anyroad, it's no use keep going over and over old ground. Sit down, love . . .' This to Nancy who was still hovering like an avenging angel, glaring at her daughter. 'And calm down an' all. You don't want to bring on another of your coughing dos. And as for you, my girl,' he turned to Doreen, 'you'll go round to that doctor's surgery tomorrow and apologise to that young lady for being so rude.'

'Just what I was going to say, Harold,' said his wife, sounding a little breathless. She sat down again thankfully in the armchair. Harold was right. Her chest felt rather tight; it really did not do her any good to get too agitated.

'Say I'm sorry? Why should I? I'm not sorry. They're all the same, them doctors, pandering to rich folk who can pay. That's what he was doing when I went round that day – and her, that girl – fussing around some dressed-up, toffee-nosed woman . . .' Her voice petered out, no longer sounding so confident. 'Anyway, I expect you've already said sorry, haven't you? "It's not like our Doreen to behave like this . . . I don't know whatever's got into her . . ." I can just hear you. Oh . . .' Doreen gave a deep sigh as she flopped down on the rag rug at the side of her mother's chair, resting her head against her lap. 'I am sorry, Mam; really I am. Not for saying what I did to her, but for upsetting you. But I felt so mad, that posh girl coming here offering us a lot of old clothes.'

'But it wasn't like that, love. They were beautiful clothes, all washed and ironed and as good as new. Our Peggy and Janey'll be thrilled to bits with 'em. And she was a real nice lass, Dr Winters' daughter, wasn't she, Harold? Asked us to call her Abbie an' all.'

'Did she? How kind of her,' murmured Doreen. 'Pretending she was just like us, was she? Don't you believe it, Mam.'

'Doreen, listen to me.' Nancy spoke sharply. 'That young woman was lonely. Don't ask me how I know, but I do. And she was real glad to be here with folk who were friendly and . . . ordinary. Because that's what she is, an ordinary lass who wants a bit of love and affection. Leastways, that's how it seemed to me.'

'Your mother's right,' said Harold. 'We've got a happy home here. Aye, I know we haven't much money and we've had our fair share of ups and downs, and tragedy an' all. But we're a lot

40

happier than some of them rich folk with their big houses and cars. Not that they can use 'em as much now, the cars, I mean, wi' t' war being on, but you know what I'm getting at. Dr Winters is a real good bloke and it seems to me that his daughter takes after him, but I'd like to bet there's not so much love in that house. Like your mother said, don't ask me how I know, but I reckon that lass, Abbie Winters, is in need of a few friends.'

'You're surely not asking me to make a friend of her, are you, Dad?' asked Doreen. 'Her and me? I don't even like her.'

'No, I'm not,' said her father. 'But you can't say you don't like her when you don't even know her. And I happen to think she deserves a bit of kindness . . . and an apology.'

'Oh, all right then.' Doreen gave a wry smile. 'S'pose I'll get no peace if I don't. Can't imagine what I'm going to say to her, though.'

'Just say you were upset when you saw her at the door, that it reminded you of . . . Tony. Tell her you didn't mean to be rude.'

'But I did, Dad. I felt like lashing out at her. Oh . . . what the heck. I'll go, I'll say I'm sorry. Goodness knows what sort of a reaction I'll get, though.'

'It'll be all right, love.' Her mother smiled at her. 'We've told you, she's a nice sort of girl. Quiet and a bit shy, like, till she gets to know you.'

'Not like me then, eh?' Doreen grinned. 'Both feet right in it. That's me, isn't it, Mam?'

Nancy regarded her fondly. 'You'll do. I know you've been upset, love. We all have . . . You're looking very nice. Are you going out?' Doreen had changed into her pink striped dress, a different one from the rather shabby one she had worn at work under her overall, and she had powdered her face as well as applying the pink lipstick her mother had noticed.

'Yes . . . that's if you don't mind? Gwen and I thought we'd have a walk into town, see what's on at the pictures later this week. I think there's a George Formby film coming to the King Edward. Unless you think it's too soon . . . Do you, Mam?'

'No, why should I, lass? You go and enjoy yerself. Our Tony wouldn't't've wanted us all to sit around with long faces. He loved George Formby, didn't he?'

'Doubt if I'll enjoy myself much, Mam. I could still cry buckets, but it'll perhaps help me to take my mind off things a bit. You don't think this dress is too bright, do you?'

'No.' Nancy shook her head. 'We decided, didn't we, not to go on wearing mourning after the funeral? Except for that black coat I got from the Co-op, of course. That'll do me for best for many a year. But I felt I had to have summat decent for our Tony's sake. Fourteen coupons it were an' all! That's a good bit of me allowance gone. Even if we had money to buy clothes we wouldn't have enough coupons ... No, yer dress is fine, lass. Pink suits you. You've got your grey cardigan to put over it, haven't you? That'll happen tone it down a bit if you feel it's too bright. Have you got your torch now, and your gas mask?'

'Here, Mam.' Doreen patted the maroon leatherette case, a Christmas present, which had replaced the utility cardboard box in which all the gas masks had been supplied. 'I won't need a torch. It stays light long enough. Besides, I won't be late. Now, what are you two going to do? Listen to *ITMA*?'

Harold and Nancy looked at one another. 'Happen we will, eh, Nan?' said Harold softly. 'It'll not do any harm, might even do us a bit of good. Beats listening to that bloomin' Lord Haw-Haw anyroad. Rotten traitor! He wants shooting. I'll go and see if Peggy and Janey have finished their homework. They like Tommy Handley an' all.'

As did most of the nation. There was a saying going around that if Hitler were to invade Britain between 8.30 and 9 p.m. on a Thursday night he would meet with no resistance; everyone would be at home listening to *ITMA*! You had to do something to cheer yourself up, thought Nancy, staring into the embers of the fire after Doreen had gone out and Harold had gone to fetch the two girls. Or at least you had to try, although she knew that no amount of Mrs Mopp or Colonel Chinstrap would ease the ache in her heart.

And apart from their own personal tragedy the war news was grim. Winston Churchill could say all he liked about 'the spirit of an unquenchable people', but facts were facts. The Desert War had started in North Africa and that General Rommel, the 'Desert Fox', seemed invincible. The little island of Malta was being continually bombarded and, nearer to home, the major

42

cities of Great Britain – Liverpool, Glasgow, Hull, Southampton, Belfast, not to mention London – were suffering terrible air raids. And, not content with most of Europe, Hitler had now invaded Russia.

These were all things that Harold had read out to her from the newspapers. Nancy didn't bother much with papers herself, apart from the *Evening Gazette* and the *Blackpool Gazette and Herald* on a Saturday. You couldn't do much about the war news anyway, good or bad. What affected her most, though she realised it might be a selfish way of looking at things, was all this blessed rationing and food shortages and endless queues. Admittedly they didn't do too badly with rationing. Being a large family the 1s 2d a week allowed for meat for each person was more than adequate. Nancy could never have afforded to spend eight or nine shillings a week on meat anyway. And it was the same with the bacon ration. Four ounces a week, which was the allowance at the moment, was more than enough, for well-off folk as well as the poorer ones, she guessed. Although Doreen had told her it would most probably be reduced before long.

No, Nancy supposed that rationing was a sensible way of distributing the food. It meant fair shares for all and she had always been good at managing – stretching sixpence to do the job of a shilling, as Harold teasingly told her. But what annoyed her intensely was all this confounded queueing that you had to do. Queueing for meat, for potatoes, for bread, for tripe – this Lancashire delicacy had become very popular recently with the shortage of meat – even for insignificant little things like hairgrips or knicker elastic. She was lucky in one respect; she did not have to queue for her groceries as Doreen brought their rations home each week from Harding's Grocers where she worked. Some women loved queueing. They made quite a hobby of it, often joining the end of a queue when they had no idea what it was they were queueing for. It was an excuse for a good old chin-wag and a chance to pull a neighbour's reputation to shreds. But Nancy had never been a gossip. She minded her own business and expected other people to mind theirs.

Some of the shortages were very aggravating, too. There was not a banana or an orange or lemon to be had for love or money, and tinned fruit and meat had disappeared completely from the shop shelves. Luckily, Doreen kept her informed as to when a supply of tinned peaches – for instance – might be coming in, and Mr Harding always made sure that one was put on one side for the Miller family. He was a good boss, Doreen said, so nice to work for and so scrupulously honest and above board you would hardly believe.

Doreen was in a thoughtful mood for much of the following day, most unlike her usual cheerful self. She was popular with the customers, always ready to chat and have a little joke. Not that she had done much of that recently, since Tony died, but she had at least managed to raise a smile and exchange a few pleasantries. If the customers noticed, however, that she was unusually withdrawn today they did not comment, assuming that her recent bereavement was troubling her again. And Mr Harding, apart from a solicitous glance and a brief enquiry, 'Are you OK, Doreen?' did not probe any further.

It kept coming over her, what on earth was she going to say to that girl Miss Winters, Abbie, or whatever her name was? It wasn't that she didn't want to apologise – she had promised her parents that she would and she did realise now, on reflection, that she had been rather rude – but she and that posh Abbie person, they were poles apart. Her mam and dad said that the girl was very nice, but Doreen still feared that she might be all snooty and look down her nose. Not that it would matter; it wasn't likely that their paths would cross again and at least Doreen would have done what she knew was right, but she did so hate to be made to feel inferior. Her mam and dad made her mad sometimes, so conscious were they of 'keeping their place' and almost venerating those they considered to be their betters: doctors, headmasters, lawyers and the like. They had been tickled pink because that girl had asked them to call her Abbie, as if she had been Princess Elizabeth or somebody paying a call on them.

Supposing there wasn't a surgery today and she had to knock at the door? And what if it wasn't the daughter who came to the door, but the doctor's wife? She had heard her father say what a stuck-up woman she was . . . Oh, what the heck! She had better

44

concentrate on the job she was supposed to be doing. The woman she was serving was looking at her in a most peculiar way.

They were kept busy all day. Friday was the day when most housewives came to collect their rations, although in this affluent neighbourhood it was often the housekeeper-companion or the daily woman who did the shopping. Or sometimes the groceries were delivered by Mickey, the errand boy, to houses a good distance away. It was towards the end of the afternoon when Doreen glanced at the queue of just five or six people and noticed, right at the end of it, the one person she had least expected, or wanted, to see. The doctor's daughter, Abigail Winters. She was wearing a sombre brown dress, a brown felt hat and was carrying a large shopping basket. She was staring down at her feet as though she, too, wished she were anywhere but here.

It was a good twenty minutes or so before Doreen had dealt with the queue ahead of her and during that time Abbie Winters had not even glanced at her. Now, as they faced one another across the mahogany counter, Doreen found herself looking into a pair of slightly puzzled, slightly apprehensive, brown eyes. Lovely, deep brown eyes Abigail Winters had, just like pools of treacle toffee. And her hair was just about the same colour, what you could see of it, because it was pinned back in an old-fashioned sort of roll round her head with most of it hidden under her hat.

Abbie gave a shy smile – Doreen's mother had said she was a bit shy – and opened her mouth to speak, but it was a few seconds before any words came. 'Hello . . .' she said, very unsurely. 'Your mother told me you worked here. I thought I recognised you, the day you came to ask . . . the day you came to the surgery. I don't usually do the shopping . . .' Her words were coming more quickly now, almost falling over one another, in fact. 'My Aunt Bertha does the shopping as a rule, but she's not well today, so my mother sent me instead . . .' She paused, looking rather helplessly at Doreen.

'I'm glad you've come,' said Doreen, 'because you've saved me a journey.' She half smiled at her, realising it was not going to be nearly as bad as she had feared. At least here she was on her home ground, or as good as.

'Saved you a journey? What do you mean?' Abbie frowned, poking her head slightly forward, the look of puzzlement still there in her eyes. For such an important person as a doctor's daughter she seemed very nervous. Doreen had not got that impression of her at all when she had encountered her in the waiting room; there she had appeared much more confident.

'I was going to come to the doctor's after work,' said Doreen, 'to say I was sorry. For – you know – for being so rude to you. My mam and dad said I had to . . .' She stopped. 'No, I don't mean that. Well, they did say I had to say I was sorry, but I decided I wanted to say it an' all. I am sorry, Miss Winters . . . real sorry. It was horrid of me.'

'That's all right. There's no need to apologise.' Abbie shook her head confusedly. 'I understood; at least I think I did. I said so, to your parents. And I was sorry – so terribly sorry – about your little brother.'

'Thank you.' Doreen hung her head. 'It was wrong of me to blame you.' She felt very contrite and humble. The girl was being very understanding. Doreen was beginning to think she was a very nice girl, just as her parents had said. She looked up again at Abbie. 'I'm sorry for that an' all. It was awful of me, the way I went on at you that day. It weren't your fault. How could it be?'

'It was understandable.' Abbie gave a rather sad smile. 'I could see how upset you were and I felt really sorry for you. I remember wishing I had somebody I cared about, the way you obviously cared about your little brother.'

Doreen looked at her in some amazement. The poor girl! What a strange thing to say. Could it be, with all her money and her parents' big house and her posh little job working for her father, that the girl was lonely? Doreen's mother had thought so. 'Yes, me and our Tony, we were very close,' she replied now. 'With me being the eldest and him the baby I looked after him a lot, y'see.'

'Yes, so your mother told me.'

'Anyroad, he's gone . . .' Doreen gave a slight shrug. 'Mam and Dad reckon he would never've made old bones; he was a frail little lad, always ailing with summat or another. We've got to try and get on the best way we can without him . . . Now,

Miss Winters, what about your shopping? Your rations, is it? Four of you, aren't there? If I could just have your books, please . . .'

Dr Cedric Winters, Mrs Eva Winters, Miss Abigail Winters and Miss Bertha Shorrock; Doreen marked the ration books. Yes, it was Miss Shorrock who usually came for the groceries. Doreen recalled a plump elderly little woman, very homely and friendly, not the sort of person you would imagine living in one of those big posh houses. But it was possible she was more of a servant than a relation; she had certainly never seen Mrs Winters doing her own shopping.

'Would you like a small tin of Nescafé, Miss Winters?' Doreen asked, as she had been told to ask all the regular customers, when all the other items had been sorted out.

'Oh, yes please,' replied Abbie. 'My mother prefers ground coffee, but we've come to the end of our supply. She's been grumbling like anything at my aunt for using that Camp coffee in a bottle, but I don't mind the taste of it.'

Neither did Doreen. It was the sort her mother used on the rare occasions they drank coffee. They were 'proper tea bellies' in their house, as her dad always said, but she thought she might take a tin of Nescafé home tonight as a treat; Mr Harding had reserved one for her. 'That lot's going to be heavy,' she remarked as she helped Abbie to pack the various items into her shopping basket. 'Are you sure you can manage it? Listen – why don't you leave it and I'll get Mickey, our errand lad, to deliver it for you when he gets back? He shouldn't be long.'

'No, no, it doesn't matter,' said Abbie. 'Thank you all the same. My mother will be waiting for it. I can manage this lot easily. I'm a big strong girl, aren't I?' She gave a rueful smile. 'That's what my mother is always telling me.'

'Well, if you're sure then . . .' Doreen gave her a sympathetic smile, though she wasn't sure why she should feel sorry for the girl. Partly because of that remark she had just made about being big, she supposed. She was undoubtedly a big girl. 'A big strapping lass' was the way Doreen's father had described her, and Doreen guessed that Abigail Winters was very much aware of, and somewhat uneasy about her height and well-built figure. Not that she was abnormally tall – five foot seven or so – but

47

the fact that she was plumpish as well made her appear bigger. Maybe that was why she stooped a little and poked her head forward, as though to make herself seem smaller than she really was.

'I'm ever so glad I've sorted things out with you, Miss Winters,' said Doreen. 'It was worrying me quite a lot. Thanks for being so nice to me. Here, I'll open the door for you.' She nipped out from behind the counter and hurried across the shop. It was empty now, no one else having joined the queue behind Abbie, which was why Doreen had been able to spare the time to talk with her.

'Just a minute . . .' Abbie put a hand out, somewhat diffidently, touching Doreen's arm as she made to open the door. 'Do you think . . . could you call me Abbie, please? I would like it so much if you did. That's what I said to your mother and father and they did . . . try.' There was an appealing, almost beseeching, look in the girl's brown eyes, then she smiled, really smiled for the first time, and the way her whole face lit up made her look almost beautiful.

Doreen found herself grinning back. 'Yes, 'course I will . . . Abbie. And p'raps I'll see you again sometime.'

'I hope so,' Abbie replied, sounding shy again. She glanced round the shop, empty apart from the two girls and Mr Harding cleaning his bacon slicer. It was getting near to closing time. 'This is a lovely shop, isn't it? It must be a real delight, working here.' She sniffed appreciatively. 'I love the smell of bacon. I remember coming in with my aunt when I was a little girl. They had huge tubs of butter then and enormous cheeses, and sides of bacon hanging from the ceiling. I remember looking at all the lovely biscuits in those glass boxes on the edge of the counter, and Aunt Bertha sometimes let me choose my favourites. Chocolate ones, of course.' Her eyes lit up at the thought. 'And I used to love those with jam and cream in the middle.'

'Can't get hold of those now, for love nor money,' Doreen replied. 'The boxes are still there,' she nodded towards the counter, 'but it's just digestives now or arrowroot or Nice biscuits.'

'It's still a very nice shop, though,' said Abbie. 'It's always so bright and clean, and colourful, in spite of the shortages.'

'We do our best, luv.' Mr Harding looked up from the bacon slicer and grinned. He did try to make his shop attractive with displays of unrationed goods – tins of custard powder, gravy browning, sauces, jams and marmalades, jars of pickles and the like – tastefully arranged on the shelves and in the window. It was a question of making a little look like a lot, but it was nothing like it was before the war. 'Thanks for the compliment. Much appreciated, Miss Winters. We'll see you again, I hope.'

'Yes . . . goodbye, then. Goodbye . . . Doreen.' Abbie smiled again in that hesitant, self-conscious way she had before hurrying out through the door.

'Nice lass, that,' observed Mr Harding as the door closed behind her. 'Didn't realise you knew her, Doreen. She doesn't often come in now, but I remember her as a little kiddie. Always with her aunt, she was. Her mother now, she's real old battle-axe. I wouldn't like to get on the wrong side of her, I can tell you! I pity that poor lass.'

'And where do you think you have been all this time?' Eva Winters snatched the basket off her daughter as soon as she came through the door, just as quickly handing it back to her when she realised how heavy it was. 'Mrs Cuthbert has been waiting goodness knows how long for that lard and margarine, to make a fruit tart.' Mrs Cuthbert was a woman who attended their church – not one of Eva's whist drive cronies, but one who was on the church cleaning rota – whose services she had procured whilst Bertha was ill. Eva would not attempt to do any cooking herself, besides, she considered she was far too busy now, doing the waiting room job that had once been Abbie's.

'Take that lot into the kitchen and unpack it. Goodness only knows what you've been doing till now. You've been gone nearly an hour.'

'I couldn't help it, Mother. There was a queue, and it always takes ages now, with ration books to be seen to and . . . and everything.' Her best intentions to stand up to her mother often foundered when she saw the angry look in Eva's eyes, a look that had been there more frequently since her father had started to take her into his confidence a little more. Abbie did not say that she had spent some time talking to Doreen Miller. She knew it would be best not to mention that young woman at all.

'Don't argue! You're forever arguing with me lately. Just do as you're told. And when you've sorted out whatever's in that basket you can give Mrs Cuthbert a hand with the dinner. There's no knowing how long she'll take if she has to do it all herself. And I thought Bertha was slow . . . Still, she's better than nobody, I suppose, while your Aunt Bertha's feeling sorry for herself. Go on . . . What are you waiting for?'

'I . . . er . . . I hadn't finished in the dispensary, Mother, when you asked me to go shopping. Father wants me to go back and finish off.'

'Then he can go on wanting! Dispensary, indeed! He used to manage perfectly well on his own until he got this ridiculous idea of the clinic. I'll have a word with your father. Go on . . . Or we'll be waiting till midnight for our dinner.'

Abbie crept into the kitchen, feeling like a naughty little girl. She knew that her mother had called her away from her work in the dispensary – work which was useful and which she enjoyed – out of spite. Eva could easily have gone to the grocer's herself, or if that idea was too, too preposterous, she could have sent Mrs Cuthbert. Aunt Bertha usually did the shopping on a Friday morning, but she had been too poorly this morning to remind Eva of the fact, which was why the job had been overlooked until late in the afternoon. Abbie knew that her aunt, far from feeling sorry for herself, was not well at all. She must be feeling ill to have obeyed the doctor's orders that she must stay in bed, something she hated doing, although Abbie was not sure what was wrong with her.

'Sorry I've been such a long time, Mrs Cuthbert,' she said as she hastily unpacked the contents of the shopping basket on to the kitchen table. 'There was a queue. Mother doesn't seem to understand.'

'Well, she wouldn't, would she?' remarked Mrs Cuthbert, a nice ordinary woman from the church, whom Abbie liked very much. Abbie was not sure whether or not there was a touch of sarcasm in her tone now, though she never spoke to Eva with anything but the utmost politeness that almost amounted to servility. Eva had that effect on some people and Abbie knew that Mrs Cuthbert badly needed the extra money; she often 'did' for the more affluent members of the congregation. 'You've not been all that long anyroad,' she went on cheerfully. 'I've been seeing to the shepherd's pie. It's a recipe I heard on the *Kitchen Front*; more potatoes and a handful of oatmeal to make the meat go further.'

Oh dear! Abbie was doubtful as to what her mother would make of such economy measures. 'Mother said you were waiting for the fats, to make a fruit tart.'

'So I was, but not to worry. Tell you what I'll do – I'll make a crumble instead; it'll be quicker. Is there any brown sugar, do you know, dear?'

'I think there might be a bit left. Mother likes it in her coffee.' She opened the glass-fronted kitchenette and reached for a stone jar. 'Yes . . . there you are, Mrs Cuthbert. Now, what can I do to help?'

'Nothing, dear. I can manage. You've yer own job to do, haven't you, with yer father? Blessed if I know why you should be helping me.'

'Mother said I had to.'

'Oh, she did, did she? Well, there's not a great deal to do now. Happen you could make us a nice cup of tea, eh? My tongue's fair hanging out for one, and I'm sure your poor old auntie'd like one.'

'Yes, so I will. Good idea.' Abbie knew her mother was safely out of the way in the waiting room – making sure that the less desirable of her husband's patients did not steal the bits of family china that were dotted around – so when she had made the tea she stealthily crept up the stairs, with Bertha's large willow-patterned cup in her hands, to her aunt's bedroom.

Chapter 4

Aunt Bertha stirred in the bed as Abbie knocked, then entered the room. 'I've brought you a cup of tea, Auntie,' she said. 'I hope I haven't disturbed you, but Mrs Cuthbert thought you might like one.'

'Oh . . . yes. Yes, thank you, dear. That would be lovely.' Bertha struggled into an upright position, leaning back against the pillows which Abbie, after putting the cup and saucer on the bedside table, quickly plumped up and arranged for her. 'Do you know, I think that little sleep has done me good? I feel tons better now. Little sleep, I say, but I seem to have done nothing but sleep the whole of this blessed day, and yesterday an' all.'

'Father says it's nature's way of getting you right again, Auntie,' said Abbie. 'I know you don't like staying in bed, but the rest will do you a world of good.' Abbie felt sure that what her aunt was suffering from, most of all, was sheer exhaustion. Admittedly there were only four of them in the house, all adults. Bertha did not have to cope with a horde of children or struggle to make ends meet – as Mrs Miller did, Abbie found herself thinking – but she was by no means a young woman. The house was large, she did the work more or less single-handedly, and she was constantly at Eva's beck and call, which, in itself must be very wearing.

'Aye, I suppose so,' replied Bertha. 'At least when I'm asleep I'm not thinking. I gets to thinking sometimes . . . especially at this time of the year.' She gave a sigh before reaching across for the cup and saucer. Abbie quickly put them into her hands.

'There you are, Aunt Bertha. It's your favourite cup. Can you manage it now?'

'Of course I can, child! Give over speaking to me as though I'm a babby! I'll be out of this dratted bed tomorrow if I have my way. It was your father that said I had to stay put. Mrs Cuthbert's here, you said? Tch, tch, tch! I reckon nothing to that. Another woman in my kitchen? That'll never do.' There was a hint of amusement, however, in her aunt's tone, and Abbie smiled back at her.

Oh, she did love her Aunt Bertha. When she looked back on her childhood it was always Aunt Bertha who sprang to mind. She recalled occasional visits to the beach with her little tin bucket and wooden spade. (Very infrequent visits, of course, as Eva did not really approve of such common pursuits, and under no circumstances had Abigail to be allowed to paddle; the sea water was filthy and full of germs.) There was a rare visit to the cinema to see an early Mickey Mouse film; trips in her father's Ford car, to Fleetwood or Morecambe, with her aunt caring for her in the back seat and cleaning her up after she had been carsick (which she always was); even little trips to the local shops, to the butcher's or baker's or grocer's – as she had mentioned to Mr Harding and Doreen – had seemed exciting when she was hand in hand with Aunt Bertha.

The woman looked small and fragile in the big double bed although she was, in reality, quite a plump person. Her chubby face had dropped into lines of weariness at the corners of her mouth, her eyes lacked their usual brightness and spirit and her iron-grey hair was flattened and in need of combing. Abbie felt that she must do something to help her. When she had recovered from whatever was wrong with her – and Abbie did not think it would be as early as tomorrow – she should not be expected to struggle on doing the work all by herself.

'Mrs Cuthbert has been a good help,' Abbie said now. 'Not as good as you, of course, Auntie. Mother's been having a bit of a grumble about her, but that's Mother, isn't it? I got into trouble, too, for being late back from the shop.'

'Oh well, your mother has to have her little say. You should know her by now, Abigail. Not that I'm saying anything wrong about her, mind . . . She's been very good to me, has Eva.' Bertha's eyes took on a contemplative look.

I'm sure I don't know what's good about the way she has Aunt Bertha run ragged, thought Abbie. But she made no comment, except to say, 'I'm sure a bit of extra help wouldn't go amiss, would it, Aunt Bertha? How would you feel about Mrs Cuthbert coming in to help you – say a couple of times a week, if we could arrange it?' Abbie had, in fact, only just thought of this and her aunt's words echoed the next thought that came into her mind.

'Oh, I don't know so much about that, Abbie. What would your mother say? They pay me a wage, you know – only a small one, mind – as well as my keep. Your mother expects me to manage on my own. As I have done this last . . . nearly twenty-two years it'll be now. Nigh on twenty-two years since your mother and father came and rescued me. He asked me to come and live with them. It was the year after they got married – January 1920, it was, when I first came here – and I've been here ever since.'

What on earth did Aunt Bertha mean, thought Abbie. Rescued her? From what? She did not enquire, however, guessing that her aunt had been speaking unguardedly and might well be regretting the remark that had slipped out. Instead she went on to talk about the suggestion she had just made regarding Mrs Cuthbert. 'I intend to ask my father – not my mother – about extra help for you, Aunt Bertha. After all, he is the one who pays the bills, isn't he, and if he chooses to employ Mrs Cuthbert then I don't see how Mother can object, do you?'

'Oh, I'm sure I don't know, Abbie love.' Aunt Bertha sounded agitated. 'I don't like to do anything to upset your mother. And neither did you until this last week or so. What's got into you lately? I've never known you to be so – well – forward.'

'Argumentative, you mean? Cheeky?' Abbie grinned. 'That's what Mother says I am. I'm nineteen, Auntie. I'm not a little girl any more. I suppose I'm just waking up to the fact and trying to assert myself, but I don't always succeed. She still manages to make me feel about so big sometimes.' She held her thumb and forefinger about an inch apart.

'Don't go upsetting her, Abbie. It's not worth it. She'll only go and take it out on you if you cross her. You know what she's like. There now . . . I shouldn't've said that. You know I try never to criticise her, after what she's done for me, her and your father, of course. The two of them; I've thanked God many and many a time for what they did for me. Goodness knows what would've become of me else. Oh, deary me, I don't know!'

Abbie looked on in some dismay as she could see her aunt becoming visibly more and more distressed. The cup and saucer were shaking in her hands and Abbie removed them from her grasp. 'Then I starts thinking . . . and thinking about it all doesn't do any good, but I can't help it sometimes. Then it brings on one of my bad attacks.'

'What sort of attacks, Auntie?' asked Abbie.

'My head, love. It's all inside my head, all the muddle and bad thoughts that won't go away. Then I start trembling all over. I can't seem to control it, but your father's very good. He knows just what to give me, to help me. That's why I've been sleeping so much. I'm all right most of the time. It's only sometimes, 'specially this time of the year, that it comes over me. It was this very day in July, you see, that he was born.'

It was as though her aunt was talking to herself. She was staring unfocusedly across the room, seemingly unaware of Abbie's presence. 'Who?' asked Abbie in the smallest whisper. 'Who was born?'

'Why, my little boy, of course. My little Johnnie. That's what I called him. Johnnie, after his father. At least, that's what I called him to myself. I don't know what they called him after they took him away from me. 'Cause that's what they did. They took him away and I never saw him again.' Bertha seemed, suddenly, to come back to the here and now. It was as though she had been miles away, in another world, another time. Now her glance became sharper, far more alert as she looked keenly at Abbie. 'You didn't know, did you, about my little boy? They never talk about him. Of course, they wouldn't, would they? That's what made it so dreadful for me, shutting it away all these years, as though it never happened.'

Abbie was almost too stunned to speak. She could scarcely take in what she was hearing and she didn't understand any of it, but she knew, instinctively, that she must not do anything at this moment that might disturb her aunt. Like asking her what she was talking about.

'Now, don't start upsetting yourself, Auntie,' she said, trying to speak calmly. 'It was all a long time ago, wasn't it? You're with people who care about you now. Father and . . . Mother.'

Although Abbie sometimes wondered if her mother cared about anyone but herself. Maybe she did, in her own peculiar way; Aunt Bertha, certainly, would speak no wrong of her. 'And me. Try and forget about it.'

'Forget? I can't forget. I would like to, believe me. I would like to blot it all out, all that dreadful time, but it keeps coming back into my mind. That's what makes me ill, just now and again. You know, don't you, Abigail, how I try to keep going? Never still, am I? It's working hard that keeps the awful thoughts away, most of the time.'

'Yes, you do work hard, Aunt Bertha,' replied Abbie. 'I don't know what we'd do without you. I've heard Father say so many a time.' She recalled that very rarely did her aunt succumb to ill health. She was, indeed, rather scornful of people who 'enjoyed being poorly' as she put it, forever moaning on about their ailments. Only now and again, Abbie remembered, did her aunt have a couple of 'off' days, as she was doing now. Eva was impatient at such times and Abbie had never understood until now just what the mystery illness was from which her aunt occasionally suffered. Even now she couldn't understand it or take in the enormity of what her aunt was saying. Was she actually saying that she had had a child, a little boy? But her aunt, as far as Abbie knew, had never been married.

'I'd like to tell you about it, Abbie,' her aunt said now. 'You don't mind, do you? They never let me talk and I'm sure it would help. And there's nobody I can talk to, is there, but you? I haven't many friends, except for a few women at the chapel, and I couldn't possibly tell them anything about myself, not that sort of thing anyroad.' She actually gave a little chuckle. 'Shocked to the core, they'd be, them Primitive Methodists.' Abbie and her mother and father attended the Church of England, whereas Aunt Bertha had always gone to the Methodist chapel. It was a good mile away, but she walked there, come rain or come shine, every Sunday evening. The Winters family attended the morning service at their church, but at that time Bertha was always at home preparing the Sunday luncheon.

She looked pensively at Abbie, her rather faded blue eyes no longer having the distraught look which had so alarmed her niece a little while ago. She sounded calmer, but still sorrowful.

'You're an adult now, Abbie, and I think you have a right to know the family secrets . . . some of them, anyroad,' she added. 'The ones that concern me at any rate. And you and me, we've always been good pals, haven't we, ever since you were a tiny little lass?'

Abbie nodded. 'Yes, Auntie, we've always been friends.' The only real friend I've ever had, Abbie thought now, but she did not voice the thought. She had not been brought up to wear her heart on her sleeve and expressions of affection did not come easily to her.

'When you came along it was like a miracle to me.' Her aunt smiled at her fondly. 'I didn't think there'd ever be any children in this house, and then you arrived. And it meant so much to me, almost as though it was my little Johnnie come back, except that you were a little lass, of course. That's why I've always made so much of you. Yes, my Johnnie . . . he would've been twenty-six years old, this very day. Well, I suppose he still will be . . . wherever he is.'

'You mean . . . you had a baby, Aunt Bertha? A little boy?'

'Yes, love. My Johnnie.'

'But . . . did you get married then?'

'No, love.' Bertha gave a sigh. 'I've never been married. That's why it was so dreadful – or so they all thought. That's why they wouldn't let me keep him.'

'But you've got to be married to have a baby, haven't you? I mean . . . there has to be . . . a man, hasn't there?' Abbie shook her head in bewilderment. 'I don't really understand.'

She recalled how, once before, when she was about fourteen or so, she had asked Aunt Bertha to explain certain 'things' to her. The sort of 'things' that the girls at school whispered about in corners. Abbie had known it would be no use asking her mother even if she had dared to do so. Her aunt was the one who always answered her questions. Not this time, however. Aunt Bertha had just looked embarrassed and said that Abbie would know soon enough, but there were certain things you must never, never do with a man, not until you were married. Now it seemed as though Aunt Bertha had done them.

Her aunt was silent for a moment, then she smiled sadly at her. 'No, love, I don't really expect you to understand, but—'

'Abigail . . . Where are you?' Her mother's strident voice and the sound of footsteps coming upstairs broke into Bertha's words. There was a peremptory knock on the door, before it was flung open and Eva appeared, in high dudgeon. 'Oh, there you are, girl. What on earth are you doing up here? I've been looking all over for you.'

'I've just brought Aunt Bertha a cup of tea, that's all.' Abbie was determined to give as good as she got. She was doing nothing wrong; on the contrary, she was doing something to help her aunt. 'You told me to help Mrs Cuthbert. Well, she didn't want any help and I thought Aunt Bertha could do with a bit of company.'

'Don't you take that attitude with me. Your aunt likes to be left alone when she's . . . like this. She doesn't want to be bothered with you nattering her to death. How are you, Bertha?' The question sounded like an afterthought,

'A lot better, thank you, Eva. The sleep's done me good, and those pills Cedric gave me . . . Don't go on at the lass. I was glad of that cup of tea – it was very kind of her – and we've been having a nice little chat, haven't we, Abbie?'

'Yes, maybe you have.' Eva frowned. 'But Abigail has work to do downstairs and that's where she should be. She made a fuss when I asked her to help in the kitchen. She said she had some work to do in the dispensary, and then what do I find but she's sneaked upstairs to waste time with you.' She turned to Abbie. 'You'd better get down there right now, to your father's dispensary, if there's such important work to be done.'

Abbie turned away, muttering under her breath, 'I can't do right for doing wrong.'

'What did you say?' snapped Eva.

'Nothing, Mother . . . Nothing at all. I'll be down in a minute or two.'

'You'll go down now!'

Abbie walked towards the door, but slowly, turning to speak to her aunt once again. She didn't know how she was daring to be so defiant, but, as she had just told her aunt, she was not a child any longer and it was high time she stuck up for herself. 'Shall I bring you some dinner up, Aunt Bertha? Mrs Cuthbert's making a shepherd's pie, and there's a rhubarb crumble to follow.' She studiously ignored her mother who was standing there drumming her fingers on the dressing-table top, positively seething with indignation. Bertha appeared to ignore her, too, as she answered.

'Do you know, I think I might be able to manage just a little of each. I've been off my food, but that little chat we had has bucked me up no end.'

'We didn't finish it, did we, Auntie? The chat, I mean. We were interrupted ...' Again she ignored her mother's gasp of indrawn breath. 'I'll come up and see you again, shall I, when we've finished our dinner? After I've helped Mrs Cuthbert with the washing-up, of course.' She glanced towards her mother, her look seeming to say, So there; forbid me to see Aunt Bertha if you dare!

'Yes ... yes, that would be lovely, dear,' replied Bertha, casting an apprehensive glance in Eva's direction. 'Off you go now, though, there's a good girl. Thank you for the cup of tea.'

'And what did you and Bertha find to talk about that was so interesting?' asked Eva as they went down the stairs. Abbie could tell that she was finding it hard to keep the lid on her temper.

'Oh, this and that,' she replied. 'I was telling her how interesting I am finding it, working in Father's dispensary. And helping in the surgery.' Without another glance at her mother she disappeared in that direction now. Abbie lied because she knew that on no account must she breathe a word of what her aunt had been saying. But she was still almost completely in the dark. She was dying to hear more; it was the most baffling thing she had ever heard in her life.

What have those two been talking about? Eva wondered as she went into the sitting room and sat down in her favourite armchair. And why was it that Abigail could talk so freely to her aunt when she never even tried to do so with her own mother? But Eva, if she were honest – and she was usually honest with herself – knew that it was largely her own fault. She had, right from the start, resented Abigail, feeling that a baby would spoil the companionship, if not love, that she and Cedric had shared.

She had believed that Cedric had loved her. In the beginning she was *sure* he had, and she had been so grateful to him for marrying her and rescuing her from the domination of her overbearing father. As she looked around her lovely home now, glorying in all her possessions, she knew she had so much for which to be grateful to Cedric. And she had tried to love him. She had tried so hard to give him the physical love as well as the companionship he had desired. But time and again the spectre of her father would come into her mind: his rigid discipline, the way he used to chastise her even when she was in her late teens. His harsh treatment of her had brought about a coldness in her that almost amounted to frigidity.

She had determined she would never resort to physical chastisement with Abigail, and never had she done so; but the same aloofness that had affected her relationship with Cedric had made her unable to accept the child and love her unreservedly as she knew she should have tried to do. She did love her. She did . . . but it was so difficult to show her feelings. She sometimes found herself being sharp with Abigail – quite nasty at times, she knew – because, deep down, she realised she was . . . jealous. Jealous of the girl's undoubted affection for Bertha, and, of late, of the companionship that seemed to be developing between Abigail and her father, ever since she had started working more closely with him.

Eva loved Cedric more than he would ever know. Why then, she asked herself, could she not tell him that she did, or show him? She did not know the answer.

Oh dear, thought Bertha when the door closed behind her cousin and her niece. Whatever had she been thinking of, blurting it all out like that, about little Johnnie and the shameful secret she had been forced to keep to herself all these years? It was not entirely true that her little chat with Abbie had cheered her up, but she had been forced to say something to get Eva off the poor girl's back. The way Eva treated that lass at times was deplorable, nor was it getting any better as the years went by, as Bertha had hoped it might.

Bertha knew that Eva had never really wanted the child, that she had been shaken rigid when she knew about the baby, but Bertha had hoped that once the child was in her arms her attitude would change and that motherhood would mellow her. But any parental love that there was came from Cedric, and he, poor man, seemed afraid of showing too much affection for the girl in case he upset his wife. Bertha loved her, of course, and had tried over the years to make up to the child for what she was missing. And the little girl, too, had helped to fill the aching void in Bertha's life; as she had just, so misguidedly, been telling her.

Bertha knew that now she had started the story, however unintentional or unwise it might have been, she would have to go on and tell the whole of it. Abbie would be back, wanting to know what her aunt had been talking about, and who could blame her? She had never been a particularly inquisitive child, probably because her parents had not encouraged her to ask questions, but as she became older she had, naturally, become more curious. And it had always been her aunt who had tried to answer her queries. Innocent little questions; such things as where did the sea go when the tide went out on the Blackpool sands, and where did the sun go when it disappeared behind the sea; why was thunder so loud; and why was the wicked queen so unkind to poor Snow White – a pertinent question, that one. Bertha had answered as best she could, because she was very much aware that she was nothing like as well educated as either Cedric or Eva. The only question she had shied away from was when Abbie had asked her about the facts of life. Bertha had left school at fourteen to go into service, and if she had not done that her life might well have taken an entirely different turn. She might even have been married with three or four children. How she would have loved that . . .

Bertha pulled her thoughts back to the present. Yes, she would have to tell the girl the whole story. Maybe it would do her a power of good to talk about it after all these years. It was suppressing it that made her ill, that brought on these occasional crises of nerves which left her helpless for a couple of days. But fancy Abigail still not knowing where babies came from, at her age. That was still the one question which, were she asked outright, Bertha knew she would be unable to answer. Abigail would have to discover for herself, as Bertha had told her once before, just what was involved in the act of procreation, the

62

coming together of a man and a woman, and about the bliss or agony, the joy or sorrow, that such an act could bring.

Bertha, looking back, thought that at nineteen – the age Abbie was now – she had certainly known what went on although she had not, of course, experienced any of it for herself. Even when she and Thomas, the footman, had started walking out together there had been 'none of that'. They had both agreed that they should wait for the wedding day, although goodness knew when that would be with the small wage they were both earning. When Bertha did experience, for the first time, the delights of love – or lust, whichever you wanted to call it – she was at an age when she should have known better. Certainly, at fourteen, which was the age she had been when she joined the Tennant household, she had been as innocent as Abigail, it seemed, still was.

It was in 1897 that Bertha had gone into service at Tennant Hall, the home of Sir Reginald Tennant, the holder of a minor baronetcy, and his wife, Catherine. The hall was a stately Georgian mansion on the border of Lancashire and Yorkshire; just into Yorkshire, in fact, near to Skipton. King George III had been on the throne when the hall was built and Sir Reginald was the fourth baronet. Many of the girls and boys from the neighbouring villages found employment with the Tennant family, and so it was that at fourteen years of age Bertha Shorrock started work there as a kitchen maid.

She proved herself to be a willing and biddable servant and she was soon promoted to nursery maid, helping Nanny Foster to take care of the three children, Reggie (named after his father, as was usual with the eldest son), Johnnie and baby Geraldine.

Johnnie had always been her favourite. He was born in 1895, two years before she joined the household. When she first met him at three years of age he was a somewhat nervous little boy, overshadowed by his brother, two years his senior, and feeling piqued by the fact that Nanny's affections, or so he thought, had been stolen by his new baby sister, who now seemed to be ruling the roost in the nursery. He was a delicate-looking child with fair curls, worn rather long, contrasting noticeably with his boisterous brother's dark straight hair, and eyes of an unusual greeny-blue colour. Bertha had taken him at once into her arms and into her heart, and thus a friendship had developed between Johnnie and the nursery maid. Although he regarded her at first as a grown-up, on a par with Nanny Foster, she was, in fact, only twelve years his senior.

When, later, she became a housemaid, then parlour maid, then chief parlour maid, she still followed the fortunes of young Johnnie Tennant. She watched with some anxiety as he went away to prep school, then to public school, fearing he would not like it, then listened to the stories of his exploits when he returned for the holidays. To her surprise it seemed that the boy did not dislike school as much as she had thought he might. He told Bertha how he had developed a love of horse riding and he was thrilled when, on his eighteenth birthday, his father presented him with a magnificent chestnut stallion. The servants guessed that this was a reward for the young man who had pleased his father by agreeing to go for military training at Sandhurst. He had finally succumbed to the pressure of his family, far more readily than it was once feared he might have done, and followed his elder brother to the academy.

He had grown into a handsome young man, less fragile-looking than he had been as a child, though still slim and pale of complexion. Bertha had assumed that he might have a young lady somewhere, maybe more than one. He was a good-looking lad and boys who went away to school often became friendly with schoolmates' sisters. That had been the case with young Master Reginald. She had seen various young women at Tennant Hall from time to time and had gathered they were there because Reggie, with the permission of his parents, had invited them. She had never actually seen Johnnie, however, in the company of a young lady. Not that it was any of Bertha's business how the young gentlemen conducted themselves, but she still took a proprietory interest in Johnnie, wanting him to be happy in the career he had chosen – or had had chosen for him – and in his marriage, when it happened.

She now had a young man of her own, Thomas Martin, the head footman. They had started walking out together when she was in her mid-twenties. Some five years later they were no nearer fixing a date for their wedding, although they were now officially engaged. Bertha, on her days off, or on the rare occasions when she and Thomas went out together, wore a tiny pearl and opal engagement ring. She took no notice of her father, who told her with malevolent delight that opals were unlucky. Father had always had a vindictive streak and Bertha was unhappy about leaving her mother, ailing with a chest complaint, in his care. Her mother had assured her, however, that she was all right.

'Don't tha worry about me, lass,' she had said the last time Bertha was at home. 'I'll be alreet. Thi father's noan so bad, not wi' me, anyroad. He does what he can. It's just you and 'im as 'ave never hit it off, goodness knows why. And our Mabel'll be 'ere next weekend.' Bertha's younger sister was in service as well, in a different part of the county. 'You've got a good feller there, Bertha. That Thomas thinks the world of you, Ah can tell. You stick to 'im, there's a good lass. He's straight, dependable, like, an' that's the sort you want.'

Bertha had every intention of sticking to Thomas. He was a good man, as her mother said, straight – Bertha would have said strait-laced. She did wish that Thomas could be a little more loving, more demonstrative, in his behaviour towards her. Their relationship had progressed little beyond a few good night kisses, and although Bertha knew it would be wrong to – well, to do what she had heard the young housemaids giggling about – before they were married, she felt she was missing out on something. Violet, the youngest kitchen maid, was the talk of the servants' hall with her goings-on with Bert, one of the grooms. And what was more she didn't care, despite a telling off from Mr Murchison, the rigid-principled butler. Thomas agreed wholeheartedly with Mr Murchison. Such behaviour from the servants of Tennant Hall was disgraceful. No matter how the members of the family might choose to conduct themselves, the servants had to be beyond reproach. Bertha, in her position as chief parlour maid, had to pretend to agree, but she longed for more light-heartedness – more frivolity – in her friendship with Thomas. Her mother liked him, though, and she would do anything to please her dearly loved mother.

When she died at the beginning of 1914 Bertha felt sadder

than she had ever been in her life, although her mother's death was not totally unexpected. And when she returned home for the funeral she knew, her relationship with her father being on no better footing, that her visits there in the future would be very infrequent. The sad event actually spurred Thomas on to fix a wedding date. Early the next year, they decided, the spring of 1915; by that time they should have been able to find a cottage to rent and saved enough money for some necessary furniture. Then Bertha, of course, would stay at home whilst Thomas continued with his work at Tennant Hall.

But the events of summer 1914, put paid to all their plans. After hostilities started in August, the first territorials ready to move in the country were those of the 6th Battalion, Prince of Wales' Own West Yorkshire Regiment, and amongst their number was Private Thomas Martin. They had been practising trench digging and manoeuvres in the woods and parks of the area for the last couple of months and when Thomas requested to be relieved of his duties to join their number, Sir Reginald was pleased to give his consent. What else could he do? He had two sons serving in the same regiment, Reggie as a first lieutenant and Johnnie, who had only recently finished his training, as a second lieutenant.

It had all happened so suddenly that Bertha felt a sense of unreality, of disbelief that Thomas should have wanted to enlist and then depart so quickly. He said goodbye to her with scarcely more than a fond kiss and a cheery wave, never a backward glance as he went off to serve his King and Country. Britain had declared war on Germany on 4 August after the invasion of Belgium, and by the end of that month Thomas had gone. Bertha began to feel she did not know this man who was treating her in such a cavalier fashion, or so it seemed to her; perhaps she had never really known him or understood what made him tick. Reginald, the elder son of the family, had also gone, but it was October before Johnnie departed.

He looked very handsome in his smart khaki uniform when he came home one day in autumn on embarkation leave. A far superior uniform in cut, material and style than the one Thomas would now be wearing, Bertha thought to herself, but the young gentleman was a commissioned officer as befitted his class and breeding. He spent much of the time riding round the country-side on Rob Roy, his chestnut stallion, always alone now his brother had gone, although the two of them had never seemed to have very much in common. Wars in the past had been fought on horseback, Bertha reflected. She could just imagine Johnnie leading a cavalry charge, resplendent in a bright red tunic; but this war, from the little she knew of it, would be fought in a vastly different way. It was all about subterfuge and concealment, hence the khaki uniform to act as camouflage from the enemy. And the news was not good. The German armies had driven the British and French to retreat from Mons and had already captured Brussels, Ghent, Lille and Rheims. They had finally been stopped, however, by the French armies and Paris had been saved. Now a line of trenches had been dug reaching from the Swiss border to the Channel.

Bertha, keeping abreast of the news in the daily paper, as she felt it was her duty to do, being engaged to Thomas, could not see what earthly use these trenches could be. But the 'top brass' must know what they were doing and it was still being said that the war would be over by Christmas. Bertha fervently hoped that it might be so, although she knew that her fears were more for Johnnie than for Thomas. She did not know whether her fiancé was already overseas, in the midst of the conflict, or not. He wrote to her, but only infrequently. She knew he was not much of a scholar, but wherever he was he would be facing it all with the humourless stoicism with which he confronted everything.

It would not be so with Johnnie. Bertha could see the lines of strain that had appeared on his young face, ageing him almost overnight, and a look of anxiety in those oddly coloured bluey-green eyes. They had not had any chance yet during his leave for one of their friendly chats and she was not very surprised when he knocked on her door quite late one evening. Late for her, that was. Eleven o'clock was the time she usually went to bed, tired after her not inconsiderable duties – Lady Tennant was an exacting employer – although she knew that the members of the family often stayed up till the early hours, Mr Murchison seeing to their needs with uncomplaining servitude. She was already attired in her white cambric nightgown, but it was high-necked and long-sleeved, decorous in the extreme, and she felt no qualms about inviting the young man into her room. This was her friend Johnnie, whom she had known since he was three years old; and she knew at a glance that the poor lad was worried out of his mind. The lines of stress were more noticeable now and his pale face looked even more wan than usual, ashen in the dim gaslight. And his eyes were dark with the fear she had seen there before.

'Bertha, you don't mind, do you?' He flopped down unceremoniously on to her bed. 'I have to talk to somebody, and there's only you, isn't there, I can talk to? Nobody else would understand . . .'

It all poured out whilst she did very little but listen. She had already guessed most of what he was telling her; how he had agreed to do his military training only because he wanted to please his father, to show Sir Reginald that he was not the lily-livered weakling he always seemed to be in comparison with his devil-may-care brother. Bertha tried to tell him that none of this mattered, that everyone was different, we were all 'how the good Lord made us', and that he had many sterling qualities: kindliness, concern for others and a lack of conceit; these were what had always struck her about young Johnnie Tennant. It would have been pointless to tell him he should have stood up to his father and refused to be coerced into something that was alien to his nature; it was too late for that. The army was his chosen career and the country was now at war. She gathered that, despite everything, he had enjoyed his training and made many good friends. It had all seemed academic, good fun more than anything when the world was at peace. Now it was at war.

'I'm a coward, Bertha. I know I am,' he murmured, taking hold of both her hands in his. 'I know what's happening over there and I'm afraid. God help me, I'm ashamed to say it. I daren't say it to anyone else, but that's what I am; frightened to death.'

'Don't you think all the others are afraid as well?' she tried to console him. 'Well, perhaps not all of them.' She couldn't see unimaginative Thomas being frightened of anything. 'But most of them. I'll bet there are thousands of young men feeling just the same way as you do, and not wanting to admit to it neither. Anyroad, what are you worrying about, you silly chump?' Playfully she punched his cheek. 'They say it'll be all over by Christmas, and you're not going overseas just yet awhile, are you?'

'None of us knows, Bertha. They tell us very little, even the officers. Unimportant ones like me, anyway. And it won't be over just yet. It'll be a long hard struggle, that's my guess.' He rested his head against her shoulder. 'Hold me, Bertha. Just hold me close, like you used to do when I was a little boy, do you remember? I could never cuddle up to my mother, nor to Nanny Foster, the way I could to you. Reggie was always Mother's favourite. And Father thinks the sun shines out of Geraldine.'

'Stop feeling sorry for yourself, Master Johnnie!' she admonished him. 'You've got a lot of friends who care about you. I happen to know you're the favourite one with the servants. Always have been, and there's none of 'em'll hear a wrong word about you. So we'll have less o' that nonsense. Come on, lad, cheer up.' Tenderly she stroked his fair curls, feeling his forehead slightly damp at her touch. 'It'll not seem so bad when you get back there with your pals, wherever it is you're going. They'll all feel the same, you mark my words, an' you'll be able to cheer one another up. I know fellows have a good laugh when they get together, don't they?'

'Sometimes.' He gave a feeble grin. 'Oh, Bertha, you've always been so good to me. Much kinder to me than even my mother. I think you are a very lovely young woman, Bertha. I think you're ... beautiful.' He raised his hand and gently touched her hair, then ran his fingers lightly down her cheek.

Bertha was touched by his words, although she had never had any pretensions about being beautiful. Attractive, maybe, in a healthy wholesome sort of way. Her dark hair was thick and curled easily, her cheeks were rosy and her teeth were white and strong – she had none that were decayed, nor had she any false ones, unlike several of her workmates. Her main complaint about herself was that she was inclined towards plumpness. Thomas, in a rare moment of lightheartedness, had called her a proper armful.

She smiled at him. 'It's the first time anybody's ever said

that to me.' She chuckled. 'Happen you want yer eyes testing.'

'Don't joke about it, Bertha. I think you are beautiful, and if that Thomas of yours hasn't told you so then he's an even bigger fool than I took him for . . . Do you miss him?'

'Yes, I suppose I do,' replied Bertha. 'At least, I did at first, but I've got used to being on my own again now. It isn't as if we saw all that much of one another, not on our own.'

'Will you miss me, Bertha?'

'Yes, I'll miss you very much, Johnnie. And I shall say my prayers for you every night and ask God to keep you safe.'

He looked steadily into her eyes for several seconds, then he lowered his face towards hers and gently kissed her lips. Bertha knew that this was the moment when she should have put a stop to all this foolishness. For what else was it but folly, allowing the young gentleman of the house to kiss her? But for some reason she did not call a halt and after his second kiss, longer and more lingering, all sensible thoughts flew out of the window. This was Johnnie whom she had cared for so much when he was a little boy. Now he was a grown man, or almost; grown up enough to be going off to war at least, but to her he was still a little boy in need of love and affection and comfort. What harm could there be in giving the lad a little comfort?

She offered no resistance when he undid the ribbons of her nightdress and began to stroke her breasts, nor when, a few moments later, he divested himself of some of his clothing. 'Love me, Bertha . . .' he murmured. 'Please, let me love you. I want to, so much. I want to remember you.'

As he kissed and embraced her and she returned his embraces she realised he was no longer a little boy in need of comfort. He was a full-blooded young man, passionate and yet so tenderly loving and considerate as he gently eased himself inside her. She guessed he was not without some experience, but that it might well be, for him as well as for her, the first time he had indulged in the full act of love. She was eager and ready for him, frustrated and unfulfilled as she had long been during her engagement to Thomas, and though she experienced a sharp stab of pain it was soon forgotten in the rapturous lovemaking that followed.

'I'm sorry, Bertha,' he mumbled when at last, satiated, he

rested in the circle of her arms. 'I thought you would have . . . with you being engaged to Thomas, I mean.'

'You thought I was a woman of experience, eh, lad?' Bertha grinned. 'No, it was the first time . . . an' it was worth waiting for,' she added slyly.

'It was the first time for me, too,' said Johnnie. 'Well – the whole way, you know what I mean. Thank you, Bertha. Thank you . . . my lovely Bertha. It means so much to me. You mean a lot to me. I think . . . I love you.'

It might have been the first time, but Bertha knew that Johnnie Tennant would be a fast learner. He came to her room twice more that week before he departed to join his regiment, and she felt no hesitation or guilt about what they were doing. She was making him happy and was helping to remove that stricken fearful look from his eyes, and that was all that mattered.

He said goodbye to her in the privacy of her room, not in front of his family or the other servants. She made sure she was out of the way when his father drove him to the station the next morning. He had promised to write to her, but she did not really expect him to do so. It would not be seemly, the young gentleman corresponding with a servant, and Johnnie would no doubt realise that when he got away from Tennant Hall. He had said he loved her, more than once he had said it, but she had taken his words as idle ones, spoken in the passion of the moment. She had not told him that she loved him in return, although she did, albeit in a protective, maternal sort of way. She loved him with all her heart in a way she knew she had never cared for Thomas.

Later she realised what an idiot she had been, not to have given a thought as to what the outcome of this moment of madness – three nights of madness, in fact – might be. By Christmas, however, she knew she was expecting a baby although, as yet, it did not show, nor had any of the other servants any suspicions. Johnnie was due to come home for a couple of days' leave, but she knew that she could not – must not – face him. As it was her turn to have the Christmas period off, a privilege she would have been happy to forgo in normal circumstances, she seized the opportunity to go home to stay

71

with her father. Her sister, Mabel, was there too, but it was a miserable sort of Christmas, the first one without her mother. She was glad to return to Tennant Hall, although she knew that before long her condition would become apparent. She was numb, almost devoid of feeling during those first few months; frightened when she stopped to think about it, but Bertha was a realist and she knew the baby was there, steadily growing day by day, and there was nothing she could do about that. It never once occurred to her that she might try to get rid of it.

Maybe the thought had been there, at the back of her mind, though never fully formed, that Thomas would come to her rescue. But when he came home on leave in the February of 1915 that idea was very quickly dispelled.

'You're putting on weight, Bertha,' he said, looking at her searchingly. He had always been one to criticise rather than praise.

'Yes, too much pudding, I dare say.' She tried to give an easy laugh. 'I never could resist the cook's jam roly-poly.' But she could not entirely disguise the uneasiness in her eyes and in her voice, nor did she really want to. She knew that the truth would have to come out and maybe it was better sooner than later. She had nobody else she could turn to, no distant relatives with whom she could find a sanctuary until it was all over, at least, none that she knew of.

Thomas looked at her again, then, 'You're pregnant!' he gasped. 'Good God . . . You're having a baby!' She watched the expression in his steely grey eyes change, almost in a split second, from puzzlement to a blazing anger. 'You are, aren't you? Don't try to deny it.' They had been walking along a quiet country lane, near to Tennant Hall. Now he stopped in his tracks, seizing her by both arms and pushing her backwards against the hawthorn hedge. 'Who is it? Who've you been mucking about with? Just wait till I get me hands on him. I'll tear him limb from limb. I'll—'

Bertha was quite a buxom young woman, as tall as Thomas and heavier, too, so she was well able to defend herself. 'Get your hands off me, Thomas Martin!' She broke free from his grasp and pushed him away. 'Yes, it's true. I don't want to deny it. I'm expecting a baby. But I shan't tell you whose it is. I've told nobody, and I'm certainly not going to tell you.' She knew in that moment that even if he should ask her to marry him straightaway, to give a name to the baby, she would refuse. Any feeling that she might have had for him had died. She realised that the anger in his eyes stemmed from hurt pride, not from righteous indignation that someone had seduced – perhaps ill-used – his young woman.

Calmly she took off her engagement ring and handed it to him. 'You'd better have this back, Thomas. You won't be wanting to marry me now.'

'You're dead right I won't! Pick up another fellow's castoff? Not on your life. You're welcome to him, whoever he is. I've got me pride.' She watched him slip the ring into his overcoat pocket. His short outburst of temper was over. Bertha felt that she meant no more to him than the uniform on his back. No, less than that, for he had shown no regret at joining up and leaving her. All that mattered to him was his insufferable pride, the self-importance that she could now see had been part of his character all along.

'I'll say goodbye to you, Bertha. You'll not be seeing me again.' He turned and strode away in the direction of the village where his family lived. Bertha stared for a moment or two at his retreating back, scarcely believing that it should all be over between them so quickly. Then she walked off in the other direction along the country lane, back to Tennant Hall.

The next day she handed in her notice, making the excuse to Lady Tennant that her father was ill and she was needed at home. It was imperative that she should get away before she started to show and where else could she go but back home to her father? She dreaded to think what his reaction would be to her startling news, but she was his own flesh and blood when all was said and done, and surely he could not refuse to give her a home. The only person in whom she confided was Daisy, the other parlour maid, and she might not have told her had Daisy not already guessed.

'You're havin' a baby, luv, aren't you?' she said when Bertha told her she was leaving. 'You'll be getting wed then, you and Thomas? Well, I can't say I blame you, hurrying things along a bit. You have to when there's a war. I dare say he'll make a good enough husband, as husbands go. A bit stiff and starchy, mind. I must say I'm surprised at him—'

'It's not . . . The baby's not Thomas's,' said Bertha. 'We've split up, him and me. I can't tell you whose it is, Daisy. But you'll keep in touch with me, won't you? I'll be at my father's . . .'

Percy Shorrock was not at all pleased at his elder daughter's news, but she had guessed aright that even he would not be so callous as to throw her out on the street. She was not needed at home, though, as she had thought she might be, to see to his needs when he came home from the woollen mill. He had already replaced her mother, it seemed, in his affections, if affection there had ever been. Maud Ainscough, who lived a few doors away, was a widow. She had not yet moved in with Percy, but she was a constant visitor, seeing to his meals and his washing and mending. Bertha knew she was there on sufferance. She had not yet given any thought to what she would do when the baby arrived in July.

It was in May that she had a visitor. Daisy came to pass on to her the tragic news that the family had recently received. Second Lieutenant Johnnie Tennant had been killed in action at a place called Ypres.

Bertha broke down immediately, screaming and sobbing, shouting that it could not be true. She was powerless to stem the tide of grief that overcame her. Her feelings of hurt and disappointment over Thomas's behaviour, her anger with herself – and Johnnie – for the heedless way in which they had behaved, her father's indifference towards her and her mother's memory; all these emotions had been bottled up inside her for months and now, at this devastating news, they finally found an outlet. Daisy stared at her in astonishment for a moment before putting her arms round her in comfort. 'Was it . . . Johnnie Tennant?' she whispered in disbelief. 'Is that why you're so upset?'

'Yes, it was Johnnie,' Bertha managed to gasp between sobs. 'He's my baby's father. But nobody else knows. And they mustn't know. You must promise . . .'

Daisy promised, but she could not stay for long and when Maud Ainscough from down the road came in she left her friend in what she presumed were the woman's capable hands.

Bertha was inconsolable, incoherent in her anguish, and it was then that she had her first nervous attack, the condition that was to trouble her, intermittently, all her life.

Her father, with Maud's willing co-operation, was only too relieved to hand his daughter over to the care of the doctor. He pronounced her temporarily deranged and had her committed to the nearest mental asylum. It was there, two months later, that she gave birth to her baby boy, and it was there she stayed until Cedric and Eva Winters took her into their home some five years later.

Chapter 5

This was the story that Bertha told Abbie later that evening. She was out of bed and dressed, and feeling much better, although she still did not feel like going downstairs and facing Eva. It was only fair, however, that she should continue with the story she had alluded to that afternoon, though somewhat abridged in parts. The girl would not understand the depth of feeling a woman could have for a man, nor the lengths she would go to to make him happy, even though that happiness might prove to be her undoing.

Abbie was speechless for a few moments. She had hardly spoken at all whilst her aunt was recounting the incredible tale. A tale of love, passion, betrayal and inconstancy – for Abbie could not help but think that this Johnnie, as well as Thomas, had been guilty of letting Bertha down – of false incarceration and humiliation. No wonder her aunt still suffered from nervous attacks. What must it have done to her to spend almost five years in a mental institution when she was perfectly sane? Abbie had thought her aunt was such an ordinary little woman; she could hardly believe that such terrible things had happened to her.

'Oh, Aunt Bertha, it must have been dreadful for you,' she exclaimed, tears welling up in her eyes. 'And I never knew.'

'Nobody knows, love, except your father and mother, and they never mention it. It's best forgotten . . . although I've never been able to forget it entirely. It all comes back to haunt me at times – that's why I'm ill. But happen I'll be better now I've talked it all out of me.'

'I can understand now why you're so grateful to my parents,' said Abbie. 'It must have been like coming out of prison.'

'It was, exactly. Not that I know anything about prison, mind, but it couldn't be any worse than that. Convicts are usually quite sane, I reckon, but some of those folk . . .' She gave a shudder.

'But you said you had no close relations, Auntie, nobody you could go to when you found out you were . . . having a baby. Didn't you know about my parents then?'

'It's a long story, love, and it doesn't really matter, except to say that they found me eventually. Your mother and I are second cousins or something like that – we share the same great-grandparents, and the same name before she was married. Anyroad, this is how it happened. Your father had a patient who was moved to . . . that place. Even now, love, I can't say the name. It's near Longridge, not all that far from here and quite near to the village where we lived, in t'other direction, of course. Anyhow, I got talking to your father. I was working alongside his patient, y'see, in the laundry, and he asked me to keep an eye on her. I think he could see I wasn't . . . you know,' she tapped at her temple, 'like most of the others. He found out my name was Shorrock – his wife's maiden name – so he made enquiries, and you know the rest. They came and rescued me. And I really think the good Lord must've been watching over me that day I met your father.'

'Where was He the rest of the time then?' asked Abbie tersely. 'God, I mean. Why didn't He see to it you were rescued earlier?'

'Oh, I don't know, love. It doesn't do any good to talk like that. Maybe He was trying to teach me something. I don't know and we can't start questioning His ways.'

'But didn't my mother know she had a relation in that . . . hospital? If you were her cousin?'

'Second cousin, dear. No . . . I don't think she knew,' Bertha replied slowly. 'It was another branch of the family, and families drift apart over the years, don't they? Sons and daughters go to live in different places. Like my sister. I thought you might've asked about our Mabel, why I didn't go there. Well, she got married and went to live somewhere near Hull. Before you could say Jack Robinson she'd got a houseful of kiddies and no room for me. But I reckon she just didn't want to be bothered . . . There was quite a lot of it in those days, girls being put away because they had illegitimate babies.'

'I'd no idea that things like that went on, though I remember that girl at our church being sent away to her aunt because she was expecting a baby. But it's not . . . it's not a crime, is it? I know it's supposed to be wrong, if you're not married. But . . . I'm sure you didn't do anything wrong, Aunt Bertha.'

'No, maybe not.' Bertha gave a rueful smile. 'You'll find out when you fall in love, but if you've any sense you'll wait till after you're married before you . . . do what I did.'

'Get married, you say?' Abbie gave a bitter little laugh. 'I doubt if I'll ever do that, not if Mother's got anything to do with it. She thinks I'm still a little girl.'

Bertha sighed. 'She's tried to do what she thinks is best for you, I suppose. And you can see why I don't criticise her, can't you? I've been only too glad to work for them, because they gave me a good home. I know you think I'm run off me feet at times, but it's nothing to what I had to do in that place, I can tell you. Talk about slave labour!'

'You worked in the laundry, you said?'

'Aye, up to me elbows in near boiling water, rubbing, possing, mangling. And ironing scores o' them stiff tunics they make 'em wear. Like prison garb, as though you've no identity of your own. What I couldn't stand, though, was all the locks and bolts. Soon as you went in a room they locked it behind you. An' all them strange folk talking to themselves. Some of 'em were violent at times. I've seen 'em put in strait-jackets, padded cells even. I told the folk in charge time and time again that I wasn't like the others, but they wouldn't take any notice of me, even the doctors wouldn't. Mind you, I think they knew jolly well I was quite sane, once I'd got over my breakdown, what sent me there in the first place, but they wouldn't admit it. I think they regarded it as my punishment, you see, love. I'd gone and had a baby without being married, and that was considered a terrible crime in those days; and I'd given a lot of folk a lot of trouble into the bargain. So they decided, between 'em, that I'd best stay where I was. Besides, I'd nowhere to go, had I, with my own family not wanting to know. Not till your father came.'

'Don't think about it, Aunt Bertha,' said Abbie gently, although she did not think her aunt was likely to have another funny turn just then. She was speaking very rationally and the look of torment that Abbie had been alarmed to see in her eyes earlier that day had completely gone. 'What about the baby, though? Why wouldn't they let you keep him? Why did you have to have him adopted?'

'It was for the best, love; they made me see that. I was in a bad way when he was born, and for quite a while afterwards. Some of the nurses were kind, though. One of them let me hold him and I could see he had fair hair . . . like Johnnie's. And blue eyes, but all babies have blue eyes, haven't they? They wouldn't let me start feeding him in case I got too fond of him. No, it was for the best, at the time at least . . . though I still think about him. I've thought of him quite a lot since the war started. I dare say he'll be in the army, like his father was, or the RAF maybe. Perhaps right here in Blackpool. Do you know, I never thought of that. He might be right here, billeted in one of the boarding houses, and I'd pass him in the street and not even know him . . . I think I would know him, though, if he looks like his father.'

'You've never tried to find him then, Aunt Bertha?'

'No, of course not. How could I? He'll have a different name, and I don't even know what part of the country he went to. Besides, I gave up all my rights, didn't I?'

'Your name will be on his birth certificate, though?'

'Aye, I suppose it will. If his parents let him see it. Often they don't.' Bertha paused significantly. 'Don't worry your head about it, love. I've told you – you came along, didn't you? You don't know what a difference it made to my life when you were born. And you've done me a world of good now. I shall be back in that kitchen tomorrow, don't you worry. And I have a feeling I might have seen an end to my funny turns an' all.'

'I hope so, Auntie.' Abbie smiled at her, then went across and kissed her on the cheek. 'Thank you for telling me all about it. I'll leave you in peace now to get a good night's sleep.'

'No . . . don't leave me just yet, love.' Bertha sounded a mite agitated again. 'What I'd really like is a nice drink of cocoa. D'you think you could make us some? Bring it up here, then we'll talk about something different, eh?'

Abbie understood that maybe it was not wise to leave her

aunt alone just yet with her painful memories. She made the cocoa and went back upstairs.

'I met such a nice girl today, Aunt Bertha,' she said. 'Actually, I'd met her before – it's the girl whose little brother died, you remember? – but we had a really good chat this afternoon. She works at Harding's Grocers. Doreen Miller, she's called and – oh, Aunt Bertha – I would like so much to be friends with her.'

'I've got some tickets for the Palace Varieties on Saturday night,' said Doreen Miller to her mother, one evening towards the end of July. 'One of the customers gave them to me. She'd booked seats and now her husband is ill and they can't go, so she wondered if I could make use of them. Nice of her, wasn't it? And d'you know what I'm going to do, Mam? I'm going to ask Abigail Winters if she'd like to go with me.'

'The doctor's daughter?' Nancy looked as though her eyes were about to pop out of her head.

'Of course I mean the doctor's daughter,' laughed Doreen. 'How many Abigail Winters do you know?'

'Mmm . . . it's a kind thought, I suppose.' Her mother, looking up from the ironing board, sounded very doubtful. 'But d'you think it's really a good idea?'

'Of course it is! Why not? Honestly, Mam, I wish you'd make up your mind. There you were, going on at me 'cause you thought I'd been rude to her. Now as I'm trying to be friendly, like, that's not right neither. Why shouldn't I ask her, for goodness' sake?'

'Because . . . well, she's the doctor's daughter, isn't she?'

'So you keep saying. And it was you that told me she was lonely, that she could do with a few friends. Or it might've been me dad that said that, I can't remember. Anyroad, it was the pair of you that made me apologise to her, and when I got talking to her I knew I liked her, much better than I thought I would. So what's wrong, eh?'

'It's all right being friendly and polite, instead of downright rude. But you don't need to overdo it, our Doreen.' Nancy picked up another flat iron that was heating on the range and started to smooth it back and forth over her husband's blue striped shirt, her lips closed tightly together in a disapproving line. 'We're not in the same class as them, luv, can't you see? Of course I want you to be nice to the lass, but I don't want to see you get hurt neither. She might be offended, you asking her to go to the Palace Varieties, just as though—'

'Just as though she's one of the common herd, like we are? The lower orders, is that what you're trying to say, Mam?'

'I'm only saying we know our place, Doreen, yer dad and me. And people like that – well, they're different, that's all.'

'Good grief! You really think they're our "betters", don't you? That sort of thinking is on the way out now, Mam.'

'Yes, maybe it is, but I can't forget what I've been used to. Anyroad, it was you that called her Lady Muck. You wouldn't even give her the time of day.'

'And when I got to know her better I changed my mind. OK? She'll be only too pleased if I ask her, Mam. I know she will.'

'All right, dear. You know best.' Nancy's sigh of irritation refuted her words. 'But what about Gwen? You usually go out with her on a Saturday night, don't you?'

'She's got other fish to fry, Mam. Her boyfriend's home on leave. Anyway, I'd already decided to ask Abbie.'

'Ask Abbie what?' said her father, coming into the room at that moment. 'Is it the doctor's lass that you're talking about, the one that came here? What are you going to ask her?'

Doreen explained for the second time and Harold Miller, unlike his wife, approved the idea.

So did Abbie when Doreen called at the doctor's house to see her. The girl walked into the waiting room 'as bold as brass', as Eva Winters reported later to her husband. 'The cheek of it! Actually asking if she could have a word with Abigail, and she hadn't even got an appointment.'

Eva was just about to send her away with a flea in her ear when Abbie popped out of the surgery for a moment, and her mother had no option but to say, 'This ... er ... this young person wants to speak to you, Abigail. I can't imagine why, I'm sure, but she'd better be quick about it. You've got your work to do.'

Abbie drew her away, out of her mother's hearing, guessing from Doreen's friendly smile that it was not a medical matter she wished to discuss. They spoke in whispers, but Abbie was aware of her mother's eyes on them all the time. Eva must have noticed Abbie's gasp of joyous surprise when Doreen told her about the variety show on Saturday evening, and her eager nod of acceptance. Yes, of course she would be delighted to go, she answered. They agreed to meet at the corner of Park Road, a convenient spot for both of them, then walk to the theatre together.

Now all Abbie had to do was to persuade her parents, more particularly her mother, to allow her to go. She dashed back into the surgery after her chat with Doreen, not giving Eva the chance to ask what the girl had wanted.

She brought up the subject when they were all at the dinner table, feeling she might have the bolstering support of her father and her Aunt Bertha. Not that Bertha's words carried much weight with her mother, but Abbie knew her aunt would be wholeheartedly behind her even if she did not say very much. They had almost finished their first course before Abbie plucked up courage to speak. She decided it would be best to come right out with it and not waste time prevaricating.

'I'm going to the Palace Varieties on Saturday night, Mother,' she said, speaking very quickly. 'With Doreen Miller. You know, the girl who called to see me today. That's why she came, because somebody has given her some tickets and she wants me to go with her.'

Eva did not speak for several seconds. Abbie could almost imagine her mother had not heard as she continued to eat the remainder of the minced meat and potatoes that was left on her plate, taking small mouthfuls as she always did, then dabbing her lips precisely with her napkin. Only when she had placed her knife and fork neatly at the side of her plate did she answer her daughter.

'The Palace Varieties?' Her lips curled in a travesty of a smile. 'With . . . that girl? Good gracious, Abigail! What a preposterous idea! Decent young ladies like you don't go to places like the Palace Varieties, and especially not with a girl such as that. How could you imagine for one moment that you might go, or that I would allow you to? No, Abigail, definitely not; it's out of the question.'

'Why shouldn't I go?' Abbie stared back defiantly at her mother on the other side of the table. 'I think it was very kind of Doreen Miller to invite me – I told her so – and I said I would go with her. I'm meeting her at the corner of Park Road on Saturday evening.' She drew a deep breath before continuing. 'And if you had listened properly to me, Mother, you would have realised I was not asking your permission. I'm just telling you that I'm going! Other girls don't have to ask their mothers every time they want to go out, so why should I?' She stopped suddenly, brought to a halt by the look of rage on Eva's face. The icy cold blueness of her eyes was accentuated by the angry red flush which was suffusing her cheeks and neck. Abbie decided that enough was enough. She didn't know how she had found the courage to be so rebellious, but she did not want to go so far as to cause her mother to have an apoplectic fit.

'How . . . how dare you?' Eva's voice came out as a strangled whisper rather than a shout of anger. 'I've never known such insolence in all my life!' She jumped to her feet with such force that the heavy oak dining chair rocked on its legs. 'Get out!' she bellowed, suddenly finding her voice again. 'Leave the room this minute. Get up to your bedroom!' She pointed her finger towards the door before wagging it menacingly in her daughter's face. 'And you don't come down until you've learned to behave yourself and are ready to apologise.'

'That's quite enough, Eva.' Cedric Winters' placid, but authoritative, tone cut across Eva's strident shrieks. 'Stay where you are, Abigail.' He put a hand out towards Abbie who, in spite of her best intentions, had already risen to her feet. 'There is no need for any of us to lose our tempers over this matter. Sit down, Eva, and just calm down as well. You're going to make yourself ill. And as for you, young woman . . .' he turned to Abbie, 'try to control your tongue a little more, although I don't suppose you meant to be cheeky.' Her father was not smiling. He was, in fact, looking rather worried, but Abbie thought she could see a glimmer of understanding in his grey eyes.

'That's right, take her side! You always do.' Eva sat down again with an unladylike, most uncharacteristic, thump. 'And I'd ask you not to undermine my authority, Cedric. If I reprimand

Abigail then I expect you to support me.' She continued to glare at Abbie across the table.

'I said leave it, Eva!' The doctor almost, but not quite, shouted. 'I can't support you – no, not even you, my dear – when I think you are in the wrong. And this time I do happen to think so. I have to agree, however, that Abigail was rather . . . er, impulsive in the way she spoke to you, but I know she will say she is sorry. Won't you, Abigail?'

At her father's stern but pleading glance, Abbie did murmur, 'Yes . . . I'm sorry, Mother. I didn't mean to be rude.' But Eva refused to meet her eyes.

'I don't see why you should be against her going to such a respectable place as the Palace Theatre,' her father continued. 'Anyway, what Abigail says is perfectly true, you know. She is nineteen years of age now and she should not have to ask her parents' permission when she wants to go out for the evening.'

'I was under the impression that twenty-one was the age of consent,' replied Eva coolly. 'And I'm of the opinion that while Abigail lives under our roof she should obey our rules. It's that girl I object to more than anything. She's not a suitable companion at all for someone like Abigail. A family like that, living hand to mouth in all that squalor. That boy caught diphtheria because he wasn't looked after properly. And to think of letting Abbie go to a variety show! Honestly, Cedric, I think you've completely lost your senses as well.'

'I've told you before, Eva, and I don't see why I should waste my breath telling you again, but it seems that you must have forgotten.' Cedric sighed. 'The Miller family are decent hard-working folk and Doreen is a most respectable and pleasant young woman. Young Tony dying was a tragedy they are still trying to come to terms with. Personally, I'm glad if Doreen is going out and enjoying herself. And as far as the Palace Theatre is concerned it's a very respectable place. We've been there on occasions ourselves, Eva, if you care to remember.'

'To the cinema, yes; not to the Varieties. Who is performing there this week, Abigail, do you know?' Eva, at last, condescended to glance towards her daughter.

'Yes, Rawicz and Landauer,' replied Abbie. 'You know – the pianists.'

'Yes, yes, of course I know who Rawicz and Landauer are. Quite able pianists from what I've heard of them. They broadcast on the wireless sometimes. Not in the same class as Myra Hess, of course, but I don't suppose it will do you any harm to listen to them. With you being a pianist yourself, I mean. No doubt it will be mostly popular, trivial stuff they will be playing.' Eva gave a derisive shrug, 'but there may be the odd piece by Debussy or Liszt. Yes, Abigail, on second thoughts I see no reason why we should not allow you to go.'

'Thank you, Mother,' replied Abbie with a show of meekness. Her mother was priceless! Never would she admit when she was defeated. Now she was making it out to be some sort of educational experience. What Abbie had omitted to tell her mother was that there was also a comedian on the bill called Max Wall. Abbie knew very little about him except that her mother refused to listen when he was on the wireless, pronouncing him crude and vulgar, although even Abbie, with her limited experience, knew that the BBC had very stringent rules about what they allowed to be broadcast. She could only guess that her mother, even though she would not admit it, must have heard him at some time on the stage and disapproved. Abbie just hoped that Eva would not decide to look in the *Evening Gazette* for the list of the artistes. It was too late though; she had already said that Abbie could go.

'But you make sure you are back in this house not a minute later than ten o'clock,' said Eva now. 'Do you understand that, Abigail? Have I made that quite clear? I will not have you wandering around the streets of Blackpool with all the riffraff that's around these days. All those RAF men and other nationalities as well. Goodness knows what might happen to respectable young ladies.'

'I'll be home by ten, Mother,' said Abbie, still very mildly. She couldn't believe how well things were going now, thanks to the intervention of her father. 'I believe the ballrooms close early anyway, so I wouldn't be late.'

'Ballroom? Who said anything about the ballroom?' retorted Eva. 'I thought you said you were going to the variety show?'

'Yes, but you can go into the ballroom with the same ticket,' Cedric broke in quickly. 'You know that very well, Eva. We used to go ourselves on the – er – odd occasion ... Many moons ago,' he added, as though to himself. 'It's the same at the Tower and the Winter Gardens, but from what I've heard the Palace is far less ... brash than those other places. I can't see that Abigail will come to any harm there. And I think we might say a quarter past ten, not ten o'clock, don't you, dear?'

'Abigail doesn't dance,' said Eva, 'so there's little point in her going into a ballroom.'

'She can watch the others,' replied Cedric evenly. 'Besides, you never know what you can do until you try.' Carefully he placed his knife and fork at the side of his plate. 'Now, are we going to have any pudding today?'

'Yes, of course we are. Bertha has made a trifle, I believe. Come along Bertha – what are you waiting for? Go and dish it out ... please. And you can put the plates together, Abigail. You shouldn't need to be told to clear the table. Come on now, get a move on!' Her mother, knowing she had lost the argument, was retaliating with a bout of bossiness, not that that was anything unusual.

Bertha had been sitting silently throughout all this inter-change of views, quite forgotten, except by Abbie. When they escaped to the kitchen, her aunt gave her a conspiratorial grin.

'My goodness, that was an argy-bargy and no mistake! You cheeky monkey, you!' Bertha nudged her. 'Fancy you answering your mother back like that. I'd never have believed it. Just watch it though, Abbie. Don't go too far, there's a good girl ... You know what she's like. But I'm ever so glad you're going to the show, I am that. And I hope you have a real good time.'

'I don't know what I'm going to wear, Aunt Bertha,' said Abbie on the Thursday evening before her outing with Doreen. 'All my dresses are so dark and old-fashioned looking, except for that green and white one, and that's ... well, it's childish, isn't it?'

Abbie knew it was a ridiculous state of affairs that, at nineteen years of age, all her clothes were still chosen by her mother, but until recently she had never thought of insisting on making her own choice. The green and white daisy dress had been a rare concession on Eva's part to the summer weather, but

87

to Abbie's mind it was more suitable for a twelve-year-old. 'Honestly, Auntie, puffed sleeves and a gathered skirt at my age. I shall feel so stupid going into the Palace dressed like that, but it's the only summery dress I've got.'

'Then buy another one,' replied her aunt, sounding very decisive. 'It's about time you treated yourself to a nice dress, Abbie. You can afford it, can't you?'

'You mean . . . go and buy one myself?'

'Yes, why not?'

'Oh, I don't know . . . although I have got some money saved up.' Eva, surprisingly, did not seem to mind Abbie having her own bank book. Indeed, she encouraged her to save and not waste her money on what she called 'silly fripperies', and until now Abbie had been obedient. 'But Mother has always insisted on going with me. I've got to admit she's not mean with money, but she chooses my clothes because she pays for them.'

'You mean she has done till now,' said Bertha. 'It's high time you started choosing your own, Abigail. Far be it from me to encourage you to rebel, but you've been doing a pretty good job of it yourself, lately, without any encouragement, haven't you?' Bertha's eyes twinkled. 'And there's nothing wrong with buying yourself a new frock. Go on – why don't you? Go into town tomorrow afternoon and treat yourself. Your father doesn't expect you to work all day, does he? And you could be back for the five o'clock surgery.'

'Yes, but I usually go into town on Saturday afternoon with Mother,' replied Abbie doubtfully. 'I don't suppose she'll want me to go with her this week, though. She's still annoyed with me about this Palace thing. She's hardly speaking to me.'

'What about yer old aunt going with you, if you don't want to go on yer own?' Bertha's face broke into a cheerful grin. 'Come to think of it, it's about time *I* had a new frock, never mind about you. I haven't used any of my clothing coupons yet and I can help you out with a few if you haven't enough. I reckon you'll need some new shoes as well, Abbie.'

'Do you think so?' faltered Abbie. In spite of her recent spell of bravado she felt apprehensive at the thought of asking her mother to give her the ration book, let alone telling her she was going shopping for clothes with her Aunt Bertha. 'I usually wear my sandals in the summer.'

'Of course you need new shoes. Don't spoil the ship for an 'a'p'orth of tar, lass. It's them flat Clark's sandals that make you look – well – a bit childish sometimes, not just the dress. You want some nice black court shoes.'

'But I'm so big, aren't I? Tall as well as a bit ... plump. That's why I don't wear high heels. Not that Mother would ever let me have any,' she added.

'They don't have to be high,' said Bertha. 'Cuban heels are very fashionable, so I believe, and your legs are nice and slim, Abbie, even though you do take after your father in build. Don't you worry, you'll look a real bobby-dazzler by the time we've finished.'

Eva said nothing when Abbie asked if she could have her ration book. She handed it to her without question, albeit distantly, and to Abbie's announcement that she and her aunt were going shopping she merely raised her eyebrows in a supercilious way. Abbie knew she was being well and truly 'sent to Coventry', but she found she didn't greatly care. She had so much to look forward to.

They both held bulging carrier bags when, at the end of their shopping trip, they climbed aboard the Marton-bound tram. Abbie, with the help of her aunt and the assistant at Sally Mae's dress shop, had chosen a rayon crepe dress in vertical stripes of pale blue and cream, unlike anything she had ever worn before. Bertha assured her that the semi-fitting style with lightly padded shoulders and pleated skirt suited her very well. She would have been very unsure on her own, but even she could tell that the black patent leather court shoes, cut low at the front and with just a medium cuban heel, that she purchased from Stead and Simpson, made her legs look slimmer.

For herself Bertha had chosen a grey pinstripe costume, rather than a dress. She said it would be useful to wear at chapel and she already had a few good blouses to go with it. It was Abbie's day, she insisted, not hers, and Abbie guessed she had only bought the costume to keep her niece company and to stop her feeling guilty at spending so much money on herself. It was at Bertha's insistence that they went into Woolworth's and bought a length of blue satin ribbon which just matched the blue stripe in Abbie's new dress.

'What's that for?' asked Abbie. 'I'm not going to wear a ribbon, Aunt Bertha. I'll look more childish than ever with a bow in my hair; unless you mean I've to tie it back.'

'No, not a bow, love. One of those – what do you call 'em? – Alice bands. I think it'd suit you if you combed your hair loose, and this'll keep it in place. I'm going to make one for you. Just trust yer old aunt.'

Abbie scarcely recognised herself when she stood in front of her wardrobe mirror the following day. It was late afternoon and, after having had an early tea, she would be soon on her way to meet Doreen. First house at the Palace started at the ridiculously early hour of 5.30. There were two houses each evening, the second at eight o'clock, to enable the whole place to close down soon after ten, to comply with the wartime restrictions. Early for most people, but it would be the first time Abbie had ever been out so late in the centre of Blackpool, unless accompanied by her parents. Her stomach was churning with butterflies already at the thought of the evening ahead, but she had to admit that she looked – well, if not exactly beautiful then at least quite attractive. She surveyed herself critically. At least her reflection told her she was as far removed from the old Abbie as it was possible to imagine.

The knee-length skirt, much shorter than anything she had worn before, and the smart shoes made her long legs – possibly her best feature – look even slimmer, especially encased in her one and only pair of sheer pure silk stockings. But it was her hairstyle that had transformed her appearance. She usually wore it in a roll round her head, a style more favoured by older women, but one her mother had insisted upon for her job as doctor's receptionist. After washing it the previous night in some specially bought Amami shampoo, her aunt had brushed her dark shining hair until it crackled. Now, assisted by curling tongues, heated in the fire, it hung in a gently curving page-boy style almost to her shoulders. It was held in place by the Alice band that Bertha had quickly made with the blue ribbon and a scrap of elastic.

Her face, however, was devoid of make-up. She had never

used any, not even the slightest dusting of powder or smear of lipstick. Even the new Abbie, beginning at last to emerge from her chrysalis, guessed that to do so would be to push her mother a little too far. Her rosy cheeks and the bright eyes that looked back at her were due to excitement rather than artifice.

'There you are; I told you you'd look a bobby-dazzler, didn't I?' said her aunt. Bertha's face, too, was flushed with pleasure. She reached up and kissed Abbie on the cheek. 'Off you go now. You'd best not be late meeting that Doreen. Have a good time, won't you, love? I shall be dying to hear all about it tomorrow. Or tonight, happen, if you're not too late back. Pop in and see me, love, before you go to bed.'

'I'll not dare be late, Aunt Bertha,' said Abbie. 'You know what Mother said. And if she catches sight of me looking like this . . .' Tentatively Abbie touched her flowing hair, 'I'm frightened she'll stop me from going, even now.'

'No, she won't,' replied Bertha. 'Even Eva knows she's lost this round,' she added quietly. 'Come on, we'll see if the coast is clear.' She opened the bedroom door and leaned over the banister rail. 'I heard her come in from town about an hour ago, but the sitting room door's shut tight. Go on, then – down them stairs – quietly, mind. You'll be out of the front door before she even realises.'

And so she was, but Abbie guessed her mother was keeping well out of the way on purpose.

Doreen was already waiting at the corner of Park Road when Abbie alighted from the tram.

'Sorry if I'm late,' said Abbie, dashing towards her.

'You're not. It's me that's early.' Doreen gave a friendly grin. 'But we'd best step on it. It starts in a quarter of an hour. We've got tickets, though, so we won't have to queue. That makes a change these days.' She turned to grin at Abbie again. She certainly seemed to be a most cheerful, chirpy sort of girl. 'I say, you do look nice,' she went on. 'You've done yer hair different, haven't you? It suits you.'

'Thank you,' said Abbie, patting at her new page-boy bob somewhat self-consciously. It felt strange to her, flowing round her neck instead of being tightly skewered back with hair grips.

'I've never worn it like this before,' she went on. 'Do you really think it looks all right?'

' 'Course it does,' replied Doreen. 'You look real nice, and I wouldn't say so if I didn't mean it. I always say what I think, me. But you know that already, don't you?' She gave a rueful smile. 'Every time I open me big mouth I put me foot in it; that's what me dad says. Honest, though, it makes you look a lot younger. How old are you, Abbie, if you don't mind me asking?'

'I'm nineteen,' Abbie answered. 'Twenty next January. What about you?'

'I'll be nineteen in March,' said Doreen. 'I thought you were a lot older than me when I first met you.' She stopped abruptly. 'There I go again! Both feet right in it. Sorry, Abbie. But that hairstyle does make a difference, you know.'

'It's all right, honestly.' Abbie laughed. 'I know I look older than I am. It's my mother's fault. She always tells me how I have to dress and do my hair. At least, she has done until now. As a matter of fact, I thought you were quite a bit younger than me. With you being small, I mean.'

'Yeah, I've often wished I could grow a bit,' remarked Doreen. 'Never satisfied, are we?'

'No, I suppose not,' said Abbie. There was a few seconds' pause in the conversation, inevitably, thought Abbie, as they didn't know one another very well yet, although Doreen did seem to be quite a chatterbox. 'It was really kind of you to invite me to come tonight,' she continued. 'I appreciate it very much . . . Doreen.'

'Don't mench,' said Doreen cheerfully. 'I wouldn't have asked you if I didn't want your company. And it's a way of saying sorry an' all.'

'Oh, don't bring all that up again,' said Abbie quickly. 'I'm just glad you've asked me. I've never been to the Palace before.'

'You what?' Doreen turned to stare at her in amazement. 'You've never . . . ? Oh, come on, you must've been.'

'No, I've never been to the variety theatre, nor the ballroom. I remember going to the cinema there once. I can't remember what the film was, but it would be something worthwhile and educational . . . My mother's words, not mine,' she added, as Doreen gave her a peculiar look. 'We only go to the cinema if

Mother thinks it will be a film that's suitable for me. We went to see *Major Barbara* last week, at the Odeon.'

'Never heard of it.'

'It was very good, actually. Rex Harrison was in it – I like him – and Wendy Hiller. It's from a play by George Bernard Shaw.' She stopped, aware that Doreen was giving her another funny look. 'But I shall enjoy it much more tonight; I know I will.'

'From the sublime to the ridiculous, eh?' laughed Doreen. 'I say, poor you. You don't have much of a life, do you, with your mother telling you what to do all the time? Sorry, I'm being dead cheeky, aren't I?'

'No, you're not.' Abbie shook her head. 'You're quite right. But I've started sticking up for myself – just a bit. Mother doesn't like it much, but I'm tired of being treated like a little girl.'

'So you've started to rebel, eh? Good for you!'

'Only mildly. There was quite an argument before she would let me come tonight. She only agreed because Rawicz and Landauer are performing.'

'Oh yes, the chaps that play the piano. There are lots of other acts as well, though. It'll be good . . . What do you do then, if you don't go to the pictures, or dancing? Where do you go?'

'Oh, we sometimes go to functions at the church we attend. Plays and socials and concerts. I perform at the concerts sometimes. And Mother has people round for dinner from time to time, and I have to sit there and make polite conversation, you know?' Doreen grinned and nodded, though she looked rather puzzled.

Abbie hurried on to say, 'I spend quite a lot of time with my Aunt Bertha as well. She lives with us and she has her own little room. Her parlour, she calls it, and we sit and listen to the wireless, or sometimes she does her sewing and I read a book. She's lovely, my Aunt Bertha. You would like her.'

'Yes, I know who she is,' replied Doreen. 'Miss Shorrock – she comes in the shop. She's always real nice and friendly. Not like some of the stuck-up folk who live on Whitegate Drive. Ooh – er . . . sorry!'

'It's all right.' Abbie smiled.

'Did you say you performed at concerts? I say, you clever thing, you! What do you do? Sing?'

'No, I play the piano. I had lessons till I was sixteen and I still enjoy playing.'

'No wonder you're interested in Rawicz and Whotsit then. I like a nice tune, me, but I don't know much about it all. I 'spect you took a load of exams an' all that at school, didn't you? School Cert or Matric or whatever they call it.'

'I got my School Certificate, yes,' said Abbie guardedly, not wanting to sound as though she was boasting. 'But I left when I was sixteen. Mother didn't want me to stay on any longer. She wanted me to work at home, for my father. And that's what I'm still doing, as you know.'

Doreen nodded. 'I left when I was fourteen, me. I had to get a job 'cause there were so many of us, y'see. Six of us kids – till our Tony went – and I was the eldest. Not that I'm dim or anything. I didn't mind school. I used to be top of the class in the Juniors, or pretty near. I was good at sums. I still am, an' it's a good job an' all with all the reckoning up we have to do at Harding's.'

'Do you like working there?'

Doreen shrugged. ' 'S all right, I suppose. It'll do, just for now. I was thinking of joining the ATS till our Tony died. But I don't think it'd be right to leave Mam and Dad just yet. They still get upset. I'd like to do something more worthwhile, though, to help the War Effort. You know what they're always saying, we've all got to do our bit.'

'That's exactly how I feel, too,' agreed Abbie. 'My father says I'm doing a very important job helping him, especially since I started doing more work in the surgery. But sometimes I feel . . .' She gave a deep sigh, suddenly wanting to confide in her new friend. 'Oh, I don't know. I feel that I'd like to get right away. I'm so . . . so repressed, so . . . smothered.' She gave a tight little smile. 'I don't suppose you know what I mean. I dare say you have a good deal of freedom, don't you?'

'Oh, I think I do understand,' said Doreen, looking at her sympathetically. 'Don't you imagine for one moment that my mam and dad don't fuss, because they do, especially Mam. Don't all parents? Never mind, eh?' She linked her arm companionably through Abbie's as they turned into Bank Hey Street. 'P'raps we'll be able to spread our wings one of these days, you and me. Both of us join the ATS, or the WAAFs, mebbe. That'd give yer mother a fit, wouldn't it? She'd be having kittens!'

Doreen's high spirits were infectious and Abbie found herself giggling back. 'Not half!' she agreed, then she smiled to herself as she thought of what her mother would say to such a common expression.

'Here we are,' said Doreen, pausing at the Palace entrance. 'Gosh, what a crowd! I told you it was a good job we've got tickets. Hang on a minute while I find them.'

Chapter 6

The Palace building, comprising a theatre, cinema and ball-room, was comparatively small compared with the Tower and the Winter Gardens. Many visitors and residents, however, preferred its friendly and comfortable atmosphere, and as soon as Abbie, with Doreen leading the way, stepped over its threshold she felt, somehow, that she would not be too much out of her depth here.

There was not much time to spare as it was almost 5.30 when they squeezed past a row of people already seated, and slid into their red plush seats some ten rows back in the stalls. The small orchestra came to the end of its overture with a blaring, slightly discordant, flourish, to perfunctory applause from the audience; then the red velvet curtains were drawn back and the show began.

To Abbie, who had never seen its like before, it was all very thrilling. The illuminated numbers at each side of the stage changed from 1 to 2 to 3, and so on as the various acts took the stage. There was a troupe of long-legged dancing girls who opened the show; then a ventriloquist with a grinning, wide-mouthed, pop-eyed dummy; a woman with performing poodles; a singing duo resplendent in evening dress who compared admirably, or so Abbie thought, with the famous Anne Ziegler and Webster Booth whom she had heard on the radio; a man who could imitate the whistles of all the well-known song birds; and, of course, Max Wall and Rawicz and Landauer.

You only had to look at Max Wall to find yourself laughing. He was, as Doreen put it, a scream, with his spindly legs encased in tight black trousers, his sticking-out bottom and his comical walk. His rubbery face could appear lugubrious and deadpan, before breaking out into a cheeky irrepressible grin. Doreen was shrieking with laughter at his quick-fire jokes, rocking backwards and forwards in her seat with uncontrolled mirth. Many of his innuendoes – about honeymoon couples, Blackpool landladies, mothers-in-law, hen-pecked husbands and the like – went over Abbie's head, but she laughed along with Doreen, whether she understood or not, determined to join fully in the carefree spirit of the evening.

> 'King Solomon had a thousand wives
> That he serenaded daily,
> But what's the use of a thousand wives
> If you've only one ukelele?'

he asked, strumming away on a tiny banjo.

Doreen thought that was hilarious. 'He's a real scream, isn't he?' she said again, dabbing her handkerchief at the tears of merriment that were rolling down her cheeks.

'Yes, he is. He's . . . ever so funny,' agreed Abbie, not understanding the joke at all. George Formby played a ukelele, didn't he? But there was nothing very funny about that. At least, George Formby's songs were funny – her mother had quickly turned off the wireless once when he was singing that rather rude one about cleaning windows – but Abbie didn't think Max Wall was referring to a ukelele like George's. She realised afresh what a very sheltered existence she had led until now. Most girls of her age, girls like Doreen, knew much more about life and its hidden secrets and mysteries. She felt quite sure that Doreen would know the answer to the problem that puzzled her, the one that even Aunt Bertha had refused to answer. She would have to ask her sometime, when she got to know her better.

Rawicz and Landauer were far more to Abbie's liking and the whole audience settled down to a mood of quiet reflection and nostalgia as the melodious music from the two grand pianos filled the theatre. There was nothing too highbrow for an audience comprised of holiday-makers – still flocking to Blackpool in this third year of the war – RAF recruits, women from the Civil Service (transferred from London), middle-aged housewives and their husbands, and local girls, like Doreen and

Abbie, out for an evening of light-hearted entertainment. Strauss waltzes, Chopin mazurkas, Sinding's 'Rustle of Spring', 'The Golliwog's Cake-walk'; the two middle-aged gentlemen in pinstripe trousers, highly starched shirts and tail coats tackled them all with technical brilliance and aplomb and a good deal of sensitivity.

'Music hath charms to soothe a savage breast.' So Abbie had learned when she was at school, and that was what she found now as she listened to the concluding item in their repertoire, the haunting first movement of Grieg's A minor Concerto, a piece she had tried to struggle through herself, after a fashion. Not that she was feeling savage or angry or whatever the poet had meant, but she had been worried about the animosity that had built up between her and her mother. It had marred, slightly, the delight of her anticipation of the evening. Now she felt her cares being soothed away by the enchantment of the music. There was a pause of a second or two after the pianists had played the final chords before the audience responded with thunderous applause.

'Those two fellows can't half play the piano. Brilliant, aren't they?' Doreen enthused as they followed the crowd up the elegant marble staircase which led from the theatre and cinema on the lower floor to the ballroom on the floor above. 'Can you play like that?'

'No, of course not,' laughed Abbie. 'Nothing like as good. When I listen to pianists like that I know that I'm very mediocre.'

'Well, I think it's dead clever to be able to play at all,' said Doreen. 'I can't do anything like that, me.'

'I expect you can do all sorts of things that I can't do, though,' replied Abbie. 'You said you were good at sums, didn't you? Well, I'm hopeless. And I can't sew to save my life. I expect you made that dress you've got on now, didn't you?'

'Yes, I did actually.' Doreen glanced at her rather sharply, then down at her pretty pink and white polka-dotted dress. 'Why? Does it look like it's home-made?'

'No . . . no, of course it doesn't,' said Abbie quickly. Oh heavens! she thought. I hope I haven't offended her. She really must be more careful of what she was saying. She didn't know

Doreen very well yet, and her first encounter with her had shown her that the girl was inclined to be touchy. 'I just guessed . . . that you might have made it. I think your mother mentioned that you made some of your own clothes.' Yes, she was sure she remembered Mrs Miller telling her something of the sort. 'And I saw some material like that in St John's market. It's really very nice. Very professional-looking. I think you're very clever to be able to sew like that. And that white edging finishes it off perfectly.'

Doreen's dress was, as Abbie said, very well made. The sweetheart neckline and the short sleeves were trimmed with a neat edge of white bias binding and the flared skirt swirled becomingly round her slim hips. Abbie found, again, that she was comparing herself unfavourably with her new friend; her neat trim figure, to say nothing of her fair hair and bright blue eyes. But that would not do any good. We were all, as her Aunt Bertha was fond of saying, 'as the good Lord made us', and there was little we could do about it. Not about our looks, but Abbie had made a start by changing the way she dressed.

'Ta very much,' said Doreen, smiling brightly, so Abbie knew she was not offended. 'I enjoy sewing. Most of me frocks are home-made or else second-hand, but I like to think I look as nice as anybody when I go out.' She patted in a self-satisfied way at her short fair hair which curled of its own accord around her head.

'You do look nice – very nice,' said Abbie, meaning it wholeheartedly. The other times she had seen her Doreen had been wearing her shop overall or – that first time – had looked less than spruce, but now she looked very pretty indeed.

'And so do you,' responded Doreen, looking at her again in an appraising way. 'That dress isn't home-made, is it? It's real smart. I couldn't wear it, of course. It's for somebody . . . Well, it wouldn't suit me. But it looks smashing on you, honest it does.'

What had Doreen been about to say? wondered Abbie. Somebody . . . what? Older, more mature, taller . . . fatter? 'No, it's not home-made,' she smiled in response. 'As a matter of fact it's new, bought specially for tonight. You may find this hard to believe, Doreen, but I had nothing suitable to wear, so my aunt and I went shopping yesterday and I bought this dress at Sally Mae's . . . Do you honestly think it looks all right?' She lowered her voice, looking almost pleadingly at the other girl, suddenly aware that the dress, smart and stylish as it was, might appear a trifle staid – 'old-maidish'? – amongst all the gay floral-patterned and brightly hued dresses she could see all around them. 'I'm not used to choosing my own clothes,' she admitted, a little self-consciously. 'My mother usually buys them, you see. Aunt Bertha said it was nice and that it suited me, but – well – she's an elderly lady . . .'

'Of course it's all right,' Doreen assured her, suddenly linking arms with her and squeezing her elbow briefly for emphasis. 'I've told you, it's real smart and I wouldn't say so if I didn't mean it. Those stripes going down make you look . . . well, you know what I mean. Not quite so . . . Oh heck! Doreen,' the girl slapped at her own wrist, 'why can't you watch your big mouth!'

Abbie laughed. 'I know exactly what you mean. They make me look not quite so fat. That's what my aunt said, and the shop assistant, though I know they were trying to be tactful.'

'I wasn't suggesting you're fat,' said Doreen. 'Of course you're not. Fatter than me, but then I'm dead skinny. And you're a lot taller than me as well, so you can carry it.'

'Yes, I know very well I'm plump,' said Abbie resignedly. 'Plump's a nicer word than fat, isn't it? Puppy fat, my Aunt Bertha calls it, and she says I'll lose it when I get older. It's her fault though, really. She's such a good cook, you see, and I can't resist her apple pies and suet dumplings.'

'I bet you could if you tried.' Doreen surveyed her critically. 'We all might have to cut down if rationing gets any worse. It wouldn't do you any harm to lose a bit of weight, if you don't mind me saying so. I've told you, I always say what I think. And you've got smashing legs, honest you have.'

'Oh . . . thank you.' Abbie found herself blushing confusedly. But the next minute she stood stock-still in astonishment as they entered the ballroom. 'Oh . . . oh, just look at that! Isn't it . . . beautiful?'

Her voice dropped to a whisper, then she gazed in silence for a few moments at the wonderful scene that confronted her. The interior of the Palace was designed in the style of the Italian

Renaissance, the ballroom being the pinnacle of the whole achievement. The gleaming parquet floor, the gilded pillars and balconies, the frescoed ceiling, glittering chandeliers and plush velvet seats; Abbie stared spellbound at it all, feeling as though she had been transported into a magic fairyland.

'Yes, it is nice, isn't it?' Doreen was looking at her with some amusement. 'Oh, I forgot. You've never been here before, have you? Yes, the Palace is a nice little ballroom, and Francis Collins' band's not bad neither. What are we going to do? D'you want to sit down for a bit or shall we stand here? We'll have more chance of partners if we stand near the floor. When I come with my friend Gwen, we usually stand just about here. Not that Gwen wants to come dancing all that often. Her boyfriend's in the army, y' see, and he doesn't like to think of her dancing with other fellows. I don't think it matters, though, me. I meanter say, it's not as if you're doing something wrong, is it, just having a dance? And these RAF blokes are usually just nice friendly lads. At least the ones I've met have been . . . I say, what's the matter? You're looking a bit worried. What's up? Have I said something wrong?'

'No, of course not. It's just that – well – I can't dance,' faltered Abbie. 'Not properly, I mean, and I shall feel such a fool if I don't know what to do. I knew we'd be coming into the ballroom, but I didn't think I'd be dancing myself. I don't mind you going on, though, if somebody asks you – and they will, of course – but I'd rather just sit over there and watch . . . if you don't mind?'

'Don't be daft! Of course I don't mind.' Doreen squeezed her arm in a friendly manner. 'But I'd much rather you stayed here with me. Nobody's bothered whether you can dance properly or not. A lot of these RAF blokes have two left feet, believe me; and they have a lot of Old Time dances here – veletas and military two-steps an' all that. You can do those, surely?'

'Yes, I can do those, after a fashion,' replied Abbie. 'They have them at the church socials we go to. And when I was at school they tried to teach us a few dance steps – just the waltz and quickstep, and we had to dance with other girls, of course; it was an all-girls school. But I was hopeless at it. And my mother's always saying things like, "Abbie doesn't dance", as though there's some sort of virtue in not doing so. So I've stopped trying. There's never been any opportunity, anyway . . . Until now,' she added doubtfully, wondering if she could, after all, be so bold as to stand at the edge of the ballroom floor with Doreen. And whether anyone would ever ask her to dance if she did so.

'Your mother sounds a real pain in the neck,' said Doreen, 'if you don't mind me saying so.' That was the second time she had said that – 'if you don't mind me saying so' – and Abbie knew it didn't much matter whether she minded or not. Doreen had said it and, what was more, Abbie agreed with her.

'Yes, I dare say you're right,' she replied. 'Mother does get me down at times, but she's always been like that so I suppose I've got used to it. She finds fault all the time. I can't seem to do right for her.'

'Why don't you stick up for yerself?' asked Doreen. 'Honestly! Being told what to do at your age, and having your clothes chosen for you. I wouldn't stand for it.'

'No, I don't think for one minute you would,' Abbie grinned. 'But I've told you, I've already started a mild sort of rebellion. Anyway, never mind about my mother. I want to enjoy myself. I've decided . . . I'll stand here with you,' she said, though still a trifle hesitantly, 'and see what happens. I don't suppose anybody'll ask me to dance, but you never know, do you?'

'Good for you.' Doreen nudged her in a friendly way. 'I bet you anything two fellers'll come along in a minute. That's what usually happens when Gwen and me stand together. Two blokes'll come and ask us. They weigh up the talent, y'see, and they usually do it in pairs. And I reckon we look as nice as anybody.'

I wish I had her confidence, thought Abbie. If only Doreen knew how nervous she was feeling at this moment; she would think she was a real scaredy-cat. Abbie couldn't imagine her new friend ever being frightened of anything or anybody. She was aware that she towered above the other girl as they stood side by side near to one of the ornate gilded pillars, but, small as she was, Doreen seemed very self-possessed and full of vitality. Abbie hoped that some of that self-assurance would be transmitted to her. Certainly, without Doreen she would never have dared to enter the ballroom, let alone stand and wait for a partner.

It was a veleta that was being danced now to the tune of 'Little Sir Echo'.

'Little Sir Echo, How do you do? Hello, hello . . .' sang some of the less inhibited girls as they swung their partner's hands, then twirled round in time to the music. Some girls were dancing together, but most of them were partnered by young men in uniforms of air-force blue. Almost all the men were in uniform. Just here and there you could see a middle-aged man dancing with his wife, or a very young man who was not yet of call-up age; but here, as throughout the whole of the town, air-force blue uniforms predominated, Blackpool being the chief training ground for RAF recruits. Abbie was hoping desperately that if someone was going to ask her to dance at all it would be soon, because this was a dance she could do. The previous one had been a foxtrot and she would have been hopeless at that.

'See, what did I tell yer?' Doreen nudged her again. 'There's two blokes heading this way. They're not bad neither. At least, one of 'em's OK . . . Bags I the ginger-haired one,' she whispered.

'All right,' Abbie whispered back. 'I don't mind. But we'll have to wait and see, won't we, which one asks us . . . ?' If she could have turned and fled at that moment she would have done so, but it was too late.

'Would you like to dance?' asked the tall gangling young man who had hesitated a moment before speaking. In the first few seconds as she looked at him Abbie noticed he had a rather long nose and his fairish dead-straight hair flopped limply across his forehead. She didn't notice the colour of his eyes, but she thought they had a glint of humour in them and he was smiling broadly as he spoke, his wide mouth revealing a set of large uneven teeth. Not out of the top drawer as far as looks were concerned, but he seemed . . . nice. And who was she, anyway, to be choosy? As Doreen had hoped, and as Abbie had known would happen, the ginger-haired good-looking one had already swept her friend on to the floor. He was much the shorter of the two, but Abbie guessed that was not the reason he had chosen the smaller girl.

'Yes . . . thank you,' said Abbie as they stepped on to the ballroom floor. 'I'm . . . I'm not very good at dancing, but I'll try.'

'Don't apologise,' said the RAF lad. 'You'll be fine. Anyway, what does it matter? I'm no great shakes at dancing myself. But you can't go into a ballroom and not dance, can you?'

'No . . . no, you can't,' replied Abbie, trying to concentrate on her steps. She was finding, however, it was not too bad. You didn't have to improvise to this dance like you had to do with the modern ones, but the end part where you twirled round always seemed to finish in rather a muddle. She was coping, though, and her partner was not swirling her round madly, thank goodness, as some of the others were doing.

'This is a nice ballroom,' said the young man. 'It's the first time I've been here. I've been to the Tower and the Winter Gardens, but I think I like this one better.'

'It's the first time I've been here, too,' said Abbie.

'Why is that?' asked her partner. 'Are you on holiday here? I thought you might be local.'

'No, I'm not on holiday – I live here,' she answered. 'But . . . I don't go dancing much. In fact I don't go at all. But Doreen – that's the girl I'm with – asked me to go to the variety show with her and so we came here afterwards. I wasn't sure that I wanted to, but Doreen did . . . Sorry,' she said as she tripped over his foot. That was what came of talking and not concentrating. She decided she had better shut up. He wouldn't want to know her life story anyway. He would disappear at the end of this dance and that would be that. She doubted if anyone else would ask her and she decided she wouldn't much care if they didn't. It was quite an ordeal. She could feel her hands growing clammy and the perspiration breaking out on her forehead.

'Don't say sorry.' He gave her hand a brief squeeze. 'There's no need. You're doing fine. And my feet are so big I fall over them myself.'

She looked at him uneasily and saw that he was smiling, and it was then that she saw his eyes were a clear bright blue. How could she not have noticed them before? They were undoubtedly his best feature in a face that was pleasant but quite unremarkable. She smiled back at him, a little more confidently. 'It's a lot different here from the church dances,' she said. 'I was afraid I'd make a fool of myself.'

'Then that makes two of us,' he replied. 'That's where I've spent my youth as well, at church hops. There – that wasn't too bad, was it?' he asked as the music slowed down and came to an end. Then, 'Shall we try again?' he said, as the band started up with 'One Day When We Were Young'.

'Yes . . . if you don't mind.'

'Why should I mind?' He laughed. 'You're a funny girl, aren't you? I don't mean that unkindly,' he added as she gave him a startled look. 'I've a feeling you're rather shy. Well, so am I – with girls, I mean, though I get on fine with blokes. My mate, Neil, though, he makes up for it. He could talk the hind leg off a donkey.'

'Neil – that's the young man who's dancing with my friend, is it?'

'Yes, with . . . Doreen, did you call her?' Abbie nodded. 'And what is your name?'

'I'm Abbie,' she answered. 'Abigail, really, but my . . . my friends call me Abbie.'

'And I hope I may be one of those, perhaps?' said her partner. Abbie felt herself blushing and she looked down at her feet as he went on to say, 'And I'm Peter. So now we know one another, don't we? And I think we're mastering this dance very well. What do you think?'

'Yes . . . yes, I think so,' said Abbie, a little more boldly. Her first instinct, she was sure, had been right. This young man, Peter, did seem to be very nice. She found herself relaxing, the feeling of clamminess and the panicky, churned-up sensation in her stomach fast disappearing as she realised that Peter, maybe, was just as nervous and shy as she was. At least he had said he was, unless he was only doing so to make her feel better. It was hard to tell, and she didn't know enough about young men to fathom their behaviour.

They were dancing near the edge of the ballroom floor, all the couples rotating in an anticlockwise direction. Around the perimeter of the dancing area there were glass panels built into the floor, beneath which were lights which changed colour as the dance proceeded, from blue to green to pink to mauve. It

106

was a very romantic setting, adding to Abbie's feeling that she was not really here at all, but in some sort of dream sequence from which she might suddenly awaken.

The dance came to an end and she stood there unsurely, clapping in a polite way as she could see those all around her doing. What did you do now, for goodness' sake? Say thank you and walk away, or wait for your partner to make the first move? She could feel herself getting all flustered again. But Peter took charge of the situation.

'Come along,' he said, taking hold of her arm. 'Let's go and see if we can find your friend Doreen and my pal Neil.'

The same thing would happen again, as it always did, Peter Horsfall had thought, as he and his mate Neil Craddock had approached the two girls who were standing at the edge of the ballroom floor. He would be left with the plain one while his friend waltzed off – or, more correctly, veletaed off – with the pretty one.

There couldn't be two more dissimilar girls, he pondered as he'd walked towards them. One of them short and slim – what he thought they termed 'petite' – fair-haired and very pretty, whilst the other one was tall and heavily built, dark-haired and very ordinary-looking. A big fat lump was how the more insensitive of his mates might have described her. But Peter always tried to be sympathetic and optimistic in his estimation of people, and he knew, also, that he was no oil painting himself. Besides, it didn't matter a scrap what people looked like, even girls – birds, as some of his mates called them – though the majority of the RAF recruits he was training with would disagree with him. And as he'd danced with Abbie, as the big girl had said she was called, he'd started to forget what she looked like because she really was very nice.

She was painfully shy. He'd been able tell by the way she'd hung her head when he spoke to her, and that had given him an empathy with her straight away. He, too, had been shy when he was growing up. That was what came of being the only child of parents who doted on him, and his unexciting job as a bank clerk had done little to improve his reticence or his social contacts. He had not been sorry when his call-up had interrupted his career. He had been in Blackpool for three months now and was enjoying his air-force training far more than he had ever thought he would. He hoped, ultimately, to become part of a flying team; a navigator, maybe, or a gunner. His instructors seemed to think he had the aptitude for this. He knew he was of more than average intelligence – his scholarship results, years ago, had proved so – he possessed a keen eye and had a calm unflappable nature, not one that was likely to go to pieces in an emergency. It was one thing, however, to feel brave when on a training course, but quite another, he was sure, when you were thousands of feet up in an aeroplane, surrounded by enemy fire. But that was quite a long way into the future; time enough to worry about that when it happened. For the moment he found that he was enjoying – again, far more than he had ever anticipated – the easy camaraderie of the other young men. He was casting off the shyness that had afflicted him for so long and was making some very good friends. Neil Craddock was one of them.

Without Neil, Peter would never have plucked up courage to go dancing. The dance halls here in Blackpool were so very different from the little *palais de danse* or the local church hall where the youth club held their dances, in the small Norfolk town where he lived. Huge glittering palaces they were here, where a country bumpkin such as himself could easily feel like a fish out of water. The Palace, though, had a far friendlier ambience than the Tower or the Winter Gardens.

That was what he had remarked on to this shy girl, Abbie, and, emboldened by her diffident smile and the way she had seemed to warm to him as the dance progressed, he decided to stay with her for a while. He had never done this before. His partners had always seemed glad to leave him at the end of a couple of dances. He had certainly never made a date with any of them as Neil had done now and again. Peter felt quite sure that Neil would do his utmost to hang on to the pretty little bit of fluff he had just been dancing with. Doreen, Abbie had called her; and he guessed that Abbie would feel more comfortable about staying with him, Peter, if her friend were there too.

It turned out just as Peter had hoped. The four of them stayed together for the rest of the evening, only separating to go on to the floor now and again to dance. Abbie seemed to be covered with confusion, however, when Neil suggested they should all go for a drink.

'What do you mean? What sort of drink?' she asked, then looked despairingly towards Peter. 'I don't drink. At least . . . not beer or anything like that. My mother would throw a fit if she thought I was going into a pub. Is it a pub?'

'I don't know, to be honest,' said Peter. 'I told you, I've never been here before. Is it, Neil?'

'Well – yes – I suppose so,' replied Neil with a puzzled half-smile, half-frown. 'A bar, at any rate. But what does it matter? You can get all sorts of drinks. Ginger beer and lemonade as well as the – er – hard stuff. A cup of tea, if you like. Don't worry, darling. We're not going to get you blind drunk. We wouldn't do any such thing, would we, Peter?' He winked at his friend.

'No, of course we wouldn't,' said Peter. 'You'll be OK, Abbie, honestly you will,' he went on, turning to this somewhat odd, but nice, girl towards whom he was already starting to feel rather protective. 'I'll look after you . . . Go easy with her, Neil,' he said to his friend in a low voice as Abbie dropped behind to walk with Doreen. 'She's a bit out of her depth here, from what I can gather. She was just starting to come out of her shell when you mentioned the drink. So no funny business, OK?' Neil could be a terrible tease with the girls.

'OK, OK.' Neil held up his hand. 'I'll behave myself. But I must say you've got yourself a right one there, mate. It sounds as though she's tied to Mummy's apron strings from that last remark. I wouldn't have stuck around this pair, but I rather fancy that little Doreen. She's quite a dish. Sorry to land you with old misery-guts there. Good grief! "My mother would have a fit," ' he mimicked. 'Have you ever heard the like?'

'Shut up, Neil. She'll hear you. She's not all that bad and I certainly wouldn't say she was miserable. Just shy, and I know how that feels. She's quite nice when you get to know her and I was just beginning to.'

'OK, anything you say, but I'd rather you than me, mate.' Neil turned round to call over his shoulder to Abbie. 'Don't worry about your mother, darling. She's not here, is she, and you'll be quite safe with old Pete and me.'

'Just what I was telling her,' Doreen called back. 'She's here to enjoy herself and I intend to see that she does. And just for your information, Neil, I don't drink neither. Nothing stronger than a shandy at any rate, but I shall have a lemonade tonight to keep Abbie company. I don't want to be getting home tiddly or my mam'd have something to say as well. Lemonade do for yer, Abbie?' she asked, as they arrived at the bar area.

'Yes . . . yes, thank you. Lemonade will be very nice,' replied Abbie, staring round a little apprehensively.

'Are you going to get 'em, Neil?' called Doreen. 'Abbie and me'll have lemonade. Look, there's a table over there. We'll go and grab it. Come on, Abbie.'

There could not be two girls more unalike than this pair, thought Peter, as he stood at the bar with Neil, waiting to be served. Not only in looks, but in disposition as well. He wondered how they came to be friends, as he assumed they must be. The bar area was really more like a café, a place that even Abbie could not take exception to, he was pleased to see. He did not want her to take fright and run off home, or retreat back into her shell again now he was getting to know her. He determined to engage her more deeply in conversation, just the two of them, to leave Neil to do his flirting or whatever it was he wanted to do with the vivacious Doreen.

The more he talked with Abbie the less Peter noticed her plainness and her plumpness. She was, in fact, not plain at all. It was only her build and her unprepossessing manner which made her seem so. When she smiled her face was completely transformed; he was glad he had been able to make her smile. Her eyes were lovely, deep brown, clear and candid, and when she was happy and relaxed, as she seemed to be as the evening drew on, they glowed with warmth and intensity. Peter felt sure there were depths to Abigail Winters, as she told him she was called, that were as yet unfathomed.

They had a great deal in common, both being the only child of somewhat overprotective parents. But whereas Peter's parents had now let go of the reins, being concerned only for his welfare and, of course, his safety – what else could they do now he was twenty-one and serving in His Majesty's Forces? – he felt that

Abbie was still ruled with a rod of iron, by her mother if not her father. She did not criticise her mother unduly, but Peter guessed there was animosity between the two of them, a lack of real love, maybe, which he, with such loving parents, found difficult to understand.

This was not the only point of contact they found. They were both musical. That was when Abbie had smiled with real delight, on discovering that Peter had been persuaded to come to the Palace that evening because Rawicz and Landauer were performing. Abbie, he understood, was quite an able pianist, though she was very modest about it, and he was an organist, his call-up into the RAF having interrupted not only his career in the bank, but his musical vocation. He had been, until a few months ago, deputy organist at his local church. He and Abbie were both, they discovered, members of the Church of England.

She was a quiet girl, gentle, unassuming and pleasant to talk to, just the sort, Peter thought, that his parents would be delighted for him to find. They danced together a couple more times, managing to synchronise their steps reasonably well, and Abbie appeared much more relaxed. She was even beginning to unbend more with Neil towards the end of the evening. Admittedly, he had been on his best behaviour, and it was Neil who suggested they should all meet there again the following Saturday, not to go to the pictures or the variety theatre, but just to enjoy the pleasures of the ballroom.

The girls were anxious to be on their way home by 9.45, Abbie more so than Doreen, so the young men walked with them as far as St John's church where Abbie was to catch a tram and Doreen a bus.

'You amaze me,' Peter remarked to Neil as they walked away, heading for their billet in Lord Street. 'I really thought you'd be hankering to take that Doreen home. What's up? Don't you fancy her now as much as you thought you did?'

'Don't want to push it, mate,' replied Neil. 'I fancy her all right, but she'll be there again next week if she's keen enough, don't you worry. And if she isn't – well – there's more fish in the sea. No, to be honest, Pete, I was thinking about you. You really like that girl, don't you? I thought I'd give you a bit of a helping hand. That Abbie'll be more likely to come along if she's got her friend with her. And if she's what you want – well then – the best of British luck!'

'Thanks, Neil,' grinned Peter. 'You're a pal.' He wasn't sure yet just what he wanted, but whatever it was, he knew he would have to take it very, very slowly with a girl like Abbie Winters.

Chapter 7

It was a couple of minutes before 10.15 when Bertha opened
the door to a flushed and excited-looking Abbie. Bertha was
relieved that the girl had arrived home before the deadline that
Eva had set. She knew there would have been all hell let loose
if she had been so much as a few minutes late. Eva had,
ostensibly, retired to bed. She was in a peevish mood, resulting
from her failure to get her own way over her daughter's visit to
the Palace Varieties. Bertha guessed that, far from being in bed
and asleep, she would be peering through the bedroom curtains
and blackout blinds ready to catch Abigail out should she arrive
home late.

Bertha, in the comfort of her own little parlour, had been
awaiting Abbie's knock. The girl did not have her own door key
although, in her aunt's opinion, it was high time she did. Cedric
was enjoying some well-deserved peace and solitude in the
sitting room. How he put up with his wife's moodiness and ill
temper at times Bertha could not imagine; and she guessed it
would be her aunt that Abbie would want to chat to when she
came in.

'I've had a lovely time, Aunt Bertha,' said Abbie, closing the
vestibule door quickly behind her. Blackout restrictions required
that not a chink of light had to show. She spoke quietly,
obviously not wanting her mother, wherever she was, to hear
her, but the softness of her voice could not disguise her
excitement. 'Where's Mother?' she asked, glancing round a
little apprehensively.

'Gone to bed,' replied Bertha.

'Oh ... that's good,' Abbie whispered. 'Come on, let's go
and make a cup of cocoa and I'll tell you all about it.'

They made their cocoa, then they sat in Bertha's snug little room, and Abbie talked and talked in a way her aunt had never heard her talk before. About Doreen, about what a nice girl she was, so friendly and amusing and not at all hostile to Abbie as she had been at first. Abbie even thought now that the other girl had invited her along because she actually wanted her company and not because she felt sorry for her.

'Of course she wants to be with you,' Bertha assured her. 'Why shouldn't she? You're a young lass, the same as she is, and I don't see why the fact you've got a bit more brass should make any difference.' It did, though, to Eva.

She said how she had enjoyed the variety show, especially the two pianists. 'They were wonderful, Auntie,' she enthused. 'I wish I could play half as well. I thought I was quite good until I heard them . . . And then, after the show, we went dancing. I was ever so nervous and I said I wouldn't dance, I was too scared, but Doreen persuaded me. And – guess what, Aunt Bertha – two RAF blokes – I mean, men – came and asked us to dance.' Bertha smiled to herself at Abbie's slip of the tongue; one of Doreen's words, she guessed. And how Eva would detest it!

'One of them's called Peter,' Abbie went on. 'He's a really nice boy, Aunt Bertha. Well, a young man, I suppose, not a boy. He's older than me, anyway. He didn't seem to mind that I couldn't dance very well. He said he wasn't very good at it either, and we stayed together all the time after that . . . and he's asked me to meet him there again next Saturday!'

Bertha could hardly believe that this was her niece talking; Abbie, who had always been so dreadfully shy, especially of young men. She had, indeed, hardly ever met any, except for the ones at church, friends of the family, vetted and approved of by her mother. Bertha looked at the girl's flushed cheeks and bright eyes, realising, with a stab of surprise, that she looked almost pretty. She began to feel fearful for her. Abigail was so naïve, so trusting, and she couldn't know very much yet about this Peter.

'You mean . . . you've got a date? Isn't that what they call it?' Her aunt smiled at her. 'Well, that's lovely, Abbie. But do be careful, dear. You don't know much about him yet, do you, and I don't want you to—'

'Oh, it's all right, Auntie,' Abbie interrupted. 'Don't worry about it. It's not a real date. Perhaps I've given you the wrong impression, but I was so amazed that someone should actually want to see me again. No, it was Neil, really, now I come to think of it, who suggested we should all meet again. He's the one that Doreen was dancing with, but I liked Peter much better.'

'And did he see you home then, this . . . Peter?'

'Oh no, of course not. He walked with us to the tram stop, they both did, then they went off to their billet and Doreen and I came home. He's a bank clerk, Aunt Bertha, at least he was in civvy street . . .' Another expression, thought Bertha, that Abbie had probably never used until this evening. '. . . and he plays the organ at his church in Norfolk. He's not really good-looking, not like his friend Neil, but he's very nice. You would like him, Auntie . . .'

And as Bertha listened she felt sure she would like him. She wondered, though, if this young man had been attracted to her niece in any way, or whether he had stayed with her out of kindness, because his friend was smitten with the delightful Doreen, maybe. She did not want Abbie to get hurt, and from the radiant look on the girl's face it would seem as though, already, she was halfway to falling in love. Or it could be the idea of being in love that attracted Abbie. At all events, Bertha was apprehensive.

'I don't think I'd better tell Mother, do you?' asked her niece unsurely, when she had come to the end of the eulogy about Peter. 'Or Father, for that matter. About Peter, I mean.'

'No, perhaps not,' agreed Bertha. 'Far be it from me, Abbie, to encourage you to be deceitful, but I think – for the moment – it might be as well to keep this under your hat. And you can be sure I won't say anything.' It could well be that the lad would not turn up next Saturday, although Bertha prayed, for Abbie's sake, that he would.

'But I'll have to tell them I've arranged to see Doreen again next week, won't I? Do you think Mother will let me go?'

'I don't see how she can stop you,' replied Bertha. 'You've already told her, haven't you, that you don't have to ask her permission. She won't forget that in a hurry, and if you can say A then you can say B. But go easy with her, Abigail. Be tactful

115

– try not to get her back up, there's a good lass.'

Bertha was glad that Eva had not been there to see the girl's face, glowing with happiness, when she came in from the dance hall. Had she done so she would have come down on her like a ton of bricks. If she hadn't been able to chastise her for her lateness she would have found something else. Oh Abbie, please be careful, Bertha whispered to herself when the girl had gone off to bed. The memory of her cousin's wrathful face and the querulous mood she had been in for the last few days filled her with dread.

The lights were turned down low in the Palace ballroom, enhancing the effect of the underfloor lighting, as the couples danced round to the music of 'I'll Be Seeing You'. It was a foxtrot rhythm, not a dance Abbie had ever imagined she could do. Nor could she. The steps she and Peter were executing involved little more than walking backwards to the music – forwards, in Peter's case – with a little turn here and there – far from the authentic foxtrot steps, but it didn't matter in the slightest. Most of the couples were no more adept than they were.

It was a slow sentimental song, one which encouraged the demonstrative shows of affection which were going on around them. Abbie could see girls with their hands on the shoulders of their partners, others with their arms entwined right round the men's necks, and some of the men's hands – well, they were everywhere; caressing hair and neck and shoulders, some even straying below the waistline of the girl's dress, stroking her . . . Well, really! Abbie looked away in embarrassment.

It was not so with her and Peter. They were dancing decorously, one of his hands clasping hers firmly and the other one resting where it should be, in the middle of her back. She felt rather discomfited that he would be able to feel the fastening of her brassiere, but there was nothing she could do about it. She could feel his slight breath on her cheek and occasionally his chin nudged against her temple – he was a tall young man, almost six foot – but he made no attempt to hold her any closer.

'I'll be looking at the moon,' sang the lady vocalist. 'But I'll be seeing you.'

116

There was a discordant flourish from the trumpets, then the dance came to an end. Peter squeezed Abbie's hand briefly as he had done at the end of each dance, then they held hands lightly as they walked off the ballroom floor. That was the only intimacy he had shown towards her, but Abbie did not mind. She wondered however she would react if he were to put his arm round her, or kiss her in front of all these people as some of the bolder RAF lads were doing. She had caught sight of Doreen and Neil once or twice during the dancing. He had been holding her tightly with his cheek pressed against hers, and when the four of them went for a drink the other two had sat together on a red plush couch, his arm around her shoulders.

And then, soon after nine o'clock, Neil and Doreen announced – or rather, Neil did – that they were going for a walk on the promenade. It was very obvious he did not want any company other than Doreen's, so Peter and Abbie stayed at the Palace on their own. Abbie didn't mind this at all. She felt, somehow, wary of Neil, not sure how to behave towards him, and she had a faint suspicion that he was laughing at her. So she was relieved, in a way, to see him go even though it meant Doreen had gone as well. Peter, no doubt, would offer to see her home, maybe even further than the tram stop. Her feelings about this were ambivalent. She could not be so churlish as to refuse to let him go in the tram with her, although it was a long way out of his way; but she knew she must not let her mother catch sight of him. The tram stop was very near to their house. Perhaps they could get off the stop before . . . Oh dear, what a problem it all was.

She had not thought about all these complications when she had been looking forward to her 'date', if it could be called that. She had been more concerned with what, and how, she was going to tell her mother she was seeing Doreen again. In the end she had said very little to Eva, except that she was going out on Saturday night with a friend – leaving her mother to enquire, if she so wished, where and with whom she was going. Eva had not done so, but it was obvious she had guessed. She had merely given her daughter a disdainful look.

The atmosphere in the house – between Abbie and her mother, and between her parents – had been far from congenial all week, but Abbie was determined to stick to her guns regarding her bid for independence. She had been cowed by her mother's dominance for too long. Eva, as always, however, intended to have the last word.

It was at teatime today that she had said, 'You are determined to defy me, Abigail, I know that. But there is one thing I insist on . . . and your father will agree with me over this. As long as you live under our roof you will obey our orders.' The look she gave her husband said quite clearly that she would brook no disagreement. 'You will be home not one minute later than ten o'clock.'

'Ten fifteen, Eva. That was what we said last week,' Cedric was bold enough to argue.

'I said ten o'clock, and I mean ten o'clock,' retorted Eva. 'And that's my last word on the subject. Just you remember, or else . . .' The threat hung heavy in the air.

All in all it had been a lovely evening and Abbie had been able to put to the back of her mind the ongoing discord with her mother. Peter and Neil had been waiting in the ballroom, as arranged, and Peter's welcoming smile had given Abbie hope that perhaps he was not meeting her just out of politeness. They chatted easily, more so than they had done the time before. Abbie learned that Peter wanted, eventually, to be part of a flying team. He told her about the training of the RAF recruits in Blackpool, much of it at the Winter Gardens. They had PT in the Empress Ballroom, morse code lessons in the Olympia and kit inspection in the Floral Hall, as well as the square-bashing on the promenade and in the streets, which attracted the curiosity of both residents and visitors, although the residents, by now, had grown very used to the boys in blue.

Peter, in turn, learned of Abbie's work with her father, far more fulfilling since she had become more actively involved in the surgery and the dispensary. She did not tell him, however, feeling it would be disloyal, of her conflict with her mother, nor of how her work as a doctor's assistant, though worthwhile, was not really to her liking; nor how she longed, without any hope of it ever happening, to get away from home. She liked Peter very much, but confidences such as those could not be given to a young man she had only just met.

'What time do you want to leave?' he asked, soon after Neil and Doreen had departed. 'I'll see you home, of course.'

'Oh . . . thank you,' said Abbie. 'I said I would be in by about ten o'clock,' she added casually. 'Mother doesn't like me to be out late, especially in the blackout.' Just as though her mother was a normal parent instead of a dictatorial harridan. 'It's out of your way though, surely. I live on Whitegate Drive, and you're in North Shore, aren't you?'

'Not to worry,' said Peter cheerfully. 'My long legs'll soon cover the distance, or I can get a tram back. What is it to your house? A couple of miles? My landlady is used to us being late on a Saturday night. Some of us, at any rate, although I'm not usually one of the culprits. Come on then, you go and collect your jacket and we'll get on our way. See you at the bottom of the stairs.'

Tonight the weather was inclement with rain threatening, and Abbie had worn a short jacket over her blue and cream dress. She had left it in the cloakroom, but now, as she searched through her handbag and purse, she realised, to her horror, that she had mislaid the little pink cloakroom ticket. She stared at the attendant in dismay. 'I'm sorry, I can't find my ticket.'

'No ticket, no coat,' snapped the attendant. 'Come on, luv. Hurry up and find it. I've a queue waiting.'

Abbie stood to one side, resuming her frantic search, but it was no use. The ticket was not there. She could only assume it had fallen out when she had used her handkerchief.

'I can't find it.' She was almost in tears as she went back to the counter. 'But I can see my coat. Look, it's that one. The navy-blue jacket.' She pointed to the coat hanging near the end of the rack.

'But how do I know it's your coat, eh?' The attendant poked her face towards Abbie in an intimidating manner. 'Don't suppose you remember yer number, do you?' Abbie shook her head. 'Well then, I've told you – no ticket, no coat. Anybody could say it were theirs, couldn't they? All I can suggest is that you wait till the end. Ten o'clock, that's when the place closes, then we can see if that's the one that's left. Sorry, luv, it's all I can do.'

'Ten o'clock!' gasped Abbie. 'I can't possibly wait till ten o'clock. I have to be—' She stopped abruptly. What a fool she would look if she said she had to be home by ten o'clock. She was sure the other young women in the queue behind her, lipsticked and powdered, teetering on high heels, did not have to be home by such a ridiculous hour. One of these girls stuck up for her now.

'Oh, come on,' said the girl behind her. 'Anybody can see she's not making it up.'

'Yeah, 'course you can,' added another voice. 'Come on, you mean old thing. Let 'er 'ave 'er coat.'

The red-faced woman behind the counter scowled and glared at the irate young women who confronted her, determined not to back down. These cloakroom attendants, in charge of coats and washbasins and penny-in-the-slot toilets, could be veritable Hitlers at times in their own little domain, and this one was no exception.

'Come on, give the girl 'er coat.'

'Did you ever see the like? Mean old cow!'

'For heaven's sake! We can't stand here all night. Let her have it.'

Confronted by such a barrage of opposition the woman at last gave way, but only to a degree.

'Very well then,' she said, with a grudging sniff. 'I've got to admit you look a respectable sort of lass, not like some of 'em. Just wait while I get rid of this queue, then we'll see.'

It was another five minutes before Abbie was able to retrieve her coat. 'Thank you, thank you ever so much,' she said, just as though the woman had done her the most tremendous favour instead of making her late. Hurriedly she put it on and dashed down the stairs.

'Peter, I'm so sorry. I lost my ticket . . . and the woman . . . wouldn't let me . . . have my coat.' She was quite out of breath by this time and she could feel her face growing red. She was sure she looked a mess, but that was the least of her worries. It was already well turned half-past nine. If they didn't catch a tram straight away she was going to be late.

'Hey, steady on, Abbie,' said Peter, putting a hand on her arm. 'What does it matter? You've got your coat now, and I guessed you must have been held up in a long queue.' He

120

smiled. 'It's always the same with you girls. Here, what is it? What's wrong?'

The face she turned towards him was anxious, although she had by now hastily brushed the stray tears away. 'I'll be late home and my mother will be furious.'

'Of course she won't,' replied Peter in an encouraging voice, taking her elbow and quickly steering her through the crush of folks towards the door. 'She won't be cross if you explain what happened, about your ticket. Anyway . . .' he gave her a puzzled smile, 'you're a big girl now, aren't you?'

Abbie knew he was referring not to her size, but to her maturity. 'You don't know my mother,' she said darkly. 'She doesn't think so.'

'Do they ever?' He gave an easy laugh. 'Come on, Abbie. Let's step on it then. Best foot forward,' he said as they emerged into Bank Hey Street and the gathering evening darkness. It was high summer, but it had been cloudy all day and dusk had fallen earlier than usual. With no streetlamps and no lights in shop windows to relieve the darkness it was a gloomy scene.

'It's not far up Church Street,' Peter went on, 'and it won't take long once we get on the tram. Stop worrying. My parents used to be just the same, almost till the time I joined up. ' "Where are you going? And who are you going with? Don't be late . . ." ' he mimicked cheerfully as they strode along quickly, past the Grand Theatre, then Marks and Spencer's and Sharple's music shop towards St John's church.

'I doubt that your mother was ever like mine,' said Abbie gloomily as they drew near to the Winter Gardens. 'Oh look, Peter – there's a tram. Quick, let's get across the road.'

But they couldn't because there was a tram coming along from the other direction and they had to wait until it had passed. By the time it had gone so had the Marton-bound tram. And it was now a quarter to ten.

'When's the next one?' asked Peter, looking at her anxiously as they stood at the tram stop by the church.

'I don't know,' she replied in a small voice. 'Five minutes, ten minutes – I'm not sure. Whenever it is it'll be too late. I can't make it now for ten o' clock.'

She felt sick with anxiety and all the joy had gone out of the evening. It was difficult to explain to anyone why she was so afraid of her mother, certainly to this young man who, she felt sure, had kindly, understanding parents. Normal ones who only fussed in the way that loving parents always did. Abbie could scarcely believe, at this moment, that she had found as much courage as she had these last few weeks to stand up to her mother. But one thing she knew: her mother's wrath would be all the worse now because of her defiance.

'Stop worrying,' said Peter, putting his arm through hers. She was glad of the companionable closeness, but it did little to relieve the misery she was feeling. 'It'll be all right, you'll see. Your mother will understand when you tell her what happened. Anyway, she won't kill you, will she? Why are you so scared?'

Yes, why am I scared? thought Abbie. It was true; her mother would not kill her, or resort to any sort of violent behaviour. It had never been Eva's way to punish her daughter physically. No, her punishments were much more insidious and far-reaching whereas a smacking would have been over and done with in a few moments. Besides, Abbie was too old for such a manner of correction, and it would have been far below Eva's dignity. When she had been a child Eva's form of chastisement had been to shut her in her bedroom for long periods to reflect on her naughtiness; to deprive her of outings or the few friends she had; once, to stop her from performing at a church concert and to make her look small in the eyes of the audience by telling them why. And her mother's brooding resentment against her could last for days and days. It was bad enough already and this was sure to make it worse. That was what Abbie feared.

'You're right, Peter,' she answered now, trying to smile. She really must make an attempt to cheer up or he would think she was a real old misery-guts. Despite the sick feeling in her stomach she gave a little laugh. 'She can't kill me. But when she's in a temper she'd scare anyone, believe me. I'll explain, though, about the ticket.' If I get the chance, she thought, which was doubtful. Eva only listened to what she wanted to hear.

'That's OK then.' Peter squeezed her arm. 'Abbie . . .' She could sense him looking at her intently and she raised her eyes to his. 'Will you meet me again next Saturday? Without the other two, I mean, Doreen and Neil? I dare say they'll want to be on their own anyway, and I would like to see you again. Perhaps we could go to the pictures instead of dancing. Or whatever you'd like to do.'

'Yes, I'd like that, Peter,' she replied, though not with the eagerness she knew she should be feeling. 'The pictures would be nice. I don't know what's on, though, and the second house is rather late.'

'Some of them are continuous,' said Peter. 'It doesn't matter what time you go in. And you could ask your parents for permission to stay out a little longer, maybe . . . ? I'll have a look at the *Gazette* and see what's on.'

'All right.' She nodded in an apathetic sort of way. Did he not understand what she had been saying? That she would be in trouble for being late. No, maybe he did not understand, but then who would? 'I mean – yes, that would be lovely, Peter. Where shall I meet you?'

'What about here? But on the other side of the road. Outside the Winter Gardens where you get off the tram. Shall we say half-past six?'

'Yes, half-past six,' she repeated automatically. 'I'll . . . I'll look forward to it. Oh look, here's the tram. Thank goodness for that.'

They sat near the front and Abbie resisted the temptation to keep looking at her watch as the tram trundled on, so slowly and laboriously. Each stop that it made – the Grammar School, Devonshire Square, Palatine Road – seemed longer than the last and she knew that she had long exceeded her deadline. They had sat in silence for several minutes and it was as the tram approached the stop near the Health Centre that she spoke. 'Peter . . . I wonder if you would mind getting off at the next stop?'

He gave her a puzzled look, then a half-smile. 'Would I mind? What do you mean? If that's your stop then that's where we get off.'

'No, not me. I mean just you – if you don't mind,' she faltered. 'I daren't let my mother see us together and she's sure to be looking out of the window. Our house is just opposite the tram stop, and if she sees us she'll—' She stopped, smiling at him unsurely. 'And I do want to be able to meet you next week.'

'OK, anything you say.' He shook his head bemusedly. She thought he sounded a little annoyed and the look he gave her seemed to be saying, What a peculiar girl. 'Is this the stop? Shall I get up now? I'd much rather see you right home, you know.'

'No,' she almost shouted. 'It would be better . . . not to. Yes – this is the stop.'

'All right then.' He stood up, looking at her confusedly for a few seconds, then, to her amazement, he stooped and kissed her cheek. 'It's OK, Abbie; I understand. I'll see you next week. I'll look forward to it. Take care now.'

He leaped off the tram, lifting his hand briefly in a goodbye wave. The last she saw of him was his tall rangy figure striding away into the darkness along Whitegate Drive in the direction from which they had just come.

The front door was flung open, heedless of blackout regulations, before Abbie was halfway up the path, to reveal the irate figure of her mother standing in the vestibule. Had she arrived home on time Eva would, no doubt, have been hiding away in her bedroom as she had been the week before. But this was too good an opportunity to miss. The opportunity, Abbie knew, that her mother had been waiting for.

'And what time do you call this?' Eva didn't wait for an answer. 'I'll tell you what time it is. It is nearly half-past ten.' Abbie knew for a fact that it was just turned quarter past, but she did not dare to argue. 'Get inside!' Her mother gave her a push and Abbie almost fell through the hall door. 'Never mind standing there on the doorstep looking gormless, just as though butter wouldn't melt in your mouth. We'll be having the ARP warden after us, not that you would care.'

Eva closed the door forcefully behind them, then turned to confront her daughter. 'Well, what have you got to say for yourself? What do you mean by it, coming in at this time when I quite clearly told you ten o'clock? I knew all along, though, that you were set on defying me. And you've been even worse since you started going around with that . . . that Miller girl. I suppose she's just gone home as well, has she? Not that her parents could care less, I'll be bound, what sort of hours she keeps. From the look of her I'd say she was allowed to run wild.

124

Well, it's not happening here, young lady. I've been far too lenient already, allowing you even to see her. And this will be the very last time—'

'If you'd let me speak, Mother, then perhaps I could explain,' said Abbie. 'I'm sorry I'm late. I didn't mean to be, but I couldn't help it.'

'Couldn't help it? Of course you could help it. What nonsense! You've got a watch, haven't you?'

The sitting-room door opened and Dr Winters appeared. Wearing his homely brown cardigan, his library book in his hand and slippers on his feet he looked so ordinary and comforting that Abbie felt like flinging her arms round him, except that she had never behaved in that fashion towards her father.

'Let the girl explain, Eva,' he said quietly. 'At least you can let her do that. You're not being very reasonable.'

'That's right. You stick up for her. I'm getting used to this. Not reasonable! I think I've been more than . . .'

'Eva! For God's sake, listen to the girl.' Abbie had rarely heard her father blaspheme, even mildly. He turned to her, giving a nod and a hint of a smile. 'Go on, Abigail.'

'I lost my cloakroom ticket,' she said, very quietly and humbly, her eyes downcast. 'We went to the Palace – to the ballroom – and I couldn't find my ticket, and the woman wouldn't let me have my coat, not for ages, anyway. Then we missed a tram.'

'What do you mean – "we"?' Eva's eyes narrowed. 'That girl – that Doreen Miller – she doesn't go home on the tram, does she? I thought she lived off . . . Central Drive.' The way her lips curled showed what she thought of such an area.

'No – I mean, yes, she waited with me for the tram.' Abbie had to resort to a white lie, but she knew her mother would be even angrier if she knew the truth, that she had been dancing all evening with a young man. An RAF recruit – an AC1 – almost as low a rank as you could have. 'Doreen goes home on the bus,' she added lamely.

'You see,' said her father, very calmly. 'There is a perfectly good explanation. I knew there would be. I knew Abigail would not be late on purpose.'

125

'You knew!' stormed his wife. 'You know nothing! Nothing of how I've put up with her disobedience for weeks now. Or if you did know you have chosen not to support me. And Bertha has gone out of her way to encourage her. Just look at her!' Eva threw a contemptuous look in her daughter's direction. 'Hair flowing round her shoulders like some . . . some tart! Is that how you want your daughter to look?'

'I think she looks very nice,' replied Cedric evenly. 'And she has said she's sorry. She didn't mean to be late.'

'Whether she meant it or not, she has done it once too often.'

'Mother, that's not fair!' Abbie was startled into resistance by the unmerited remark. 'What do you mean, once too often? It's the first time I've been late.'

'And the last,' said Eva ominously. 'It's not just your being late I object to. It's the way you've been behaving for the past few weeks. Well, you won't get the chance to be late again because you are not going out, not for a month. You will stay in and read, or knit socks . . . or help your Aunt Bertha, seeing that you seem to enjoy spending so much time with her. But you are – not – leaving – this – house!' Eva banged her fist against the banister rail in emphasis.

'You can't make me do that!' gasped Abbie. 'It's . . . it's ridiculous!'

'I can and I will. And it's you that's ridiculous,' retorted Eva. 'Gadding around with that no-good girl, you know she's not a suitable friend for you. You can do your father's errands, of course, and you can attend church. I may even allow you to go to the play that the Dramatic Society are performing. I am not unreasonable, Abigail. But as for anything else – no, most definitely not. And in future I trust you will learn to choose your friends more carefully.'

'I am really very worried about Abigail,' said Eva to her husband after the girl had gone up to bed. 'I know you think I am being hard on her, but it is for her own good, Cedric. She will thank me for it one day. After all, we don't want her to turn out like . . . Well, enough said about that the better.' Cedric did not answer, but after a wary look at his downcast eyes Eva continued. 'One can't be too careful with girls of her age. I'm so afraid she will get into bad company and . . .'

'I would have thought she was far too sensible to do that,' Cedric interrupted and Eva could tell from his stern glance that he was still none too pleased with her. 'You must try to trust her, Eva. She's growing up now. In fact she is, already, quite a grown up young woman. You can't keep her tied to your apron strings for ever.'

'Of course not, Cedric, and I don't want to, but you must see . . . One has to be cruel to be kind, sometimes.' She smiled coaxingly at him, anxious not to incur his displeasure any further.

'Very well, my dear.' His half smile was one of resignation rather than affection. 'I accept that you have Abigail's best interests at heart. But . . . try to be a little more lenient with her, hmm? You know she is not really a wilful or a disobedient girl, like you make her out to be sometimes.'

Eva nodded. She had the feeling at times that Cedric could see right through to the heart of her. She was concerned about Abigail's welfare. What mother worth her salt would not be? But she also knew, if she were honest with herself, that what Cedric said was true. She did not want to let go of the control she had always exercised over their daughter, a control that it seemed was gradually being taken away from her. She had noticed Abigail's growing allegiance with Bertha and the way her cousin always tried to defend the girl; the comradeship that was developing between Cedric and Abigail; and now, not least, this undesirable friendship with a young woman from a most unsuitable background. Eva knew she had to stake her claim on her daughter's life before it was . . . too late.

Chapter 8

Abbie cried herself to sleep that night, something she very rarely did. She had never considered herself to be an emotional girl. There had, indeed, been very little for her to be emotional about. Until now. She had been growing to like Peter Horsfall very much; she had even begun to think that he might like her, too. Now the friendship was finished before it had even started. Peter would never wait a month for her. He would think she had stood him up, and by the time she was allowed out again, he would have got friendly with another girl, and who could blame him?

Why did he ever look at me in the first place? Abbie asked herself as she thumped at her hot pillow, feeling the scalding tears of disappointment and misery running down her cheeks. I'm fat and plain, I get tongue-tied whenever a man speaks to me, and I have a mother who treats me like a naughty little girl. She was wishing she had never set eyes on Peter Horsfall. What you never had you would never miss. She hadn't spent enough time with him to get to know him well, but already she had felt he was a kindred spirit and that the spark of liking they felt for each other might grow and deepen. Now it was all ruined by a domineering mother who was determined her daughter would have no life of her own.

When she awoke in the early hours of the following morning after just a few hours' sleep she felt much calmer. She stared into the blackness of the room, the dark unrelieved by even the tiniest sliver of light creeping through the blackout blinds. Abbie had never been afraid of the dark. The darkness could be very comforting. She had always been of a philosophical frame of mind and as she lay there, quiet and still, her bout of frantic – uncharacteristic – weeping over, she came to the conclusion that her friendship with Peter would have been doomed anyway. She realised now that even as she had agreed, at the tram stop, to meet him again, she had known, deep down, that this would not happen.

Her mother would never have approved of him for the simple reason that he had not been chosen by her. Abbie would have had to tell her mother about him sooner rather than later, because she had never been a deceitful girl. And then the inquisition would have started. Suitable though he may have been – and Abbie was sure that Peter had a highly respectable family background; moreoever he had been a grammar school boy and was a churchgoer – Eva would have found fault with him. And what young man would continue seeing a girl whose mother was always carping and criticising? Abbie persuaded herself that it would have come to nothing in the end.

But she had to let Peter know that she could not meet him. It would not be fair to have him standing outside the Winter Gardens believing that she had let him down. She would have to see Doreen. Her mother could not object, surely, to her popping into the shop to have a word with the girl. Eva could not watch her twenty-four hours a day. Or if Abbie was unable to leave the house her aunt would be sure to be calling in at the grocer's. Doreen would, no doubt, be seeing Neil, and he could pass a message on to Peter. Neil would have a good snigger about it, she felt sure, but what did it matter? She, Abbie, would not be seeing either of those young men again.

She caught her aunt on her own for a few moments later that morning before she was due to leave for church with her mother and father. Bertha, clad in her voluminous apron, was just starting to prepare the joint of meat for roasting, a ritual which took place every Sunday whilst the Winters family were at their devotions. It was a half-shoulder of lamb this week. It looked a little scrawny and under-sized, sitting in the centre of the large tin, but it would be delicious, as always, when served with the crispy roast potatoes at which Bertha excelled, rich brown gravy and at least two or three vegetables. The carrots and peas and a large cabbage were lying at the other end of the scrubbed pine table awaiting attention, together with a few sprigs of mint, ready to be chopped finely and made into mint sauce. The war, as yet, had made very little difference to the Winters' family's Sunday dinner, although the meals throughout the rest of the week were more austere, often concocted from recipes on the wireless programme *Kitchen Front*, or the *Food Flashes* shown between the big films at the cinema. Bertha was an excellent manager. Just how good she was, Eva, who considered such trivialities as food and rationing beneath her, had never realised. Normally Abbie would have been looking forward to her Sunday dinner. She felt calmer this morning, but still too hurt by her undeserved punishment to be much interested in food.

Bertha gave her a sympathetic smile. 'I take it things didn't go too well last night, love? I couldn't help overhearing. I was in my little parlour when you came in and I thought, By Jove, she's for the high jump now! I'd've let you in myself, you know, but I knew your mother was already waiting there. I felt sick with worry when it got to quarter-past ten, but I knew you wouldn't have done it on purpose.'

'She wouldn't listen, Aunt Bertha! It's so unfair. I did try to explain, but it was any excuse to stop me from seeing Doreen. She's trying to break up our friendship. But there's something even worse, Auntie. You remember me telling you about Peter, that RAF lad?'

'Yes, of course I remember.' Bertha spoke cautiously, with one eye on the kitchen door.

'Well, he asked me to meet him again, next Saturday, and now I can't! You know Mother says I've to stay in for a month, don't you?'

'Yes, I did hear, love.' Bertha lowered her voice. 'But I daren't interfere – you know that, don't you?'

Abbie nodded solemnly. 'I know, but I thought my father might've stuck up for me. What's the matter with him? Is he frightened of her or what?'

'I reckon he's tried, love,' said Bertha with a sigh. 'But he has to live with her more closely than either you or me. But there . . . I mustn't say too much. I'm sorry about that Peter, though. He sounded a real nice lad.'

'He was – I mean, he is. And I've got to let him know. Could you call in the shop, Aunt Bertha, and tell Doreen what's happened? Then she can get a message to him.'

131

'I could,' Bertha said guardedly, with another glance towards the door. 'But there's nothing to stop you telling her yourself, is there? You'll be doing errands for your father so you could nip in and see her. Nobody'll know,' she whispered. 'And I don't see as how that could matter anyway . . .'

'Abigail, where are you? I've been waiting ages.' Her mother's voice called from the hall and the next second the kitchen door was flung open. Eva was immaculately dressed, her fox fur slung round her shoulders and a tiny green hat with a veil, which exactly matched her Moygashel suit, tilted forward over one eye.

'She came to see if I needed any help,' said Bertha, untruthfully, 'but it's all under control. Thanks for asking though, love.' She grinned at Abbie, half closing one eye in the merest suggestion of a wink. 'Off you go now. Enjoy your service.'

Poor lass, thought Bertha, as she watched her niece trail dispiritedly after her mother. Yesterday she had been so carefree and happy, looking forward to seeing that nice-sounding young man again. And now, all the sparkle had gone out of her. But she might have known. It was only to be expected. Eva could be the very devil when she was roused, but Bertha could not see, for the life of her, that the poor girl had done anything wrong. Being a few minutes late home was neither here nor there, but Bertha knew – and Abbie knew, too – that this was just an excuse. The only offence Abbie had committed was to carry on seeing Doreen Miller against her mother's wishes. Eva, no doubt, would be highly delighted if she knew she had managed to put the kibosh on a budding relationship with a young man, but the less she knew about that the better. Bertha, at that very moment, made up her mind she would do her utmost to see that Eva did not ruin Abbie's friendship with that nice girl as well. It was about time the lass had a real friend and it seemed to her that Doreen would do her niece nothing but good. Bertha had only a few friends of her own, women from the chapel she attended who occasionally called in to share a cup of tea with her in her little parlour. She could please herself whom she invited into her own room, and if she chose to invite Doreen Miller then there was nothing Eva could do about it. If she ever knew.

'Honestly, Abbie, I can hardly believe what you're telling me. Your mother has actually forbidden you to go out for a whole month? It's flippin' ridiculous! She can't do that. How's she going to stop you? Is she going to lock you in your room? Why can't you just . . . go? I know I would!'

'You wouldn't say that if you had a mother like mine,' replied Abbie ominously. 'It's different for you, Doreen. I don't think you realise how different it is. Your mother's a reasonable woman, and she's nice and kind . . . I think she's lovely, your mum,' she added wistfully. 'But mine is . . . well, it's no use. I know you don't understand, but I have to do as she says. About staying in at night, at any rate. And I know jolly well that that's what she objects to and what she's determined to put a stop to. It's the idea of me going to the Palace on a Saturday night. She hates it. She'd be as mad as anything if she knew I'd come here this afternoon, but she can't be watching me twenty-four hours a day. Anyway, she's safely out of the way at her whist drive and I'm supposed to be doing some deliveries for my father. I managed to do them before I came here.'

The two girls were walking round Stanley Park lake, Abbie with her eyes continually straying to the Cocker memorial clock, visible from nearly all over the park. She must be back before half-past four when her mother would return from her afternoon with the Mother's Union women, but as it was only a quarter of an hour's walk from her home to the park she had plenty of time. She had made haste with her errands, and by making out that she had a lot of deliveries to do when there were really only a few she had given herself time to spend with Doreen. Her friend had been busy when she went into the shop late on Monday afternoon, and unable to exchange more than a few words with her. Doreen had sensed the urgency in Abbie's voice, however, and she had suggested they should meet at Stanley Park gates on Wednesday afternoon, which was half-day closing for the Blackpool shops. Abbie had been determined she would be there. Her mother had deprived her of enough already. She was not going to stop her from spending an hour or two in the sunshine, mingling with the holiday-makers who, invariably, on one day of their week's holiday, paid a visit to Blackpool's lovely municipal park.

'What your ma objects to, more than anything, is you being friendly with me, isn't it?' said Doreen. 'You don't have to try and wrap it up, luv. I know only too well what she thinks about me.'

'Oh, I don't know that it's that,' said Abbie, trying to be tactful. 'It would be the same whoever I was going with. It's the thought of me going dancing, that's the top and bottom of it. And she thinks I've been defiant lately, giving her cheek, as she calls it, so she's putting a stop to it.'

'For God's sake, Abbie, you're nineteen! You're not a kid!'

'I know, I know, but that's the way it is. It's the way she is and I've got to put up with it. For the moment, anyway. But the worst thing is – I won't be able to see Peter . . . He asked me to meet him again on Saturday night,' she added, a little shyly.

'He did? Gosh, that's great. You really liked him, didn't you? And . . . you can't go? Are you sure you can't? There must be something you could do. Honestly, Abbie, you can't let your mother stop you from going on a date. Why don't you tell her you're meeting a young man, and not me? I've told you, it's me she objects to.'

'You must be joking!' Abbie gave a bitter laugh. 'Tell her I've got a date? She'd hit the roof and never come down. No, that's the last thing I could ever tell her . . . and don't ask me why. I don't know why. I just . . . can't. I'm all right, Doreen, really I am. I was terribly upset at first and I'm still disappointed, but I know I've got to accept it. I was wondering, though, if you could get a message to Peter for me? I don't want him to be standing there waiting. Perhaps Neil could tell him.'

'Sorry, luv. No can do.'

'What do you mean? You're seeing Neil again, aren't you? Oh, I see – you're not seeing him till Saturday night, is that it?'

'No, I'm not seeing him at all,' said Doreen, very forcibly. 'Not after the way he tried it on on Saturday night. I ought to have known, though. I was an idiot to go on the promenade with him. We stopped and had a kiss or two under the colonnades. Well, I didn't mind that, but then . . . honestly! His hands were everywhere: inside me dress, up me skirt. I kept telling him to stop it, but he took no notice. Then he tried to get me on to the sands, under North Pier. He said it would be more private, like. Would you believe it? He must've thought I was protesting because there were a few people around. But I told him, "You can get knotted, mate! I'm not that sort of a girl." Anyroad, I managed to get me knee up and gave him a kick where it hurts. Then I ran. Praise the Lord he didn't follow me. I got on a bus at Talbot Square an' I'll bet I was home before you.'

Abbie was staring at her in open-mouthed amazement. 'Gosh! I'm glad you managed to get away. You must have been awfully frightened.'

'Not so much frightened as bloomin' annoyed that he thought I'd do . . . that.'

'What do you mean? Do what?'

'Well, you know. Go the whole way. I never have done. I've been brought up properly, y'know. Me mam's ever so strict about things like that. She's not bossy and domineering like your mother, but she's always told me I should have respect for meself and not let fellows mess about with me. And so I never have done.' Seeing Abbie's puzzled frown, she stopped. 'Sorry, p'raps I shouldn't be talking to you like this. You've never had much to do with fellows, have you, Abbie?'

'Nothing at all,' said Abbie. 'And I don't mind what you say, honestly I don't. I'm intrigued. Nobody has ever talked to me like that before and nobody would ever tell me . . . what I wanted to know. I don't know what happens, you see. Not that I've ever asked anybody except Aunt Bertha, and she wouldn't tell me. Except to say that I'd know when I fell in love, and that I hadn't to do it before I got married.'

'You mean . . . you don't know at all how it happens?' Now it was Doreen's turn to be amazed.

'Not really,' replied Abbie. 'I have some idea – I'm not stupid – but I don't know for sure. I haven't any brothers or sisters like you have, and at school when they used to talk about . . . things, I was never part of it. Some of the girls weren't very nice to me at school. Not that you could blame them, I suppose. I was so . . . peculiar.'

'I don't think you're peculiar.' Doreen took hold of her arm. 'Come on, let's sit down here for a bit.' They sat on a form near the children's boating area, where the ducks and swans often waddled out of the water. 'I think you've been too lonely for too long. That's all that's the matter with you, and that mother of yours is not going to spoil our friendship, not if I've got owt to do with it. Sorry – I mean, anything to do with it. I'm trying to speak proper an' all, since I met you.'

Abbie laughed. 'I don't care how you speak. I'm just glad you want to talk to me at all, and to be my friend. I can't believe it, really. My aunt says she's going to ask you round for supper one night soon. I often sit with Aunt Bertha in the evening and Mother won't know you're there. Anyway, I don't care if she does. She might be able to stop me from going out at night, but she can't stop Aunt Bertha from inviting a friend round.'

'Good for you.' Doreen nudged her in a matey sort of way. 'I'd like that. I like your Aunt Bertha. But about that other ... thing, I'm amazed you don't know. With your father being a doctor an' all.'

'A very discreet one.' Abbie smiled. 'He's only just started to let me see the patients' records. No, Father would die with embarrassment if he had to tell me anything like that.'

'Come to think of it, I suppose I only learned about it through playground gossip,' said Doreen thoughtfully. 'And by putting two and two together. I had brothers, of course, and they're made a little bit different from us. Anyway, I suppose it's quite simple really, though it sounds a bit odd when you describe it . . .' Doreen, who had no inhibitions, did so.

Abbie blushed slightly, looking not at Doreen, but at the distant view of trees fringing the lake, the bridge spanning the narrow part, and the Cocker clock, which now said ten minutes to four. She had thought it was something like that, but it was a relief to have it explained. She had felt such a fool, not knowing at nineteen years of age. She decided to change the subject.

'I used to come here when I was a little girl,' she said. 'Aunt Bertha used to bring me to feed the ducks. Goodness knows what they eat now, poor things. You're not supposed to feed them now there's a war on.'

'Be blowed to that!' replied Doreen. 'I never come to Stanley Park without a few crusts.' She pulled a paper bag out of her shoulder bag and scattered a few bits of bread on the path at the edge of the lake. 'Come on, Donald Duck, and you, Daisy Duck, or whatever yer name is. Come and 'ave yer dinner. This lot'll've gone before any nosy park keeper comes along.'

The crusts disappeared in an instant, fought over not only by the ducks, but by an elegant swan who condescended to swim to the side, and a couple of seagulls who dive-bombed out of the sky at the sight of the feast.

'That's it then.' Doreen folded up the empty paper bag and put it carefully away in her shoulder bag. Paper bags were not things to be thrown away; they could be used time and time again. 'Come on, we'd best be making a move, hadn't we, or your mam'll be on the warpath. Here, hold on a minute.' She took hold of Abbie's arm as they stood up. 'We never decided what to do about letting Peter know, did we? I tell you what,' she went on as they walked off in the direction of the main gates, 'I could meet him for you and tell him what has happened. Don't worry,' she added, looking at Abbie's anxious face, 'I won't run off with him or anything like that. He's not my type . . . but I wouldn't anyway. You know that.'

'It wouldn't matter much if you did,' said Abbie glumly. 'I know he'd never want to see me again, not after this. And who could blame him? Honestly, fancy getting into trouble for being late home at nineteen years of age!'

'She'll get fed up one day, your mam, of bossing you around, especially if she can see you're not upset by it.'

'But I am! I can't help it.'

'Then try not to let her see how she's getting to you. Now, d'you want me to meet Peter for you, or don't you? Just say the word.'

'Yes, please, if you would, Doreen. Half-past six, outside the Winter Gardens. Just tell him . . . I'm very sorry.'

'Where's Abbie?' asked Peter when he saw the lone figure of Doreen hurrying towards him along Church Street. 'She's not ill, is she?' He looked concerned and Doreen could tell that he did care about her friend. As Abbie had said, Peter was a nice sort of lad, very different from his mate Neil.

'No, she's not ill,' said Doreen, 'but she can't come. She's asked me to come and explain . . . and to tell you she's sorry.'

137

Peter gave a puzzled frown. 'You'd better tell me then.' He frowned even more when he heard the reason, that Abbie was being punished for being late home. 'Good grief! Who would believe it, in this day and age? I thought girls were being given a lot more freedom, with the war being on. I dare say you are, aren't you, Doreen?'

'Sort of,' she replied. 'My parents like to know where I am, but my mam's a very different kettle of fish from Abbie's. She's a right old battle-axe, Abbie's mam.'

'So I gathered.' Peter looked very distressed. 'She didn't say much, but I could tell she was in a real old state when she lost her ticket and knew she'd be late. Look, Doreen, let's go for a walk on the prom or somewhere. We can't stand here all night, and I don't suppose you feel like going to the pictures, do you?'

Doreen grinned to herself. She didn't quite know how to take that remark, but she realised that Peter did not possess the same slick assurance when talking to girls as his friend did.

'No, 's all right,' she answered. 'Let's have a walk. I feel like a bit of fresh air, but I told me mam and dad I wouldn't be very long. I told them where I was going and they thought it was a real shame about Abbie. But they weren't surprised. Dr Winters is our doctor, y'see, and they know his missus an' all. She's a real old cow . . . if you'll forgive the language, Peter.'

As they walked northwards along the promenade she explained to Peter how she had first met Abbie. She told the tale truthfully, as was her way, including the fact that she hadn't liked the other girl very much at first. 'But she's real nice when you get to know her,' she added, with a sidelong glance at Peter. 'P'raps her mother might give way after a week or two. Pigs might fly, I suppose, but you never know. Then p'raps you could see her again? I know you liked her a lot,' she added boldly.

'Yes, so I did,' said Peter. 'But it's no use, I'm afraid, Doreen. We've got our marching orders. We're being posted, quite a lot of us. It's the next stage of our training. So even if I had met Abbie tonight it would have been for the last time. Neil's going as well,' he added, 'but I don't suppose that will worry you very much, will it?' He even managed a wry grin.

'You're not kidding it won't!' retorted Doreen. 'Thinks he's a right little Casanova, doesn't he?' She was not sure what Neil had told his friend, but he would have been sure to have put his own interpretation on the facts, probably saying that he had got tired of her.

'You're well rid,' said Peter. 'You deserve somebody better than Neil. I know what he can be like with the girls. But, for all that, I have to say he's a very good mate to me. I'm glad we'll still be together.'

'Where are you going?' asked Doreen.

'We're not sure. It's all very hush-hush, but we guess it'll be one of the big air fields in the east of England. That's where they fly from, you know, on the bombing raids.'

Doreen felt herself go cold. Peter was such a nice bloke and so many of them didn't come back. She hoped that wherever he went he would keep safe.

'At any rate, I should be nearer home,' he added, with an attempt at cheerfulness. 'My parents will be pleased about that. Come on, we might as well have a cup of tea while we're here.'

They found a snack bar on the promenade and sat there for a while, chatting about this and that. Peter was easy to talk to once his initial reserve had broken down and Doreen began to understand what Abbie had found so appealing about him. Afterwards they leaned against the railings near North Pier, gazing out over the stretch of blue-green sea. It was usually more grey than blue, but as the sun began its descent its rays miraculously changed the colour of the ocean to an iridescence reflected from the sky's glowing shades of rose and vermilion, the edge of each dark cloud fringed with gold.

'That's something I shall miss,' said Peter, nodding towards the horizon. 'I'd never seen sunsets like that till I came to Blackpool. But all good things come to an end, I suppose . . . sometimes before they've even started. Do give Abbie my . . . best wishes, and tell her I'm very sorry I won't be seeing her again. If I'd met her tonight I'd probably have asked her to write to me, but the way it's turned out I don't suppose there's much point in that, is there?'

Why ask me? thought Doreen. It was up to him to make the decision. 'I'll give you her address, if you like,' she said.

'No, better not,' said Peter, rather sadly. 'It's no use deluding myself. It could never amount to anything, and it's not fair with me going away. I'll just have to think of her and me as ships that pass in the night. A pity, though. She's a grand girl. And so are you, Doreen. Thanks for coming to tell me. Come on, I'll see you home.'

Doreen did not argue. She had stayed out longer than she'd intended and already dusk was falling. They walked quickly through the streets of town, then along Central Drive to her home.

'I live up there,' she said, stopping at the corner of the narrow street of terraced houses. 'Thanks for seeing me home, Peter. You don't need to come any further. I'll be OK . . . A bit different from Abbie's neck of the woods, isn't it?' she added.

'It doesn't matter where you live, Doreen,' said Peter gently. 'I've told you – you're a grand lass. Abbie's lucky to have such a good friend.' He stooped and kissed her cheek. 'Good night, Doreen . . . God bless.'

Yes, he is nice, thought Doreen as she stared at his retreating figure. But it had never once entered her head to flirt with him, or him with her, she guessed. It would not have been fair to Abbie.

Chapter 9

'There's something in this morning's paper that might interest you two,' said Bertha, with a decided gleam in her eye, one evening in December. She pointed to a headline in the *Daily Express*. 'There, what do you think of that, eh?'

'*Conscription for Women*.' Abbie and Doreen read the words that seemed to leap out at them from the page, then looked at one another for a few seconds before eagerly devouring, with their eyes, the rest of the paragraph. It was short and to the point. Women, between the ages of twenty and thirty-one were to be conscripted to do war work and registration would begin in January. They were to be given a choice between joining the auxiliary services – the WRNS, the ATS or the WAAF – or serving in civil defence or industry. Married women living with their husbands and those with children under fourteen were the only ones who were exempt.

'Yippee!' yelled Doreen, nudging her friend excitedly. 'That's you and me, kid. Your mam won't be able to tie you to her apron strings any longer. You'll have to join the army, luv.'

'Conscription. That means it's compulsory, doesn't it?' said Abbie. 'That you have to go?'

''Course it does, you fathead! Aren't you pleased? Isn't it just what you've been waiting for? A chance to get away from here?'

'Yes . . . yes, of course,' replied Abbie, though a little unsurely. 'But . . . I'm not twenty, am I? I'm only nineteen.'

'You'll be twenty in January, Abigail,' replied her aunt crisply. 'And like Doreen says, I thought it was the chance you'd been waiting for.'

'So it is. Yes, I do believe it might be.' Abbie nodded soberly before turning to her friend. 'But you're certainly not twenty,

141

are you, Doreen? You won't even be nineteen till March.'

'Oh heck! I'm not, am I? But it won't make any difference. They won't stop me from joining up if I want to, and I do want. It's what I've wanted for ages, but I decided to wait a bit when our Tony died. But I'm sure Mam and Dad wouldn't stand in my way now. What d'you think, Abbie? Which shall it be? I rather fancied the ATS at one time; now I think I might like to be in the WAAF. My friend Gwen's in the WAAF now, you know. She thinks it's great. I don't suppose I'd be sent to the same place, but it would be good if you and me were together, wouldn't it, Abbie? I wouldn't want to join the WRNS though – I think I might be seasick.'

'I doubt if they'd let you go on the ships, anyroad,' replied Bertha. 'You'd be doing the office jobs, I reckon, or serving in the canteen or stores or whatever. It's only the men that'll do the dangerous work. What's the matter, Abbie? You're looking a bit down in the mouth. I thought this news'd buck you up no end. Your mother won't be able to stop you from doing this, you know. Even Eva won't be able to argue with His Majesty's Government.'

'I wouldn't be too sure, Aunt Bertha,' said Abbie gloomily. 'She'll have a jolly good try. It says industry as well, doesn't it? She'd probably insist that I went to Vickers Armstrong. I know she was dead against the idea before, but it would mean that I wouldn't have to leave home. If she let me do anything at all . . . I wouldn't put it past her to say I'm doing an important job where I am, working for my father.'

'Oh dear, I never thought of that.' Bertha sounded worried. 'Maybe you are. Perhaps it counts as what they call a key job, working with a doctor. Don't think for one minute that I'm trying to get rid of you, Abbie, nor you, Doreen. I don't know what I'd do without you two lasses cheering me up like you do. You've made me feel young again. But there's a war on and they keep telling us we all have to do our bit, and if it means parting with you two for a while then I know I'll have to put up with it. The war won't last for ever.'

'I shall be firm,' said Abbie. She set her mouth in a determined line before she went on speaking. 'I've made up my mind. When I'm twenty I shall go. I don't know where, not yet, but I'm not going to let Mother stop me. And I've just got to get away from this awful job with Father. I thought it would be great at first, working in the surgery instead of just messing about with appointments and the waiting room, but I'm not cut out for it, really I'm not.'

'I thought you liked it,' said Doreen. 'You've never complained very much before, have you?'

'No, I suppose I haven't,' said Abbie. 'That was the way I used to be, wasn't it? It was how I was taught to behave, to keep things to myself. Now I'm finding it's much better to talk things over with friends.' She smiled, still rather shyly, at Doreen. 'Aunt Bertha was always here, of course, but we never used to discuss things all that much, did we, Aunt Bertha? Important things, I mean.'

'No, not till just recently,' replied Bertha. 'There've been changes all round since Doreen here came on the scene, and many more to come, I'll be bound. What's up then, Abbie? What don't you like about it, working with your father.?'

'I like the dispensary well enough,' said Abbie. 'It's the surgery part, when I have to help him with the victims of accidents and things like that. We have to deal with what Father calls minor injuries in the surgery – but they don't seem all that minor to me. One little boy had fallen down in the street and his knee was gashed open nearly to the bone. My father put a couple of stitches in and the little lad was ever so brave. It was me that turned green, I can tell you. Like I did when I had to help him with lancing a carbuncle on the back of some poor man's neck. I had to hold the bowl. You'd never believe the stuff that came out of it. I very nearly passed out. But Father said I'd been a great help. I think he's trying to toughen me up a bit and I daren't complain. If I did Mother'd have me back tidying the magazines and arranging the flowers as quick as a wink.'

'So you're admitting it's more worthwhile, what you're doing now?' observed her aunt.

'Yes, obviously. But I don't like it. I never wanted to work for my father in the first place, not even when I left school. But Mother insisted.'

'What did you want to do?' asked Doreen.

'I don't honestly know. Do you know, I was never allowed to make any decisions of my own, or think for myself,' said Abbie, wonderingly. 'Goodness knows what I might have been if I'd been encouraged to make up my own mind.'

'A teacher, p'raps,' said Doreen. 'You're dead brainy.'

'Maybe ... I might have liked to work in a library. But I know I would never, never have chosen to be a nurse. Father would be far better off with a trained nurse, you know, rather than a squeamish coward like me.'

'You're not a coward at all,' said Doreen. 'If you were then you'd go back to tidying them bloomin' magazines, wouldn't she, Aunt Bertha?' That was what Doreen called Abbie's aunt now. 'I think it's dead brave of you to have carried on when it makes you feel so sick. I think it'd make me feel sick an' all. I looked after our Tony quite a lot, but there was never anything – you know – real nasty.'

'Just think about this, though, Abbie. And you, too, Doreen,' said Bertha. 'You might have to see worse sights than the ones you've described if you joined the ATS or the WAAF. I know they wouldn't put you in the middle of the fighting, but – well – we are at war, after all. And war is never pleasant.'

'I know,' replied Abbie. 'I realise that. It had just occurred to me, as a matter of fact, and I was thinking what a silly frightened thing I must sound, cringing at a drop of blood. It's nice of you to say I'm brave, Doreen, but I don't feel very brave, I can tell you. But if I was helping the War Effort I don't think I would mind. I wouldn't have to, would I? Besides, I would be doing something I wanted to do, something I had chosen, not something my parents had pushed me into.'

'An' I'd be there with you,' said Doreen brightly. 'Whatever happens, kid, we'll be in it together. I've made up my mind. What you do, I'll do an' all. Let's sleep on it, eh? We've got till January to decide. Now, are we going to listen to *ITMA*? It's nearly time.'

Doreen had fallen into the habit of calling round at the Winters family's house at least once, sometimes twice, a week. The first time she had been invited by Aunt Bertha, but now she needed no invitation. The three of them enjoyed their cosy evenings together, especially as winter drew on. Sometimes they listened to their favourite programmes on the wireless, not only *ITMA*, but *Monday Night at Eight*, *Garrison Theatre* or *Happidrome*, or whatever happened to be on. Or she and Abbie would chat comfortably, Aunt Bertha joining in between the complicated stitches of the jumper she was knitting or between the pages of her *Woman's Own*.

It was invariably Bertha who answered the door to Doreen, Eva Winters very rarely condescending to do such a menial task. The doctor's wife knew only too well that she was there, however, though probably not how often. But there was little Eva could do about the steadily growing friendship between her daughter and Doreen Miller. Doreen was treated to a frosty glance whenever the two of them chanced to meet, which was very rarely. But Doreen knew that this was a battle that Abbie had won.

After Abbie's month of being 'confined to barracks', as Doreen put it, the two girls had resumed their occasional visits to the cinema or the Palace Varieties, usually on a Saturday. They had gone dancing afterwards, but they had not met any more young men with whom they might strike up more than a passing acquaintanceship. Doreen had watched her friend, however, growing in confidence and becoming, slowly but surely, much less awkward in her manner and, consequently, more attractive. She was even beginning to lose weight.

Aunt Bertha's little parlour was a home from home to Doreen. She had been surprised at how much like her own home it really seemed. As she spent more and more time there she realised afresh what she had probably always known, that it was not elegant furnishings and costly possessions that made a true home. If she were honest she supposed she had envied Abigail Winters at first, which had added to her initial animosity towards the girl. The Winters family had so much and the Millers so little.

A peek into Eva Winters' luxurious lounge had convinced Doreen that this was not what she thought of as a home. The room had no heart, no feeling of being lived in. The green velvet curtains and the perfectly matching carpet, the costly china, silver and cut glass and the little tables with spindly legs, they all looked as though they belonged in the pages of *Ideal Home*, the magazine that Doreen had seen lying on a coffee table – she thought that was what they called it – in this elegant, but soulless, room.

A greater contrast than that with Bertha's room could not be imagined. Here was where Doreen felt was the real heart of the house, just as the household itself revolved around the person of Bertha, though it was possible that none of the Winters family realised how much. With the red plush curtains drawn against the winter darkness, and the flames from the fire causing the brass coal scuttle and fire irons to gleam, the place felt like a refuge, not only from the cold outside, but from all the dreadful things that were happening in this third year of the war. Maybe not in Blackpool – the town, mercifully, was escaping the worst of the bombing raids – but in many, many towns and cities of Britain. The rag rug on the hearth, made from hundreds of pieces of multicoloured material, was very similar to the one in Doreen's home, but Bertha's red floral-patterned carpet, though it was almost identical in design to the one in the Millers' living room, was not nearly so shabby and threadbare. The fireside chairs, too, and the oak table and two dining chairs were examples of good, solid, though rather unfashionable furniture. Doreen guessed that Eva Winters had furnished this room for her cousin with articles she no longer required. It was Bertha's own touches that made it so homely and lived in, something that you did not feel in the rest of the house, the parts Doreen had seen, at any rate.

The chair backs and cushion covers had been embroidered beautifully by Bertha, and the runner on the sideboard was edged with a crochet border that she had also worked. She had pointed out to Doreen some of the mementoes she had brought back from her infrequent holidays: a copper lustre jug from Morecambe, a box lavishly decorated with shells from Southport, and a pair of Staffordshire pottery cats, which sat at either end of the sideboard, she had bought right here at a saleroom in Blackpool because she liked their smiling faces.

Standing on the mantelpiece and decorating the walls were family photographs, just as there were in Doreen's home. Doreen could not help but notice that most of them featured Abbie. Abbie as a baby, as a sturdy little girl in a white sunbonnet and somewhat long dress, as a schoolgirl in a most unflattering gymslip, and one as she was now – or had been until recently – an ungainly looking girl, appearing much older than her years, who was smiling rather self-consciously at the camera. There was a wedding photograph of Eva and Cedric Winters, the doctor looking as though his high starched collar was choking him, and Eva wearing a headdress and veil that was pulled low over her forehead and shoes with very pointed toes. Doreen wondered if Bertha had hung it on the wall out of politeness.

There were hardly any photos of Bertha herself, just one of her holding little Abbie by the hand, and one of Bertha and another girl in very old-fashioned dresses that came right down to the floor. Doreen knew, of course, that Bertha was quite old and this must have been taken in the early years of the century. Goodness – forty years ago! Bertha said, when Doreen enquired, that it was her sister, Mabel, although she didn't seem to want to talk about the girl – well, old woman she would be now. She pointed out another photograph, brown-tinted and very faded, of a gentle frail-looking lady she said was her mother. But there did not seem to be any pictures of her father. Doreen had gathered there was some sort of mystery about Aunt Bertha, but even the outspoken Doreen knew it would be impolite to enquire too closely. Maybe Abbie would tell her more in her own good time.

For the moment Doreen was only too pleased to have been welcomed into these lovely cosy surroundings. She was so glad she had decided to make a friend of Abigail Winters, the girl she had once thought of as the doctor's stuck-up daughter. It just went to show how wrong you could be. She liked to feel that the friendship was not one-sided; that not only was she, Doreen, learning more about books and music, for instance, and how to speak more correctly, but that Abbie might be learning something from her as well. Learning how to mix with all sorts of different people and to overcome the shyness

147

and awkwardness that had beset her for so long.

The week before Christmas Doreen had been given an afternoon off work by her understanding employer in order to do her Christmas shopping, and Abbie was fitting her work at the dispensary around her friend's free time so that they could spend a few hours together. They had met at the corner of Park Road, as they had done the very first time they'd gone out together.

'There's something I want to show you,' said Doreen as they walked along Church Street. 'Look, there it is.' There was an empty space between the shops where a variety of bills and posters, mainly ones of war propaganda, were displayed on a hoarding, and Doreen was pointing to one of these.

'What? "Is Your Journey Really Necessary?" ' said Abbie. 'Is that the one you mean? I'm not thinking of going anywhere so it doesn't apply to me.'

'No, you chump, not that one!' said Doreen. 'The one next to it. And we're both thinking of going somewhere soon, aren't we? Don't forget, it's nearly January, call-up time. How does that appeal to you, eh?'

The poster she was indicating pictured a cheerful bonny-looking girl dressed in a white shirt and khaki trousers with a bundle of wheat tucked under her arm. She was smiling broadly, showing dazzlingly white teeth and pointing to the slogan above her head. 'Come and help with the Victory Harvest,' it read.

'What do you mean?' Abbie gave a puzzled frown. 'How does what appeal to me?'

'That! That girl,' said Doreen. 'Honestly, Abbie, I know you're a lot brainier than me, but you don't half act dim sometimes. She's a land girl, isn't she? How d'you fancy joining the Women's Land Army? You've heard of it, haven't you?'

'Of course I've heard of it,' said Abbie, a trifle huffily. 'But I wouldn't have thought it was for girls like us. They work on farms, don't they? What would you and I know about working on a farm? I've never even done any gardening. Father has a man round to do the garden, to trim the hedge and mow the lawn, although—'

'Oh well, he would, wouldn't he? It's all very well for folks who can afford gardeners.'

Abbie was not sure whether or not there was any malice in her friend's remark. Probably Doreen, as usual, was only joking, but Abbie hurried on to say, 'Don't be like that! I was just going to tell you that Mr Evans – the chap who does our garden – has dug the back lawn over to plant vegetables. Digging for Victory, you know. It was Father's idea. He said we must do it to be patriotic, but Mother nearly went mad! About what you were saying, though. That land girl; just look at her! She's a real country lass. I've never even set foot on a farm. I've never seen a cow any closer than over a hedge, and I doubt if you have either, Doreen. They won't want girls that have been brought up in the town, like we have.'

'Then that's where you're wrong,' said Doreen. 'You don't know everything, Abbie Winters. Most of the girls that join the Land Army are town girls, just like us. Most of 'em have never done any digging or hedging or mowing or whatever it is they do. If they're anything like me they haven't even got a garden to dig. A poky back yard, that's all we've got. But it makes no difference; I bet they'd still take me.'

'How do you know?' asked Abbie. 'And how have you heard about all these other girls?'

'I've heard people talking in the shop. And one woman was telling me how much her daughter likes it. She joined last summer and she's at a farm in Herefordshire. I don't know where that is, but she thinks it's great, this girl. And she lived in Palatine Road, so she wouldn't have been used to the country, would she?'

'Herefordshire . . . That's on the borders of Wales,' said Abbie thoughtfully.

'All right, clever clogs. I don't want a geography lesson,' said Doreen, laughing. 'Not right now . . . D'you think you might fancy it, though? I know I would.'

Abbie was silent for a moment. Then, 'Do you know, I do believe I might,' she said, sounding a little surprised. 'Yes, why not? If it's like you say and a lot of them are town girls . . . What would we have to do to join? Does it say?'

Together they studied the wording at the bottom of the poster.

' "You are needed in the fields! Apply to the nearest employment exchange for leaflet and enrolment form . . ." '

'Shall we do it?' said Doreen. 'This afternoon?' Her big blue eyes were alight with enthusiasm, and Abbie felt herself responding eagerly.

'Why not?' she said again. 'By the time we've filled in the forms and everything it'll be after Christmas, and then in January I'll be twenty and Mother won't be able to do anything about it. I'd better not say anything, though,' she went on as they set off walking along Church Street again. 'Not till Christmas is over. I don't want to get her in a worse mood than she's in already. What with Mr Evans digging the garden up and me telling her about conscription for women she's in a real old way with herself.'

'What did she say when you told her?' asked Doreen.

'She said, "Don't be silly, Abigail! It doesn't mean girls like you." I told her it meant everybody, but she said, "Huh! We'll see about that!" And so I've not mentioned it since. Christmas'll be bad enough without upsetting her any further. She's invited the Sidebottoms to come for dinner.'

'The who?' said Doreen, with a giggle. 'Did you say the Sidebottoms? Who are they?'

'Oh, just some friends of my parents,' said Abbie indifferently. 'Friends of Mother, really, rather than Father. Mrs Sidebottom's one of her whist drive cronies and Mr Sidebottom's in insurance. Mother has a policy with him. And they've a son called Sidney.'

'Sidney Sidebottom!' Doreen giggled again. 'That's a name to go to bed with, isn't it? How old is he?'

'Sidney? I don't really know,' said Abbie. 'About twenty-five or so, I suppose. I'm not sure. I've never thought about it.'

'He'll be in the army then,' said Doreen, 'if he's twenty-five.'

'No, he isn't,' said Abbie. 'He'll be coming with them on Christmas Day, more's the pity. It's bad enough having the two of them, but with him as well . . .'

'Why isn't he in the army?' persisted Doreen.

'I couldn't say.' Abbie shrugged. 'I've never been interested enough to find out. I think he has a weak chest, and he wears glasses so maybe they wouldn't take him. I don't know.'

'Sidney Sidebottom!' Doreen nudged her, then burst out laughing. Abbie found herself joining in, though she wasn't sure what she was laughing at.

'What's so funny? What are you laughing at?' she said, the ripples of hilarity that her friend had provoked making her voice louder than it should be, especially in the middle of town. Whatever would her mother say about such uncouth behaviour? She could feel tears of merriment springing to her eyes, something that had never happened before she met Doreen.

'His name!' shrieked Doreen, clinging to her friend's arm. 'Sidebottom! Those bottom names always make me giggle. There was a boy in our class at school called Eric Winterbottom and all us kids used to giggle like mad when the teacher said his name.'

'I don't see why,' said Abbie, trying to be serious. 'The poor lad; his name's not so much different from mine, is it?'

'No, I s'pose not, but there's no bottom attached to yours.' Another peal of laughter erupted from Doreen, and Abbie, in spite of herself, laughed out so loud that a passer-by gave the two girls a reproving glance.

'Some of the kids used to call him Chilly Bum!' cried Doreen, causing them both to laugh even louder. This was something Abbie had never experienced all the time she was growing up: a friend with whom to share a joke and a giggle. Only now did she realise what she had been missing. Life could – and should – be fun, not deadly serious all the time. Even though the thing they were laughing at was trivial – quite silly and childish really – Abbie was beginning to appreciate what a tonic laughter was and how it could make you feel so much better to let your hair down in this way.

'I knew a girl called Shufflebottom once,' she giggled.

'You didn't! You're making it up. Give over, Abbie; you'll have me wetting me knickers.'

'No, honestly; Alice Shufflebottom, that was her name,' said Abbie, nodding soberly in an attempt to quell her mirth. 'She was in our class, but nobody laughed very much. You weren't

151

encouraged to laugh at the school I went to. We were supposed to be demure young ladies ... And we'd better stop giggling now. We'll get turned out of Sweeten's bookshop if we behave like this.'

'Yes, so we will.' Doreen tried to smother the rest of her chuckles as they approached the town centre. Blackpool was crowded with Christmas shoppers and the ubiquitous RAF lads, walking about in twos and small groups. They always seemed to have plenty of time to spare between their training and square-bashing.

'Have you decided which book you're going to get for your aunt?' Doreen asked as they went in at the front entrance of Sweeten's and up the narrow aisle. 'She likes that bloke Thomas Hardy, doesn't she? She lent me a couple of them, but they weren't exactly a bundle of fun. I enjoyed 'em, I must admit, but that one about Tess made me cry me eyes out.' They stopped at the shelf of classics, all attractively bound in leatherette. 'There they are. Brontë, Dickens, Thackeray ...' Doreen began to read out the names. 'Arnold Bennett – who's he when he's at home? Never 'eard of 'im. But I'd hardly heard of any of 'em, had I, till I met you? D'you know, one of these days I'm gonner start collecting me own books, like you and Aunt Bertha do, instead of just getting 'em from the library. I think it 'ud be lovely to have a house full of books. I can't afford it yet, though. Food and clothes are more important in our house than books ... One day, though. Now, which are you going to get for her?'

'If you'd stop nattering for a minute I might be able to concentrate better,' said Abbie with a smile. 'As a matter of fact, I'm going to get her something a bit more up to date this time, if they've got it in stock. *The Crowthers of Bankdam* it's called. It was only published last year. It's about mill owners in Yorkshire. I know she enjoyed *Inheritance*, and she used to live in Yorkshire ...'

With the help of an assistant Abbie was able to find the book by Thomas Armstrong for her aunt, and she also bought a leather – well, austerity leatherette really – diary for her father. She had already bought an art-silk paisley-patterned scarf for her mother, and this year, to her great joy, there had been another present for her to buy. Listening to Doreen's easy chatter about books she knew she had made the ideal choice for her new friend. A copy of *The Good Companions* by J. B. Priestley was already wrapped, ready to be given to her at her next visit. It was a happy carefree book that she felt sure Doreen would enjoy. And she knew that her aunt had bought the girl a copy of *Under the Greenwood Tree*, one of Hardy's more light-hearted works, so already Doreen's desire for her own library was beginning to be realised.

'I'd like to buy summat – something – for Aunt Bertha as well,' said Doreen musingly. She was fingering a leatherette bookmark from a box on the counter.

'There's no need,' said Abbie. 'You have so many people to buy for, Doreen, with your big family, and Aunt Bertha wouldn't expect you to.'

'That's not the point, is it?' said Doreen sharply. 'I want to say thank you to her. She's been real kind to me. I'll get her one of these. It's not much, but I know she'll use it.'

'A Blessed Companion is a Book,' it said on the red bookmark that Doreen chose, and Abbie agreed that her aunt would be well pleased.

A visit to Woolworth's provided Doreen with the rest of the presents for her family. Gilt collar studs and cuff links for her father; a glittering brooch for her mother, which Abbie helped her to choose – one that was not too gaudy; bath cubes for her sisters; and a jar of brilliantine for her fifteen-year-old brother who had just started work as an errand boy at Harding's Grocers.

'We've got to make an effort,' said Doreen as they came out of Woolworth's into the semi-gloom of Bank Hey Street. It was only four o'clock, but already the winter dusk was falling. 'It'll be a sad sort of Christmas, though, the first one without our Tony. I remember last year I bought him some animals for his farm. He never liked toy soldiers and guns and forts, like some lads do. His farm's still there on the bedroom floor. Me mam hasn't had the heart to move it.'

'I'm so sorry,' said Abbie, tucking her arm through her friend's. 'I can imagine how sad it will be, especially for your mum and dad . . . Come on, shall we go and collect those forms about the Land Army? That'll be something to look forward to, won't it?'

The gift that thrilled Abbie most that Christmas was the one from Doreen. It was a powder puff in the centre of a pretty georgette handkerchief, just like the ones she had seen girls patting their noses and cheeks with in the cloakroom of the Palace. With it was a small box of Pond's face powder. It was the most frivolous thing she had ever possessed. She had opened it in secret and she knew it would have to be used in secret too, until such time as she was able to escape from home. Escape; what a word to be using, even in her thoughts, but that was what she felt it would be like to get away from home. Powder and lipstick may well be frowned upon for land girls – she didn't know – but however strict the authorities were she knew it could not be worse than her mother's domination.

Abbie was trying hard, at the moment, not to upset Eva too much. She had filled in her application form for the Women's Land Army – the WLA, as it was usually called – as had Doreen. They had decided to post them together after Christmas when the yearly glut of mail had been dealt with. They didn't want to risk their precious forms being lost in the post. Then it would be just a question of waiting for an answer – an interview, maybe – and, of course, plucking up the courage to tell her mother what she had done.

Christmas followed the usual ritual with the Winters family, the only difference being that this year there were seven of them sitting round the dining table instead of four. Bertha was always allowed to dine with the family on Christmas Day, even if there were guests, which was only right as it was she who had cooked the meal almost single-handed. Abbie had helped with the preparation of the vegetables, but Eva, as always, had not lifted a finger in the kitchen. All she had been concerned about was making sure that both she, and the sitting room, were in an immaculate condition to receive their guests.

Eva was quite the lady of the manor in her pale blue twinset and pearls, smiling from the head of the table whilst Bertha scurried back and forth from the kitchen with the plates of chicken and tureens of vegetables, roast potatoes, and sage and onion stuffing. Turkeys could not be obtained at any price this year, at least not from the shops; and as Cedric abhorred the black market Eva had not pursued this source. The chicken that Bertha had procured from the local butcher was, however, quite adequate. There would be very little left over to make sandwiches at tea time, but Doreen had saved a tin of red salmon for Bertha from Mr Harding's stringently distributed supply. It had taken a goodly number of their precious points – the points system had been introduced in November – but as it would impress their guests Eva had considered it well worth it. She knew little of points anyway, she had told Bertha when her cousin had informed her about the salmon. It was what she paid Bertha for, to worry and work out the budget on their behalf.

'Abigail, I think it would be a good idea if you and Sidney were to go for a walk,' said Eva, when they had all listened to the King's speech, another Christmas Day ritual, but one to which Abbie did not object; it made her feel patriotic and very proud to be British. But what on earth was her mother thinking of? She, Abbie, had never exchanged more than half a dozen sentences with Sidney Sidebottom. He attended the same church, that was all, and when the two of them met it had always been in the company of other people. And that was just how Abbie wanted it because the fellow gave her the creeps.

'It'll put some roses in your cheeks, dear,' her mother smiled, 'and I'm sure you and Sidney would find such a lot to talk about.' Roses in her cheeks, indeed! Abbie fumed inwardly. What an inane remark, and what the dickens would she find to say to him? But she did not dare refuse. It would be most impolite to Mr and Mrs Sidebottom to spurn the company of their son. They were a pleasant enough couple, but singularly lacking in personality. She couldn't understand why her mother should want to be friendly with them.

'Rather! What a good idea, Mrs Winters.' Sidney was rubbing his large white hands together in a way that made Abbie's flesh creep, although she had always considered him harmless enough. Sometimes, in fact, she had felt rather sorry

155

for him, knowing what it felt like to be unattractive in comparison with one's peers. Sidney, at twenty-five – which was the age she guessed him to be – was already balding, his hair falling in oily strands over his shiny head. His chin receded away into his stiff collar, above which his prominent Adam's apple wobbled. That was soon covered, however, by the fawn scarf he wound round his neck and tucked beneath the lapels of his fawn raincoat.

'I'm ready now, Abigail. We'll take a turn round the park lake, shall we?' His pale grey eyes, reminding Abbie of a codfish on a slab at the fishmonger's, blinked at her rapidly from behind his steel-rimmed glasses. 'Wrap up warm now. It's cold out there.'

A fawn trilby, covering his bald patch, completed the overall picture of fawnness – of nonentity – that typified Sidney Sidebottom. But Abbie had been wrong in assuming that he would have little to say for himself. She need not have worried about what to say to him because it was Sidney who did all the talking. About himself.

'You're a lot thinner than you used to be, aren't you?' he said, peering at her in what she considered a very bold way as they set off walking along Whitegate Drive. 'You used to be quite plump, didn't you?'

'Yes, maybe I was,' she replied in a toneless voice. 'But we all have to tighten our belts. There is a war on, you know.' And you are not part of it, she wanted to add, but if Sidney was aware of her thoughts he certainly did not show it. He talked and talked, on and on, about his job in the same insurance office as his father, his clients, his boss – for whom he had no time at all; his prowess at chess – he played with his father every night and invariably won; and his collection of birds' eggs.

'I'm cold,' Abbie said eventually, knowing she sounded petulant, but she really was frozen. It was a raw, damp day with a bitter east wind blowing across the lake. 'Let's go back, shall we? Aunt Bertha will have the tea ready,' she added, a little more graciously.

'Very well, Abigail. Whatever you say.' Sidney gave her a hurt look and they walked back in silence. At least there will be salmon sandwiches for tea, thought Abbie, and very soon it would be time to post her application to the Women's Land Army.

Chapter 10

Abbie knew she couldn't possibly wait until the evening to tell Doreen her good news. There was only a short queue at the grocer's when she went in at four o'clock, and when she reached the counter there was, fortunately, no one behind her waiting to be served.

'I've got it!' She waved her letter triumphantly in front of Doreen's face. 'An interview at the Town Hall. It came this morning. Have you got one as well?'

'Yes, I have. An interview next Wednesday. Is that when yours is? I was going to tell you tonight and I was keeping my fingers crossed like mad that you'd got one an' all . . . as well. And so you have. I say, kid, isn't it great?' Doreen's eyes were glowing with excitement and you could have heard her voice right outside on the drive.

Mr Harding, slicing bacon at the other end of the counter, looked across and grinned. 'She's been like this all day. I've never seen her so full of beans. It's a good job that there interview's on a Wednesday afternoon, eh, Doreen? Or else you wouldn't've been able to go, would you?'

'Aw, get on with yer bother, Mr Harding!' said Doreen. 'You'd've given me some time off, I know you would.'

The grocer's smile confirmed that he was, indeed, only joking. 'I shall miss you, though,' he said. 'I can't pretend otherwise. But I can't stand in your way when you're off to serve your King and Country. I dare say it might count as a key job, working in a food shop. If you wanted to take the easy option you'd be OK here for the rest of the war, but that wouldn't be your way, would it, Doreen?'

Doreen shook her head. 'Not really, Mr Harding. I know I've got to do summat – something – more challenging. Anybody can wrap up butter and cut coupons out, can't they?'

'Not as quickly as you can, Doreen.' Mr Harding looked regretful for a moment. 'So you're going to be a land girl as well, Miss Winters?' He turned to Abbie. 'And what do your parents think about that, eh?'

'Er . . .' Abbie looked down at her feet. 'I haven't told them yet.'

'What!' shrieked Doreen. 'You haven't . . . ? Honestly, Abbie, you've been humming and hawing for the last couple of weeks, ever since Christmas. And now the letter's come you still haven't told her.' Doreen knew, as did Abbie, that the stumbling block would be her mother, not her father. 'How did you manage to read the letter then without her seeing it?'

'Aunt Bertha knows about it,' said Abbie. 'She's been watching the post for me every morning. It's usually her that picks it up from the mat anyway, not Mother. I'll tell her – I mean I'll tell them both tonight, really I will. I won't put it off any longer, honestly.' Abbie looked imploringly at her friend. 'Keep your fingers crossed for me, though, won't you? Or say a little prayer to your Holy Mother, or whatever it is you do.'

'Course I will.' Doreen's glance was somewhat pitying. 'You really are a prize chump, though. Fancy leaving it till the last minute like this. I tell you what – I won't come round tonight after all. If yer mam claps eyes on me it'll only make matters worse. So you'd better jolly well get in there and tell her! *Tell* her, mind, not ask her. She can't kill you.'

'I wouldn't be too sure.' Abbie's smile was humourless. 'I can't begin to imagine what she'll say, or what she'll do.'

'She should be proud that she's got a daughter like you,' said Mr Harding. 'She may well surprise you, Miss Winters. She may be pleased. Anyway, whatever happens, you can be sure you're doing the right thing. Now – I don't suppose you wanted to buy anything today, did you?' he added with a twinkle in his eye.

'Oh – er – no. I'm sorry.' Abbie looked down at her hands, empty of any shopping basket. 'I just came to tell Doreen—'

'It's OK; I understand.' Mr Harding winked. 'Tell Miss Shorrock, though, would you, that we've just had an allocation of tinned fruit? I've saved a tin of peaches for her.'

160

Abbie waited until the evening meal was over, knowing that once she dropped her bombshell there would be very little more food eaten and Aunt Bertha's delicious stew would go cold on the plates. As it was, she had eaten very little, although her mother did not seem to have noticed. There were just the three of them sitting at the dining table now whilst Bertha, as previously arranged with her niece, busied herself with the washing-up. Cedric was enjoying an after-dinner cup of tea, a common 'working class' habit in Eva's eyes, one which she deplored. As there was no ground coffee left, nor even any Nescafé, she preferred to go without a post-prandial beverage.

'Mother . . . I've got something to tell you. You as well, of course, Father.' Abbie took a deep breath. 'I've decided . . . I'm going to join the Land Army. I've got an interview at the Town Hall next Wednesday.'

'You're what? Did I hear you correctly, Abigail? Did I actually hear you say you were joining the . . . Land Army?'

'Yes, you heard correctly, Mother.' Abbie knew that her mother was not in any doubt, that sarcasm was just another of her weapons, often used to try to discomfit others. 'I've got an interview at the Town Hall . . .'

'Yes, yes – I heard you the first time, although I thought for a moment my ears were deceiving me.' Eva put her hands to her ears then stroked her fingers down the length of her neck, all the while staring at her daughter. 'You've got an interview . . . I see. And what makes you think for one moment that they would take you? You've never touched a spade, or a rake, or whatever else they use in all your life.'

'That's hardly my fault, is it, Mother, that I haven't done any gardening? Or that I've been . . . well, that I've had such a sheltered upbringing. They won't care, anyway, that I haven't had any experience. They're taking all sorts of girls from all sorts of backgrounds, so I've heard.'

'So you've heard! Yes, I dare say you have, and I can guess who you've heard it from. I wouldn't have to look very far to see who has put you up to this.' Eva paused, then her eyes softened a little. 'You're a well-brought-up girl, Abigail. Yes, I know you've been sheltered, as you call it. Any mother would try to protect her daughter from . . . from some of the things that go on in this wicked world.' She glanced at her husband who, so far, had not spoken. 'Anyway, Abigail, it's out of the question. You can forget the Land Army, or anything else for that matter. Other girls might have to join the ATS or the WAAF, but not you.' Abbie was surprised to see her mother smile, almost fondly, at her. 'You work for your father, who happens to be a doctor. Nursing is a reserved occupation. I've been making enquiries.'

'Just a minute, Eva.' Cedric Winters spoke quietly, but with an air of authority. 'Abigail is not a nurse, nor, I believe, does she want to be.' He looked questioningly at his daughter. 'I'm right, aren't I, Abbie?'

'Yes, Father. I've tried to help you, as best I can, but I'm not really—'

'She's not really cut out for it, Eva. That's what she's saying, and I respect her for it. I have decided . . .' The doctor made a steeple of his fingers, pausing for a few seconds before he went on. 'I have decided to advertise for a nurse to help with the practice. It's too much for me to cope with on my own, especially with the new clinic. I have already placed an advert in this week's *Evening Gazette*. Somebody local would be ideal, or if that fails I can advertise in the medical journals.'

Eva, for once, looked too dumbfounded to speak. Cedric smiled vaguely in her direction before continuing. 'My timing could not have been better, the way things have worked out, but then I guessed that Abigail might have something up her sleeve. You go right ahead, my dear. Join the Land Army if they will accept you – and I'm sure they will – and I for one will be very proud of you.'

'Cedric! What on earth are you saying? What has got into you? You can't let her join . . . Not Abigail! It's not suitable for a girl like Abigail.' Abbie was amazed to see that her mother's eyes were slightly moist and, moreover, she thought that the unshed tears might be ones of desperation rather than of anger. Could it be that her mother did care for her? That she might possibly be sad at the thought of losing her?

Cedric looked sympathetically at his wife. 'Abigail will be twenty next week, my dear. We must not forget that. And neither you nor I can stand in the way of the Government. Women are being conscripted, and it would be very wrong of us to try to stop our daughter from doing what she knows to be her duty. Just look at it this way: if she doesn't join the WLA then they may well conscript her into the ATS, and I know you wouldn't care for that, would you, Eva?'

'I don't care for any of it,' replied Eva. 'Not for women. Let the men go and fight their wars if they want to. If it was left to the womenfolk to decide there would never be any more wars, I can tell you that.'

Cedric gave a grim smile. 'Yes, I'll go along with that. I'm sure you're right. But unfortunately it's the men who make all the decisions, isn't it? And we have to do as we are told. Let her go, Eva.' His voice was gentle and persuasive. 'You have no choice anyway.'

Eva was silent. She stared down at her tightly clasped hands, not looking at either her husband or her daughter.

The interview at the Town Hall was a formality and both Abbie and Doreen, to their delight, were told they would be accepted into the Women's Land Army. Their uniforms and details of their training would arrive through the post in due course. All they had to do now was go home and await instructions. Abbie's birthday, the following day, was something of an anticlimax. Where would she be next year, for her coming of age, she wondered. As far as she was concerned it was this birthday, her twentieth, that had proved to be a watershed, giving her for the first time a glimpse of the freedom ahead.

Eva's attitude had mellowed. Abbie was surprised at the change in her and was telling herself that this time, maybe, her mother was being forced to admit defeat. She could not help but smile to herself, though, at the way her mother could change her mind as and when it suited her. She well remembered, when her father had first suggested she should assist him in the surgery, how her mother had protested most vehemently. On no account was their daughter to be allowed to help with matters which she, Eva, considered unseemly. Now, when it meant that it might prevent her from joining the Land Army, it was perfectly in order for Abbie to play the part of a nurse. For Abbie knew that that was all she was doing: playing a part.

Eva was polite, though not exactly cordial towards the new nurse whom Cedric had appointed to help in the practice. Faith Summers was a young woman who lived locally, near enough to travel to and from the surgery each day on her bicycle. In her mid-thirties, small, dark-haired and quietly confident, her old-fashioned name seemed to suit her admirably and Abbie warmed to her immediately.

'So now it's summer as well as winter in the surgery, Father,' Abbie said, remarking on the coincidence of their names.

'Yes, I had noticed,' her father smiled. 'As a matter of fact, it was one of the reasons I appointed Nurse Summers. Not the only reason, of course. Her qualifications are good and she has a gentle, unassuming manner; and the patients like her, although I know it's early days yet. But her name seemed like a good omen. I'm not superstitious, but I believe I've made the right choice.'

Abbie was concentrating almost entirely now on her work in the dispensary although her thoughts were often elsewhere. She was eagerly awaiting the instructions which would tell her where, and when, she was to start her big adventure, the Women's Land Army.

Dr Winters had been called away to a family funeral. A telegram had arrived one Friday morning at the beginning of February saying that his eldest brother, Jacob, had died, and his sister-in-law had requested that he should come at once. The funeral was to be held on Tuesday, but Cedric knew that his sister-in-law, a dithering, far from competent sort of woman, would be glad of any assistance he was able to give her with the arrangements. He was amazed at the docility with which his own wife had agreed to the plans. It would not be sensible, she agreed, for them both to travel to Birmingham, especially as one was continually being asked 'Is your journey really necessary?' And she had never got on all that well with Jaocb and his timid little wife, Bella. She would 'hold the fort' in his absence, Eva told him, smiling disarmingly, although there was, in truth, very little for her to do. He quickly arranged for a locum, a retired doctor who lived in the area, to take charge of the surgery on the Monday and Tuesday, and Nurse Summers, of course, was an invaluable help. He set off on Saturday afternoon with a clear conscience.

'We are having a visitor this afternoon, Abigail,' said her mother when they returned from church on Sunday morning. Eva was smiling quite charmingly. She had smiled much more readily just recently. 'Sidney is calling round. I have asked him to stay for tea. You will be in this afternoon, won't you, dear?'

'Yes, Mother; I wasn't thinking of going anywhere.' Abbie gave a slight frown. 'But they are your friends, Mother, not mine. It is really nothing to do with me, is it, if you invite the Sidebottoms to tea?'

Eva tutted impatiently. 'You didn't listen, Abigail. I made no mention of Mr and Mrs Sidebottom. Sidney, I said. He's coming on his own. He wants . . . he wants to talk to you.'

Abbie's heart sank. She had, of course, heard her mother correctly. She had known that Sidney's mother and father had not been mentioned. And she felt sick at the thought of what Sidney might want to talk to her about. She had had her suspicions when the two of them had been sent for that walk in the park on Christmas Day, but as he had made no further move since that time to suggest that he desired her company, she had decided she must have been mistaken.

'You have a visitor, Abigail.' Her mother's eyes held a roguish gleam, Abbie thought, as she flung open the door of the sitting room and ushered Sidney inside. 'There you are, Sidney. Make yourself at home and I'll leave you two young people on your own for a while.' Her conspiratorial smile as she departed was for Sidney, not for her daughter.

'Abigail . . .' The young man advanced towards her with his hand outstretched and she had no choice but to get up from her chair and take hold of it. It felt cold and clammy, like a fish, and Abbie remembered how his pale grey eyes had reminded her of the self-same creature. 'How nice to see you again. How well you are looking.' As if he hadn't already seen her that morning at church. She recalled, now, how she had been aware of him staring at her from the adjoining pew and when she had caught his eye he had smiled sheepishly and looked away.

'Yes . . . thank you. I'm very well, Sidney. Sit down, won't you?' She perched on the edge of her chair and he sat down, cagily, in the one opposite. 'And you are . . . well, are you?'

'Oh yes, yes. As well as can be expected.' He gave an affected little cough. 'I have rather a weak chest, as I think you know. But I've learned to live with it and apart from that I'm well . . . very well. Mustn't grumble, as they say.' He gave a neighing laugh.

'I'm joining the Land Army,' said Abbie, in a decisive voice. 'I'm just waiting for my call-up. Did my mother tell you?'

'She . . . er . . . yes. She did say something about the Land Army,' muttered Sidney. 'But I didn't think it was definite. And I don't think . . . I mean to say . . .' He took a deep gulp and his Adam's apple wobbled alarmingly. 'You don't have to join the Land Army, Abigail. You don't have to join up at all . . . because the reason I've come to see you is because . . . I want to ask you if you will . . . marry me.'

'Marry you? But . . . why? Why do you want to marry me, Sidney?'

'Well, that's a pretty silly sort of question, isn't it?' Sidney sounded indignant. 'It's because . . . because I care for you. I have always admired you, Abigail, and I know you would make me a good wife. And . . . and I know I would make you a good husband.' He was quite clearly confused, and Abbie would have felt sorry for him had she not been so blazing angry.

'I've got a good job, Abigail, and good prospects. There is every chance I will get promoted soon and . . . and I would be able to provide for you. You would never need to work – to go out to work, I mean. My mother has never worked outside the home. I know some women are working, now there's a war on, but it's not something I would ever want a wife of mine to do.'

He was getting into his stride now, no longer sounding so unsure of himself. But it was the mention of the war that did it. A war in which he – or his wife elect, God help her! – obviously wanted no part.

'Whose idea was this, Sidney?' Abbie's voice was sharp and Sidney's face, as he looked at her, began to wear something of a hangdog expression.

'What . . . what do you mean?' he stammered. 'Whose idea?

It was my idea, of course. I've told you, Abigail; I admire you and . . . and I want to marry you. I come from a good family. You can't deny that. And I know yours is a very acceptable family with . . . with your father being a doctor and . . . and everything. So I had a word with your mother and—'

'My mother! Yes!' Abbie interrupted. 'You and my mother have cooked this up between you, haven't you? She's determined to stop me joining the Land Army so she's dragged you in as the last resort. And that's what it would be, believe me, Sidney, to be married to you. Do you really think I would ever consider marrying you, even if I wanted to escape war service? Which I don't! I want to do my bit to win this war, which is quite obviously more than you are prepared to do.' She stopped at the wounded look in his eyes, aware that she might have said too much.

'I say, Abigail; there's no need for that. They won't have me in the army. I've got a weak chest and then there's my eyesight. There's no need to take that attitude just because you've decided you don't wish to marry me.' He sounded peevish, like a small boy who had lost a game of marbles.

'No . . . I'm sorry, Sidney. What I said was uncalled for,' replied Abbie. 'The reason you are not in the forces is your own affair. It has nothing to do with this present matter. But nobody is going to stop me from joining up! Nobody! Can't you see, Sidney?' she went on, more reasonably. 'It's not a good idea at all, you and me. It would never work out. I'm sure you don't really want to marry me at all, not if you think about it sensibly. Anyway, you should have been asking my father, shouldn't you, not me? I'm only twenty, you know. Old enough to join up, but not old enough to get married without permission. You would have had to ask my father first if you wanted to . . . to marry me. Which I know you don't.'

'Yes, I do!' persisted Sidney. 'And I was going to ask your father when he gets back from Birmingham. Your mo—I mean, I thought it was better to ask you first. Now I shan't bother asking him!' His usually pale face was quite pink with indignation as he leaped up from his chair. 'And you can tell your mother I won't be stopping for tea. Tell her . . . tell her it was kind of her to ask me. She's a nice woman, your mother. I like her!' he added defiantly. 'But I'm not going to stay where I'm not wanted.'

He flung open the sitting-room door and dashed out, almost colliding with Eva, who was standing outside. Abbie guessed she had been there for some time; most likely she had heard every word. Eva, however, did make some attempt to cover her discomfiture. Never must she be seen to be at fault.

'Sidney – you're not going, are you?' For the young man was already snatching his coat from the hallstand. 'I was just coming to see if you would like a cup of tea, before we have our main meal?'

'No thank you, Mrs Winters. There's nothing for me to stay for.' Sidney did not even glance in Abbie's direction. 'Your daughter will tell you why.' He darted out of the front door and down the path, struggling into his fawn raincoat as he fled, his long fawn scarf trailing from his pocket like a snake. He had forgotten his fawn trilby hat, but did not come back for it.

'You silly girl!' Eva turned on her daughter as the front door slammed shut. 'You'll never get another chance like that. A nice, polite, well-brought-up young man like Sidney Sidebottom. From such a respectable family, too. His father's in insurance, and so is he. I know it isn't quite the same as being a doctor, but . . . Oh, I feel so angry with you!' Abbie, to her surprise, could see tears welling up in her mother's eyes before she flounced into the sitting room, closing the door firmly behind her.

And there was I thinking she might be getting more used to the idea, thought Abbie. Were there no limits to which Eva would go to try to get her own way, to prevent her daughter from doing her bit for her country? Marriage to Sidney Sidebottom! Surely her mother couldn't have imagined for one moment that Abbie would agree to it? But it did have its funny side and how Doreen would laugh when she told her friend the incredible tale. For the moment, though, Abbie did not feel much like laughing. She was so furious with her mother, and distressed, too, that the two of them were at loggerheads again just when she had thought that things were improving. As to what her father would think, Abbie had no idea. She hoped he might take her side as he had been doing increasingly of late, but you could never tell. Parents sometimes considered it their duty to stick together.

Cedric Winters arrived home to a household that was the very personification of its occupants' name. An icy chill pervaded the atmosphere of his home, and between his wife and daughter particularly the frostiness was palpable.

'Well, you had better tell me what is wrong, hadn't you?' he said eventually after a very silent mealtime. Bertha, right on cue, bustled into the kitchen leaving the three members of the Winters family on their own.

'What's wrong? I'll tell you what is wrong,' replied Eva. 'It's that daughter of yours. She has only gone and turned down a proposal of marriage.'

'Marriage?' Cedric's beetling brows closed together in a frown. 'What do you mean? Marriage ... to whom?'

'To Sidney Sidebottom,' replied Eva. 'He came round to ask Abigail to marry him ... and before you say anything,' she continued quickly, as Cedric opened his mouth to protest, 'he fully intended asking your permission first, Cedric, but you weren't here, were you? So he decided to go ahead and see what Abigail thought about it. And the silly girl went and turned him down. That is why I am so cross with her. As far as I am concerned it wouldn't matter if I never set eyes on her again.'

'I see.' Cedric looked seriously at both his womenfolk, first at Abbie then at his wife; then as he looked at Abbie again she thought she could detect a glint of amusement in his eyes. 'You have read *Pride and Prejudice*, haven't you, my dear?' he said.

'*Pride and ...*? What on earth are you talking about, Cedric?' His wife shook her head irritably. 'We are in the middle of a family crisis and you are going on about some book or other? Honestly, of all the—'

Cedric ignored her. 'It seems to me, Abigail, that the same calamity faces you as faced Miss Elizabeth Bennet.' He raised his eyebrows and Abbie saw she had not been wrong. His eyes were positively twinkling.

'Oh yes, Father, I see,' she replied, a smile spreading across her face as she realised to what he was referring. 'You mean ... ?'

'I mean that if you were fool enough to marry Sidney Sidebottom then I would most certainly never want to see you again. And your mother has said she does not wish to see you again if you *don't* marry this young man. A ticklish problem, isn't it? The same dilemma that faced Elizabeth when she refused to marry Mr Collins.'

'For goodness' sake shut up about that silly book, whatever it is you're going on about.' Eva was not a great reader. 'It's Abigail we should be thinking about. Do you mean that you are not going to support me, Cedric? You will stand by and let her turn down the chance of—'

'The chance of what, Eva?' said Cedric, in what was quite a patient voice. 'Of marrying a pompous, self-opinionated . . . and cowardly . . . young man? Abigail is worth a hundred of Sidney Sidebottom and if you didn't know that then it is time you woke up to reality.'

As Eva pushed her chair aside and fled from the room Abbie was surprised to see she had tears in her eyes. 'Mother, don't—' Abbie began to cry out, but Cedric caught hold of her outstretched hand.

'Let her go, Abbie,' he said gently. 'She'll get over it. It's all nonsense, anyway, her saying she doesn't want to see you again. Of course she does. And I can't really believe she wanted you to marry that . . . that nincompoop.'

'It seemed like it,' replied Abbie. 'It's any excuse, though, isn't it, Father, to keep me out of the Land Army, to make me do just what she says.'

'Your mother . . . has always thought she knows what is best for you,' said Cedric slowly. He paused, then, 'She does love you, you know,' he went on, 'though she sometimes has a strange way of showing it. The top and bottom of it now is that she doesn't want you to leave home.'

'I'd have had to leave home if I'd married . . . him.'

'Yes, maybe you would. But your mother would still have been able to keep an eye on you. If – when – you join the Land Army you'll be beyond her reach. That is what is worrying her.' He paushed again, shaking his head sadly. 'When you were a little girl, Abbie, I left your upbringing to your mother. Maybe it was wrong of me, but I think it is what most fathers do. But now . . . well, I've tried to make her see that she must let you go. She is only making matters worse.' He stopped abruptly. 'Leave it to me, my dear. It will be all right, you'll see. I shall miss you when you go, Abbie, far more than I can say. I'm afraid neither of us – your mother and I – have ever been much good at showing our feelings. But you will be missed, by both of us. And it seems to me that the sooner you get your marching orders from the WLA the better it will be. Your mother will come round, though. I'll make sure she does.'

It was one of the longest speeches Abbie had ever heard her father make. She looked at him in some bewilderment as he suddenly got up and left the table, almost as if he were embarrassed at having said so much.

'How you had the nerve to invite that lily-livered creature here in my absence, I just can't imagine.'

Abbie had never heard her father speak so angrily. She hadn't been intending to eavesdrop, but she had no choice. The voices of her parents were clearly audible through the bedroom wall.

'Yes, yes, I know what you've already told me.' She could imagine her father raising an admonitory hand as her mother tried, in vain for once, to plead her case. 'He was going to see me, but I wasn't here. It seems very strange to me, though, that it all took place while I was out of the way. And Sidney Sidebottom! Good gracious, Eva, what on earth were you thinking of? A weak-kneed coward like that, who won't do his bit for his country.'

'His doctor has said he's unfit, Cedric. It's hardly Sidney's fault, is it, if he has a weak chest? I think it could be worse than we imagine, actually.'

'Then why are you so anxious to marry our daughter to him if he's going to be an invalid? Weak chest, my foot! If you ask me he's got an obliging doctor. I can tell you, Eva, if I were his doctor he wouldn't have got away with it . . .'

Abbie could hear only the low hum of voices now and she guessed her parents had moved out of earshot. Then a few moments later it was her mother's voice she could hear, shrill and sounding quite distraught.

'You know I've always tried to do my best for her, Cedric. It wasn't easy, especially at first, but you left it all to me. I've tried so hard to love her ... I do love her, but I've had to be strict with her, can't you see? I didn't want her turning out like ... well, you know who I mean.'

Abbie frowned to herself. Like Aunt Bertha, she supposed. Aunt Bertha who had had a baby without being married.

'When there's bad blood in a family it can so easily come out again. You can't be too careful. I've tried to keep her on the straight and narrow and I thought I'd succeeded until she met that girl. If she was married she would be safe, that's what I thought. If she goes away how will I know what she's doing, what sort of company she's keeping? I do love her, you know, Cedric. I don't want to lose her. I don't want her to go away.'

Abbie was astounded to hear her mother's words.

'You've got to trust her, Eva. She's a good girl. She knows what is right and what is wrong.' Abbie's father was speaking placatingly now. 'You don't need to worry about Abigail, my dear. She will never go off the rails. Try to be kind to her, though, before she goes. I know you can be, if you try. Let her see that you really do ... care about her.'

Abbie didn't hear her mother's reply.

Once again Cedric had taken Abigail's side, but Eva was getting quite used to that. She lay wide awake in the suffocating blackness of the room, listening to her husband's rhythmic breathing – he always fell asleep so quickly, as though he didn't have a care in the world – and feeling very sorry for herself. Cedric and Abigail; Bertha and Abigail; Doreen and Abigail ... or Abbie, as they all insisted on calling her. The girl, it would seem, had so many allies. But never was there any feeling of closeness, of kinship, between Eva and Abigail. And now Eva feared she might have alienated her daughter even more with – what her husband considered to be – her rash and foolish action. Had she really expected, or wanted, Abigail to marry Sidney Sidebottom? she asked herself now in a rare moment of honesty. Probably not, but she had been desperate. She could not bear to think of losing the girl or imagine how empty her life would seem if Abigail went ahead with her plan and joined the Land Army. Cedric, increasingly, seemed to be losing interest in his family life, and with Abigail away the chances were that he would become even more involved with that blessed clinic of his.

What could she do to make him take notice of her, Eva, again? One thing she could do was try to be kind to the girl, as her husband had asked. Eva decided, as the tears of frustration and loneliness rolled from her eyes, that she would make a special effort. After all, she did love Abigail. Surely it would not be all that difficult to show her, now and again, that she really did care for her.

Chapter 11

'Can you ride a bike, Abbie?' Doreen asked, one evening at the beginning of March.

'No, I'm afraid I can't,' Abbie replied. 'I've never had a bicycle. It's very busy where we live with it being one of the main roads into Blackpool. And then there are the trams, of course; rather a hazard for people on bicycles. My mo—I mean . . . no, I can't ride a bike.'

She had been about to say that she had never been allowed to have one. It was just one more instance of how her mother, always ready to anticipate the risks and dangers, had over-protected her. Many of the girls at her private school had had bicycles, but Abbie had been transported back and forth in her father's car; or if it did not fit in with surgery hours her Aunt Bertha had walked with her and come to meet her. This had gone on until she was thirteen or so. It would have been most embarrassing being met out of school, even by her much-loved aunt, but Aunt Bertha had had the good sense to wait round the corner. And Abbie had usually been on her own anyway. She decided, however, not to mention her mother now. Eva appeared to be quite a changed person. She had started speaking to her daughter again, not effusively, but politely enough. Her father's promised word to his wife must have been effective because Sidney Sidebottom had not been mentioned again. Neither, it had to be admitted, had the WLA. But Abbie did not want to start her friend off again on the old, old story of how repressed she had been.

'Why?' she asked now. 'Why do you want to know?'

'Because if you can't ride a bike, then you'd best get learning,' replied Doreen, 'before we get called up.'

'Learn to ride a bike?' Abbie frowned. 'What's that to do

with joining the WLA? If you'd said learn to ride a horse it might make more sense. And no, I can't ride one of them either. But why a bike?'

'Because it's the way the land girls get to their farms, you chump,' said Doreen. 'On bikes. Honestly, I thought you'd've known that.'

'How should I know? I don't know the first thing about the WLA, not really. How come you know?' Abbie often found she was slipping into the free and easy vernacular used by her friend, but she did not correct herself. It made them seem closer, and with every day and week that passed their friendship was, indeed, growing firmer.

'Cause I've been talking to that woman whose daughter's a land girl,' said Doreen. 'She told me about the bikes, and I thought to meself, I bet Abbie can't ride a bike. Listen, we've got a couple in our shed. They've seen better days, but at least they're ladies' bikes, with most of us being girls, y'see. I'll teach yer, shall I? It's as easy as winking really. You just get on and go.'

The next Wednesday afternoon, Doreen's half-day, found Abbie somewhat timorously mounting the rusty black bicycle and, with her friend holding on to the saddle, wobbling up and down the length of Doreen's street. It was, in fact, a lot easier than she had anticipated, and the determined streak that Abbie had discovered in herself over the past few months helped considerably. After a few tries she found she was no longer wobbling so much, and when Doreen let go of the saddle she was concentrating so hard that she didn't notice. There she was, actually riding a bicycle, with Doreen and her mam and her two younger sisters, Janey and Peggy, who had just returned from school, madly cheering her on.

It was at the Millers' home, too, that Abbie first tried on her Land Army uniform. It had arrived by post in a huge parcel the week after she had learned to ride the bike. After checking with Doreen that hers had also arrived she took the whole lot round to Doreen's home that evening, to have what Mrs Miller called 'one of them mannequin parades'.

'Eeh, don't they look smart, Harold?' Mrs Miller enthused, clasping her hands together in delight as the two girls paraded before the assembled family in their green jerseys and ties, cream shirts and khaki corduroy trousers. All the clothing felt stiff with newness and Abbie wondered how she would ever be able to walk in those heavy boots. And as for the khaki greatcoat, that also weighed a ton! When Doreen put hers on she pretended to stumble and fall down with the weight of it, which had everyone in fits of laughter.

'I like the titfer,' said Billy, the brother who was now an errand boy at Harding's, winking at Abbie. 'Very smart, i'n't it? Shouldn't think it'd be much good, though, when you're mucking out them cowsheds. It'll keep falling off into t'cow muck, won't it?'

'That'll do, our Billy,' said his mother. 'We'll have less of yer cheek. They look very nice, both of 'em. I feel so proud, I do that!' Nancy Miller's eyes were moist, and Abbie guessed, as the little woman smiled at them both, that the unshed tears were ones of affection rather than sadness. Moreover, Abbie felt that she, as well as the woman's daughter, was a recipient of that warmth and tenderness.

'What does yer mother think about it all, Abbie?' Nancy Miller asked gently. 'Has she got more used to the idea now?'

'Yes, I think so, Mrs Miller,' replied Abbie. 'She's very quiet about it, but I think she's more resigned to it now. She doesn't ... er ... actually know about the uniform yet. Aunt Bertha answered the door to the postman and ... well, I haven't shown it to her yet.'

'Then you'd better do so,' said Mrs Miller quite sharply, in a way in which she would never have spoken to the doctor's daughter when she first got to know her. But Abbie was almost like one of the family now. 'She's yer mam when all's said and done. I know she's happen been a bit strict with you sometimes. Our Doreen's told us about it, but I'm sure she loves you and she'll miss you, like I'll miss our Doreen. So think on now; show her your uniform, like you're showing us, there's a good lass. Eeh, isn't it exciting? Next week and you'll both be off ...'

'Very nice, dear,' was all Eva said when Abbie stood before her that evening, dressed once more in all her WLA finery. 'I have to admit it's a smart uniform, although it won't always look as smart as that, not when you're . . . doing whatever it is you'll have to do.' She did not smile, but her eyes softened just a little. 'It's your choice, Abigail. Not what I would have chosen for you, but at least you should be out of danger, hidden away in the country.' Her mother stopped speaking and looked away. She appeared to be biting her lip lest she should show any emotion.

Eva seemed perfectly in control of herself, however, when she said goodbye to her daughter the following week. She kissed her on the cheek and told her to take care of herself and not to forget to write. Abbie's parting with her aunt was more demonstrative, Aunt Bertha unashamedly weeping then wiping her tears on her flowered apron. Abbie's father was driving her to the station, calling for Doreen on the way, and Abbie felt it would be a relief when they were on the train with Blackpool far behind them. Saying goodbye was awful. Even though she had looked forward to this day, her first day of freedom, for so long, it was still awful.

It was obvious that Doreen felt the same and the two girls said very little to one another until they had changed trains at Preston for the one which was bound for Yorkshire. They had been pleased – more than pleased, in fact; almost ecstatic – when they had discovered they were both being sent to the same hostel, near Malton in Yorkshire. On the second train they met several other girls, all bound for the same destination, and in the excitement of shared confidences – where had they come from? What did they do in civvy street? Did they have a boyfriend? (or a husband, which one or two of them had) – Abbie forgot for a while the anxiety and sadness she had seen in the eyes of her father and aunt and, to a lesser extent, in her mother's.

She was glad she had learned to ride a bicycle because, as Doreen had said, this was the usual form of transport for the land girls. Sometimes, if the training farm was quite a distance away, the girls would be taken to and fro in an army lorry, otherwise they used bicycles. And what bicycles! The ones in Doreen's shed had been the Rolls-Royce of bikes compared with some of these. They were heavy-duty machines, khaki-coloured with a carrier at the back for a raincoat or extra footwear. There were twenty-four girls in the hostel and the same number of bikes, but as many of them had faulty brakes or no lights it was a question of first come, first served.

It was the same with the sandwiches for the lunchtime break, which the girls had to make up themselves before breakfast. The early risers got the sardines or corned beef, otherwise it was cheese – the mousetrap variety – or, of all things, beetroot! Abbie had never heard of, or ever imagined, there could be such a thing as beetroot sandwiches. But she was to get used to them as she got used to lumpy pillows and mattresses, iron bedsteads, bare wooden floors, antiquated oil stoves and rising at 6 a.m.

Both she and Doreen were too bewildered by all their new experiences, and often too exhausted as well, to consider whether or not they were homesick. They both got on well with the other young women. Abbie was surprised how easy she found it to talk to them, these girls from a variety of backgrounds, but she knew that a lot of her new-found confidence was thanks to Doreen. Working in the fields with sacks tied round their shoulders to prevent the rain from trickling down their necks was not pleasant, but the sight of the Yorkshire countryside – the early springtime green in the hedges, the new-born lambs in the fields, and the sweet-smelling air – compensated for the less welcome aspects of their new life.

When Abbie looked in the mirror as she approached the end of the four-week training period she could scarcely recognise the rosy-cheeked, healthy-looking girl who looked back at her. Her brown eyes were glowing, she had lost the few spots that had marred her complexion, and, what to her was the most important of all, she had shed the remainder of the surplus weight she had been carrying around since her childhood. Living in the country obviously suited her – she might almost be an advert for a WLA poster – but she had the good sense to know that this was only the beginning. So far they had only been playing at it, but soon they would all be sent to proper live-in farms. She was keeping her fingers crossed, and saying a little prayer each night as well, that she and Doreen would be sent to the same farm.

They could hardly believe their luck when they heard that the two of them were to go to Four Winds, a farm near Malton, owned by a farmer called Mr Rawnsley.

It had seemed easy enough on the training course, learning to milk a 'mock' cow, a wooden contraption with four rubber teats, and they had also had some experience with milking machines. But the reality was very different. Only the large farms had mechanical milkers. On the smaller ones the job was still done by hand, and Abbie, after only a few tries at the training farms, had not yet mastered the art. Here, at Four Winds, there were times when she almost wept with the pain from her blue swollen hands, her fingers red raw from pulling at teats that seemed unwilling to yield even the tiniest drop. Occasionally an odd tear would plop into her milking bucket before she told herself to snap out of it and jolly well get on with the job. Whatever would her mother think if she could see her now, she sometimes mused, as she lifted a cow's tail to comb off the clinging crusty dung, then plunged her cloth into a bucket of icy water to wash its udders before starting to milk. And the thought of Eva's horror did afford her some slight amusement although she and Doreen were finding that life at their first live-in farm was, indeed, no laughing matter.

Four Winds was well-named, suffering the blast of winds from all four directions across the Vale of Pickering. This part of north Yorkshire was not generally considered to be the most bleak, not when compared with the moors or the more remote dales. The low-lying valley contained much rich pasture land, but the place seemed bleak and inhospitable in the extreme, probably because of the unlovely character of the farmhouse and the unwelcoming attitude of its occupants; Mr Rawnsley, the farmer, more so than his wife, but the two girls soon realised that Mrs Rawnsley had to do as she was told.

The two girls had arrived there at the end of April when the days were lengthening and the chill of winter and early spring was diminishing a little. They did at least have the summer to look forward to, they told one another later, in an attempt to cheer themselves up, because they had both realised, after a first look at the place, that their comparatively carefree training days were at an end and that real life in the WLA was to begin in earnest. And it would not be an easy life.

Their first glimpse of Four Winds showed that the greystone farmhouse, the sheds, barns and outbuildings all had a dilapidated, neglected appearance, and the interior of the house was no better. The kitchen was cold and cheerless, with a stone flagged floor, a shabby rag rug providing the only shred of covering. A small fire burned half-heartedly in the huge black range and no curtains hung at the grimy cobweb-festooned windows, only the regulation blackout blinds. Abbie noted with some surprise the gaslight which hung from the whitewashed ceiling – she had never before been in a house that did not have electricity – and, next to it, a long yellow flypaper almost black with the dead bodies of flies and bluebottles. The fact that it hung right over the table which stood in the centre of the room made her stomach churn in anticipation. Was this where the family had their meals, she wondered.

Mrs Rawnsley, a wiry little woman with sharply pointed features, whose face wore a furtive half-frightened expression, had welcomed them – if her derisive sniff could be called a welcome – when they had arrived in the army lorry, and only when they had followed her into the kitchen and deposited their heavy bags on the floor did she make the effort to speak to them. Her words confirmed Abbie's worst fears.

'This is t'kitchin,' she said. 'We 'ave us meals in 'ere, most o' t'time. We only use t'dining room on a Sunday, or at Christmas, happen . . . Come on, I'd best tek yer to yer room. You can manage them bags, can't yer? Our Billy's out in t'fields, and Mr Rawnsley an' all. Not that he'd . . .' They were to learn that she often left her sentences unfinished. 'Anyroad, come on . . .'

She led the way through a door that opened off the kitchen, up a narrow twisting staircase. They stopped briefly at a tiny landing, then they went up an even twistier flight of steps to the attic room.

' 'Ere y'are then. I'll leave yer to get yersels sorted out.' Mrs

181

Rawnsley opened a creaking door, then quickly disappeared.

The room, up in the eaves, was large enough as far as floor space was concerned, but as the roof sloped steeply it was only possible to stand upright at one end. There were two single beds covered with faded counterpanes, two bentwood chairs, a shabby dressing table with a fly-blown mirror and an equally shabby wardrobe with a badly fitting door hanging half open. A marble washstand held a large plain white bowl, badly crazed, and a jug, and on the towel rail at the side there were draped two grimy-looking towels. The single light fitting, hanging from a beam in the ceiling, was, of course, a gaslight.

Abbie's heart sank. 'Do you suppose there's . . . a toilet?' she whispered. 'I'm dying to go.'

'Shouldn't think so,' replied Doreen with a complacent shrug. 'No such luck, I'm afraid, luv. Else they wouldn't have that, would they?' She pointed to the third item on the washstand, a sturdy white chamber pot which stood on the ledge at the bottom.

'Oh dear . . . I couldn't,' said Abbie. 'At least . . . not now.'

'There'll be one in the yard,' said Doreen cheerfully. 'Like we have at home. I'm used to it, y'know, trekking down the yard with me torch. Let's leave our stuff for a few minutes, shall we, and go and ask Mrs Rawnsley where it is? Come to think of it I could do with a wee-wee. She's a bit of a misery-guts, isn't she, Mrs R.? I wonder what he's like?'

Mr Rawnsley was in the kitchen when they had cautiously made their way down the two flights of rickety stairs. He was an undersized man, rather gnome-like, with sparse ginger hair that stuck up in tufts and black beady eyes. 'Oh, yer've arrived then 'ave yer?' was his unceremonious greeting. 'Aye, the missus told me you were 'ere. You'd best have rest o' t' day to settle yersels, I reckon, then it'll be a five o'clock get-up for yer to see to t'cows. Our Billy'll show yer t'ropes.'

'Five o'clock?' Doreen was bold enough to query. 'We got up at six when we were in the hostel.'

'Oh aye, well, you were on yer holidays there, weren't yer?' Mr Rawnsley gave a malicious sneer rather than a smile. 'It's five o'clock 'ere. That's only in t'winter and spring, mind,

182

when t'cows are laying in. In summertime – that'll be in a week or two – you'll have to go and fetch 'em in from t' fields afore yer start milking. So don't get too used to yer extra half-hour in bed. It won't last . . .'

Abbie looked at her friend in despair. However would she survive, rising at five o'clock, four thirty in the summer? And in such miserable inhospitable surroundings as these with such a strange couple as their hosts seemed to be. At that moment Abbie almost wished herself back home – even marriage to Sidney Sidebottom seemed, fleetingly, to be not such a bad alternative – but Doreen's companionable wink and grin put heart into her.

During the next few weeks, throughout her battles with troublesome, evil-minded, fiercely kicking cows – always they were to prove her biggest bugbear – Abbie gave silent thanks many, many times for Doreen. How she could have survived, or would ever survive, without the bolstering companionship and cheerfulness of her friend she could not imagine. Some farms required the help of only one land girl. How dreadful it would have been if she had been here on her own.

The girls were not miserable all the time, however. For instance, there were the Saturday night dances in nearby Malton to look forward to. Abbie knew she would never have had the courage to go there on her own, nor to brave the censure of Mr Rawnsley, who strongly disapproved of such goings-on. Malton was the Guards' headquarters and the Coldstream Guards played rousing military two-steps, quicksteps and barn dances at the assembly rooms every Saturday night. Abbie and Doreen had been to a few of these dances whilst they were on their training course and had thoroughly enjoyed them.

'But I don't see how we can go to them now,' Abbie said dejectedly to her friend after their first week at Four Winds. They had both been too tired even to consider an outing the first Saturday night, but they knew they would have to find some form of relaxation, some escape from this dreary farm-house and its even drearier inhabitants or else they would go mad. 'How can we get there? It's a lot further than it was from the hostel. And Mr Rawnsley'd never let us go, you know he wouldn't.'

'Pooh! I'm not scared of him,' declared Doreen. 'I don't see how he can stop us. It's nothing to do with him what we do in our spare time. Look here, Abbie, if we want to go to the dance then we're bloody well going.' Her language had become much more colourful since the training course. 'That sanctimonious old so-and-so isn't going to tell us what to do. He's not our keeper. If he tries to stop us I shall report him to the authorities. Come on, luv; don't be such a cowardy custard. Your mother's not here now to boss you about. I thought you were starting to stick up for yerself.'

'But how would we get there?' Abbie asked again.

'On bikes. How else? There's a couple of ramshackle things in the shed. I've seen 'em and they're no worse than the ones we've used before. Mrs Rawnsley says we can use them.'

'All right then. I'm game if you are,' said Abbie, a little timorously. 'We'll ask him, shall we?'

'No, we won't. We'll tell him,' replied Doreen.

And so, together, the following Saturday, they braved the lion in his den; namely Mr Rawnsley washing his hands and arms at the slopstone after an afternoon spent mucking out the cows. One thing they were bound to say in his favour was that he never asked the girls, or his son, to do any job he was not willing to tackle himself, and he did his share of the dirty, less agreeable jobs as well as the more pleasant ones. He was there in the kitchen when they returned from their first Saturday afternoon excursion to Malton – Saturday being their half-day – with his wife who was cutting doorsteps from a huge loaf. Their tea, thought Abbie, watching the woman spread bright yellow margarine sparingly over the bread. This, with bloater paste or plum jam – or beetroot – was the usual fare for their tea, their main meal, such as it was, being taken at midday.

The girls glanced at one another uneasily. Even Doreen seemed to have lost some of her bravado. 'Let's take our coats off first,' whispered Abbie. It would be as well to let the farmer finish his ablutions before they broached the subject of their night out.

When they re-entered the kitchen Mr Rawnsley, his braces dangling over his heavy tweed working trousers, was drying his hands on an unsavoury-looking grey towel which might once have been white ... or pink? At all events, it was very little different from the ones that hung in the girls' bedroom.

'Mr Rawnsley ...' Doreen began.

'Yiss. Wha'd'yer want?' His beady black eyes peered over the top of the cloth in his hands – he was giving his face a good rubbing down, too – and his sparse ginger hair stood up in peaks.

Doreen gave an audible swallow before going on. 'Well, we were wondering if ... No, we weren't wondering,' she added more decisively. 'We wanted to tell you, Abbie and me, that we're going out tonight. We're going back into Malton and ... and we thought we'd better tell you, that's all.' The last few words came out in a rush.

'Goin' back to Malton?' Mrs Rawnsley paused in her task of setting the table, a pile of earthenware saucers in her hand. They were so thick and heavy they reminded Abbie of dogs' bowls. 'But you've only just come in. Why are you goin' out again?'

'Because we're going to a dance,' said Abbie, feeling that it was not fair to leave all the talking to Doreen. But once the words were out she began to regret them. Maybe they shouldn't have admitted where they were actually going because the farmer and his wife stared at them as if they had declared they were going to commit a murder.

'A dance?' Mrs Rawnsley put the saucers down with a loud clonk. 'You're goin' all that way back to Malton to go to a ...? Then why didn't you stay...?'

'Shut thi' trap, woman. Leave 'em to me.' Mr Rawnsley scowled at his wife. 'I'll deal wi' this. You gerron wi' yer woman's work, mekin' t'tea, or whativer yer supposed to be doin'. I'll sort them two lasses out. Why didn't they stay in Malton? Huh! They want to tart 'emslves up, no doubt, like painted Jezebels. Like that other hussy we had here afore.'

'Nothing of the sort, Mr Rawnsley,' interrupted Doreen, and Abbie thought how brave she was. She, Abbie, was practically shaking in her shoes. 'As a matter of fact, we'll be going to the dance in our uniforms. We're supposed to wear them all the time. We only came back for our tea.'

'Aye, that's right. Eat us out of house and home,' mumbled Mr Rawnsley.

Doreen continued as though he hadn't spoken. 'And to tell you we were going to the dance. So now we've told you.'

'Hey, you watch yer tone wi' me, missy!' The farmer glowered at her. 'Yer under my roof – both on yer – and it's up to me and t'missus to see that yer behave yersen. The one we had afore were a right load o' trouble and it ain't goin' to 'appen again. Not if I've got owt to do wi' it. I don't hold wi' dancing. T'other 'un used to go dancing, tarting 'erself up to catch t'fellers, but we soon got rid of 'er.'

'Now that's not really true, Alec,' said Mrs Rawnsley, very bravely, Abbie thought. 'It was her that—'

'Shurrup, woman!' Mr Rawnsley turned on his wife. 'I've warned you afore about stickin' yer oar in when I'm tellin' t'tale. 'Er left, didn't 'er, and that's that.'

His wife lowered her eyes and scurried away to the other end of the kitchen like a scared little rabbit. Poor woman, thought Abbie. Why on earth didn't she stick up to him and give as good as she got? He was 'nobbut the height of six penn'orth of copper', as her Aunt Bertha would say, and Abbie didn't imagine for one moment that he was a violent man despite all his bluster. But he was narrow-minded and vindictive and he had an acid tongue. He had his wife and his slow-witted son, Billy, well and truly under his thumb, but he had no right to treat his land girls in the same way. She wondered what 'the one we had afore' had done to displease him so much.

'Sithee, both on yer.' The farmer put his hands on the edge of the table and leaned forward. 'I don't hold wi' dancing. I've telled yer so. But I can't stop yer, short of locking yer in yer room and I'll noan do that. I'm a reasonable man . . .' Abbie felt a smile pulling at the corners of her mouth in spite of her trepidation and she didn't dare look at her friend. '. . . but look 'ere. You'll be back by ten o'clock, sharpish, or you'll find that there doower locked and bolted and you'll have to spend t'neet in t'cowshed. I'm warnin' yer!'

'OK, Mr Rawnsley, we'll be back by ten o'clock.' Doreen's voice was expressionless and she cast a contemptuous glance at the awful little man, but Abbie was glad she had the good sense not to argue any further. 'Won't we, Abbie?'

Abbie nodded. 'Yes, we'll be back.' She was reminded forcibly of her mother and how she had insisted she was home from the Palace by ten o'clock. And of how she had lost the only chance she had ever had of a date because of her mother's intransigence.

'Come on, the pair of yer; get yer tea.' Mrs Rawnsley, scurrying back to the table with a huge brown earthenware teapot, cast them what Abbie interpreted as a sympathetic glance and a half-smile. 'How'll yer get to Malton then? It's a fair stretch, an' I don't know about t'buses.'

'The same way as we went this afternoon,' replied Doreen. 'On our bikes. Well, your bikes they are really, but you said we could use them.'

'What? Yer going to ride all that way there and back? It'll be getting dark afore . . .'

'We'll be all right, Mrs Rawnsley,' said Abbie, turning her head away slightly as she spread the pungent bloater paste on her bread. 'There are lights on the bikes and it doesn't go dark till quite late. Anyway, that's how we got into Malton when we were doing our training, on bikes.'

'But that hostel were nearer, weren't it? Only just down t'road.'

'Give over molly-coddlin' 'em, woman.' Mr Rawnsley scowled at his wife. 'If they want their pleasures then they mun pay for 'em.' His words, mumbled through a mouthful of bread and bloater paste were muffled and particles of the gooey mess dribbled out on to his chin. He took a slurping gulp of tea before wiping his shirt sleeve across his mouth. 'And think on, what I've telled yer. Ten o'clock.'

Neither of the girls bothered to answer and the rest of the meal passed in near silence as did most of the mealtimes. Billy, the fifteen-year-old son, never contributed much to the conversation. Abbie felt sorry for the lad. He was the image of his father: short, but more thickset and inclined to be bandy-legged, but without his father's alertness or, mercifully, his malice. Abbie had heard Billy talking in gentle tones to Gertrude, the cow that was her own deadly enemy, and to Cain and Abel, the two cart horses. The lad had an affinity with animals that he certainly did not have with humans, but that was hardly surprising, considering his background. Who could have any rapport with such as Alec Rawnsley? Abbie wondered whyever Mrs Rawnsley had married him in the first place.

She said as much to Doreen as they got ready for the dance in their attic bedroom. Getting ready, however, consisted only of washing their hands and faces in the icy cold water in the bowl, combing their hair and applying a little fresh powder and lipstick. Abbie, since leaving home, had started to use a little make-up, on occasions such as this. They would be wearing their uniforms, as Doreen had already said.

'I wonder why she married him,' mused Abbie. 'Old Rawnsley. He's such an awful little man, isn't he? Just imagine . . .' Getting into bed with him, was what she was thinking, but she didn't say it. Abbie had come out of her shell a lot, but she was still nowhere near as outspoken as some of her land girl friends.

Doreen, however, never once to mince matters, voiced her unspoken thoughts. 'Perhaps she had to.' She gave a giggle. 'Happen they'd given way to consuming passion in the hayloft and she was in the family way. With "our Billy". Can't you just imagine them in the hayloft? Or perhaps she was a timid virgin and he seduced her . . .'

Abbie now looked back in some amazement at how ignorant and naïve she had been before she met Doreen. Living and working in the country, it was impossible for her to remain in ignorance about the 'facts of life'. She would never forget her first sight of the farm bull mounting one of the cows. That had been at one of the training farms and it had taken all her self-control not to run away in horror. Now she was quite used to such sights.

'Yes,' she said, smiling, as she continued with the unlikely fantasy about the farmer and his wife. 'Perhaps she was the farmer's daughter and he was the hired hand . . . and he was determined to have his wicked way with her.' She had read one or two rather lurid romances that Doreen had lent her, a change from the classics and more serious books she had always read before. She found herself laughing out loud at these wild imaginings. 'Oh dear, you've got to laugh, haven't you?' she said, wiping the tears from her eyes. 'If you didn't laugh you'd cry. That's what Aunt Bertha was always saying. Alec Rawnsley in the hayloft with ... what's she called? I don't know, do you?'

'No,' giggled Doreen. 'He never calls her anything but "woman" or "hey you!" '

'It sounds like a Thomas Hardy novel, doesn't it? *Tess of the D'Urbervilles* or something like that. You've read that, haven't you, Doreen? Do you remember? Tess discovered she was pregnant ... It puzzled me at first when I read that. I didn't understand how she could be.'

'But you know now.' Doreen grinned at her. 'Yes, your Aunt Bertha lent it to me. Wasn't there that chap in it that was all religious? Maybe that's what it was with old Rawnsley.' She nodded thoughtfully. 'Too much religion; it can do funny things to you. Perhaps that's why he seduced her. You've got to admit the fellow's got religious mania. Him and his bloomin' morning prayers.'

Bible reading followed by morning prayers was the routine in this gloomy household. This took place after breakfast, which was after the cows had been milked. It had been useless for Doreen to protest that she was a Catholic, not a Primitive Methodist, which was what the Rawnsleys were. The farmer still insisted that she must attend and to argue would only make matters worse.

'I suppose we'll just have to put up with it,' Abbie said now. 'There's nothing else we can do. Maybe some of the other girls are no better off than we are.'

'We'll find out tonight,' said Doreen. 'I say, Abbie, I wonder what that girl did? You know, "that hussy that was here afore", that old Rawnsley was on about. Sounds as though there was one hell of a row.'

'And she packed her bags and left,' added Abbie. 'Mrs R. let the cat out of the bag, didn't she? He wanted us to think he'd sent her packing, but it sounds as though it was the other way round.'

'We can always complain to the authorities if it gets too bad,' said Doreen. 'Maybe she did complain, "that hussy". And things here are certainly far from perfect. How you put up with bread and jam for breakfast, Abbie, I can't imagine.'

'It's Hobson's choice, I'm afraid,' replied Abbie. 'I can't stand that awful fatty bacon, that's why I have bread and jam. I could have porridge if I wanted, but I couldn't eat that either. Not the way she makes it; it looks like pig swill. Don't worry, I'll survive.' Personally Abbie couldn't imagine how Doreen could stomach that revolting fatty bacon, eaten cold, which was the standard breakfast in the Rawnsley household, swilled down with gallons of strong black tea. 'I must admit, though, I'm missing my aunt's cooking,' she mused. 'Speaking of Aunt Bertha . . . she had a baby once. It reminded me, talking about seductions and all that.'

Doreen was staring at her in amazement. 'Your Aunt Bertha? I didn't think she'd ever been married.'

Abbie gave a rueful smile. 'You're as bad as me. That's what I said when she first told me. She hasn't . . . been married. It was like – you know – what we've just been talking about. She worked in a big house and he was the son. One of the gentry, a Lord, or the Lord's son or something.'

'Gosh!' Doreen's eyes were like saucers. 'Poor Aunt Bertha. And . . . what happened to it, the baby, I mean?'

Abbie told her the story, or as much of it as she knew. 'So nobody ever talks about it. I shouldn't've told you really, but it just reminded me of her, talking about Tess and all that. I know you won't ever let on you know, will you?'

'Of course I won't.' Doreen was looking very sad. 'Poor Aunt Bertha,' she said again. 'Couldn't she try to find it? How dreadful, having to give your baby away and not knowing where he has gone.'

'I think it would be almost impossible,' replied Abbie. 'He would have a different name and everything. I don't see how . . . I have thought about it, especially since we came to Yorkshire. The big house was in Yorkshire. Not near here, though. I think it was near Skipton. But it would be no use. No, Aunt Bertha's all right now, I think, and she says she's been a lot happier since you and I got friendly. She likes to hear our chatter, she says. I didn't chatter much before I met you. That reminds me, I must write to her.'

'I'll write as well,' said Doreen, still looking very anxious.

Abbie was reminded afresh what a kind-hearted girl her friend was. 'We'd best not let on too much about this place though, had we? We'd best tell a few white lies, eh, and say it's lovely? That's what I said to me mam and dad when I wrote. Don't want 'em to worry . . . Now, are we ready then? Coldstream Guards, here we come. Let's hope they're worth all the effort.'

Chapter 12

It was good, when they arrived at the Assembly Rooms, to meet up with some of their friends from the training course and exchange notes as to the congeniality, or otherwise, of the farms to which they had been sent. Abbie and Doreen soon knew, as they had guessed all along, that they had struck unlucky.

'Oh no, don't say you're with old man Rawnsley?' said Olive, one of their former colleagues. 'At Four Winds? Oh, I say, you poor devils!'

'Why? Do you know about him?' asked Abbie.

'I'll say I do. Not personally, thank God – I've never met the old blighter and I hope I never will – but the girl I'm working with knows him. She was there last year and she said it was the most miserable time of her life. Until she told him where he could stick his flamin' pitchfork! Well, I don't suppose she actually said that, but she complained and they moved her. There she is, look – that ginger-haired girl dancing with the tall bloke. She's called Heather. She'll tell you all about old Rawnsley.'

Abbie and Doreen looked knowingly at one another. Heather must be 'the one as was here afore', the 'hussy' that Mr Rawnsley had told them about. The music came to an end and Olive beckoned to Heather as she came off the dance floor with the tall guardsman. 'Heather – have you a minute?' The girl didn't seem sorry to leave her partner – he did look a long streak of misery – and she came across to them. 'What do you think?' said Olive. 'These poor devils have ended up at Four Winds.'

Heather was an arresting-looking girl with bright ginger hair curling almost to her shoulders, vivid red lips and nails to match and a curvaceous figure that strained at her green jumper and khaki breeches. They seemed to be much tighter fitting on Heather than on the other girls. It was easy to see that she and Alec Rawnsley would not have seen eye to eye.

'Oh God, how dreadful! I wouldn't wish that on my worst enemy.' Heather pulled up a chair and sat down beside them. 'Tell me all about it . . .'

And so they did. Their shrieks of laughter echoing across the room caused many a head to turn in their direction, as they exchanged horror stories about the awful food and the even worse company in the near prison-like atmosphere of Four Winds.

'You don't have to put up with it, you know,' Heather assured them. 'You can complain to the War Agricultural Committee and they'll send somebody round to see you and have you moved. You have to have a good reason, though. They won't move you unless it's absolutely necessary.'

'That's what I keep telling Abbie,' said Doreen. 'That we should complain. What made you leave? What was the last straw?'

Heather gave a hoot of laughter. 'You never spoke a truer word. That last straw! You've hit the nail right on the head. That's where he found us, you see, on a pile of straw behind the barn in the top field. It was a hot day – the end of September, you remember how hot it was last autumn – and we were . . . what can I say? Less than adequately clothed!'

'Who? You and who?' asked Doreen.

'Tom, their farm hand. The last one – he's gone now; he was due to be called up. We'd gone for a picnic, y'see. It was his last weekend and – well – one thing led to another. Then along comes old man Rawnsley. You should have heard him! He nearly exploded. I was a harlot, a whore, a brazen hussy! I wanted locking up. And then – guess what? – Tom punched him on the nose. "How dare you speak to Heather like that?" he said, and he gave him the most almighty thump. You've never seen anything like it. Blood everywhere. Old Rawnsley hopping about and holding his nose, and Tom with his trousers . . . well, you can imagine, can't you?'

'Gosh!' Abbie was almost too stunned to speak. 'What a

fantastic story!' Doreen, too, seemed to have been rendered speechless for once.

'But I suppose . . . if you were meant to be working . . .' said Abbie.

'Were we heck as like! It was Sunday, my day off and Tom's as well. I sometimes go home on a Sunday – I only live in York – but with it being Tom's last weekend I decided to stay there. And so we were . . . well, I've told you. I know it sounds funny, and I suppose it was really. Like a "What the Butler Saw", on Bridlington prom, but Rawnsley wasn't laughing, I can tell you. Neither were we. It ruined everything, him coming along.'

Heather paused for a moment, not smiling now, although she had laughed as she recounted the tale. She stared into space looking pensive.

'Was he your boyfriend then, this Tom?' asked Abbie.

'Yes, I suppose you might say he was . . . is,' replied Heather. 'We'd got quite friendly, Tom and me. I'd been there two months and we'd started going around together. Rawnsley didn't like it, but there was nothing he could do about it, and he knew Tom would be called up before long. Which he has been. He's stationed near the south coast.'

'And . . . is he writing to you?' asked Abbie. She hated to think that the horrid old farmer had completely ruined everything.

'Yes, we're still keeping in touch. But that doesn't stop me from getting out and having a good time.' Heather gave a wink as she glanced around. 'They get some very dishy Coldstream Guards here. And I'm stopping us from dancing, aren't I, nattering on like this?'

'Never mind about that,' said Doreen. 'You haven't finished your story, have you? What happened afterwards? You said you complained.'

'So I did, eventually. At first I thought to myself, well, maybe Rawnsley did have cause to be annoyed. We were behaving improperly, or so he thought, on his land. He didn't do anything while Tom was still there. He went off on the Tuesday – Tom, I mean – to have a few days at home before he joined the army. And it was then that Rawnsley took it out on me. He took the bikes away so that I couldn't go out. "That'll stop yer gallivanting!" he said. And he wrote to my parents, telling them what I'd been up to. Fortunately Mum's quite broad-minded and she had met Tom, so it didn't matter. But it might've done. He was just trying to stir up trouble, nasty old devil. But the last straw was when he locked me in my room.'

'He never!' gasped Doreen.

'Oh yes, he did. On the Saturday night. I couldn't've gone out anyway – I'd no bike – but that's what he did. So I wrote and complained. I didn't half lay it on thick, I can tell you, and they sent somebody round and had me moved. Incompatibility of temperament, they called it, him and me. I'm surprised they've sent anybody else there, to be honest. And I'm surprised he's agreed to have any more land girls, but I suppose he had no choice. All the farm workers have been called up.'

'So it's us or nobody,' said Doreen. 'Thanks for telling us, Heather. It explains a lot. But I should imagine Rawnsley knows how far he can go now. He won't dare to lock us in. He mentioned it, didn't he, Abbie? But he said he was a reasonable man – just imagine! – and he wouldn't do that. Huh! If he's a reasonable man then I'm the Queen of Sheba!'

Abbie nodded. 'So he did. But there are no more farm hands for us to get friendly with, are there?' she added seriously.

'Only our Billy,' laughed Doreen.

'Poor Billy,' said Abbie, feeling suddenly sad. What a miserable life he led, to be sure.

'Never mind him.' Heather jumped to her feet. 'Come on, girls. It's a Paul Jones. Time to grab ourselves some handsome guardsmen.'

'So now we know who the mysterious "hussy" is,' remarked Abbie as they cycled back along the country lanes, in plenty of time to meet the curfew at ten o'clock. 'Quite a lass, isn't she, that Heather? She seems very fond of Tom, although she wasn't short of partners tonight, was she?'

'We all did OK for partners if you ask me,' said Doreen. 'There weren't many dances when we were wallflowers. Us land girls seem very popular with the soldiers.'

'But not with the local girls,' observed Abbie. 'I must admit I feel sorry for the local girls. There they are, all dressed up in their pretty frocks and high-heeled shoes, and there's us in our jumpers and breeches and great clumping brogues, and we get most of the partners. They must think it's most unfair. I noticed we were getting quite a few dirty looks.'

'Well, we're doing our bit for our country, aren't we?' said Doreen. 'The lads appreciate that. You're too soft-hearted, Abbie. You know what they say – "All's fair in love and war." Come on, we'd best pedal a bit harder or we'll find t'doower locked.'

'And we'll have to spend t'neet in t'cowshed,' added Abbie. Their bicycles wobbled as they shrieked with laughter and they were lucky not to end up in the ditch.

The Saturday night dances proved to be an occasional high-spot relieving an otherwise bleak existence at Four Winds. The only consolation to the girls was that it was summertime, and even though summer in Yorkshire could sometimes be almost as cold as winter, especially at half-past four in the morning, at least the days were light, with Double British Summertime ensuring that it did not go dark until about eleven o'clock. Their days, when they were not busy with the cows, were spent in the fields, carting hay, raking, hoeing or muck spreading, cleaning out the pigsties or whitewashing the walls of the cow shed; this on a rainy day when even Mr Rawnsley had to admit that it wasn't fit to turn a dog out. They soldiered on, telling themselves they were helping the War Effort and that it couldn't be for ever, although it was difficult to see an end in sight.

Their departure, when it arrived, came suddenly. One Saturday night in mid-July they were cycling back from the dance in Malton when Abbie discovered her front tyre was punctured. She found herself wobbling and quickly dismounted.

'Oh, drat it!' she exclaimed. 'Look what's happened. It's as flat as a pancake. I'll have to walk.'

Doreen got off her bike and joined her. 'Yeah, so I see. Nothing we can do about that. We've got a kit of sorts, but there isn't time to stop and mend it. Come on, let's get walking then. We haven't much time – we were a bit later leaving than we should've been tonight. My fault, I know. I got talking to that nice sergeant. I thought he might ask to see me again, but no such luck!' Doreen started off up the lane, pushing her bicycle. 'Come on, Abbie. Get a move on.'

'No . . .' Abbie grabbed hold of the back of her friend's jumper. 'Don't be silly. It's daft us both walking. I'll walk, and you ride on ahead and tell them what's happened.' She glanced at her watch. 'Gosh! It's ten to ten. I hadn't realised it was so late. Go on, Doreen; you're going to be late if you don't hurry.'

'I'm not going to let you walk on your own. Did you really think I would?' said Doreen indignantly. And Abbie had to admit to herself that if it had been the other way round she would have said the same thing. She was grateful to her friend for offering to stay with her now. Abbie had never entirely conquered her fear of some aspects of country life. Admittedly it was not all that dark at the moment, but bats sometimes swooped low as dusk approached, owls hooted and ordinary trees and bushes seemed to assume weird and menacing shapes. But which was worse, she wondered, to walk home alone or to face, together, the wrath of old man Rawnsley?

'But . . . what about Mr Rawnsley?' she muttered.

'Oh, to hell with him!' said Doreen. 'He can't lock us out, I don't care what he says. And if he does then we'll get him! You heard what Heather said. This might be our chance, Abbie.'

Abbie gave a rather fearful smile. 'OK. I won't say no to the offer of company. Thanks, Doreen. We're in it together then?'

'I'll say! All for one and one for all, eh? Except that there's only two of us. Come on, let's step on it.'

They were further away than they thought, a good mile and a half, and it was nearly half-past ten when they finally propped their bicycles against the wall and knocked on the door. It was usually left on the catch for them to walk in, but now, as they had feared, it was locked and bolted just as Mr Rawnsley had threatened.

They knocked several times, but in vain. The house was in complete darkness, not that a glimmer of light would have showed anyway with the blackout restrictions, but the place appeared forbidding and hostile, and Abbie got the impression they could knock till doomsday and not be admitted. A snatch of a poem they had learned off by heart at school flitted through her mind. ' "Is there anybody there?" said the Traveller,

198

Knocking on the moonlit door;' Except that they weren't travellers, and there was no moonlight, save for a tiny sliver of a crescent shape just visible in the dusky sky. What a time to be quoting poetry, if only to herself, she thought, as Doreen lifted the cast-iron knocker and pounded it yet again.

Then the curtains were drawn back in an upstairs room, the sash window was lifted and Mr Rawnsley's angry face looked out. His hair stood up in tufts like a hedgehog and he was clad in broadly striped pyjamas and a button-up vest which showed at the neck.

'Stop that din!' he yelled. 'It's enough to wake the dead. I warned yer, both on yer, and now you'll see as I mean it. Yer come back 'ere at midnight and expect to be let in? Huh! Yer can find someweer else to sleep. Go on! Be off wi'yer, yer young hussies!'

'You let us in this minute or else we'll stand here banging all night.' Doreen raised the knocker and let it drop again with a resounding clang. 'Is that loud enough for you? I can knock louder than that, I'm warning you!'

'Doreen ... stop it!' Abbie seized hold of her hand. 'You might make matters worse,' she whispered. 'We'll have to try and make him see reason. Mr Rawnsley,' she called, as the farmer stood back, making to shut the window. 'Wait a minute, please. We couldn't help it, really we couldn't. I had a puncture, so we had to walk. We'd have been back ages ago if it wasn't for the puncture. And it isn't midnight, is it? It's only half-past ten. Let us in ... please.'

'Don't plead with him, for goodness' sake,' muttered Doreen. 'That's what he wants, to have us crawling to him.'

'Well, I don't fancy spending the night in the cowshed, even if you do,' retorted Abbie. 'He'll let us in,' she added in a low voice. 'I think he's just afraid of losing face, the silly old fool!'

The farmer was still scowling, but at least he wasn't ranting and raving any more. He seemed unsure as to what to do; as Abbie said, he was no doubt afraid of having to back down.

'Oh, for goodness' sake, Alec, let them in, then we can all get to sleep,' said an irritable voice in the room behind him.

Mr Rawnsley didn't deign to answer his wife. Without a word to the girls he slammed the window shut.

They waited on the doorstep. 'D'you think he'll open the door?' whispered Abbie.

'He'd better, or I'll start again.' Doreen made to lift the knocker, then put her hand down. 'Nasty old devil! Anyway, he's gone too far this time. We'll get him, Abbie, don't you worry.'

The door opened, but it was the farmer's wife who stood there, not Mr Rawnsley. Her hair was covered with a pink sleeping net and her flannelette nightdress, high-necked and reaching to her feet, was bright pink as well. A light-hearted sort of colour, thought Abbie, for such a down-trodden dispirited person. But at least she had had the courage this time to stand up to her husband and persuade him to let them in, even if she had to do the job herself.

'Come on in, both on yer,' she said, quite kindly. 'You must be frozzen to death, standing theeyer.'

'Thank you, Mrs Rawnsley,' they both mumbled as they stepped inside. Abbie realised that she was cold, very cold, but she had only just noticed. Even though it was July it was a chilly night with a raw wind and rain threatening.

'Ne'er mind 'im,' the woman went on, speaking in a low voice. 'He meks a lot o' din, but 'is bark's worse than 'is bite. He wouldn't've done it, y'know. Not agin ... I reckon 'e's learned 'is lesson,' she added, as if to herself, and Abbie guessed she was referring to the trouble they had had with Heather. 'He's noan so bad really, but we 'ave to live wi' 'im so it's as well to humour 'im. He's t'boss, so we mun do as he says.'

It was the most they had ever heard Mrs Rawnsley say, but then they had hardly ever seen her without her husband hovering near.

'We couldn't help it,' said Abbie as they made their way up the dark stairway. 'I really did have a puncture. I'm sorry we had to disturb you.'

'Well, ne'er mind that now,' said the woman. 'You'd best be off to yer beds. It'll soon be half-past four. Night-night, sleep tight,' she whispered coyly as the girls left her on the landing before climbing up to their attic room.

'Oh heck, I forgot to go to the whotsit,' said Doreen as they undressed. The privy, as it was usually called, was at the rear of the farmhouse, in the yard, and the girls paid a nightly visit before retiring, but in the excitement they had forgotten.

'Oh yes, same here,' replied Abbie. 'I'm all right at the moment, though. I went at the dance.'

'Well, I'm not,' said Doreen. 'I shall have to use the guzzunder.' She reached under the bed which was where they had decided to keep the huge chamber pot. 'You don't mind, do you? Needs must, I'm afraid.'

'Of course not,' said Abbie, turning her back and stepping into her pyjamas. When they first came to Four Winds Abbie would have been acutely embarrassed at such a situation. But mucking in together, the way they had had to do, she had lost much of her former reticence. Even now, though, she was still not so uninhibited as Doreen. She decided she would 'go' later when her friend had gone to sleep; Doreen always seemed to drop off before she did. She thought again, as she snuggled down beneath the coarse blankets, how sad she would be if she ever had to leave Doreen. Especially when her friend called out, 'That's it, Abbie. We'll get him now. We'll have to do something and get ourselves moved.'

'Mmm . . . yes. You're right; we will,' replied Abbie. But had Doreen realised that it would be very unlikely they would be moved to the same farm? After they had made a complaint they were almost sure to be separated, in case they made any more trouble. Not that it was their fault, of course. But she would think about that tomorrow. She was too tired now to worry her head about it. Her last thought, when Doreen had dropped off to sleep and she had nipped out of bed to do what was necessary, was that it was Doreen's turn tomorrow for the morning milking. On a Sunday, as a great concession, they were given a couple of hours off in their turns. And tomorrow it was Abbie's turn for a lie-in. Poor old Doreen . . .

Things moved rapidly after that. The next morning Mr Rawnsley behaved as though they were not there and his wife said very little. In the afternoon, which both girls had off, they composed a letter and, after they had repaired the puncture, they cycled into Malton to post it. It was not long before a woman from the War Agricultural Committee came to Four Winds to see the two of them, then the Rawnsleys, separately.

They never found out what was said to the farmer and his wife, but the woman seemed sympathetic and agreed that they would be moved very shortly. After all, it was the second complaint – and there may well have been others before – that they had received about Mr Rawnsley, although the woman did not admit to this. She made no comment about their request to be put together – Doreen had persuaded Abbie that there was no harm in asking – but her pursed lips and slight frown made them fear the worst. Indeed, when the posting came a few days later they were doomed to disappointment. They were both to stay in Yorkshire, but Doreen was to go north, to a farm near Northallerton, whereas Abbie was bound for Wharfedale in the West Riding.

They were taken as far as York in an army lorry provided by the authorities. Neither the farmer nor his wife had been there to say goodbye, which, under the circumstances, was probably understandable. They had wondered if Mrs Rawnsley would dare to brave her husband's displeasure and exchange a few words with them, to wish them well, maybe; but since the visit of the War Ag. woman the pair of them, Mr and Mrs Rawnsley, seemed to have closed ranks. The slight thawing in Mrs Rawnsley's attitude and the unguarded words she had spoken the night they were late were not to be repeated. Now, more than ever, she seemed subservient to her husband. She had hardly spoken to the girls at all for the last few days, and they were relieved when the lorry finally turned out of the gates of Four Winds on to the rutted cart track, then on to the lane they had cycled along so often to Malton. They were silent companions, though, both aware of the parting that lay ahead. Abbie, for her part, was afraid to speak lest she should burst into tears.

She was surprised, when they stood together on the platform in York station, beneath the magnificent high glass roof, that it was Doreen who was the first one to shed tears. They had watched a monster of an engine pulling a train bound for London chuff noisily away, and they knew that Abbie's train for Leeds would be here in only a few moments, that is if it ran to time, which was somewhat unlikely these days. But at all events it would not be long and the realisation that they were to be parted for the first time in four months was hitting them forcibly. Four months was not a lifetime, admittedly, but so much had happened to them, such an abundance of shared experiences – both funny and not so funny, happy and downright unpleasant – that it seemed much longer and they had grown as close as sisters. Indeed, Abbie often looked upon Doreen as the sister she had never had.

'Oh, kid, it's awful,' wailed Doreen, pulling a khaki handkerchief out of her breeches pocket, then blowing her nose furiously. She dabbed at her streaming eyes, unable to keep the tremor out of her voice. 'I didn't mean to do this, honest, 'cause I know how you're feeling, and I said to meself, I won't cry 'cause it'll only go and upset Abbie. But I can't help it . . .' She gave a gulp. 'I don't know how I'll manage without you, not now. I mean, we've been through such a lot together, haven't we, you and me?'

'Of course you'll manage,' said Abbie, tears pricking at her eyelids, though she was more determined than ever now not to break down. It was strange: maybe Doreen was not quite as tough as Abbie had thought. 'You've always coped, haven't you, far better than I have? It was you that stuck up to old man Rawnsley. I'd have been stuck in that awful room all summer if it hadn't been for you. I'd never have dared to ask him if we could go to the dance, not on my own. Come on, love.' She put her arm through Doreen's. 'We mustn't give way. We've got to be brave. We'll look a right couple of idiots if we both start blubbing.'

'Yeah, you're right.' Doreen gave a loud sniff, then shoved her handkerchief away. 'Listen, I'll write as soon as I can. Or p'raps you can write first, eh? You're better at words than me, aren't you? But I'll reply, honest. I've got your address and you've got mine.' Addresses that didn't mean very much as yet; they were both going into the unknown. 'And p'raps we could manage to have some leave at the same time, then we could meet.'

'In Blackpool, you mean?'

'Yes, that's what I meant. It seems ages since I saw me mam and dad and Billy an' all of them. Oh heck, I'd best shut up or

I'll start again.' Doreen gave another loud sniff.

'Or maybe, if we only had a day off,' said Abbie, 'we could meet somewhere between Leeds and Northallerton? We'll look at a map. It's not a million miles, is it? In fact it's not really very far at all.' Abbie was sounding much more cheerful than she was feeling.

'No, it only seems like it,' mumbled Doreen gloomily. 'Yes, that might be a good idea . . . Look, it's here, your train. At least I think it is.'

It was, in fact, the Leeds train. Abbie gave her friend a quick kiss on the cheek, the first time she had ever done so. 'Goodbye, Doreen. Take care of youself, won't you?'

'You an' all. Take care, luv.' Doreen put her arms round her friend and gave her a hug, then, without a backward glance Abbie scrambled aboard with her case and bulging bag and managed to find just one unoccupied seat in a corner of a compartment. An obliging soldier pushed her belongings on to the rack and by the time the guard had blown his whistle and waved his green flag she had managed to compose herself. Doreen looked so lost and alone, waving furiously as the train pulled away. I wonder when I'll see her again? Abbie thought. Plans could never be made with any certainty, not in wartime.

It was not far to Leeds, but the train made a stop at each minor station. There was no telling where they were because all the signs, both on railway stations and on roads, had been removed. Presently, though, they drew near to what was obviously a major station.

'Is this Leeds?' Abbie asked.

'Sure is, love,' the soldier answered. 'Here, I'll help you off with your stuff . . . Cheerio.' He waved as she staggered off along the platform. 'Take care now . . .'

'You too,' she called back. There was an easy camaraderie that prevailed these days, especially amongst those in uniform. Abbie felt her spirits lift a little, though she was still anxious about what might lie ahead. But whatever it was she knew it could not possibly be as bad as her experience at Four Winds.

As soon as she set eyes on Mr Dobson, the farmer, waiting outside the station with his shabby Ford car, Abbie felt that she would be made welcome. He was the very archetype of a farmer: short and stout, with ruddy cheeks and a broad grin, dressed in a well-worn tweed jacket and flat cap.

'I reckon you're Abigail,' he said, holding out his hand. 'How d'yer do? I'm Mr Dobson, but you can call me Alf. Most folks do.'

'How do you do, Mr Dobson?' Abbie smiled shyly. 'I might call you Alf when I've got to know you better. It seems . . . well . . .'

'A bit familiar, like?' The farmer chuckled. 'Don't you worry about that, Abigail. I can tell just by looking at you that you're not one of them forward lasses. Come on, let's get yer stuff into t'boot, then we'll be mekin tracks.'

'Thank you,' said Abbie, 'but would you please call me Abbie? It's what most people call me. It's what I prefer.' It seemed ages since she had been called Abigail. She had not been back to Blackpool since she had left there towards the end of March.

'OK then, Abbie it is.' Mr Dobson grinned at her. 'We've another lass at home, another of you land girls. She's called Constance, but she likes to be called Connie. Abbie and Connie. I reckon you'll get on a treat, the pair of you. The last 'un we had was taken ill and had to go back home. She was a delicate little lass though. 'Er couldn't stand the life. Some can and some can't. I dare say you can cope, can't you? You look a strong healthy sort of lass.'

Abbie was glad he hadn't said 'big and strong', which was what people used to say, or think, even if they didn't say it. Thank goodness she was no longer so big. She was still tall, of course. There was nothing she could do about that, but she had learned to 'walk tall' and carry her height with confidence now she had shed her unwanted fat.

'Yes, I seem to be able to cope pretty well, Mr Dobson,' she answered. 'Although it was all very new to me when I first joined the WLA.'

She looked out of the car window as they left Leeds behind, heading towards Wharfedale. The moors around Ilkley were already purpling as the heather started to bloom, with here and there bright yellow patches of gorse amidst the boulders of limestone and stretches of dark millstone grit – a sombre scene, though awe-inspiring. But as they dropped down again to the valley of the Wharfe the scenery changed. Here the lower slopes of the fells were more wooded, with pretty greystone villages nestling amongst rich pasture land. It all looked so peaceful and idyllic it was hard to imagine that the country was at war and that, not so far away, the cities of Hull, Sheffield, Leeds and Bradford were in danger of attack from enemy bombers.

Daisy Bank farm, the home of the Dobsons, lay roughly midway between two of these old-world villages. Smoke puffed cheerfully from the farmhouse chimney and, in contrast to the place she had left behind, Abbie noticed that the barns and sheds were in good repair, with their doors painted bright green. The yard was swept clean and the farmer's wife, waiting at the door with a broad smile of welcome, wore a spotless white apron. Abbie felt at home at once, but – oh – how she wished Doreen was with her. They could have been so happy here together, she felt sure. At that moment her longing for her friend was like a pain deep inside her.

Connie Seddon was a good-natured Yorkshire lass, not very tall, but quite buxom, with powerful muscular arms that could shift a bale of hay or lift heavy milk pails with a minimum of effort. She came from the Bradford area, and though she had had no experience of farming, her previous job having been in a small bakery, she had taken to the work, as she said to Abbie, 'like a duck to watter'. She was friendly and amiable, and Abbie felt sure they would get along well enough even if they did not have the same close friendship she and Doreen had shared. Connie was inclined to be brusque and outspoken. Abbie was finding this was a Yorkshire trait, although, of course, Doreen had never been afraid of speaking her mind.

'There are quite a few big houses in this area, aren't there?' Abbie asked her new colleague about a week after her arrival. 'You know, where the gentry live?' Her thoughts, since coming to this part of Yorkshire, had strayed frequently to her aunt and the extraordinary tale she had once told her. She remembered Aunt Bertha telling her how she had been in service near Skipton, although she didn't think she had ever heard the name of the actual house – or hall, or manor, or castle, maybe – mentioned.

'Aye, any amount of 'em,' Connie answered cheerfully, looking up briefly from her task of cutting turnips. These were for the sheep to eat, and Abbie was engaged in forking the vegetables into the cutting machine, whilst Connie was turning the handle to cut the turnips into pieces resembling potato chips. 'Why, are yer thinking of goin' round hob-nobbin' with 'em?' she went on with a grin. 'I reckon they'd be glad to see yer, with yer bein' a doctor's daughter, an' all that. Let's see; there's Shibden Hall, then there's Temple Newsam near Leeds. Which of 'em d'yer fancy?'

Abbie laughed. 'No, nothing like that, I can assure you. It's just that my aunt was in service – ages ago, of course – in one of the big houses near here, and I wondered which one it was, that's all.'

'Why don't you ask her?'

'Yes, I might, the next time I write,' replied Abbie, although it was doubtful that she would do so. Since telling her of that incredible story, possibly in an unguarded moment, Abbie guessed, her aunt had never again referred to the matter.

'And there's Tennant Hall,' Connie continued. 'That's near Skipton, getting on towards Lancashire. And Harewood House, o' course. Oh, I say.' She put on a mock refined accent. 'D'you think your aunt might have worked there? That'd be summat to swank about, wouldn't it? They're Royalty as lives there, ain't they? Or as near as meks no difference. The Earl of Harewood; isn't his missus the King's sister?'

Abbie smiled. 'Yes, I do believe she is. But I'm pretty sure Aunt Bertha didn't work there. It doesn't matter.' She gave a slight shrug. 'I was just curious, with being in the area, that's all.'

Tennant Hall, she thought to herself. Yes, perhaps that was the one. It was quite near to Skipton. But what on earth could she do about Aunt Bertha and her long-lost baby, little Johnnie? Nothing at all. She had thought for a time, after hearing the story, what a fairy-tale ending it would be if the mother and son were to be reunited after all these years. But Aunt Bertha herself had made her see how impossible that would be. And how could she, Abbie, go knocking on the door enquiring if they had once, in the dim and distant past, had a servant called Bertha Shorrock? The idea was ludicrous, not that Abbie had ever seriously entertained it. She was just curious, that was all; but the niggling little thought at the back of her mind kept recurring, saying to her how wonderful it would be, if only . . .

Chapter 13

The Italian prisoners of war first came to Daisy Bank farm in the late summer of 1942, to help with the harvest: the threshing of grain and the gathering of crops, both root crops and fruit from the orchards. They were driven in a military truck from their camp each morning and dropped off at the various farms in the area. Abbie had encountered Italian POWs before when she and Doreen had been riding their bikes in the country lanes near Malton. They would shout and laugh and blow kisses at the girls from the lorry. Some of their friends, whom they saw from time to time at the Saturday night dances, had told them that some of the cheeky POWs had actually thrown love letters to them, written on toilet paper, from the back of the lorry. The general consensus of opinion was that they were, in the main, bone idle and that they fancied themselves no end as Romeos. It had to be admitted that most of them were incredibly handsome and they added a bit of sparkle to the mundane working day. But, when all was said and done, they were the enemy. It wouldn't do to get too friendly with them. That was what the land girls had told one another, although, individually, each girl had her own opinion about these personable young men.

When Abbie first noticed Carlo Bellini he was standing on top of the threshing machine. They seemed to be working together well as a team, these Italians, and to know exactly what they were doing. Abbie didn't think they looked lazy, not these three at any rate. The one called Carlo – she had heard his colleague speaking to him, in Italian, of course, but she had caught the name – appeared intent on his job, taking the stooks from his mate, severing the binder twine and feeding the loosened straw into the drum. He looked as though he had done this job before.

Of all the jobs on the farm Abbie was finding that threshing was the one she disliked more than any other. It was even worse than dealing with the cows! The dust got everywhere, into your clothes and hair and eyes, making them itch like mad and red raw with rubbing at them. Then there were the rats and the mice, always to be found in a harvest field. Abbie had never been able to overcome her fear of these creatures, especially the rats, although she found even the mice bad enough. The land girls took a turn at most things: pitching up, cutting the strings and feeding the machine, humping sacks of grain, or carrying the chaff in a big hessian sheet.

This was the job Abbie was doing when the rat came running from the bottom of the sack, right across her feet. She gave a scream, dropped the sheet and ran – not very far, just a few yards across the field to get away from the vile creature. She felt such a fool behaving like that, especially in front of those Italians, but she couldn't help it. Rodents of any kind filled her with loathing. She returned a little shamefacedly, hoping she didn't look as white round the gills as she felt.

'Sorry,' she muttered, picking up the corner of the sheet again. 'Sorry, Connie.'

'Yer daft 'a'p'orth!' said Connie, laughing loudly. 'You can't bear 'em, can you? Can't say I blame you, although they don't worry me overmuch. I'm used to 'em, see. We used to get 'em in t'bakehouse now and again.'

Abbie cast a quick glance at the men on the machine and saw that two of the three looked amused, as well they might, but the third one, the one called Carlo, was looking at her with eyes that were full of sympathy. She smiled at him and he smiled back, then quickly turned back to his work.

'Take this soup out to the Italians, would you, Abbie?' said Mrs Dobson at midday. 'You can carry it in the pan, and there are three mugs to pour it into. And some bread and cheese. Happen you'd best go with her, Connie. There's quite a lot to carry.'

Her husband turned round from the sink where he was washing his hands. 'We've been told we haven't to fraternise with the ... er ... prisoners. Anyroad, they've brought their own lunch, haven't they? They're supposed to have done.'

'If I can't offer three hard-working fellows a cup of soup and a bit of homemade bread then it's a poor do, Alf Dobson. You told me yerself they've worked like trojans ... even if they are supposed to be the enemy.' Amy Dobson cast her husband a scornful glance.

He sighed. 'I'm only telling you what they've told me, the War Ag. people. It's the rule – no fraternising.'

'Then it's a rule made to be broken, that's all I can say.' Mrs Dobson banged the lid down forcibly on the pan. 'Fair enough, we don't need to be the best of pals with 'em – I haven't invited 'em into the house, have I? – but while they're working on our land they're entitled to a bit of courtesy. They're somebody's sons, poor lads.'

The Italians were sitting by the hedge in the nearest field. They had just taken out their sandwiches, but their eyes lit up at the sight of the steaming vegetable soup and crusty bread.

'*Sì grazie! Minestrone ... Molto buono!*'

The one called Carlo looked intently at Abbie as she handed him the mug. '*Grazie, signorina* ... Thank you. You are ... how do you say? OK now?'

She smiled at his use of the colloquialism and nodded. 'Yes, thank you. I am ... OK.'

'You do not like ... the rats, no?'

'No.' She gave a shudder and frowned. 'No, I don't like rats. I don't even like mice. Silly, isn't it, working on a farm, but there it is.'

'Come on, Abbie.' Connie was pulling at her arm. 'Let's leave 'em to get their lunch. And ours'll be going cold an' all.'

'All right. I'm coming ... Goodbye then.' Abbie smiled shyly at the three men.

'*Arrivederci*,' they chorused, grinning happily; well, as happy as they could be seeing they were prisoners, poor lads, thought Abbie.

She noticed that Connie hadn't spoken to the men and neither did she talk to Abbie as they walked back to the farmhouse. It was understandable, Abbie supposed. She had heard that many of the Italians had been captured in the desert in North Africa, and that was where Connie's boyfriend, Jack, was fighting. Her colleague was bound to regard them as the enemy far more than she, Abbie, did. Jack might even have come face to face with them.

She encountered Carlo again that afternoon when she found herself working next to him, lifting a row of sugar beet. She couldn't help but answer him when he spoke first.

'The soup was – very good. We like it.'

'I'm glad,' replied Abbie. 'Mrs Dobson is a good cook . . . You speak very good English,' she added. It was an obvious remark, the sort one always made to a foreigner, although Abbie hadn't met many. It was true, though; he did seem to understand what she was saying and to be able to reply.

'*Sì. Poco* . . . a little. More than a little, perhaps. We learn it at school. And my father, he has an *albergo* – hotel, do you say? – near the *lago di Garda*. We have English guests. And so I learn to speak.'

'You're Carlo, aren't you?' said Abbie, standing upright for a moment to ease her aching back. 'I'm called Abbie.' She didn't see any reason why they shouldn't know one another's names. He seemed a pleasant young man. He was tall, a little taller than she, and probably thinner than he ought to be, with black wavy hair and soulful deep brown eyes. Very handsome in a foreign sort of way.

'*Sì.* I am Carlo Bellini.' He, too, stood up straight. 'And you are . . . Abbie, you say? I have not heard that name, I do not think.'

'Yes, it's short for Abigail. But I like Abbie best. Abigail is rather a mouthful.'

He looked puzzled. '*Mi scusi?* Mouth . . . full?'

Abbie laughed. 'I'm sorry. I just meant Abigail is rather an unusual name. I prefer Abbie.'

He nodded and smiled. She wasn't sure that he understood, but he must have done because he replied, 'OK, I will call you Abbie. If you wish?'

She nodded, suddenly embarrassed that she might have said more than was wise. They said little more that day, but worked alongside one another in a companionable silence. Abbie was aware, now and again, of Connie watching her, but after they had finished their day's work, the girl did not mention that she had seen her colleague 'fraternising' with one of the Italians, if, indeed, she had noticed.

By the end of that week most of the harvest was gathered and there was no longer the need for the three POWs to work on the farm. It was decided that only one of them should continue to work at Daisy Bank, and it was Carlo Bellini who was chosen – by the authorities, not by the Dobsons – to do so. Abbie was pleased when she heard the news, though she did not show it by so much as a smile or a favourable comment; but, secretly, her spirits lifted and she felt a warm glow inside her.

The Italians stayed late that last night and as dusk was falling Mrs Dobson brought a picnic supper out to the field. Jugs of steaming cocoa, ham rolls, buttered scones, cakes and pastries for all the helpers. As well as the Dobsons, the land girls and the Italians there were several men – too old or too young for the armed services – from the nearby village who had come to help with the harvest. Abbie could not remember a meal ever tasting so good, or feeling such a sense of wellbeing. There was a beautiful harvest moon, round and golden, and as it rose higher and higher the work continued until the last load had been pitched up on to the wagon and secured by ropes.

'Abbie . . . see here. I have something for you.' Carlo was suddenly at her side, speaking in a low voice. 'I must not stay . . . The lorry it will soon be here.' He reached into his jacket pocket. 'See . . . I have made this for you. Not mouse.' He chuckled. 'I think you do not like mouse. It is bird . . . *uccello*, we say. You like it, I hope?' He placed in her hands a tiny wooden bird, beautifully carved in every small detail.

She gave a cry of delight. 'Oh, Carlo, it's lovely. You say . . . you have made this? You carved it?'

'*Sì* . . . I carve. Italians are good, we think, with the wood carving.'

'Very good. *Molto buono*.' She smiled at him. 'It's wonderful; so lifelike. Thank you very much indeed.'

'I think . . . I may not see you again. But now I know I am to stay here. Mario and Roberto, they go to some other farm. I am lucky, I think.' He looked at her intently. 'I am happy to stay here . . . with you.'

'I'm pleased as well, Carlo,' replied Abbie. 'Happy that you are staying.' She glanced around rather nervously, aware that they had been talking together for more than a few moments. She was wondering who might be watching, possibly disapproving. But they did not seem to have been observed. Most people were drifting away in the direction of the farmhouse. Connie was turning round though, wondering where her colleague had got to.

'Good night, Carlo . . . I must go now,' Abbie said, edging away reluctantly. 'Thank you again for the bird. *Uccello* . . . is that how you say it?'

'*Sì* . . . *uccello.*' He nodded and smiled at her. '*Buonanotte.* Good night . . . Abbie.'

She pushed the tiny wooden carving deep into the pocket of her breeches and hurried away after Connie. It wouldn't do to let her see Carlo's gift. It was only a little thing, to be sure, but Abbie saw it as a sign that their friendship, though tentative as yet, might deepen.

Everyone came to like Carlo. You could not but help admire his politeness and willingness to tackle anything he was asked to do. He wasn't exactly friendly at first, but then he wasn't given much encouragement to be so, certainly not by Mr Dobson or by Connie. They were courteous to him, but always kept him at a distance. Amy Dobson, however, had taken little notice of her husband's strictures. Since his fellow prisoners had moved to other farms and he was on his own, Carlo had been invited to eat his midday meal in the farmhouse kitchen with the family. Although he was never overly companionable, neither was he servile in his attitude towards them. Just respectful and agreeable. Quite soon their token resistance was broken down and they came to regard him as another farm hand who was working along with them, being given responsibility at times as well as just being expected to obey orders.

Abbie, from the start, had had an amiable relationship with him, although she tried hard not to let it show that she was attracted to him. Which she was, more and more as the weeks went by, as she was sure he was to her. It had started with the gift of the bird, then continued with the odd smile and sidelong glance at one another when they were sure they were not observed. They had started to find reasons for being in the same place at the same time, picking the same row of potatoes, for instance, or sharing the task of muck spreading; an unpleasant job, but one which had to be done, and which was made more bearable to Abbie by Carlo's cheerful presence. For when he was with her he cast aside much of his reticence, giving her a glimpse of what he could be like . . . if he were not a prisoner of war.

'This job seems to come easily to you,' Abbie had remarked to him. 'Farming – you have done it before?'

'Yes, I have done the farming. My uncle has a farm, not too far from where we live. I help, at busy times, like I do here.'

'You live near Lake Garda, you said?'

'*Sì*, Limone, near the lake. I am *cameriere* – waiter, you say – in my father's hotel. Limone, it is very beautiful. The lake it is so blue, and there are mountains and orange and lemon groves. It is what the name means – *Limone* – the place of lemons. It is *molto bello* . . . very beautiful.' He opened his hands wide in an expressive gesture. 'Perhaps, one day, you will see my village . . . Abbie?'

Abbie could not be sure whether these were idle words, or not; whether Carlo was hinting that the two of them might have a future together, one day, when the war was over. Or maybe he was just saying that the place where he lived was so very beautiful that Abbie would be sure to want to see it for herself. She was aware that when he spoke of his homeland there was a faraway look in his eyes and, fleetingly, a glimpse on his face of the anguish he must be suffering as a prisoner in a foreign country.

It was hard to remember sometimes that he was a prisoner, until, at the end of the day, the lorry came to escort him back to his camp. He was never allowed to spend a night away from it, nor to go outside the boundaries of the farm, even on business. At least he was luckier than some, he had told Abbie, in his only slightly faltering English. He was able to come out and do

215

work he enjoyed, in the open air, with good food . . . and pleasant company, he had added with a smile.

'Is the food good,' Abbie asked him, 'in your camp?'

'Not always so good. Not like the food of Signora Dobson. But it is – how do you say? – so-so.' He moved his head and his hand in an eloquent, very Italian, gesture, one which made Abbie's heart contract with her ever-growing awareness of him. 'No pasta, no ravioli. And spaghetti, it comes from tin, I think. Not real spaghetti. And so many times we have the potatoes and gravy. Always, you English, you have the gravy, never the good sauces like we serve in my father's hotel. And the beetroot . . . ugh!'

Abbie laughed. 'I agree with you about the beetroot.'

'All the same . . .' he shrugged, 'is not too bad. We have stove to keep us warm, wood to burn. Plenty blankets. *Sì* . . . we are OK. Quite OK.'

It was the high perimeter fence, Abbie understood, that Carlo found the hardest thing to accept, and the guard towers and the soldiers with guns. And the women from the nearby village – usually it was the women, not the men – who shouted abuse at them and even made rude gestures; making him more than ever aware that he was a prisoner in an alien land, he who had never wanted to fight in the first place. He had enlisted because he felt it was his duty.

'We Italians, we do not like the fighting,' he told her. 'We are not like the Germans, not a warlike race. We like the music and art and always things that are beautiful. War, it spoils everything.'

Thousands of British men, too, thought Abbie, had enlisted for the self-same reason, because they considered it to be their duty. And now they were forced to regard one another as enemies. What a tragedy it all was.

Letters from his home seemed to arrive fairly frequently. Abbie sometimes found him reading them in a corner of the barn. He had two sisters, he told her and a brother who, like him, was in the army, but not a prisoner.

'You haven't got . . . ? You're not . . . married?' she had asked him tentatively, soon after they had first spoken together.

'No, I do not have . . . a wife,' he had answered. And if there had been the slightest hesitation in his reply Abbie had chosen not to notice it.

When he kissed her for the very first time, just before she was due to go home to Blackpool for the Christmas holiday, she felt quite sure that he felt the same way about her as she did about him. He had not said he loved her, but then how could he? she told herself. He was not free to do so. His kiss was gentle and undemanding, a friendly kiss, rather than one of passion. But for Abbie, it was her first kiss ever, and that alone was sufficient to fill her with wonderment. Peter had kissed her on the cheek, she recalled, that time she was late home – how long ago and far away that seemed now – but it was not like this. This was a real kiss, on the lips, and his arms were round her, as she had so often longed for them to be.

'You are so lovely, Abbie,' he said, stroking her hair. They were standing in the corner of the cowshed where Abbie, with Carlo's assistance that day, had just finished the milking. His words thrilled her far more than any words she had ever heard. She, Abbie Winters, was being told she was lovely? The girl who had been so fat and ungainly, who had looked in the mirror so many times, despairing of what she saw there? Was it possible that the ugly duckling she knew she had been was really, as in the fairy story, becoming a swan? 'I will miss you when you go home,' whispered Carlo. 'Tomorrow, you say, you go home?'

'Yes, just for a few days. I will be back soon. I will miss you too, Carlo . . .'

He kissed her again, and this time she felt the pressure of his lips a little more, and she clung to him a little more closely. This was all very new to her, but she felt sure that she could soon learn all there was to be learned.

'Happy Christmas, Carlo,' she whispered.

'*Sì*. . . . Happy Christmas, Abbie. We say "*Santo Natale*" in Italy. Holy Christmas. Is nicer, I think.'

'Yes, I think so, too,' replied Abbie softly. '*Santo Natale*, Carlo . . .'

It was Abbie's first experience of a Yorkshire winter. Blackpool could be cold enough, to be sure, in the wintertime and at other

217

times as well, when a howling gale blew in from the Irish Sea and twenty-foot-high waves crashed over the sea wall, drenching everything and everyone in their fury. They really had to be seen to be believed. But there was not the same intense cold she had experienced here.

'Aye, it's a couple of coats colder here than it is where you come from,' Mr Dobson had told her cheerfully. It was an expression she had not heard before; a coat colder, or even a couple of coats, but it did seem to sum up the numbing cold and the face-freezing wind which came with the first snow of the winter. The snow had come early. The tiny crystals of ice, borne on blizzard-type winds, clung to the hair and eyebrows and forced their way under doors, through keyholes and window crevices. But the countryside, if you could stop thinking for a moment about how cold you were, was breathtakingly beautiful. A wonderland of sparkling brightness, each tree and bush fringed with an edging of white lace and each rooftop, barn and shed looking unfamiliar and magical, like something off a Christmas card.

The cows now 'lay in' ready for milking, instead of having to be fetched in each morning from the fields. And in the cowshed, as she had said goodbye to Carlo, Abbie had not been aware of the cold. It was a cosy place, warmed with the steaming breath of thirty animals, and redolent with the familiar smell of cow dung, warm straw and fresh milk. Cows were still not Abbie's favourite creatures and never had she been able to conquer her mistrust of them. She had been kicked on the shin several times and had suffered the indignity of a load of cow muck – she could not, even now, bring herself to use the less delicate word to describe it! – right in her face while she was milking. But as she stood there, with Carlo's arms around her, the cowshed seemed to Abbie the most desirable place in the world.

'You'll get used to t'cold, like you've gotten used to everything else, Abbie lass,' Mr Dobson said as she gathered her belongings together ready to depart for the station. The farmer was running her and Connie to Leeds in the Ford car. 'Connie here, she's used to it, being a Yorkshire lass. But you're a grand little pair of workers, both on yer. I've got to give credit where it's due. I reckon we've been right lucky with our land girls, what say you, Amy?'

'I'm sure we have.' Amy Dobson smiled at them both. 'Have a good Christmas, both of yer, and there's a little something here for yer mam and dad. Say nowt though.' She tapped her nose eloquently as she handed each of them a cardboard box tied securely with string. 'Not to anybody else but your family, I mean. It wouldn't do. But you've deserved it and what the eye doesn't see . . . Goodness, I hope you can manage it with all the rest of yer luggage.'

Abbie was glad of her heavy greatcoat on this freezing cold morning and she appreciated the truth of Mr Dobson's remark. Several coats colder on this side of the Pennines, she would guess. She said goodbye to Connie at Leeds. Her colleague had only a short train journey to Bradford, whilst Abbie was starting a much longer journey eastwards. Not that it was all that far 'as the crow flies' from Leeds to Blackpool, but travel in wartime seemed abominably slow, the trains stopping at every small station and at other times in between, in the middle of nowhere and for no apparent reason.

It was, as Mrs Dobson had feared, something of a struggle with her luggage, but, as had happened on Abbie's previous journey, there was a good-natured serviceman – an airman this time – to assist her.

It was with mixed feelings that she contemplated her few days' leave at home. It would be good to see them all again, of course: Aunt Bertha and Doreen, and her father and . . . mother. She felt a twinge of guilt at the way she always put her mother at the end of the list. It would be great to see Doreen again and catch up on all the gossip about their new farms. They had exchanged a few letters, but had not been able to arrange a meeting midway between the two places, as they had hoped. Abbie had not told her friend anything about Carlo, in fact she had not even mentioned him, and she hugged the secret thought of him tightly inside her now. She would probably tell Doreen about him, even if she told no one else. After all, there wasn't really anything to tell, not yet, but she felt sure there would be before long. It had been such a wrench saying goodbye to him, but it was not for long; in a few days' time she would be back.

The young airman sitting opposite her grinned as she happened to catch his eye. She smiled back warily then looked away, reminded momentarily of Peter Horsfall. She wondered how he was going on, whether he had started flying yet; that had been his aim. It was a pity the way their friendship had been curtailed when it had started off so promisingly. But with Peter there had been none of the thrill she had felt each time Carlo whispered her name.

After the train had crossed the border into Lancashire the snowy landscape gradually gave way to the usual browns and greens. In Blackpool there had been no snow at all, as yet.

Her father met her at the station, and it was so good to see him again. Her parents and her aunt all seemed pleased to see her. Even her mother's smile of welcome and the kiss on her cheek seemed to be genuine and there was an unmistakable glint of a tear in the corner of her eye. But then her mother had to go and spoil things.

'Goodness, you've lost a lot of weight, Abigail,' said Eva, when Abbie had taken off her overcoat. 'And I don't know that it suits you either.' She put her head on one side, pursing her lips in a critical way. 'You'll be as thin as a bean-pole if you don't watch out. Aren't they giving you enough to eat at that farm? You've had your hair cut, too,' she added with a slight disapproving sigh. 'It doesn't look like you at all.'

Abbie wondered if her mother would really have preferred her to remain as she had been before, buxom and unattractive. She had had her hair cut, at Connie's suggestion, at a posh hair stylist's in Leeds. She found the short style much easier to manage and she had discovered she had a slight natural wave in her hair which now curled attractively – or so she had thought – around her face.

She patted her hair now, in the way she had seen Doreen do, as though she knew it suited her. 'It's easy to keep tidy like this,' she said dismissively. And it's my hair; I can do what I like with it, she added, but only to herself. It would not do to start an argument with her mother when she had only been home for five minutes. 'And of course I'm getting enough to eat,' she went on. 'Mrs Dobson's a wonderful cook – almost as good as Aunt Bertha.' She smiled at her aunt who was clearly over the moon at seeing her beloved niece again. She hadn't said very much, but she could not stop beaming and looking at Abbie in wonderment as though she could not believe what she was seeing.

'Mrs Dobson has sent you this,' said Abbie, handing the cardboard box to her mother. 'I'm not sure what it is. A few things they produce on the farm, I should imagine.'

Eva raised her eyebrows. 'We don't need charity, Abigail, whatever it is. I'm sure the farmer's wife, Mrs ... Dobson, or whatever you call her, thinks she is doing us a favour, but ...'

Cedric Winters gave a little tut of exasperation, so quiet it could hardly be heard. 'Let's have a look at what the woman has sent us,' he said. 'I'm sure it's very kind of her and I'm not going to turn my nose up at some real farm produce.' He took the box from his wife, marching purposefully into the dining room where he placed it on the table. 'Have you a pair of scissors, Bertha –' he appeared to be ignoring his wife – 'so that I can cut the string?'

'I think we'd best try and undo the knots,' replied Bertha, 'not cut it. String's precious now, and it could be used again. Here, let me have a go, Cedric.'

She carefully pulled at the knots in the string. 'There, that's done,' she said, standing back. 'Go on, open the box.' There was a slight glint of amusement in her eyes as she nodded at Cedric, before turning to grin at Abbie. 'It's like Christmas already, isn't it?'

Dr Winters pulled back the lid, then started to place the articles one by one on the table.

'Not on my chenille cover, please, Cedric!' said his wife. 'You should have taken it into the kitchen.'

'It's all right, my dear,' answered the doctor, quite amiably. 'We'll stand them on a newspaper. Here we are – no problem at all.' He took a newspaper from the magazine rack at the side of the fireplace.

The box contained a slab of creamy butter wrapped in greaseproof paper, and about the same amount – a good half-pound – of Wensleydale cheese. The Dobsons' farm was in Wharfedale, but Abbie knew they had friends in the nearby dale. There was a jar of Mrs Dobson's home-made lemon cheese, several rashers of home-cured bacon, half a dozen eggs and a small chicken.

'My goodness!' exclaimed Bertha, clapping her hands together in delight. 'That's a feast and no mistake. It's ages since I clapped eyes on bacon like that. Mr Harding does his best, but it's wafer-thin sometimes, not much taste in it. And a few ounces a week doesn't go far. And just look at them brown eggs! Real farm bacon and eggs on Christmas morning. How about that, eh?'

'Yes, I should say so,' said Cedric, beaming. 'Your farmer's wife has done us proud, Abbie.'

'I thought you didn't approve of the black market, Cedric,' said Eva. 'And we've already ordered a chicken for our Christmas dinner. Bertha will be collecting it from the butcher's tomorrow.'

'So we'll have chicken tomorrow as well,' replied Cedric. 'We'd better eat it while it's fresh. Or tonight, maybe?' He looked enquiringly at Bertha. 'Or have you already planned the meal?'

'It was only going to be a make-shift meal tonight, I'm afraid,' said Bertha, 'using up odds and ends. This chicken'll be a real treat. I'll go and get it in the oven now, shall I, then it can have a good couple of hours?'

Eva, who obviously thought she was being ignored, spoke up now. 'Do just as you wish, Bertha. Whatever I say doesn't seem to matter much.' She turned to look at her husband. 'When all's said and done this is black market produce. I thought you didn't approve of the black market,' she repeated. 'How many times have you told me—?'

'Black market, my foot!' replied Cedric. 'This is a gift, that's all, and I, for one, am very glad of it. Come along, Eva, my dear.' He seemed to be trying hard not to let his exasperation show. 'Don't let's spoil our daughter's homecoming. We're all so pleased to see you again, Abigail. The place isn't the same at all without you . . . Is it, Eva?'

'No, of course it isn't,' Eva answered quietly. She turned to smile at her daughter. 'We're very pleased to see you home again, Abigail,' she said, still very quietly, but her eyes were

warmer than Abbie had ever seen them. 'We have missed you
. . . all of us.'

Chapter 14

Abbie decided not to wear her uniform greatcoat. It weighed a ton and she was glad to be rid of it for a while, as she was glad to exchange her corduroy breeches and green jersey for a skirt and jumper of a different colour.

'Where are you off to?' her mother asked when she saw her in the hallway fastening her tweed coat.

'I'm going to meet Doreen,' said Abbie, not at all timidly or apologetically. 'She's home on leave as well. It will be good to see her again.' She turned to the hall mirror, tying a multi-coloured headscarf firmly beneath her chin. She had decided against a hat. All her hats seemed old-fashioned to her now. Headscarves were the thing these days. She had got used to wearing one to protect her ears against the biting Yorkshire cold, and it would be ideal, too, for the Blackpool breezes.

'Hmm . . .' said Eva. She paused as if deliberating what to say. Then, 'You look like a factory girl in that thing,' she said. 'Why don't you wear a nice hat?'

'It'll keep my ears warm, Mother, and they're quite the fashion now. Didn't you know?' Abbie answered cheerfully. At least her mother had not said anything derogatory about Doreen.

'Hmm . . .' said Eva again. 'Well then . . . have a nice time with your . . . friend. Don't be late back now. Your Aunt Bertha has an idea she wants to make a bacon and egg pie with some of the – er – produce you brought.'

'Good!' Abbie smiled broadly. 'That'll be great. I'll be ready for that after a walk on the prom.' She hesitated, then on an impulse she leaned forward and gave her mother a peck on the cheek. 'Tara, Mum,' she said. 'I won't be late.'

It was the first time she had ever called her anything but Mother, and Eva seemed rather taken aback. Neither would she approve of the casual farewell – Tara, indeed! – thought Abbie, grinning to herself as she closed the door behind her. But in spite of missing Carlo it was good to be home again, and she was trying hard, as she thought her mother was doing too, to put all their previous animosity behind her. In her new-found confidence she felt the best way to treat her mother was to be cheerful and self-assured and never to let herself be intimidated.

She had arranged, by letter, to meet Doreen the afternoon after they both arrived home. It was the day before Christmas Eve and they met, as they had done so many times, at the corner of Park Road and Church Street. Doreen was already waiting there and they both beamed with delight as they caught sight of one another; but they did not hug and kiss in the street. They were both a little unsure about what to do, but their diffidence did not last more than a moment or two.

'Gosh, it's great to see you again, luv!' Doreen, as usual, was the first to speak. 'You look bloomin' marvellous! You've lost even more weight, haven't you? Come on, let's get moving. It's a bit nippy standing here.' She tucked her arm into Abbie's and they set off down Church Street towards the promenade.

'Yes, I'll be as slim as you if I carry on like this,' agreed Abbie. 'Not that I'd ever be anything like as dainty,' she added, her former lack of self-esteem surfacing for a moment. 'I don't think my mother approves of me being slim. And she didn't like my headscarf either. She says I look like a factory girl.' She gave a chuckle. 'I'm glad to see you've got one on as well.'

'Yes, I never wear owt else on me head now,' said Doreen. 'Oh – pardon me! – anything else, I should've said. I've got out of the habit of talking proper, y'see,' she gave her friend a nudge, 'now as you're not with me. They're broad Yorkshire up in Northallerton. Trust your mother, eh? Don't suppose she liked you coming to meet me neither, did she? How is your mam?'

'She's OK,' replied Abbie. 'If you mean health-wise. I think we're getting on better than we did. I'm determined not to let her upset me, you see. And she didn't actually say anything about me coming to meet you.'

'Wonders never cease,' mumbled Doreen. 'And how's dear

old Aunt Bertha? And your father, of course – mustn't forget him.'

'They're all fine,' replied Abbie. 'How about your family?'

'Mam's not been too well.' Doreen sounded less cheerful now. 'She's had another bad do with her chest, her usual bronchitis, you know. My dad persuaded her to go along to that clinic your father has. She was really taken with him, and that new nurse of his, Nurse Summers. And then your dad came to visit her at home, without being asked. That was kind of him, Abbie . . . I'm real sorry about what I said about him – y'know, when our Tony died – 'cause I know now what a good chap he is.'

'I thought we'd decided to forget all about that.' Abbie gave her a mock-reproachful look. 'Shut up about it, eh? So your mother's on the mend, is she?'

'Oh yes, she's not so bad now, ta. It's bucked her up no end me being home, of course. You'll pop round to see her, won't you, before you go back? She'd be ever so pleased.'

'Of course I will. I don't go back till Monday. How about you?'

'Yes, same here . . .'

They crossed the promenade to the sea side, then started to walk northwards. And as they walked Abbie told her friend about Carlo. She just couldn't keep it to herself any longer.

Doreen, unusually for her, went very quiet. Abbie thought she could even sense a slight reproach in her friend's glance.

'You don't approve?' Abbie asked.

'It's got nowt to do wi' me. I can't say whether I approve or not,' said Doreen. 'How the heck can I? I don't even know the fellow. But you must be careful, Abbie. You know you're not supposed to fraternise, as they call it. We've had 'em working for us as well and I know how charming some of these foreigners can be. And that's what this . . . Carlo is. He's a foreigner, and he's one of the enemy an' all.'

'You wouldn't say that if you met him,' said Abbie, feeling, and sounding, rather indignant. 'He's a lovely young man and so polite and respectful. You can't help but like him. Everybody likes him.'

'Oh aye.' Doreen nodded knowingly. 'You've told yer mother

about him then, have you?' She gave a mischievous grin.

'No, of course I haven't. What do you take me for? A complete idiot? I haven't told anybody – not yet – except you, that is. There isn't really anything to tell . . . at the moment. But he's told me all about his home, and he says he would like me to see it. So what else could that mean? I think he's leading up to something.'

'Honest? You really think there might be something more? That this Carlo might ask you to marry him?'

'Not yet. Of course not. But he might, when there's some sign of the war ending. We won't be enemies for ever, you know.'

'No, I know what you mean. Especially about us being enemies. It isn't right that ordinary people like us, and this Carlo, should be enemies just because we happen to be on different sides in some stupid war.' Doreen sighed. 'I'm sure he's very nice, luv. But I don't want you to get hurt, that's all. Try not to read too much into it. What do a few kisses amount to when all's said and done? He's lonely and a long way from home, and you're a nice girl who's been kind to him. A very pretty girl an' all. You look smashing with your hair like that.' Abbie's headscarf had blown off in the stiff breeze and it was then that Doreen had noticed her stylish hairdo. 'And talk about slim! Wow! I'd never've believed it.'

'Thank you.' Abbie was flattered. 'But I think you're wrong about Carlo. I think we really do mean something to one another. At least . . . he does to me.' She fell silent for a moment, wondering if she could possibly have been mistaken. It was so easy to let doubts creep in when they were apart, but other people could not possibly understand about the closeness that had built up between them. When she saw him again next week she would realise how silly she had been to let Doreen's words upset her, as they had done for a moment.

'Have you told your Aunt Bertha?' asked Doreen quietly.

'No, I've already said, I haven't told anybody else. But I think I will.' Abbie made a sudden decision. 'Yes, I jolly well will. I'll tell Aunt Bertha. I know she'll be pleased for me. Aunt Bertha always sees two sides to every problem, and I know she'll understand.' Her aunt would understand, of course, after what had once happened to her. 'And don't forget, I'll be twenty-one next month,' Abbie told her friend, with a touch of defiance. 'And then I'll be able to do whatever I like, and nobody will be able to stop me.'

'OK, keep yer hair on.' Doreen grinned. 'I don't think we'd better walk any further, do you? Or we'll end up at Fleetwood.'

They had been walking at a good pace and now they stopped, leaning on the railings almost opposite the Boating Pool, a favourite haunt of children, both local and visitors, during the summer season. Now the place was closed for the winter, the wooden animals on the automated ride hidden away under their tarpaulin sheet. Here and there Abbie could see the shape of a tall-necked giraffe or an elephant, or the stripy leg of a tiger peeping out. The pool itself was empty of its gay paddle boats and the whole place looked forlorn and neglected.

'I used to love the Boating Pool when I was a kiddie,' Abbie remarked. 'Aunt Bertha used to bring me.' She turned to her friend. 'I expect you used to come too, didn't you?'

'Very rarely,' replied Doreen. 'A penny bun cost sixpence in our house, y'know, with all us kids. Eightpence if you count me mam and dad.' Abbie knew it was only a figure of speech about the buns. Mrs Miller did all her own baking. They would never have had any money for shop-bought cakes. She regretted being so tactless. Of course they wouldn't have been able to afford the Boating Pool.

'Sorry,' she said. 'I wasn't thinking. It just brought back happy memories, that's all.'

' 'S all right,' said Doreen. 'I know what you mean. Yes, I used to love it an' all. I have been here – but not as often as the "privileged clarsses".' She put on a mock-refined accent, then she burst out laughing and Abbie joined in. She knew Doreen well enough now to know when she was joking.

'It's grand to be home, isn't it?' said Doreen. 'There's no place like Blackpool, even out of season. In fact I think I like it better when it's quiet.'

The tide was out, but the stretch of gold-brown sand was deserted, except for a few people, mostly alone. Abbie could make out the figure of a solitary airman, hunched up in his blue greatcoat and, further away, another serviceman with his arm around his girlfriend. There were still quite a lot of them in the town although many of them would have gone home for Christmas leave. The sky and sea were grey. There would be no glorious sunset tonight.

Abbie suddenly felt cold and she gave a shudder. 'Come on, let's see if we can find a café and have a cup of tea before we go home. I think there's one near Gynn Square. Then perhaps we'd better get a tram back to town. It'll be dropping dark before we know where we are.' And she had told her mother she would not be late, although she didn't say that.

'D'you feel like going dancing tonight?' asked Doreen as they turned round and started to walk back. 'Or to the pictures or something?'

'I'm not sure,' said Abbie. She didn't really feel like it at all. 'I don't mind. I'll go if you want me to.'

'No, it's OK,' said Doreen. 'I'm not too fussy about it neither. I just thought you might like a night in town, but I 'spect you're like me, aren't you? Glad to be home . . . But I must admit I was a bit sorry, in some ways, to leave Northallerton.' Abbie was aware of a wistful note in her friend's voice and she turned to look at her.

'Oh . . . and why is that? Or can I guess?'

Doreen grinned. 'You're not the only one, you know, who's met somebody that's rather special. At least . . . I think he is,' she added, a trifle defiantly, Abbie thought. 'Although it's too soon, yet, to know if anything'll come of it. He's nice though. The funny thing is,' she turned to look thoughtfully at Abbie, 'I reckon he'd be a lot more suitable for you than he is for me.'

'Who would? Come on, tell me more,' said Abbie. 'You've got me intrigued now. Who is he?'

'He's called Norman,' replied Doreen. 'Norman Jarvis, and he's the farmer's son. Yes, I know it's one thing land girls are not supposed to do,' she went on as Abbie raised a questioning eyebrow along with her knowing little smile. 'To fall for the son of the family, but sometimes it just can't be helped . . . and you don't need to look at me like that, Abbie Winters!'

'Like what?' Abbie laughed. 'I'm not looking at you like anything, honestly I'm not. I was just thinking how pleased I am for you. As you say, I should think it's inevitable with you working so closely together. Come on, what's he like?'

'Well, that's just it,' said Doreen. 'He's . . . very ordinary really. To look at, I mean. Not tall, dark and handsome, like your Italian bloke. He's quite a few years older than me – he's twenty-nine – and he's . . . like I said, ordinary, not very tall, but not very small neither, with straight brown hair. He has lovely eyes, deep brown, like yours, Abbie. But he wears glasses. That's one of the reasons he couldn't go in the army, 'cause he doesn't see too good. But he's always studying an' all, so that doesn't help his eyesight. He went to college, to learn about farming all scientific, like. That's why I said he would be more suitable for you than me. Funny, isn't it?'

'Not really,' said Abbie. 'Not if you . . . love him?'

'Well, I like him a lot. A heck of a lot,' said Doreen. 'But I think it's a bit soon to be talking about love, don't you?'

'Maybe,' said Abbie evasively. 'And you think he likes you too? Well, he must do, I'm sure.' Nobody could help but like Doreen. 'I hope it works out for you, Doreen, if it's what you want.' How much less complicated it would be, she was thinking, if she, Abbie, had had the good sense to fall in love with someone so eminently suitable, so steady and ordinary. But love didn't work like that. You couldn't choose when to fall in love, nor with whom. Love chose you, sometimes taking you completely unawares.

Doreen told her more about Norman Jarvis as they drank their tea in a little café near Gynn Square. About how he had tried to join the army, but had been turned down not just because of his eyesight but because – to his great embarrassment – he had flat feet.

'I've never understood what difference that makes,' said Abbie, puzzled. 'What does it matter?'

'It's the marching, you fathead!' said Doreen. 'They do a lot of that in the army and if you have flat feet you can't keep up with the others, can you? Honestly, for somebody who's dead brainy you aren't half stupid at times!'

Abbie smiled, never offended now by Doreen's less-than-tactful remarks. 'I thought farmers were exempt from military service anyway.'

'So they are, but that doesn't mean they can't volunteer if

231

they want to. Norman was disappointed. He says he feels guilty when he sees fellows in uniform, but I tell him it doesn't matter. He tried, didn't he, and that's what counts. He's really nice, Abbie . . . You'd like him.' Doreen's shining eyes revealed her feelings even if she had said she didn't know whether or not it was love.

Abbie smiled. 'I'm sure I would. Isn't it nice how we've both met somebody special?'

They decided they would spend the evening with Aunt Bertha rather than go out on the town. Doreen was a little surprised and, if she were honest, more than a little fearful, when the door opened immediately at her knock, almost as if it had been anticipated, and there on the doorstep was Mrs Winters, not Bertha or Abbie as she had expected. She was more surprised than ever when Eva Winters greeted her, if not effusively, then with a degree of civility.

'Oh, good evening . . . er . . . Doreen,' she began. 'I heard Abigail telling her aunt you were coming. Yes, Bertha looks forward to having someone different to talk to. Come in, won't you?' Eva actually smiled, just the slightest curving of her lips, but Doreen, almost rooted to the spot in her astonishment, took it to be a smile.

'Hurry up . . . Doreen.' Doreen got the impression that Mrs Winters had been about to call her 'girl', but had thought better of it. 'Or else we'll have that wretched little ARP man on to us.' She ushered her through the vestibule and into the hall. 'Yes, as I was saying, Bertha will be glad of some fresh company. She loves to chatter when she gets the chance. I'm afraid her horizons are somewhat limited . . . Ah, there you are, Bertha.' Her cousin, looking very flustered, had just appeared in the hall. 'I beat you to it tonight, you see.' Eva's smile seemed almost triumphant.

Bertha's face was a study of disbelief, so was Abbie's, coming down the stairs at that moment; especially as Eva went on, speaking, it seemed, solely to Doreen. 'Perhaps you might like to come in the sitting room and have a cup of tea with my husband and me before you go home . . . Doreen? And you as well, of course, Abigail, and you, Bertha.' Her smile, like that of some grand duchess at a ball, encompassed them all now. 'I'm sure you don't want to spend all evening in Bertha's tiny little room. Perhaps you could make us all a pot of tea at nine o'clock, Bertha?'

'Rightyho.' Bertha's answer was curt, with not a trace of the servility she had used to show. 'I think we'd prefer cocoa though, the three of us. Wouldn't we, girls? That's what we usually have.'

'Just as you wish.' Eva's smile was a little condescending. 'I'll leave you to your . . . chatter.' She swept into the sitting room, leaving the three of them looking at one another in bewilderment.

'Well, I'll be . . . What d'you make of that?' said Bertha in a loud whisper. 'Here, take your coat off, Doreen love. It's grand to see you again, it is that. Go on, the pair of you, into me little parlour.' She followed them in and firmly closed the door behind them. 'I don't care if it is tiny, it's a real little palace to me. That mother of yours, Abbie – she's a proper caution and no mistake. I wouldn't care, but it's her that put me in here in the first place. Happen she's forgotten that, eh? Not that I'm complaining about it. It's a real snug little room when the wind's howling outside. I wouldn't swap it for Buckingham Palace. I say, that's a turn-up for the book, isn't it, us getting invited for our supper?'

'Oh heck! I'm not so sure about it,' said Doreen. She sat down on the rag rug, tucking her legs beneath her and holding her hands out to the flames of the fire. 'I'll be frightened of dropping me plate or spilling me tea – sorry, cocoa,' she grinned, 'in the saucer. What's she up to, eh? Why is she being so friendly all of a sudden? Well, I don't know as you could call her all that friendly . . .' She still thought that Eva Winters looked as though she had 'a poker up her bum', as she had heard her father say. 'But different at any rate. What's got into her?'

Abbie gave a slight shrug. 'Let's just accept it, shall we? She's been making more of an effort to be reasonable since I came home, hasn't she, Aunt Bertha?'

Bertha nodded, a little doubtfully.

'I think Father might have had a quiet word with her; maybe he's asked her not to . . . spoil things for me while I'm at home.' She sighed. 'I'm just relieved we're getting on better. I know my mother's something of an enigma, but that's the way she is, I'm afraid.'

'You and your big words!' said Doreen. 'What d'you mean – enigma? What's that when it's at home?'

Abbie smiled. 'All right – a mystery then, a bit of a puzzle.'

'She's that all right,' said Bertha darkly. 'Not that I'm saying anything wrong, mind . . . She's been good to me, has Eva,' she added, as she so often did. 'Now, come on, girls. I want to hear all about the Land Army. I've already heard some of Abbie's tales, of course. Eeh, that Mr Rawnsley! He was a right one, wasn't he? I dare say you were glad to see the back of him, eh, Doreen? How about your new place? Are you happier there . . . ?'

It was Abbie who went into the kitchen at a quarter to nine to put the kettle on, leaving Doreen alone with her aunt. Bertha didn't waste a moment. She leaned forward confidingly and Doreen could guess what was coming. 'Here, what d'you think about our Abbie and that Italian chap?' she asked, speaking in a low voice.

'Oh, she's told you then?' replied Doreen. 'Yes, she said she was going to tell you. She said she thought you would understand because . . .' She stopped abruptly, realising she was not supposed to know anything about Bertha's past indiscretions. Abbie had told her in the strictest confidence. 'Because . . . you are always so understanding. We'd best not say too much though, or she'll hear us.' She dropped her voice lower, although it was doubtful that they could be heard over the rattle of teacups and the hiss of the kettle.

'I don't care if she does hear,' said Bertha. 'I'm not going to say anything that I haven't already told her. Oh yes, I understand all right.' She gave a sad little smile. 'I haven't forgotten what it's like to be young, Doreen. But I've told her what you've probably told her yourself. To be very careful, not to go and do anything silly. Not just – well, you know what I mean – not just that, but to remember we're at war with 'em. That poor lad, that Carlo, he's a long way from home. No doubt he's lonely. Aye, I remember another young fellow once that was lonely . . .'

Bertha stared into space, her eyes darkening suddenly as though with a remembered pain. Doreen made no comment, nor by even so much as a questioning glance did she let on that she had noticed; but she guessed what the older woman was thinking about. Bertha quickly recovered herself. 'Aye, it's easy to get carried away, but I don't want her to get into bother. With the authorities, I mean. They'd take a dim view of it, fraternising with the enemy, as they call it. But I've been trying to tell myself that Abbie's a sensible lass. She won't do anything she shouldn't. And happen it'll all blow over, eh, Doreen? Happen she'll realise there's no future in it, 'cause for the life of me I can't see as how there ever can be.'

'I think she's been swept off her feet, if you know what I mean,' whispered Doreen, glancing towards the kitchen door. 'Maybe it's the idea of it all that she likes – you know, being in love, 'specially with somebody a bit different, like. And with her never having a proper boyfriend before, p'raps it all seems dead romantic, like the pictures. Like Clark Gable and Vivien Leigh, y'know?'

'Yes, I see what you mean.' Bertha sighed. 'She hasn't had much romance in her life, poor lass, not up to now. But the pictures isn't real life, is it? I just hope she'll be sensible, that's all.' She wasn't bothering to speak quietly now, and Abbie, coming in from the kitchem with a laden tray, grinned at her.

'That's me you're talking about, isn't it? I knew you would as soon as my back was turned. I'll try to be sensible, Aunt Bertha, don't worry . . . but I've spent twenty years being sensible, haven't I? Now I want to enjoy myself.'

'I don't want to see you hurt, that's all,' said Bertha gruffly. 'Nor you neither, Doreen, although I must say that chap you've been telling us about does seem to have his head screwed on the right way. Anyroad, I've had me say and that's that. Come on, let's go and see how the other half lives, shall we? Just remember one thing, girls.' She looked at them seriously. 'We don't drink out of the saucer. Now – think on!' She wagged her finger reprovingly, sending them into gales of laughter.

'No, and we don't dip our biscuits in the cocoa,' giggled Abbie, 'nor do we blow on it to cool it down.'

Doreen joined in the laughter, at the same time thinking that they had been known to do all those things in her free and easy home. Though not when Abbie Winters visited them.

Chapter 15

It had been an odd, spiritless sort of Christmas, Abbie mused as she travelled back, alone, to the West Riding of Yorkshire. Doreen, also, was going back that same morning, but as her farm was in the North Riding she was travelling by a different route. Abbie was glad, in a way, of the solitude – a time for quiet reflection away from the chatter of her friend – although Christmas would, indeed, have been an even gloomier celebration if it had not been for Doreen's company, livening things up from time to time.

Christmas in the Winters household had never been noted for its fun and frivolity, Eva always managing, one way or another, to spoil things, if not by her perversity, then by her silly attempts at pretension. Abbie recalled, with an inward smile, how her mother had put on her 'grand duchess' manner last year when the Sidebottoms had visited them. This year, thank goodness, they had not been invited; she had caught sight of Sidney Sidebottom in church on Sunday, but he had quite studiously avoided looking at her.

There had been just the four of them for Christmas lunch, then tea, and the day had dragged unbelievably. Abbie had found herself longing to be back in the now familiar farmstead, and not just because she missed the company of Carlo. Even milking the unfriendliest of the cows or swilling out the pigsty would have been preferable to the frustrating boredom of a day spent with such a disparate family.

It was not that Eva had been difficult these last few days, not since her gripe about the 'black market' food that Abbie had brought home. She had seemed to be making a special effort to be nice to her daughter; but Abbie had noticed – and Aunt Bertha had commented on it, too – the brooding silences that

237

frequently overcame her. Most uncharacteristic, these silences, because Eva had always had a great deal to say.

The first time Abbie had been aware of it was when Doreen had been invited into the sitting room for supper. Eva had hardly spoken to the girl. It had been Dr Winters who had made her feel at home and with whom she had chatted, quite unrestrainedly, as was Doreen's way, about the Land Army and about her family at home. Eva had sat there staring into space. Abbie had thought that maybe her mother was regretting her impulsive decision to invite 'that girl' to sit with them. But Eva had seemed lost in a world of her own and when Abbie had spoken to her she had stared at her bewilderedly as though she could not make out who she was. This had happened a few times since, and Abbie was concerned. It was almost as though her mother was losing contact with reality.

Abbie had even mentioned it to her father, but he had dismissed it as, 'Just the war, my dear; it's getting to all of us. Don't worry about your mother. I'll take care of her . . . You have to admit she's been rather more – er – amenable.'

Abbie knew this was true. Maybe this was what worried her; it was unlike Eva to be submissive. She was realising she did have a certain affection for her mother. Maybe it was true that absence made the heart grow fonder.

But then, as the train crossed the border into Yorkshire, her thoughts, inevitably, returned to Carlo. She had deliberately made herself not think of him, for the last couple of hours at least. She was trying to bear in mind the words of her Aunt Bertha and Doreen. She had overheard quite a lot of what they had said to one another while she was in the kitchen; that she was, maybe, infatuated, in love with the idea of being in love. It was, after all, she tried to tell herself, her first experience of the emotion – you could hardly count the brief friendship she had had with Peter Horsfall – and her former insecurity and lack of self-esteem began to take hold of her again. By the time she arrived back at Daisy Bank farm she had almost convinced herself that her feeling for Carlo could be nothing more than infatuation, and that he had never really cared for her; it was just in her mind.

Until he smiled at her, and then she knew she was suffering

from no delusion; he really did care. As before, they started to make excuses to be in the same place at the same time, as if by chance. Then they began to plan their meetings more carefully; in the cowshed or barn or apple orchard, in a far field or secluded copse well away from the farm buildings – and from prying eyes. Their meetings, of necessity, had to be kept secret. Abbie was quite sure that neither Connie nor Mr and Mrs Dobson had any idea about their friendship. They had been very discreet and were most circumspect in their dealings with one another when they were in the company of others.

Abbie found herself more and more thrilled by his kisses, the first real kisses she had ever experienced, and by his words of endearment. '*Cara mia, Abbie . . .*' he would whisper. 'You are so lovely.' But she was forced to admit to herself, as time went by, that they were not really words of love. Certainly not words of lifetime commitment; he had still not even told her that he loved her. And always, when his kisses started to become more passionate and demanding, he – not Abbie – would draw back, as though he were holding himself firmly in check. Abbie was glad that he did – or so she told herself – and admired him the more for his self-restraint.

She remembered Aunt Bertha's words of caution, that she must on no account be tempted to do anything silly, and though her aunt had not enlarged upon what she meant by 'anything silly' Abbie had understood. Her aunt had warned her once before that the act of love was something to be saved until she was married. She looked back in some bemusement now at the ignorant, completely naïve, girl she had been at that time. She realised now what the act of love involved – how could she not, working on a farm? – although not from her own personal experience. It had sounded so odd when Doreen had described it to her, quite unemotionally; but now, when Carlo kissed her, there was a feeling of longing deep inside her and a most peculiar sensation that she had never known before in those secret, intimate parts of her. It would be so easy . . . and she appreciated now what had happened to Aunt Bertha all those years ago. It was becoming more and more apparent however, that Carlo was not going to tempt her to give herself to him in that way; but she felt sure he was exercising his self-control only until such time as they were no longer enemies.

Her twenty-first birthday had passed with no celebration other than a few cards from home, plus those from Doreen, Connie and the Dobsons, and a cake baked by Mrs Dobson which they all, including Carlo, shared at teatime. There had been no presents apart from the one Carlo gave her; another exquisite carving, this time of a squirrel, which he had handed to her in the seclusion of the barn. The gifts from her family – a string of pearls from her parents and a Parker fountain pen from her aunt – had been given to her in advance at Christmas, and Doreen promised to give her her present when next they met. She was rather short of funds at the moment, she had written, in her usual matter-of-fact way. The day, more than anything, signified to Abbie that she was now of an age to take care of herself. No longer did she need to ask her parents' permission for anything. She could even get married without their consent.

It was in the early spring that Abbie began to notice the definite change in Carlo. He was no longer making excuses to be with her; rather, he seemed to be avoiding her. She became aware that he was concentrating too attentively on his work, whatever it might be – driving the plough, cutting kale or attending to the cows – pretending he hadn't seen her when she knew perfectly well that he had. She began to feel sick with worry. The change had seemed to coincide with a letter he had received from home. She had seen him reading it in a corner of the barn, but when he saw her approaching he had shoved it away in his pocket instead of telling her, as he often did, some snippet of news about his brother or sisters. She hadn't commented about it at the time. There was no reason, after all, why he should tell her about his letters if he didn't wish to do so, but a few days of his odd behaviour convinced her that it was time she found out what was troubling him.

She caught up with him one lunchtime in the field behind the cowshed. He was sitting by the hedge with his packed lunch of sandwiches and an apple spread out in front of him. That was another strange thing; all this week he had declined Mrs Dobson's invitation to dine with the family, excusing himself each time by saying he was in the middle of a job he wanted to finish. It didn't seem this way now. He was quite clearly taking his ease. He accepted the mug of tea that Abbie proffered – she knew she had to have a good reason for confronting him – murmuring his thanks, then, after a sidelong glance he looked away.

'Carlo . . .' She crouched down on the ground beside him. 'What's wrong? There's something troubling you, isn't there? Is it me? Have I done something . . . ?'

'You, Abbie? Oh no, not you. You could never do anything wrong. You are so good . . . Much too good for me,' he added, almost in a whisper. 'No, *cara mia*, it is not you.' He was silent for a moment and Abbie waited. Then, 'I am the one, not you,' he said. 'I think perhaps . . . I have not been – how do you say? – honest . . . *onesto*.' His deep brown eyes were regarding her keenly now, no longer attempting to avoid her glance, and she felt a chill strike right to the heart of her. He didn't love her. Of course he didn't; if he had loved her he would have told her so before now, but, fool that she was, she had gone on hoping, waiting . . . He didn't even want her any more. She knew that this was what he was trying to say. It was what she had known for several days now, but she had tried to close her mind to it.

'What do you mean, Carlo?' she asked. She hardly dared look at him for fear of what she might see in his face. Indifference instead of affection? And yet his eyes, even now, seemed full of concern. 'What is it . . . that you haven't been honest about? You must tell me.'

He took hold of her hand now. 'Abbie, I do care for you, very much. You must believe me. To meet someone like you . . . so far from home; to be your friend . . . it is so good. But it is – how do you say? – like a lovely dream. Not real life. You understand what I am saying?' Abbie didn't answer. She understood only too well what he was saying; that he had never been serious about her, it was all a dream, a fantasy. She let him go on talking.

'In Italy, Abbie, always it is the family that is important. My father, my mother, my brother and my sisters. I must not do anything that would . . . hurt them, that might harm my family.'

And yet you can hurt me, Carlo, her mind was crying. 'In

England, too,' she replied, 'the family is important.' She could not let him think that the Italians were the only ones with family values. It was Doreen, however, of whom she found herself thinking. Doreen, with her brothers and sisters and her loving parents; a big family, united in their joys and in their sorrows, something that she, Abbie, felt she had lacked.

'Sì . . . I know. But there is something else I must tell you, Abbie. You see . . . there is someone else, at home, in Limone.'

'Another girl, you mean? You are . . . engaged to be married?' An even worse thought now occurred to her. He had denied it very quickly, she recalled, when she had asked him, but maybe he had not been speaking the truth. 'You are . . . married?' she asked in a whisper.

'No, no, no . . . not married. But she is a very dear friend. Maria, she is a friend of my family. My family will be so hurt, I think, if . . . How can I say this to you, Abbie?' He was still holding her hand and he began to stroke her fingers.

She pulled her hand away, clasping both together tightly in her lap. 'You must tell me, Carlo. All of it. I want to know.' She didn't know how she was managing to sound so calm. She listened impassively, outwardly at least, as Carlo told her, falteringly, but in surprisingly articulate English, about his friendship with Maria, the girl from his native village.

They had grown up together, attending the same school and the same church, and it was always assumed that one day they would marry. Signor Valli, Maria's father, was the accountant who took care of the book-keeping for the hotel, so the families were bound by ties other than friendship. And, of course, both families were Roman Catholic, and for one of their members to marry outside of the religion would be severely frowned upon. It would mean, indeed, a complete severing of all family ties. And this was what Abbie, deep down, had always known, though she had not allowed the thought to take shape in her mind; her deluded mind, she now realised.

'But what about the letter?' she asked him when he seemed to have come to the end of his story. 'Last week you received a letter from home, didn't you? Was it something in the letter that made you change your mind about me?' In all probability, though, the change of heart had not been so sudden, she told herself. Carlo must have always known that he was not free to love her.

'Ah yes, the letter. *Sì . . .*' he replied. 'You are right. It was the letter that made me think. It was from my mother. Maria, she has been ill. Her chest . . . her lungs.' He pointed to his own chest. 'Never has she been strong, but these last few weeks she has been very ill. They think, for a time, she might not get better. But now she is recovered. My mother write to tell me.'

Abbie was astounded. This poor girl had been lying ill and all the time Carlo, who was supposed to be engaged to her, had been flirting – yes, that was all he had been doing – with an English girl. Hurt as she was Abbie was beginning to see him for the philanderer she feared he must be. 'You knew she was ill,' she gasped, 'and yet you went on seeing me?'

'No, no, no . . . it was not like that. I did not know Maria was so ill, not till my mother tell me in her last letter. She did not want to worry me. There was nothing I could do, so far from . . . from my home. I was wondering why Maria had not written.'

'*She* wrote to you? Some of those letters . . . ?' Abbie was realising, to her horror and dismay, that some of the letters she had seen him perusing must have been from Maria.

'*Sì* – well, of course. She wrote, sometimes. We are friends, I tell you. Always we were friends, since we were children. But you . . . you mean so much to me, Abbie. I do not wish to hurt you.'

'I don't think so, Carlo. I don't think I mean very much to you at all; not really.' Abbie rose to her feet. Suddenly she didn't want to listen any longer. She looked down at his dark curly hair, at his deep brown eyes in that lean handsome face, still gazing at her so intently, and it seemed, to her amazement, as though she didn't know him any more. She even began to feel her desire for him waning. She had been so sure she had loved him, but now she was realising that what Doreen and her aunt had said to her must have been true. He was far from home and she had been kind to him. That was all it was. His feeling for her was shallow. She could not think of Carlo himself as a shallow person. His animated way of talking, his varied interests, his concern for the animals surely refuted this. But her regard for him was diminishing even as she looked at him.

What she was experiencing more than anything else was a deep disappointment; in herself, in him, and that the feeling she had thought they had for one another could never now be acknowledged. And she could not help but feel relief, too, that their love – or what she had mistaken for love – had never been consummated.

'What will you do?' she asked. 'Are you going to stay here on the farm?' She was surprised at how detached she sounded.

'Yes, of course. Why not?' Carlo looked surprised. 'They send me here. It is not for me to decide.'

'You could ask to be moved.'

'You . . . want me to go?'

'I don't know, Carlo. Maybe it would be for the best.'

'But I like it here. Mr and Mrs Dobson are very kind to me. If I ask to move it look as though I am not happy.'

'Very well, Carlo. Please yourself.' She turned and walked away, aware of him staring confusedly at her retreating back.

She was never to know whether Carlo had, in fact, said anything to the authorities, or whether they were the ones to make the decision, but within a week he had been transferred to another farm.

Connie had made no comment about Abbie's friendship with Carlo. Abbie, indeed, had persuaded herself that her colleague – she could not think of Connie as a friend – knew nothing about it. It was only when the young Italian had gone that the other girl made any reference to him at all. And now, when she did so, Abbie realised that this in itself was significant; the fact that Connie had behaved all along as though Carlo was not there.

'So we've seen the last of him then,' she said, as they prepared for bed on the day that Carlo had, so suddenly, disappeared. 'Good riddance to bad rubbish, that's what I say.' She looked meaningfully at Abbie, as though waiting for her reaction, but Abbie kept quiet. 'I couldn't stand the fellow,' she went on. 'Sucking up to Mrs Dobson, getting himself asked into her kitchen when he knew damn well he was supposed to keep his distance. But I reckon they're all alike, these smarmy Italians. They don't half fancy themselves.'

'Oh, I don't know about that.' Abbie, even though her opinion of Carlo had changed somewhat, could not join in outright condemnation of him. She sat down on the stool by the dressing table, picking up a brush and running it through her hair with a display of nonchalance that she certainly was not feeling. 'I don't see how they can all be alike, any more than we are. I thought Carlo was quite a nice sort of chap.'

'Aye, I had noticed.' Connie's tone was brusque and there was not a trace of humour in it, nor in her eyes as she continued to look searchingly at Abbie through the fly-blown mirror. 'I'd've had to be bloody blind not to notice you and him.'

'What . . . what do you mean?' Abbie put down her brush and spun round to face the other girl,

'What the hell d'you think I mean? You and that Eyetie, canoodlin' in t'barn, up to yer monkey tricks in t'far field. And you thought as how none of us knew? You must be even greener than you look, Abbie Winters.'

Abbie discerned a look of contempt, almost of hatred, on Connie's face and she began to feel very disturbed; quite frightened, in fact, although she wasn't sure of what she had to be frightened. Carlo had gone now. She and Connie had never been friends. She had not found she was able to warm to her particularly, but she had thought they had rubbed along well enough together as working colleagues. Now she was not sure.

'You've got it wrong, Connie,' she said, as calmly as she could and not entirely truthfully. 'Carlo and me . . . there was nothing like that. I'll admit I liked him. We got on well together and . . . and he used to tell me about his home and his family. That was all.'

'Oh, that was all, was it?' sneered Connie. 'Pull the other one. It's got bloody bells on it!'

'We were just good friends, I tell you. That was all.' Abbie, to her consternation, realised her voice was getting louder. 'I must admit I'm sorry he's gone,' she added, more quietly, 'but that's the way it is in wartime.'

'Aye, you're not bloody kidding!' Abbie had never heard her colleague swear quite so much and realised she must be in rather a disturbed state. ' "That's the way it is in wartime," ' she mimicked. 'Don't you forget it, Abbie Winters. Oh aye, it's

245

wartime all right, and they're our enemies, and my Jack may well be giving his life, for all I know, fighting such as that . . . that blasted Eyetie. I haven't heard from Jack for ages. God knows if he's still alive . . .'

'Oh, Connie, I'm so sorry,' gasped Abbie. 'I didn't realise.'

'No, you wouldn't, would you? Your sort never do.'

Abbie wasn't sure what she meant by 'your sort', although she knew that the two of them were poles apart as far as family background was concerned. Just as she and Doreen were, but in that case it didn't matter. But she realised the girl was very upset and that she, in part, because of her friendship with 'the enemy' was responsible.

'I'm sure Jack will be all right, Connie,' she said. 'If he wasn't . . . you would have heard, wouldn't you? And it takes a long time for the mail to get through.'

'Aye, I keep trying to tell meself that,' said Connie, in a flat sort of voice. She gave Abbie another very searching look. 'I didn't like what you were doing. It's no good pretending I did.'

'Then why didn't you say something before, when Carlo was here?' asked Abbie. 'If you thought you knew something . . . although you were wrong, I can assure you.'

'None of my business, is it?' Connie's eyes were cold and hard. 'But it would be Mr and Mrs Dobson's business . . . if they knew. If they were to find out.'

Abbie felt herself go suddenly cold. 'Do they know, do you think? About Carlo and me?' As soon as she had uttered the words she wanted to retract them. Damn! She had as good as admitted it now.

Connie's eyes narrowed. 'I though you said there was nothing in it? "We were just good friends," ' she mimicked again.

'So we were,' replied Abbie. 'I wouldn't want them – Mr and Mrs Dobson – to think there was anything else.'

Connie shrugged. 'I can't say whether they know or not. Happen they do, happen they don't. Anyroad, he's not here any more, is he? Happen you'd better ask yerself why he was moved so sudden, like. Night-night . . . sweet dreams.' There was nothing at all friendly about the girl's good-night words as she jumped into bed, pulling the blankets tightly around her.

Worried about Jack or not, in a few moments Connie was fast

asleep and snoring rhythmically, whilst Abbie lay awake for half the night. The very next day Carlo's replacement arrived, another Italian prisoner, a much older man in his forties. Abbie decided she would keep her distance from this one. Not that she need have worried. Luigi was a taciturn sort of fellow who hardly knew any English, speaking only when he was spoken to. But he worked hard and that was all that really mattered on the farm.

Just as she never knew why, or at whose request Carlo had been moved, neither was Abbie ever to know the reason for her own removal to a farm in East Anglia. It was a few days later that she received the communication from Headquarters to say she was being transferred to Heathcote Farm near East Dereham in the county of Norfolk. This was to take effect from the end of March; the date given was only a couple of days hence. She was to make her way to Norwich station where transport would be provided to take her to the hostel. She was to stay in a WLA hostel this time, and not on the farm.

'We're sorry to see you go, lass,' said Mrs Dobson, on the morning of her departure. 'Aren't we, Alf?'

'Aye, so we are. But happen it's all for the best, eh?' Mr Dobson's glance was kindly; he had never been anything but kind to her, but Abbie noticed a hint of censure in his glance now, as well as regret. Or was her guilty conscience making her imagine it?

The fact that Connie was nowhere to be seen as she rode away in the car with Mr Dobson was significant. So were the farmer's words as he said a last goodbye to her at Leeds station. 'I'm sorry for the way things have turned out, lass. It weren't our doing, you know, the missus and me. We don't want to lose yer, but we had no choice. They don't like that sort of thing, y'know, and Connie . . . well she can be a bit spiteful, like. I reckon you're best away from her, Abbie lass. Cheerio then.' He held out his hand. 'It's been nice knowing yer.'

'Goodbye, Mr Dobson.' She had never got used to calling him Alf. 'And . . . thank you. Thank you for being so kind to me.' She could only guess that Connie had complained about her to the authorities and she was being removed to a farm and hostel well away from any POW camp.

Chapter 16

For each six months they served the land girls were given a red cloth half-diamond to sew on to their greatcoats. Abbie had two of these now, forming a full diamond on her coat sleeve. She had been in the WLA for just over a year and already she was on her way to her third farm. The hostel she was bound for would be her fourth set of digs, counting the first hostel where she and Doreen had done their training.

Abbie was thoughtful as the train clattered along the track, on the first stage of her journey to Norfolk. She would have to try and keep her nose clean, she decided, or she would be getting a name for being a troublemaker. The very idea was ludicrous. She, Abbie Winters, who before she joined the Land Army had been almost afraid of her own shadow, had twice been removed from the scene because of complaints. The first time, of course, the complaint had been hers; hers and Doreen's against the tyrannical Mr Rawnsley. But now she was the one being complained about, or so she guessed. It would be all the same, she surmised, in the eyes of the War Ag. Committee: this is a young woman they must watch.

She had never been to East Anglia before, and as she gazed through the carriage window she was surprised, and a little dismayed, at the bleakness of the scene. She had thought that the Fylde countryside was flat and uninteresting, but in the Fylde there were, at least, clusters of trees and small coppices here and there to add a touch of variety to the landscape. The vista here was characterised by the sparseness of trees; only occasionally was there a clump of two or three, seeming to huddle together for comfort, bending their trunks against the severity of the wind that blew constantly across the fens. Much of the area had been given over to the Air Ministry and they passed, frequently, groups of Nissen huts at the side of vast airfields. The roads between the fields were long and straight, cutting through the marshland to the distant coast, unlike the twisting country lanes Abbie had been used to near Blackpool. The expanse of sky seemed vast, never ending, and there was a clarity of light here, an iridescence in the pale azure blue, that added a touch of beauty to an otherwise unpromising scene.

The WLA hostel was a manor house, not too far from the city of Norwich, requisitioned for the duration of the war. Much more sumptuous than the first hostel she had stayed in, thought Abbie, when she first set eyes on the Georgian house, built of dark red brick, and inside she was impressed by the polished floors, high ceilings and sparkling chandeliers, the wide staircases and carved balustrades. Admittedly, the beds provided for the young women were of the regulation type, with iron bedsteads, hard mattresses and army blankets, but it was a good deal more pleasant to sleep in a room with rose-patterned wallpaper and pink curtains than in a barren Nissen hut.

Abbie found she was to share a room with three more girls and they made her feel welcome at once. They were used to chopping and changing, they told her. Like Abbie, some of the young women at the hostel had been in two or more digs before this one, and as they didn't ask why she had been moved from West Yorkshire she didn't tell them. It was sufficient for Abbie that she felt she would be able to settle down here. Indeed, she had no choice; she knew she had to like it or lump it, but it would be easier if she could be on good terms with her room-mates.

Looking back she realised she and Connie had never got on very well, having had very little in common. At one time it would have been well nigh impossible for Abbie to muck in with a set of girls she had never met before. She had had to do so at the first hostel, but there she had had the bolstering companionship of Doreen. Here she was on her own; but she was learning, gradually, to adapt to each new set of circumstances. At least this billet was a pleasant one, and the next day, when she met Mr and Mrs Heath, the tenants of Heathcote Farm, she found they were very pleasant, too. Maybe she would be able to settle down here for the duration of the war, however long or short that might be. There was certainly no end in sight as yet.

She tried to push all intrusive thoughts of Carlo and the hurt he had caused her, plus her feelings of embarrassment and guilt at being such a fool in the first place, firmly to the back of her mind. She was being given a fresh start.

'There's a dance at the sergeants' mess on Saturday night,' said Brenda, one of Abbie's room-mates, when she had been there a couple of days. 'Coming?'

'Er, yes ... I don't see why not,' replied Abbie. 'Where is it?'

'The aerodrome down the road. The home of 102 Squadron – my boyfriend's squadron,' said Brenda. 'There are quite a number of airfields in this neck of the woods – Bomber Command, you know. But this one's the nearest. It's only about half a mile away.'

'How do we get there?'

'On our bikes. How else?' Brenda grinned. 'Same way as we get to our farms.' Abbie thought again how lucky it was that she had learned to ride a bike, at Doreen's insistence, before she joined the WLA. What a fool she would have looked if she had not been able to do so.

'We have dances here now and again,' said Brenda. 'They let us use the big dining room with the carpet rolled back and the furniture pushed to one end. They put on a bus from the airfield to bring the fellows – and the girls as well, of course; quite a lot of the WAAFs come. But we prefer it at the mess; it's more free and easy somehow. And they've got a smashing little band. Only three of them; piano, drums and saxophone, but they sound real professional. The fellow that plays the piano – I think he's one of the flight sergeants – he's as good as that Rawicz and Landauer any day.'

Rawicz and Landauer ... Abbie was suddenly transported back in her mind to the Palace in Blackpool, the first time she went out with Doreen, the night she met Peter Horsfall. Almost two years ago. She hadn't thought much about Peter lately – her friendship with Carlo had made her forget so many things – but moving into East Anglia had brought him into her thoughts again. She remembered that he had been posted to one of the airfields in the east of England, but she had no idea which one; there were so many of them. For all she knew he may well have been moved again, or it was possible that he may no longer be there. He might have 'bought it'. That was the expression the RAF used when someone was missing or killed. He had wanted to fly, she recalled, and so many of the air crew, young men like Peter, failed to return from their bombing mission. The thought had saddened her and that night she had said a little prayer, the first time she had thought of him for ages.

It was the first time Abbie had seen an aerodrome at such close quarters, a vast level expanse on the skyline as they approached on their bicycles. Beside the huge hangars there was a glass-fronted watch tower, and a tall water tower with other lower buildings clustered around them, and on the other side of the runway what looked like hundreds of Nissen huts. Brenda, whose boyfriend was a member of an air crew, had told Abbie that there were twenty such crews, each of seven men, and as the ratio of ground crew to aircrew was ten to one the population of this particular base must be well over a thousand. And these airfields were liberally scattered over the whole of this area of East Anglia. Thousand upon thousand of young men – and women – fighting in this relatively small area, many of them involved in nightly bombing missions, in defence of their tiny country. The thought was mind-blowing, but at the same time, thought Abbie, it made you feel very proud to be doing your bit. She was glad she had kept her uniform on tonight. During the time she had been in the WLA she had learned to wear it with pride.

As they rode closer they could see the four-engined Lancaster bombers ranged round the rim of the landing field with the identification of the squadron painted in a dull red on the dark grey sides of the aircraft. At various points around the perimeter the white windsocks swung stiffly in the strong March wind, and on the roof of the watch tower the cups of the anemometer whirled constantly.

Brenda, who had been many times before, knew her way around. 'We'll leave our bikes here,' she said, propping her machine up against the corrugated iron wall of one of the larger huts. 'They'll be OK. Nobody'll pinch 'em. The problem, of course, is remembering which one is yours.' There were half a dozen similar bikes there already so Abbie, Brenda and Hilary, the other girl who had come along, left theirs a little distance apart.

The dance was already well under way and, as they entered, a quickstep was being danced to the tune of 'Don't Sit Under the Apple Tree'. The room, at a first glance, appeared to be a mass of air-force blue, just as the dance halls at Blackpool had seemed to be, Abbie recalled – not surprising as this was an RAF base and many of the girls dancing wore the WAAF uniform. Here and there, however, there was a bright splash of colour, a red or yellow or floral dress worn by a local girl, but there did not appear to be a single man who was not in uniform. Abbie, again, felt glad she had on her dark green jersey and khaki breeches. Not as attractive, maybe, as a pretty dress, but the girls of the WLA were always made very welcome at dances and they were seldom without partners.

Brenda disappeared on to the floor almost at once with the young sergeant who had been waiting for her. Gosh! He did look young, thought Abbie, no more than eighteen or so, with his fresh complexioned baby face and short blond hair, but Brenda had told her he was twenty-one, the same age as Brenda herself, and Abbie. The two of them had recently got engaged and planned to get married before very long.

Abbie and Hilary sat down on two of the iron-framed chairs that surrounded the dancing area and Abbie stared around. There was no disguising the fact that this was a Nissen hut, but a few red, white and blue streamers and Union Jacks strung across the ceiling added a touch of gaiety and the whole atmosphere was one of cheerfulness and *joie de vivre*. The little band on the dais at the far end of the room sounded, as Brenda had said, very professional. All three of them were members of 102 Squadron. The drummer with his rhythm section of side drum, kettle drum and cymbal was well into the swing of things, his black hair flopping across his brow at each pulsating movement. They were playing a waltz now and the wail of the saxophone seemed just right for the soulful tune of 'Russian Rose'. This was not Abbie's favourite instrument. To her a saxophone always sounded shrill and slightly discordant, but this ginger-haired lad certainly knew his stuff, throwing back his head and pointing the silver instrument to the ceiling at each crescendo.

The pianist was good, too, his touch in this particular number delicate and poignant. He was making the keys positively sing although the instrument, quite obviously, was not a good one; an old-fashioned upright that had seen better days, typical of many to be found in NAAFIs and smoky bars. It was strange how people never seemed to notice the pianist unless he – or she – was either very good or very bad. Abbie, as a pianist herself, knew this to be the case. She had glanced at this pianist, the third member of the group, but by far the least showy. Now she looked at him again, admiring the way he was able to coax such a melodious sound from such a tinny instrument.

He had fair hair, cut very short in what they called a crew cut, a style favoured by the American GIs who were now here in full force. He had a rather long nose and thin features and he sported quite a large moustache as did many of the RAF flying men. Although he was sitting down Abbie could tell he was tall, his long legs only just fitting beneath the piano keyboard.

And as she looked at him her heart suddenly gave the most tremendous somersault. She opened her mouth in a startled gasp and nearly cried out aloud. No! It couldn't be. But when she looked again she knew that it was. It was Peter Horsfall. It was the crew cut and the moustache that had fooled her. The Peter she had known had had longish hair and was clean-shaven, but as she looked now at the longish nose and the slightly hooded eyes, she knew it was him.

'Would you like to dance?' said a voice at her side and Abbie was jolted out of her reverie.

'Er, yes . . . thank you,' she said, taking to the floor with the young corporal. But her mind was not on her dancing. 'Could you tell me the name of the pianist?' she asked her partner. 'You see . . . I think I know him.'

'Yes, that's Sergeant Horsfall,' said the young man, giving her an odd look. 'Peter, they call him. But not me; I don't call him Peter. I don't really know him, only by sight. He's air crew and I'm . . . well, I'm ground crew. There's not the same glamour attached to us,' he added, a trifle wistfully, Abbie thought, and at once she felt sorry.

'Don't say that. You're doing an important job. And you're a corporal, aren't you?' She smiled at him, trying to set him at his ease in a way that she would never have dreamed of doing at one time.

'Oh yes, I'm no longer an "erk",' he grinned. 'As a matter of fact I'm a fully trained fitter, Group I, for what it's worth, same as I was in civvy street.'

Abbie resisted the urge to crane her neck as they danced past the small platform at the end of the room, but her partner must have been aware of her interest.

'You do know him, Peter Horsfall? He's the bloke you thought he was?' he asked.

'Oh yes,' she replied. 'It's him all right. I thought it was, but I wanted to make sure. He wasn't a sergeant, you see, when I knew him. He was only AC1. I met him in Blackpool – that's where I live – before I joined the Land Army. But I didn't recognise him at first. He didn't have a moustache then, and now he looks older, somehow,' she added.

'Not surprising,' said her partner. 'Some of the blokes age rapidly when they start flying. Others never get a chance to.' The last few words were spoken quietly, as if to himself, and Abbie felt herself go cold. 'I'm Terry, by the way,' he said, recovering himself and smiling at her. 'Short for Terence. And you are .. ?'

'Abbie, short for Abigail.'

'Well, Abbie, you land girls are doing a grand job . . . I think I'll go and ask your friend for a dance now,' said Terry as the waltz came to an end. 'I can tell you're just dying to go and say hello to your old mate.' Abbie felt sorry she had made it so obvious.

'No, it's all right,' she said, feeling a little unsure of herself again and somewhat conscience-stricken that she had talked about Peter rather than concentrating on her partner. She was nervous, too, at the idea of approaching Peter and starting a conversation. 'I mean . . . yes, you must go and ask Hilary to dance. That's what she's called, my friend; Hilary. But I can't really go and talk to Peter, can I? Not now; they'll be starting to play again soon.'

'It looks to me as though they're having a bit of a break,' said Terry. Peter was sorting through a pile of music and the drummer had just lit a cigarette. 'Off you go. Don't be shy!' He grinned at her. He really was a very pleasant young man. 'I'll go and chat to Hilary. She looks like a nice girl.'

'She is,' said Abbie, wondering why he hadn't asked the other girl to dance in the first place instead of her. She had still not entirely got over the surprise she felt whenever anyone asked her for a dance. Terry had already gone and there was hardly anyone in the centre of the floor but herself. With a hundred butterflies dancing inside her stomach she walked to the end of the room and stood by the piano. Peter looked up curiously.

'Hello,' she said. 'It's Peter, isn't it? Do you . . . remember me?'

Peter's blue eyes were puzzled for a moment, just a very brief moment, then the light of recognition dawned in them and, with it, a look of pure delight. 'Abbie!' he exclaimed. 'Is it really? You look so . . .' He didn't finish the sentence and Abbie wondered what he might have been going to say. So slim? So different? So much more attractive, maybe? 'I would hardly have recognised you,' was what he went on to say. 'Good gracious! What a surprise, but what a wonderful one. How lovely to see you again.'

There was no doubt that he was pleased to see her, and for a moment Abbie felt tongue-tied. She could only stand there, smiling at him, as he got up from the piano stool, then leaned forward and kissed her on the cheek.

'It's . . . it's lovely to see you again, too, Peter,' she managed to say at last. 'I didn't know it was you, not at first. You look . . . different.' It wasn't just the moustache and the hair, she realised. As she had said to her dance partner, Terry, Peter looked older, and now she was looking at him more closely she could see lines around his eyes and mouth that had not been there before.

'It's the moustache, I dare say.' He grinned at her and she noticed again, as she had when she had first met him in the Palace ballroom, that his teeth were large and rather uneven. But attractively so and they were certainly not nicotine-stained like those of many of the servicemen. 'Listen, Abbie, we must

256

get together and have a chat and a few dances. No, I won't be playing all night,' he added, at her questioning look. 'We have a break halfway through the evening, and then a bloke plays the piano accordion for most of the second half. I'll have to go now. They're waiting for me.' The other two members of the trio were casting curious and amused glances in their direction. 'See you later, Abbie.' He took hold of her hand and gave it a squeeze before sitting down again at the piano.

'Aye, aye, you're a dark horse, Peter . . .'

'She looks like a bit of all right . . .'

She heard the comments of the drummer and saxophonist as she walked off the dance floor and she suddenly felt about ten feet tall.

It was about half an hour before the trio finished their stint, during which time Abbie was asked to dance several times, and she noted with pleasure Terry's growing interest in Hilary. Hilary Meadows was a quiet girl, quite pretty in a mousy sort of way, and inclined to be shy. Abbie empathised with her and was pleased to see her emerge from her shell as Terry chatted to her and asked her for several more dances. As for Abbie, she found herself looking forward immensely to the time when Peter would join her. He smiled and winked at her a few times as she danced past and she felt a warmth suffuse right through her, from the top of her head to the tips of her toes. Not a feeling of desire, such as she had known several times when she was with Carlo; a desire that had ended, time after time, in disappointment and frustration, and, in the end, in guilt and embarrassment and anger at her own stupidity. No, this was a feeling of affection and friendship, of kinship, and the presentiment that it was . . . oh, so right. Abbie felt, in meeting Peter again, that things were back on their right course, that she was, in a sense, coming home.

'Come on, let's go and have a drink,' he said, when, at last, he joined her, taking her arm and guiding her to the other end of the room where there was a small bar area. 'Lemonade, is it, Abbie? If I remember correctly you're not fond of the hard stuff, are you?' His eyes were twinkling good-humouredly and she was aware that he was teasing her, but very kindly.

'Oh, I'm a big girl now, Peter.' She smiled at him. 'I mean

257

. . . I've grown up a bit since those days. I'll have a shandy, if you don't mind.'

'I just can't get over it, meeting you again like this,' said Peter, as they sat down at one of the small tables. 'So you're in the Land Army? I take it you've not been in this area long, or I would have come across you before?'

'No, less than a week,' she told him. 'The billet's at the manor house down the road, but my farm's near East Dereham. I was in Yorkshire at first, doing my training, and for the first two farms. With Doreen Miller. You remember Doreen?'

Yes, he remembered Doreen; and Abbie was distressed to hear that Neil, the lad he had been friendly with in Blackpool and who had been posted along with Peter to Norfolk, had been killed in a bombing raid. Abbie had not liked Neil particularly and she recalled how Doreen had very quickly sent him packing, but she was sad to hear of his death, as she would be to hear of the demise of any young airman.

'We weren't in the same crew,' said Peter. 'But he was a gunner, same as me. Six months ago it was he bought it. I still can't get over him not being here. He was so very . . . so very much alive, was Neil. And such a daredevil. I really believe he thought he was indestructible. But . . . it happens. Chaps you've been laughing and joking with in the barrack room, having a drink with 'em the night before, maybe, and suddenly, the next day, they're not there any more. That's something I've never got used to . . .' He was silent for a moment, his eyes out of focus as he stared grimly across the room. Then, just as quickly, he looked back at Abbie and smiled. 'However, we must not be morbid. How is your mother? How did you manage to persuade her to let you join the WLA?'

'She didn't really have any choice, Peter. I was twenty a few months after . . . after I met you, and I would have been called up if I hadn't volunteered. It was either this or the ATS or WAAFs. Mother's . . . well, she's OK, I suppose. I think we get on better than we used to. Maybe it's a question of absence making the heart grow fonder, as they say. What about your parents? They live not far from here, don't they? They must be pleased that you're so near, and I'm sure they're very proud of you. I see you're a sergeant now.'

'It's automatic promotion, Abbie, when you're air crew. I'm being considered for officer training, actually. I may well go in for it when I've finished this tour of ops. Fingers crossed, of course ...' He didn't say why he would cross his fingers; whether it was for being accepted on the course, or for finishing the tour safely. 'Mum and Dad would be proud of me then, all right. Yes, they were very pleased when I was posted to Norfolk. My home's in Wymondham so I'm able to get there quite easily when I'm not flying.'

'Yes, I've heard of Wymondham,' said Abbie. 'Near Norwich? Wy – mond – ham; that's how it's spelled, isn't it, but it's pronounced "Windham".'

'You must come home with me and meet my parents,' said Peter. 'Soon ... You will, won't you, Abbie?'

'Yes, of course I will,' she replied. They looked at one another without speaking for a few seconds, and Abbie knew in that moment that she would be seeing Peter again and again. She had lost him, but now, by some miracle, she had found him and she knew that their relationship was something that was meant to be. 'I'm so happy, Peter, that I've met you again,' she said.

'Same here, Abbie.' He leaned across the table, taking both her hands in his. 'When Doreen came to tell me – you remember? – that you couldn't meet me, I was disappointed. But then I thought, Oh well, maybe it's all for the best. Your mother, you know ... I knew you were having problems with her. But now – oh, Abbie, I just can't believe it. And how different you look.'

'I'm not as fat, you mean.' She gave a rueful smile.

'You're slimmer, certainly, but I didn't mean that. It's ... everything. Everything about you seems different. That's why I was a bit startled when you came and spoke to me. You look younger, and yet, in a way, you seem much older than that shy girl I met in the Palace ballroom.'

'I've grown up, Peter. That's what you mean, isn't it?' She knew exactly what he meant. Her new hairstyle – short and easy to manage – and her slimmed-down figure, to say nothing of her WLA uniform which, she knew, suited her, had done a great deal to make her look younger than the old-fashioned, almost matronly girl, she had used to be. But she was older in her ways and much more self-sufficient now she was no longer under the thumb of her mother. She was learning to adapt to new people and new circumstances, and having her heart broken – but now completely mended, she thought, as she looked at Peter – had only added to her experience. 'Joining the Land Army has made me grow up and pretty fast, too,' she told him, 'although I'm still not always terribly sure of myself. I missed Doreen dreadfully when we were first separated. She wasn't with me at my last farm and I was so nervous at the thought of being without her. But – well – I managed somehow.'

Peter was still holding her hands across the table. 'I'm sure you're doing fine, Abbie,' he said gently. 'Just fine. And now you've got me, haven't you?' He shook his head wonderingly. 'Just fancy, meeting you again like this. It's Fate, isn't it? It must be.'

'I think so, too,' she replied softly.

'Come on, you've finished your drink, haven't you?' Peter gave her hands a squeeze, then let go of them and rose to his feet. 'Let's get out of here. We can't hear ourselves think.' A boisterous group had formed round the piano now and the strains of 'Bless 'Em All' echoed across the room. 'Let's take a walk outside.'

'Won't you be needed again, to play for the dancing?' asked Abbie.

'Not for a while yet,' said Peter. 'Charlie there plays his accordion for a good half-hour or so, then the three of us take over for the last few dances. That lot'll get kicked off the piano now.' He nodded towards the dais where a young airman – another sergeant – was strapping a huge piano accordion on to his chest. 'Sorry we can't have the last waltz together, Abbie, but we'll have a dance or two, shall we, when we come back? See if we remember all we learned at the Palace?'

He put his arm round her as they left the sergeants' mess and they strolled through the grounds, between the Nissen huts, neither of them feeling the need, for a few moments, for words. There was a crescent moon, a sprinkling of stars and dim blue lights shining, very faintly, from low buildings on the horizon. The darkness was comforting and companionable. Abbie knew that the nights with a full moon – what they called a 'bomber's moon' – were the ones to dread. In a small copse at the edge of the airfield Peter drew her into his arms and kissed her, gently, lovingly . . . just the once, but she knew this would be the first of many kisses. She put her head on his shoulder and they stood there in silence for several moments, their arms wrapped tightly round one another, savouring the joy of their rediscovery of one another. Eventually – it seemed that she had stood there for ages with Peter's arms around her, feeling loved, at peace and so very happy – he kissed her again. Then they walked, not really caring where they were going, round the perimeter of the airfield.

Peter told her how he had met Alan and Mike, the other two members of the trio, and how they were very much in demand for dances and concerts. This was the group that played when a dance was held at the WLA headquarters where Abbie was billeted. And Abbie told him, making him laugh out loud, about the dreadful Mr Rawnsley and her and Doreen's experiences at Four Winds farm. She did not tell him much, however, about her last farm, certainly nothing about Carlo Bellini, although she felt she would do so in time. There must be no secrets between them. Already Peter had asked her to see him again. Tomorrow, Sunday, he was taking her to Wymondham to have tea with his parents. There was a bus which stopped near the airfield – only a couple of times a day, however – but Peter assured her that his father would run them back in his van. As a master joiner he had a petrol allowance, and it was only a matter of a few miles.

When they returned to the hut Charlie, the accordionist, was playing a slow, soulful melody and a pretty girl in WAAF uniform was crooning into a microphone.

> 'I'll be looking at the moon,
> But I'll be seeing you.'

Abbie recognised the song at once.

'They played that at the Palace,' she said. 'Do you remember, Peter?'

'Indeed I do.' He put his arm around her and they took to the floor, dancing closely together as were all the other couples on the bare unpolished wooden boards. It was a far cry from the Palace ballroom, but Abbie had never been so happy in her life as she felt Peter's cheek against hers and his arm encircling her, drawing her ever closer.

She listened as the WAAF girl sang a second song, the one about having smoke in your eyes. Yes, she had had smoke in her eyes when she had given her heart to Carlo. She had been blind. As it said in the song, all who loved were blind. But this time her eyes were wide open, seeing clearly, and she had never been as sure of anything as she was at that moment – that her feeling for Peter, a small flame as yet, would grow and grow.

Chapter 17

Abbie was made instantly welcome at Peter's home. It was a sturdily built semi-detached house on the outskirts of the town. Abbie guessed, as she took in the solid furniture and Axminster carpets, the fitted cupboards and shelves in nearly every room – Mr Horsfall's handiwork – and the evidence, in spite of the war, of a well-stocked larder, that the Horsfalls were what her Aunt Bertha would call 'comfortably off'.

Peter's mother and father were, indeed, comfortable sort of people, warm-hearted and kind and generous, and after her initial shyness which their friendliness soon dispersed, Abbie found herself liking them more and more. She soon began to feel more at ease in their homely living room than she had ever felt in her mother's elegant lounge and dining room. There was an aura of warmth and hospitality which made her think of Aunt Bertha's little parlour – although the Horsfalls' room was much larger – and of Doreen's home, too, though there was no hint of shabbiness or deprivation here.

Peter and Abbie met whenever they could, usually on a Sunday, which was Abbie's day off. As she explored the area in his company she began to change her mind about the bleakness and barrenness of this part of the country. Wymondham itself was a quite delightful ancient market town with an interesting Abbey Church. Peter told her the story of why the abbey had two large towers. In the fourteenth century the church had been shared by the townspeople and the monks from the priory. When the monks built an octagonal tower, at the same time erecting a thick wall to seal themselves and the high altar off from the parishioners, the townspeople, in retaliation, built the square west tower even larger than the one built by the monks.

It was not in this church, however, that Abbie heard Peter

play the organ, but in the much smaller parish church near his home. He still deputised, occasionally, for the regular organist; and Abbie was impressed at how expertly he performed the stirring organ voluntaries, psalms and hymns, when, only the night before, he might have been playing popular dance tunes with his group from the camp.

'I was never allowed to diversify like that,' she told him. 'If my mother heard me playing pop music on the piano she used to go mad. I remember once I was trying to play 'In the Mood'. I'd even gone so far as to buy a sixpenny copy from Woolworth's – I don't know how I dared, really – and Mother stormed in and nearly slammed the piano lid down on my hands. "Rubbish!" she said. "How dare you play such rubbish? You're ruining your style. If you want to play, then for heaven's sake play properly." Honestly, you should have heard her! And that was only a few months before I joined up.'

Peter smiled grimly. 'I'm not surprised you were glad to get away. I gathered when you refused to let me take you right home – remember? – that your mother was something of a martinet. I hope she's realised by now that you're not going to be intimidated by her any longer. Which reminds me, when am I going to meet the lady? I will have to sooner or later, you know, because you and I . . . well, we were made for each other, weren't we, Abbie?'

It was a Sunday afternoon in early June and after the morning service at Peter's church and the customary Sunday dinner cooked by Mrs Horsfall the two of them were walking round the old part of the city of Norwich, another place which Abbie was coming to love as she became better acquainted with it. Or it could have been that she had fallen in love with Peter, as he had with her, and now even the most commonplace surroundings were touched with a magical glow when they were together. He had told her, several times, that he loved her, and she had replied without any hesitation that she loved him, too. Now, at the top of the cobbled Elm Hill, Peter stopped and, in the shadow of the elm tree, he drew her into his arms. There was no one else around as he gently kissed her, saying again, 'Don't you think so, Abbie? We were made for each other.'

'Yes, I think so too,' she said softly, snuggling her cheek

against the blue serge of his jacket. She had met Peter again only two months ago, but it seemed like much longer. They had spent all their free time together between Peter's 'ops' and Abbie's farm work, and they both knew they were very much in love, unreservedly so. That they would spend the rest of their lives together was inevitable. She was not the least bit surprised at his next words; in fact she had been anticipating them, looking forward to them for weeks now.

'Will you marry me, Abbie?'

'Yes, Peter; of course I will.' She did not even need to think about it. It was what she had wanted him to ask her ever since she met him again.

'So . . .' he said, when he had kissed her once more, 'when am I going to meet your mother? And your father too, of course. I must do things correctly and ask your father if I can marry you. Although I don't really think we need their permission, do we?' They sat down on the circular seat that surrounded the tree and Peter took her hands in his. 'Next Saturday we'll go and choose a ring,' he said, stroking the fingers of her left hand, 'and then perhaps we could both wangle a forty-eight-hour pass and go to Blackpool. As soon as we can, eh? Don't be frightened,' he said, at her anxious look, putting an arm round her shoulders and giving her a squeeze. 'I can be very charming when I want to be, and I'll make your mother like me. You just see if I don't. Anyway, what can she possibly object to? A fine upstanding fellow like me, all my own teeth and hair, and not bad-looking either. I ask you!'

'Oh, Peter, you are an idiot.' Abbie fell against him, laughing. They got on so well together in every way. He was always able to make her laugh and calm her fears. 'Of course she'll like you. How could she fail to? I'll see what I can do about getting a couple of days off. I'm due for some leave.'

But Abbie knew, however charming and respectable and honourable Peter might be – and he was all of those things – her mother would still try to find something of which to disapprove.

Peter might have known Abbie for only a couple of months, not counting the brief time they had spent together in Blackpool, but he knew already that this was the girl with whom he wanted to spend the rest of his life; however long or short it might be, but he tried not to think too much about that. His parents liked her very much and had shown no surprise or even a hint of any misgivings when, the weekend after Peter had proposed to her, he took her home to show off the ring and to tell them that they planned to marry in a few months' time. Before the end of the year, they hoped. By that time Peter should have finished his present tour of ops and, with a bit of luck, might have been accepted for his officer training course.

Before that, however, they had to break the news of their engagement to Abbie's parents in Blackpool; and that, as Peter had known all along, but had tried to make light of to Abbie, was likely to be the stumbling block. Mrs Winters sounded a real old battle-axe from the odd things Abbie had let slip about her, although he knew she always tried not to be too disloyal. She was a tender-hearted girl, his Abbie. Doreen, also, had told him what a so-and-so the doctor's wife was. But however difficult the woman might be, Peter was determined he would win her round.

He could hardly believe his luck – or Fate, or providence, or a sheer bloody miracle; whatever it was – at meeting Abbie again. It was not surprising that he had failed to recognise her at first because she had changed almost beyond belief. He had become quite fond of the shy, awkward and – it had to be admitted – buxom and not terribly attractive girl he had met in Blackpool. But he had been forced to come to the conclusion that it would be pointless to try to continue their friendship. He was being posted and she was virtually a prisoner in her own home. So since that day until the time she appeared in front of him at the sergeants' mess dance, he had scarcely given her a thought.

The Land Army girl smiling at him so winsomely was, in the common parlance of the RAF, quite a 'popsie'. Tall and slim, but not too slim. The green jersey and khaki breeches showed off her curvaceous figure to perfection and her short dark brown hair waved prettily around her cheeks. Her face was still quite rounded. She had always had a bonny face and he remembered the dimple in her cheek when she smiled, but the rosiness of her complexion was something new, the result of healthy outdoor living, Peter guessed. It was her eyes, however, that made him recognise her after that initial moment of uncertainty; her dark brown eyes glowing with warmth and delight at seeing him again.

His parents had taken to her at once. She was a very kind, gentle sort of girl, friendly, too, and very easy to get along with once you had broken down the barrier of her innate shyness. That mother of hers had a lot to answer for, Peter thought, remembering the self-effacing insecure girl she had been, traits which, thankfully, she was beginning to lose.

And now, in the mid-June of 1943, he was to meet this woman who had been the cause of their initial separation. If it had not been for Mrs Winters he would have seen Abbie again in Blackpool as he had arranged to do; he might have corresponded with her and even met up with her from time to time. Pointless, though, to say 'if'; the important thing, the wonderful thing, was that he had met her again and had known at once that this was 'it'. Peter had had only a few girlfriends, and just one or two casual dates with WAAFs at the camp since moving to Norfolk, but it was the first time he had fallen in love. And he knew it would be the last. He was damned if Abbie's domineering dictatorial mother was going to spoil things for them. He was determined to marry Abbie as soon as possible, before anything happened to stop them. He was not quite sure what he meant by 'anything', but there was a niggling feeling at the back of his mind, despite his bravado, that it would not be all plain sailing.

What was more, he now had the added worry about his mate. This would have to happen before he, Peter, was due for his forty-eight-hour pass. He had been hoping for a carefree weekend in which he could forget, temporarily, all his nightmares and fears; fears he had talked about to no one, not even Abbie. But now the spectre of Sandy and what had happened to him – what could so easily happen to any flier – would be there with him all the time he was away.

Abbie had amazed herself at her own bravery. She had decided to make a long-distance call home rather than putting her request – or, more correctly, her ultimatum – in writing. You were allowed only a few minutes for a trunk call and by the time she had told her mother her news the time would be up. This way her mother would not be able to say that she didn't know, that she hadn't got the letter. Besides, writing a letter was rather a coward's way out.

She had made the call from the phone in the basement of the manor house, in the lobby next to what was once the butler's pantry. The WLA girls were allowed to use the phone provided they signed in the appropriate book and the money was collected once a week. It was the first time Abbie had availed herself of the facility. She could, she knew, ring the airfield for news of the returning bomber crews. Several girls, anxious about their boyfriends, did this, but Abbie felt sure they must be regarded as rather a nuisance. Surely the WAAFs on the switchboard had more important matters to deal with? Besides, Peter came to see her, if it was at all possible, each time he returned from an op. If there was any delay she knew it was because of the briefing after a raid and the necessary rest and recuperation period. She knew if there was ever a longer delay – for whatever reason – then she would know soon enough. She tried not to dwell too much on the dangers and she never talked about them to Peter. He had told her how he found it hard to come to terms with the loss of his comrades, but he never discussed the actual flying. He had returned from an op two days ago and now there would not be another one until they returned from the weekend in Blackpool. Abbie felt sure she was experiencing as much trepidation now about breaking the news to her mother as Peter felt at flying over Germany.

Don't be so ridiculous! she told herself as she lifted the receiver to speak to the operator. There can be no comparison. 'Nothing venture, nothing win . . .' The words of a favourite Gilbert and Sullivan song drifted into her mind as she waited for the call to go through. How did it go on? 'In for a penny, in for a pound, It's love that makes the world go round.' Well, that was appropriate at any rate. She loved Peter very much and it was the thought of his love for her that was giving her confidence now.

'Hello, hello. Who is it?' It was her mother speaking, sounding agitated.

'Hello, Mother. It's only me, Abbie. Nothing to worry about . . .'

'Abigail! What on earth . . . Why are you ringing? You've never done it before. Giving me a turn like this . . .'

'I'm sorry, Mother. I didn't mean to alarm you. I just wanted to ask you . . .' She took a deep breath. 'To tell you that I'm coming home for the weekend and . . . and I'm bringing a friend with me. That will be all right, won't it, Mother?'

'Er – yes . . . yes, I suppose so.' Her mother sounded hesitant. 'I can't think of any reason why not. It's very strange, though. You've never . . . Yes, we will look forward to seeing you, Abigail, your father and I. And your Aunt Bertha of course.' She was speaking much more decisively now. 'Which reminds me, I will ask Bertha to make up the bed in the spare room for your . . . friend. Or will she be willing to share with you? I know you must be used to sharing in the – er – Land Army.'

If Abbie had not been in such a state, her stomach churning and the fingers of the hand that was not holding the receiver tightly crossed, she would have laughed out loud. 'No, Mother,' she said. 'That won't be possible. We will need the spare room, if Aunt Bertha would be so kind. You see . . .' She took another deep breath. Come on, Abbie, she said to herself. You can do it. 'My friend isn't a girl. It's a young man. He's called Peter and he's in the RAF.' She was speaking quickly, above the audible gasp and then the cries of, 'What! What are you saying?' coming from her mother. 'As a matter of fact, Mother, Peter is my fiancé. We got engaged last weekend and . . . and he's looking forward to meeting you and Father. I've written to tell you all this. You should get the letter tomorrow.' Abbie had decided to write as well, to make the news doubly convincing. 'But I thought it was better to . . . to talk to you about it as well . . .' She stopped speaking, fully expecting a tirade of disapproval and censure from her mother, instead of which there was an ominous silence. She wondered if her mother had put the receiver down, very quietly, but she knew that was not likely. It was quite possible she might have slammed it down though, in which case Abbie would have heard it.

'Mother . . . ?' she said, tentatively. 'Are you still there?'

'Am I still here? Of course I'm still here. Where else would

I be? I'm just ... unable to believe what I'm hearing. Did I really hear you say you'd got engaged? To some young fellow in the RAF? Behind my back, without even telling me about it ... or your father?'

'I'm telling you now, Mother,' replied Abbie, surprising herself at her boldness. 'I am twenty-one now, after all, and I don't need your permission to get engaged ... or to get married, for that matter.' Abbie knew that she sounded a great deal calmer than she was feeling, but her mother's reaction was only what she had expected. She was determined not to back down and the thought of Peter, even now, was giving her confidence.

'What! Just you wait till your father hears about this. Getting engaged, indeed! Talking about getting married. I never heard such—'

'Calm down, Mother. Father will understand. I know he will. And so will you, when you meet Peter. He fully intends to have a chat with Father ... and with you. To let you see that his intentions are honourable. That's the correct thing to do, isn't it? And we do want your blessing, Mother.' All Abbie could hear at the other end of the phone was the sound of her mother's laboured breathing. 'Anyway, we will see you this weekend, Mother, Peter and I. It will only be a flying visit – a forty-eight-hour pass – so we will arrive on Friday night. I think it will be quite late, so expect us when you see us, OK?'

There was no reply, but to her relief, at that moment, Abbie heard the pips signalling the end of the trunk call. 'Oh, there's the pips. I'll have to go now. Goodbye, Mother. Give my love to Father and Aunt Bertha. Goodbye ...'

There was a few seconds' silence, then, 'Goodbye, Abigail,' said her mother. The receiver went down with a decisive, threatening click.

Abbie found that not just her hands, but every part of her was trembling and, to her consternation, she burst into tears. There was no one around to see her and she quickly made herself snap out of it. She was meeting Peter in an hour's time and on no account must she let him see how much her conversation with Mother had upset her. She only hoped that by the time Saturday came her mother would be more resigned to what must have been alarming news. Abbie had every confidence that her father – much more understanding of late – would be able to make his wife see reason.

When she met Peter she noticed his preoccupation at once and, straightaway, that old feeling of insecurity came over her again. Was he having second thoughts? Had he changed his mind about meeting her parents after she had plucked up courage to make the arrangements? And, heaven knows, that had taken some doing. Arrangements which she knew, even now, could be broken by a letter from her mother saying that it would not be convenient for her to bring her 'friend' home for the weekend. She doubted that even her mother would go to such lengths, but she would not feel secure until she and Peter were safely in Blackpool and inside her home.

'What's the matter?' she asked, somewhat fearfully, noting the abstracted look in his eyes. 'You look worried. It's not . . . your leave hasn't been cancelled, has it?' The thought occurred to her that, if it had, then the evil moment – Peter's meeting with her mother – would have to be postponed, but that was a cowardly way of looking at things.

'No, no; nothing like that.' He smiled at her, but she could tell that it was a forced smile. 'There's nothing the matter.'

'You've not changed your mind . . . about meeting my parents? Or about . . . about me?'

'Abbie, what on earth are you saying?' Peter stopped in his tracks, and underneath the spreading branches of an oak tree, the one solitary tree in the secluded lane along which they were walking, he drew her into his arms. He kissed her lovingly, longingly, then he said, 'Don't talk such nonsense, darling. As if I could ever change my mind about you. There's nothing the matter, really there isn't. At least, nothing that has anything to do with us, with you and me . . . Now, did you get it sorted out, about the weekend? It's all fixed, is it? What did your mother say?'

'Oh . . . not very much,' replied Abbie guardedly. 'She was . . . surprised, I think. But it will be all right, once she's met you. I know it will.' She couldn't help sounding apprehensive, but Peter made little of her doubts.

'Of course it will be all right,' he said, sounding very

271

confident. 'Don't worry. I'll be with you, darling, and I'll be as nice as pie to your mother, you'll see. She won't be able to resist me.' They stood by the oak tree for several minutes. There was no one in sight and Peter's kisses and embraces began to grow more ardent. 'Come on,' he said, eventually, sighing as he let go of her. 'Let's go and have a drink and make arrangements for the weekend, shall we?'

Arms around one another they made for the country inn in the tiny hamlet near to the manor house. But once inside Peter was still preoccupied.

'Peter, what is it?' Abbie took hold of his hands. 'You say it's nothing to do with . . . us, but I know there's something troubling you. Can't you tell me? That is . . . if you want to.' She realised, belatedly, that it might be something to do with flying, and fliers seldom wanted to talk about that.

And so it was. 'OK then,' said Peter. He clasped hold of her hands tightly, as if afraid to let her go. 'I'll tell you about it, if only to convince you that it's nothing to do with you and me. It's my mate, Sandy. You know who I mean, don't you?' Abbie nodded. She had met the young man, but only briefly – a pleasant, friendly lad, a much more outgoing person than Peter, or so he had seemed to be.

'I'm worried to death about him.' Peter stared into space for a moment, not speaking. Abbie waited, then he went on. 'I'm the rear gunner, as you know, and he's the mid-upper. At least he was until he suddenly . . . well, he lost his nerve, went completely to pieces, poor devil. He's gone away for a while. He just can't cope with it all, you see.'

'LMF, you mean?' asked Abbie. She had heard before about air crew members who had gone berserk with the strain of it all. Sometimes they were stripped of their rank, demoted to AC2 again and sent away so that they couldn't influence their comrades. They had 'LMF' stamped on their papers; Lack of Moral Fibre.

'Not exactly LMF,' Peter replied. 'They've given him the benefit of the doubt and he's gone home for a good rest. It had been coming on for quite a while and the squadron leader knew he'd been trying hard to overcome it. Then . . . he just snapped. Just refused to set foot in the bloody plane. It was frightening,

I can tell you. But it could happen to anybody.'

'Oh dear, that's dreadful. What brought it on? Anything in particular?' Abbie guessed that the fear could be made worse by a horrific experience. But she should have known, if that was the case, that Peter would be unlikely to tell her.

'Oh, this and that,' he answered, but she knew that his casual tone was a front. 'Could be any number of things. Some regard it as an easy option, you know, being taken off flying. They've got their feet back on terra firma and they won't fly again at any price. But Sandy's not like that. He'll be back when he's got himself together. I feel sure of it.'

'And what about you, Peter? You're OK, are you?' Abbie was feeling very uneasy about him.

'Me? I'm just fine . . .' But he didn't sound fine and she was not convinced. 'It shook me, like I said, about old Sandy. But . . . I'm OK, honest.'

'How many ops have you done?' She had never asked that question before, and she might have guessed that he would not tell her.

'Oh . . . quite a few. I've passed number thirteen anyway, on this tour. That's always the dicey one. Just bloody superstition, of course, but we're always glad when it's over.' And Abbie knew that it was the thirtieth operational flight that marked the end of a tour. 'Anyway, that's enough of all that. I've told you the story . . . so let's forget about it now, eh? So, about this weekend. There's a train from Norwich at about six o'clock, I think. I'll check and make sure . . .'

Peter had not spoken to Abbie about his fears, about his dread, one that was common to every gunner, of burning to death in a flaming gun turret. Or of how it might so easily have been him and not Sandy who was guilty of showing LMF. When a bomber turned to escape an enemy aircraft the most hazardous position was that of rear gunner. Not only was there the danger, but there were other problems to contend with as well. The cold up there was intense. Frequently Peter found he had to pull long icicles from his oxygen mask while blinking his eyes to keep the lashes from freezing up. He had seen some horrific sights. A damaged plane descending to the sea with the pilot trapped, helpless, beneath his transparent canopy, then the waters closing round him; a sudden great eruption of light as high explosives and fuel converted a bomber and its occupants to a ball of flame. And the sight of German cities burning below him, and knowing that he was, in part, responsible, made him wonder time and again what the hell he was doing there.

But he couldn't talk of any of this to the lovely girl he had, so amazingly, rediscovered. That, in itself, was like a miracle and had gone a long way to making him forget, if only temporarily, when he was with her, the horrors of this seemingly endless war. He had fallen in love with her almost instantly. Now they were engaged and he wanted to marry her just as soon as he could. Perhaps, with a lovely girl like Abbie waiting for him his fears would start to diminish. At all events, the thought of her smiling face and the love in her deep brown eyes was putting new heart into him when the going got tough. He was more determined than ever that he must come through it all safely.

Abbie was amazed at her mother's docility during that weekend, especially after the reaction she had encountered over the phone. She could only think, as she had hoped would be the case, that her father had managed to talk her round and make her see that Abbie was a grown-up woman now, capable of making her own decisions. She was not exactly effusive in her welcome of Peter, but that would have been too much to hope for. But she was quite charming – at least, as charming as Abbie had ever known her to be – playing the part of a perfect hostess and never anything but polite. It was a distant sort of politeness, admittedly, but she had raised no objections even when Peter told both her and Abbie's father that they would like to get married before the end of the year. If they were in agreement? he asked. Abbie knew it would make no difference whether they agreed or not; that was what they fully intended to do.

Her mother had not replied to this, but had bowed her head briefly, as if in acquiescence. Aunt Bertha, needless to say, was delighted to meet Abbie's young man, and her approval of him was most apparent. Her father, too, though he did not say overmuch, was obviously favourably impressed with Peter. The warmth in his usually inscrutable grey eyes as he shook hands with Peter, offering both of them his congratulations and best wishes, could not be denied.

'And the wedding will be here, in Blackpool?' Dr Winters had asked. 'I know it would mean so much to Abigail's mother, and to me, if it could be at our own parish church. Where Abigail was christened and confirmed.'

'We thought ... er ... yes, quite possibly, Father,' Abbie replied, glancing uncertainly at Peter. They had not got round to discussing any final details, but it was more likely to be a quiet affair, either in a register office or at Peter's own church which was, after all, more convenient for them. That was what they had, tentatively, been considering. But if it was a question of keeping on the right side of her mother ... 'We haven't fixed a date yet,' she said, noticing that her mother was not meeting her eyes, 'nor any details, but we'll let you know as soon as we have decided about ... everything.'

Eva was still very quiet, right up to the time of their departure. She shook Peter's hand, then kissed Abbie's cheek saying, 'Take care of yourself, Abigail, and you, too ... er ... Peter. I am pleased to have met you.'

She smiled at them both, but in the split second that Abbie's eyes met those of her mother she was startled by the questioning glance she saw there. Abbie felt a stab of apprehension. She knew, at that moment, that her mother had not accepted her engagement as she had so foolishly believed.

Peter, however, had noticed nothing amiss. 'Well, that wasn't too bad, was it?' he said, when they had left Dr Winters at the station on Sunday afternoon and embarked on the Preston-bound train for the first stage of their long journey back to Norfolk. 'I think I was well received, don't you? Your Aunt Bertha's a love, isn't she, just like you told me she was. And I really admire your father. He's a perfect gentleman and I'm sure he's a wonderful doctor.'

'And ... my mother?' asked Abbie. 'What did you think of her?'

'To be quite honest, darling, she was not the ogre I had been led to expect,' said Peter. He grinned. 'Or perhaps it was me. I told you I'd charm her, didn't I? No, I shouldn't think we've anything to fear there, Abbie. She was quiet, I'll admit. She doesn't give much away, does she? But I should stop worrying about her if I were you. I think she's beginning to see reason. And if you want to get married in Blackpool then that's OK with me.'

Abbie smiled back at him. 'Yes, maybe that's not such a bad idea. We'll have to see what your mother and father think about it, won't we?'

But Abbie could not forget the look she had seen in her mother's eyes as they said goodbye. She didn't voice her fears to Peter, however. He would say she was imagining it.

Chapter 18

'Getting married, indeed! Have you ever heard such nonsense? As if a couple of kids like those two could even consider getting married. Where would they live? And, what is more to the point, what would they live on? Our Abigail has been used to only the very best of everything. How can a young fellow like that – the son of a jobbing carpenter of all things! – hope to provide a suitable home for Abigail. It's ridiculous. The whole idea . . .'

'That's quite enough, Eva. For heaven's sake, let it drop!' Cedric's raised voice broke into his wife's tirade. He was finding lately that it was the only way of dealing with her, to speak sharply to her and then when, hopefully, she had calmed down a little, to adopt a more reasonable coaxing tone. In spite of his anger at her outburst and his deep-seated worry about her state of health – her mental health, more than anything – Cedric could not help but feel a tinge of amusement at her words. It was on the tip of his tongue to remind her that some very great men, indeed, the greatest man who had ever lived, had been the son of a 'jobbing carpenter'; but he thought it best to hold back that remark.

Instead, 'You go on and on like a gramophone record,' he said, trying to smile at her and, thus, lighten the atmosphere. 'You've told me the same thing half a dozen times at least since Abbie and Peter went back. And that was only a few hours ago. Why didn't you speak your mind while they were here? You are not usually reticent, are you, my dear, about saying what you think?'

All the while watching her through the dressing-table mirror he carefully tied the cord of his poplin pyjamas, then, in his usual meticulous way, folded his shirt, trousers and underwear, laying them in a neat pile on the pink Lloyd Loom chair beside the bed. His wife did not answer, continuing to cream her face and neck with languid smoothing movements. For a woman in her mid-fifties she was still remarkably unlined, although small wrinkles, indicative of the strain she was suffering – or pretended to be suffering – had appeared just lately at the corners of her mouth and eyes. Cedric found it hard to believe that the war could affect her so much as she claimed it did. The shortages were not nearly so bad in this household as they were in some other, poorer, homes. Rationing, on the whole, was a fair way of distributing the food, and they could, at least, afford to pay for little extras when they were available. It was Bertha, anyway, who always had, and still did, cope with the household affairs. He was surprised at how much Eva seemed to be missing Abigail. He would have thought she might be relieved at the girl's absence, once she had got used to the idea of Abbie defying her and joining the Land Army – heaven knew, there had never been all that much love lost between the pair of them – but since their daughter's departure Eva's tension and irritability had been getting steadily worse. Now she was as taut as a violin string, ready to snap at any moment.

She narrowed her eyes as she answered him. 'You had told me in no uncertain terms, hadn't you, Cedric, that I wasn't to go upsetting Abigail? That I had to try and make it a pleasant weekend for them. And so I did. Good gracious, I should hope I know how to behave, how to conduct myself properly. People like us have to set an example, Cedric, and that young man would be able to see we are people of some breeding. No, I may not have said what I think, but the very fact that I didn't say very much would be answer enough. You mark my words, that Peter will be having second thoughts about marrying Abigail now he's seen what sort of family she belongs to. And if he doesn't . . . well, time will tell. And all sorts of things can happen in wartime.'

'You are surely not suggesting that Abigail's young man is in any way inferior to us, are you? For goodness' sake, you must face up to the facts, Eva. In my opinion, Peter Horsfall is a very respectable, very well-brought-up young man. Highly intelligent, and you could not wish to meet a more pleasant fellow.'

'Pleasant enough, I suppose,' Eva continued to examine her perfectly manicured nails. 'Yes, I have to agree he was pleasant, but he was trying to get round us, don't forget that.'

'And he thinks the world of Abigail,' Cedric continued. 'As she does of him. I couldn't help noticing the way they looked at one another. I was really touched by it, Eva, my dear . . . and I thought I was too old and set in my ways to be moved by – er – that sort of thing. But that young couple are really in love and—'

'In love! What nonsense you talk, Cedric. How can a girl like Abigail know anything about love? She's far too young, too . . . innocent, too immature altogether for . . . for that sort of thing.' Two spots of high colour glowed on her cheeks as she picked up her hairbrush and started to pull it furiously through the rigid sausage-like curls. She had visited the hairdresser, as she did every week, only a couple of days ago. Now, in a few moments, her neatly coiffured hairstyle was reduced to a halo of unsightly frizz. 'Just look at my hair! That stupid girl has ruined it. I told her not to set it so tightly, but do they ever listen? No!'

She twisted round on the dressing-table stool to glare at her husband. 'I ask you, what can Abigail possibly know about being in love? She hardly knows this . . . this Peter at all. But it won't last, I can tell you that. I really don't know why I'm concerning myself about it because it will all come to nothing.'

'I wouldn't be too sure about that, Eva,' said Cedric, trying to speak calmly. She was getting into one of her rages again and he was worried. The best thing to do was to try and appease her, to persuade her to stop fretting and to make up her mind that what must be, must be. And even he, worldly-wise but often sceptical old doctor that he was, could see that his daughter and that young man were made for one another. If only Eva could begin to see it too, and be happy for them, how much better she would feel. 'She has known Peter for quite a while,' he continued, 'and I happen to think he is a very suitable young man for Abigail. I do wish you could try to see it that way, my dear. This isn't just a casual pick-up, you know, or whatever expression they use nowadays. There are any amount of those in wartime, I realise that, and those sort of marriages don't always last. But they are so happy together – anyone can see that – and I'm sure their marriage will be . . . just fine.'

'Why can't they wait till the end of the war, and see how they feel by then? They'll have changed their minds, I'll be bound.' She was sounding a little less sure of herself.

'I don't think so, my dear. From what Peter was telling me, he developed a . . . fondness for Abigail the first time he met her. That was in the Palace ballroom, right here in Blackpool. Then they lost touch, but as soon as he saw her again—'

'I didn't know that,' interrupted Eva. 'They met in the Palace, you say? It's the first I've heard of it. The deceitful young madam! Do you mean to say she was seeing him, that Peter, all the time she was supposed to be with that Doreen girl? That explains it all. So that's why she kept sneaking off on a Saturday night, because she was meeting that—'

'Oh, come on, Eva, be reasonable,' said Cedric. 'It isn't fair to say she kept sneaking off to the Palace. From what I can recall she only went a couple of times and then . . . well, you remember what happened then, don't you? She was late home and—'

'Yes! And I forbade her to go any more! But I had no idea she was meeting some RAF lad. So it was a pick-up after all, you see. He's just a lad she's met in a dance hall. That's not the place to meet a marriage partner! But I put a stop to it, didn't I? Yes, I remember now . . .'

'Let it go, Eva, please.' Cedric sighed. 'You're working yourself up again, all about nothing. They have met again, haven't they, Abigail and that nice young man? And it seems to me as though it was meant to be. He *is* nice, and I shall go on saying so; very friendly and courteous; just the sort of young man I always hoped she would meet.' But had never imagined that she would, Cedric could not help thinking to himself. Her mother had kept her on such a tight rein, denying her any real girlhood and, though he was loath to admit it, Abigail, at one time, had not been the sort of girl who would attract an admirer. But Peter Horsfall had liked her and remembered her, which only showed what a worthy sort of person he was.

'Come on, love.' Cedric smiled at his wife as he turned back the billowing pink satin eiderdown and climbed into the bed between the pristine white sheets. He patted the side of the bed where Eva slept. 'Come on, Eva, my dear. Don't fret yourself any more. It won't do any good. You'll make yourself ill and all to no avail. You must try to see . . . what will be, will be. Abbie won't change her mind, neither will Peter. Try to be happy for them. Personally I'm glad he's somebody we can approve of . . .'

'You can, you mean,' muttered Eva.

'. . . rather than . . . well, she might have met up with some really undesirable sort of fellow, although I think we can trust Abigail to be pretty discerning.' He was, in point of fact, thinking of Sidney Sidebottom, but he knew better than to mention that incident now. His wife had had no objection then, he recalled, to the idea of Abigail getting married, even to a twerp like that. But it had all been instigated, of course, so that Abbie could be kept under her mother's thumb. Eva's plan had been foiled, however, as had her previous scheme to keep the girl away from the dance hall. Poor Eva. That plan had backfired on her with a vengeance. 'Come along, love,' he said kindly. 'Try and get a good night's rest, then you'll perhaps feel better about things in the morning. I know you're very tired. We were very late getting to bed last night.'

'Stop treating me like a child, Cedric. I'm perfectly all right. There's nothing the matter with me. I know when I'm tired and when I'm not, so don't you start telling me what's good for me.' Nevertheless she got into bed now, lying rigidly to one side, as far away as possible from her husband. 'It wasn't my fault, anyway, that you and that Peter sat up talking half the night.' She turned her back on him, humping the sheet and fleecy blanket around her.

It had been Eva's fault, though, thought Cedric, that she had insisted on staying up as well last night. Her eyes had been drooping with tiredness, but she had sat there in the lounge with him and Peter and Abigail – Bertha had retired at her usual time of ten thirty – hardly entering into the conversation at all, but afraid, he knew, of missing anything. Afraid too, he guessed, of leaving the young couple on their own. Eventually, with a sigh of vexation, she had gone up to bed, unable to control her drooping head and her yawns any longer. Cedric had remained only ten minutes or so longer, and it was then that Peter and

Abbie had told him about how they had first met. He had had no qualms about leaving them on their own. Heavens above, they were an engaged couple and were entitled to some privacy, and he trusted them both not to let things get out of hand.

His wife had been asleep when he entered the bedroom, her gentle snores indicating that she was not feigning sleep, as she so often did. She had slept only fitfully, he knew, since the night she had received the astounding phone call from Abigail. She had carried on so alarmingly that night that he had feared she might have a fit of some sort. He had had to resort to shaking her and gently slapping her face – something he had never done before – to bring her out of her rage. She had stared at him confusedly then, for a few seconds, as though she did not quite know who he was, which had greatly disturbed him. After that first outburst she had appeared to calm down somewhat, though she had not, of course, let the matter drop. That was Eva's way, to worry away at a problem like a dog with a bone. Even now, after she had met the young man concerned, she was still striving against the inevitable. Cedric was only surprised that she had behaved as well as she had throughout the weekend, but, as she said, she did know how to conduct herself when needs be.

She seemed to be sleeping peacefully now but, just in case she could hear him, he leaned over and kissed her cheek. 'Don't worry, Eva,' he said gently. 'It will all be just fine, you'll see. Good night; sleep well, my dear.' She did not answer.

Even if she had been awake he would not have taken her into his arms as an overture – possible, but by no means probable – to making love. It had been a long time, many years, in fact, since he had done so. Any love that there had been between them had gradually dwindled away over the years, and now Cedric was not sure whether he loved her or not. There was a certain fondness remaining, on his part at least, and the familiarity with one another which came from long years spent together. But did that amount to love? Probably not. He was quite sure that she did not love him, but then, he asked himself, did Eva really love anyone?

That father of hers had a lot to answer for. Cedric was convinced that her harsh upbringing had gone a long way towards making Eva the woman she was today. Her mother had died when Eva was a little girl, leaving her only child to the mercies of a dictatorial – Cedric guessed sometimes abusive – father. He had been unable to stop Eva from marrying as she had been well over the age of consent, and Eva had vowed, once she left home, that she would never see her father again. In point of fact he had died soon after their marriage. Cedric had felt sure he could encourage this lovely, though somewhat strange, girl to love him, especially once her father had gone. Eva had been beautiful – she was still was – but aloof and most definitely embarrassed by the intimacies of marriage, and the situation had not improved over the years. Poor Eva . . .

The way she was reacting over Abigail's engagement might suggest that she cared for their daughter, wanting only the very best for her. Eva had insisted, more so of late, that she did love Abbie, but Cedric guessed, rather, that she was afraid of losing her control of the girl.

Her influence had been greatly reduced since Abbie left home. Now, he surmised, she could see Abbie and any hold she still had over her slipping out of her grasp altogether.

'Please God, look after Abigail and Peter,' he muttered silently, after he had recited the words of the Lord's Prayer to himself, something he did every night before settling down to sleep. A habit left over from childhood; ingenuous, maybe, but perhaps it did some good; who could tell? 'Please let things sort out for them before . . . before something awful happens.' He was not sure himself just what he meant. 'And please help my wife to see reason. And, please God, help me to love her . . .' As so often happened, he fell asleep in the middle of his prayerful thoughts.

Eva was not asleep, but she knew her deep breathing had fooled Cedric into thinking she was. She lay motionless, waiting for the change in his breathing pattern which indicated that he was sleeping. Then she rolled over on to her back, staring into the darkness relieved only by a tiny chink of light creeping round the edge of the blackout curtains. Her eyes soon adjusted to the gloom, but she was restive and knew that sleep was still far, far out of her reach. Stealthily, so as not to wake Cedric, she got out of bed and crept across to the window, drawing back the heavy pink curtains which had been lined – very competently, she had to admit, by Bertha – with ugly black sateen material. It was much lighter outside than it was inside the room, Double British Summertime lengthening the daylight until half-past eleven or so.

She stared out at the familiar scene. The wide road with the tram tracks, silver in the faint moonlight, stretching away on either hand; the tall trees, their trunks painted in zebra-like stripes of black and white, which edged the road, giving it, to Eva's mind, an air of graciousness and dignity; and the houses opposite, solidly built and imposing-looking, though not so impressive as this house, the doctor's residence, standing in its own grounds. Yes, this was undoubtedly one of the best areas of Blackpool in which to live. Eva nodded complacently to herself and even smiled, before the thought of Abigail and that RAF lad took over again, submerging all else that was in her mind.

She frowned, setting her mouth in a grim line, feeling the tension which was never far away of late causing the muscles in her neck and shoulders to tighten and her temples to begin to throb with the incipient headache. She was damned if she was going to let Abigail marry a commonplace, tuppenny-ha'penny airman like that Peter Horsfall. Oh yes, he was nice enough, she supposed. He had been extremely polite to her, but underneath his good manners she had perceived a strong will and determination to get his own way. She knew, too, that what he was doing was admirable, taking part in bombing missions over Germany, though he had not spoken much about it. But he was so . . . so ordinary, not at all the sort of young man she would have chosen for Abigail. Besides, they knew nothing about the fellow's background except for the little he had told them. How Cedric could allow his daughter to marry without first meeting the lad's parents she could not imagine. But Cedric seemed to have lost all sense of proportion and fitness these days.

Well, Peter Horsfall would find out that she, Eva Winters, also had a will of iron and she would soon put a stop to all this nonsense. Abigail did not know what was best for her. How could she, a young girl who had been so carefully brought up and shielded from the wicked ways of the world? Eva found herself whimpering a little at the thought of her daughter loose in the big wide world with no one to advise her about what she should do. Only her mother knew what was best for her, but how could she do anything to help her when she was so far away? Eva had been surprised at how much she had missed Abigail since she'd joined the Land Army – another ridiculous idea! – and she had realised, belatedly, that this feeling she had amounted to love.

She had not believed, at first, that she could ever grow to love the child, the tiny red-faced baby that had been put into her arms, looking so much like Cedric and not a bit like herself. She had never wanted a baby. That had not been part of her plan at all when she married Cedric, but things did not always go according to plan, not even for Eva Winters. But she had tried, as she had vowed to herself she would, to do her best for the child. Now she knew that she loved Abigail. She missed her and she wanted her back. She would not rest until the girl was back home where she belonged. Once she was home she would soon forget all about Peter Horsfall; her mother would make sure that she did. And she was determined that she would make it happen.

It was on the Thursday of the week following the visit of Abbie and Peter that Dr Winters came home from his visiting, late afternoon, to find his wife in a state of collapse. She was sprawled on the settee in the lounge, her face deathly pale, appearing at first glance to be unconscious. She did not move when he opened the door, but as he dashed over to her with the words, 'Eva, what on earth is the matter?' she opened her eyes, gasping his name.

'Cedric . . . oh, Cedric, thank God you're here! This pain, this dreadful pain.' She clutched at her chest. 'I thought I was going to die . . . and I thought you'd never come back.' She held out her arms to him and instinctively he put his arms around her, holding her close.

'Eva, my dear, whatever is it?' It must have come on very suddenly, whatever it was, because she had been as right as rain at lunchtime. Quiet, maybe, but she had been unusually quiet for several days now, ever since Abbie had gone back; and since that outburst on Sunday night she had scarcely mentioned their daughter and her young man. 'It sounds like a bad attack of indigestion to me. You say the pain is in your chest? Heartburn, most probably. Those Cornish pasties Bertha made were rather heavy, I must admit.' He rubbed at her hands which felt cold and clammy. 'Have you taken anything? Milk of Magnesia or Rennies? When did it start?'

'Soon after lunch. Soon after . . . you went out. You . . . and Bertha.' Eva's voice was feeble, the words coming in short staccato bursts. 'Can't you see? It's my heart. It's not . . . indigestion, Cedric. I'm having . . . a heart attack.'

He looked at her in alarm, but common sense prevailed. 'Surely not, my dear,' he said gently. 'You've never had a bad heart, have you?' He reached for her wrist. 'Your pulse rate seems normal. Possibly a shade rapid, but . . .' He was quite worried. There was obviously something the matter, but he could not believe it might be her heart. Suddenly Eva slumped sideways, gasping for breath as she lay against the cushions of the settee.

Cedric dashed out into the hall and took his stethoscope from his bag. The examination, in which she did not co-operate at all, only told him that her heart appeared to be quite in order. He knew as a doctor, however, that when the spasms of a heart attack had passed the heart could quite quickly revert to its normal functioning, making an examination comparatively useless. He did not like the look of things, though. She was certainly suffering from something, heart attack or no, and he knew he must get a second opinion. At the moment she seemed to be unconscious, although with Eva you never could tell. He hated himself for feeling so sceptical and he was just debating with himself what was the best thing to do when he heard Bertha opening the front door. Thursday, he remembered, was the afternoon she went to her women's meeting at the chapel. It was also an afternoon on which he did not have a surgery so Nurse Summers would not be coming in. Eva would have been all on her own. Conveniently? He tried to brush away the mistrustful thought, but . . .

'Cedric, I wonder if I could ask you something? A small favour . . . Good gracious! Whatever has happened?' Bertha, coming into the lounge, stopped and stared aghast at the sight of her cousin sprawled out in what looked like a dead faint. 'Eva . . . oh, Eva.' She ran over to her, taking hold of her hand. 'Oh, Cedric, whatever is it? She's not . . . ?' She looked at him fearfully.

'No, she's far from dead, Bertha,' said Cedric quietly. 'She's had an attack of some sort. She thinks it's her heart. I'm not . . . too sure. But I must do something. She certainly seems to be in a bad way and I'm taking no chances.' Making a sudden decision he rose to his feet. 'I'm going to ring for an ambulance. If it was a heart attack and I failed to do anything I would never forgive myself.'

'Yes, yes, of course you must get an ambulance. I don't like the look of her at all. Hospital's the best place for her. We mustn't let anything happen to Eva. Oh dear, oh dear . . .' Bertha kneeled at the side of the settee, holding on to Eva's hand. 'She's been so upset lately. She hasn't said much since Abbie went back, but I could tell.'

'Just look after her for a moment, would you, Bertha, while I go and phone?' Cedric went out into the hallway to ring the hospital, still not entirely sure that he was doing the right thing. But he did need a second opinion about his wife, about her mental state as much as anything. He was not a psychiatrist and knew little about ailments that were not physical. If he could get her into hospital then they would be able to help her in whichever way she needed. He was assured that an ambulance would be with them as soon as possible.

'She's not come round,' said Bertha, looking very scared, as he went back into the room. 'She's been tossing her head and moaning a bit, but she doesn't seem to know I'm here. What do you think she'll say, though, when she finds herself in hospital? I know that's where she ought to be, but knowing Eva . . .'

'I don't much care what she thinks, Bertha . . . Oh, don't get me wrong,' he added quickly as Bertha looked at him in some alarm. 'I care about what's happening to her, although God knows what it is. Yes, I know what you'll be thinking. I'm a doctor, aren't I? But I still don't know everything. I've been worried about her mental state for some time,' he said, almost in a whisper and with an anxious glance at his wife. He was not at all sure what, if anything, she was hearing. Her eyes were still closed, but that did not mean she was not alert in other ways. 'I'm not suggesting she's insane, you understand,' he went on, his voice almost inaudible, 'but she gets quite beside herself at times. I scarcely know how to deal with her.'

'What about them pills you used to give me?' said Bertha. 'They worked wonders, didn't they, when I used to have my funny turns. Not that I've had one lately, thank the Lord. No, that all seems to be a thing of the past. Have you never suggested that she might take something, to calm her down, like?'

'No, I haven't,' Cedric sighed. 'I daren't, to be honest. She would only say I was making out she was mental and that she didn't need medicine. But if someone else were to suggest it . . . I'm hoping they will sort her out when we get her into hospital. Her condition isn't like yours anyway, Bertha. When you used to have your little attacks it was depression, wasn't it, and bad headaches? Besides, we always knew what was causing them, didn't we, in your case? You not being able to leave go of the past. I'm so glad you've managed to put it all behind you now, Bertha.'

'And I think we know what's causing Eva's problem, don't we, if she is sometimes a little bit . . . strange?' said Bertha. 'There was all that awful time she spent with her father and she's never . . . well . . . forgive me, Cedric, but she's never entirely forgotten, has she? You know . . . about the . . . other thing.'

'No, I don't suppose she has, although she never refers to it.' Cedric crouched down at the side of his wife, looking at her bemusedly. He raised one of her eyelids and she did not flinch. She appeared to be in an unconscious state. 'But she did come to care for Abigail, in her own way. Now she's gone – Abbie, I mean – I think it's left a gap that Eva doesn't know how to fill. She can't get used to not having someone to boss around.'

'There's me,' said Bertha drily.

Cedric gave a wry smile. 'I think it's water off a duck's back now, isn't it, Bertha? It's hearing that Abbie's getting married, of course, that has made her worse. I'm not saying it's caused this attack, or whatever it is. I don't know . . . I only know she'll have to get used to the idea of Abbie and Peter, because it's going to happen. Oh, thank goodness, here's the ambulance. You stay here, would you, Bertha, and see to things while I go with them to the hospital? I can't say what time I'll be back.'

Eva stirred a little as the ambulance men lifted her on to a stretcher and carried her out, but she did not seem to care what was happening to her or ask where she was going. She only came to herself fully when she was in the hospital bed in the private room that Cedric had insisted upon. She looked puzzled at seeing, not only her husband, but a strange doctor in a white coat, and a nurse at her bedside.

'Cedric . . .' she called, reaching out her hand and trying to lift her head from the pillow.

The nurse was at her side at once. 'Lie still, Mrs Winters. Don't worry about anything, dear. You're going to be fine.'

'What . . . ? Where am I? What's happened?'

'You're in hospital. You've had a heart attack, just a little one, but you're going to be all right,' said the doctor. 'We'll just let you have a word with your husband, then we'll be back to see to you. Five minutes, Dr Winters.' He nodded at Cedric.

'Feeling a little better now, are you, dear?' asked Cedric when they had gone.

'Yes . . . yes, I think so,' said Eva, sounding puzzled. 'Oh yes, I remember now. That pain, that dreadful pain. I told you, didn't I, that it was my heart. But you didn't believe me.'

'Of course I believed you,' replied Cedric gently. 'I was worried, that's all. You'd never had anything like that before. But they'll look after you very well in here and I'll come in to see you whenever I can. You'll have to stay here for a little while. You don't mind, do you, dear?'

'No, why should I mind? The doctor said I'd had a heart attack, didn't he? So I know I'll have to stay here. I haven't been feeling well for quite some time. You will write and tell Abigail, won't you, Cedric? Let her know that I'm ill.'

'You're not going to be ill for long, Eva,' said Cedric firmly. He stooped and kissed her cheek. 'Make up your mind you're going to get better, there's a good girl. Yes, of course I'll let Abbie know. I'll have to go now, dear. Goodbye . . . I'll see you very soon.'

'Goodbye, Cedric. Thank you for . . . taking care of me.'

Cedric hoped he had only imagined the look of satisfaction in her eyes.

There was a delicious smell of cooking when Cedric arrived home in the early evening. Bertha hurried into the hallway to greet him. 'What did they say? Is it a heart attack? She's getting better, is she?'

'Yes, she's recovering and they're keeping her in for a while for observation.' Cedric took off his coat and the bowler hat that he always wore, winter and summer alike, a mark of his profession. 'I'll tell you about it – as much as I know, that is – over dinner. Goodness, that smells good. I hadn't realised how hungry I am.'

The beef stew, which Bertha had prepared earlier that day and which had been simmering in the oven the whole time he had been out, was truly delicious, as were the fluffy white mashed potatoes at which she knew she excelled. She smiled at Cedric, gratified at the way he was tucking into his meal.

'There's nowt wrong with your appetite, lad, and that's a good sign. She can't be in any danger or else you wouldn't be eating like that. Eeh, she had me worried, though, when I first set eyes on her. They think it was her heart, do they?'

'Well . . . yes,' replied Cedric guardedly. 'They seem to think she'd had a minor heart attack. That is what the symptoms suggest. But I wouldn't be surprised myself if it was just a severe nervous crisis. I've told them about that and they've said they will keep her in for a few days and do various tests. They're not all that busy. It isn't as if Blackpool was an area where there are a lot of bomb casualties, thank God. Although when I say that I feel guilty, thinking of all the poor folks in London and Plymouth and all those other places.' He shook his head sadly. 'Anyway, they found her a private room, which I knew she would want. We'll be paying quite a lot for it, of course, but that doesn't matter. There again, I feel guilty when some folk can't even afford to see a doctor when they're ill.'

'Don't be so hard on yourself, Cedric,' said Bertha. 'You do all you can and more to help people. I know several folk who have had reason to thank you for that clinic you're running. I reckon you've saved the lives of more than a few. Aye, I know we've had very little bomb damage here, but there's no reason for us to wear a hair shirt because of it, is there? Eva was quite settled then when you left her, was she?'

'Yes, I think so. She insisted that I must write and tell Abigail that she'd been taken ill. That seemed to be her chief concern, although I may be doing her an injustice. I will write to Abbie, but I don't see any cause for alarm. I certainly don't want the girl dashing here posthaste. I doubt if she would be able to get leave anyway; she's only just been home.'

'They'd let her come if it was urgent, surely?'

'Let's hope it doesn't come to that,' said Cedric darkly. He knew his wife only too well and guessed what was in her mind. Whether this attack had been brought on by herself or whether it was genuine it made no difference. He was determined that Abbie was going to stay where she was and marry that nice young man. 'You were about to ask me something when I came home this afternoon, Bertha,' he went on, in an attempt to change the subject, although he had, in fact, only just remembered. 'Didn't you say something about wanting to ask me a favour? What is it? I'm sure it will be nothing too demanding, knowing you.'

'Yes, that's right. I did want to ask you . . .' Bertha sounded a trifle hesitant, but she was smiling and her eyes were shining as though she might have some special news to impart. 'You see . . . I had a letter a few days ago from an old friend. No, that's not strictly true. The letter was from her son, and he says he'd like to come and see me. It's somebody I used to know ages ago, when I worked at the Hall, but she died, sadly, and her son . . . well, he says he'd like to get in touch with me. He wants to come up to Blackpool when he gets some leave. He's in the army, you see, stationed down south . . . and I thought, perhaps, he could stay here for a night or two?' Bertha was speaking quickly, her words almost falling over one another, and Cedric looked at her in some surprise.

'Yes, of course, Bertha,' he replied. 'Any friend of yours is welcome here. You know that. But I didn't realise you had kept in touch with anyone from that period of your life. I know it's a time you've always tried to forget. And . . . this young man? Do you know anything about him?'

'He might be an impostor, you mean? Or just after me money?' Bertha laughed. 'Aye, I've got a few bob tucked away, but I don't think he's got designs on that. I think he's genuine enough, but I shall know when I meet him. If I don't like the look of him then I'll let him stay in a boarding house, which is, actually, what he suggested. But if he's ... who I think he is ... ?'

'Yes, yes, of course, Bertha,' said Cedric again. 'I think you're a pretty good judge of character. Who did you say his mother was?'

'Daisy, the lass who was a parlour maid along with me,' replied Bertha hastily. 'Didn't I say? I thought I'd told you. Yes, she was the only one I ever kept in touch with. It was a blow to me when I heard she'd died.'

'But now you can look forward to meeting her son,' said Cedric. 'Good, good. It's nice to have something to look forward to. That stew was delicious. Thank you, Bertha.' His eyes twinkled. 'Dare I ask if there's a pudding?'

What Bertha had told Cedric was not strictly true, but she couldn't tell him the truth – she couldn't tell anyone – until she knew definitely for herself. And it seemed almost too incredible, too impossible, to believe.

It was true that she had had a letter a few days ago from a young man, but he was not Daisy's son. She had kept in touch, though only spasmodically, with Daisy, who had managed to find out somehow – probably from that awful asylum place – where she was living. They had exchanged Christmas cards and the odd letter until Daisy's death two years ago. Daisy's son had written to tell Bertha about this, but that was all she had ever heard from him.

No, this letter was from a young man who signed himself William J. Armstrong. 'Dear Miss Shorrock,' the letter read. 'I am not sure if you are still at the address I have been given. I have been informed that you went to live in Blackpool many years ago, but I realise you may have moved again since that time. Anyway, I hope you will receive this and I hope this news will not be too much of a shock to you. I have reason to believe that we might be related. I was born on 15 July 1915 ...'

Bertha's heart had missed a beat at this, but had almost stopped altogether when she went on to read of his place of birth: the very asylum where she had given birth to little Johnnie!

The letter went on to say that he had, in fact, only discovered that he had been adopted when both his parents, who were living in Southampton, had been killed in an air raid. He had found his birth certificate and it had been a tremendous shock to him to learn the truth.

'Johnnie, Johnnie . . .' Bertha whispered to herself in the privacy of her little parlour, hugging the letter to her breast. Could it be possible, after all this time? How had he found out about her? Probably the same way that Daisy had discovered her address. How she had longed for this to happen. In the beginning, when she had first come to live in Blackpool, she had even thought of making a search herself, but she had dismissed the idea as impossible. Just recently it hadn't hurt so much, so involved had she become in the doings of her beloved Abbie and that nice friend of hers, Doreen; and, lately, that lovely young man that Abbie was going to marry.

But now . . . could she really be about to meet someone of her very own? The address was a camp near Salisbury where his regiment was stationed. Thousands of soldiers were in the south of England, Bertha knew, preparing for something called a Second Front, whenever that might be. He was due for leave in a few weeks, he said. Would it be possible for him to come and see her?

Bertha did not reply straight away. She could scarcely believe it and kept reading and rereading the letter. But now, now she had plucked up courage and mentioned it to Cedric – it was easier, somehow, when Eva was not there – she would write to him this very evening. Of course, there was always the chance, she told herself, that it might not be true. He could be an impostor. But how, and for what reason? She was sure, though, that as soon as she set eyes on him she would know.

Chapter 19

Abbie was surprised to receive the letter from her father telling her that her mother was in hospital with a suspected heart attack. Her first reaction was one of shock combined with a slight feeling of guilt. Supposing her mother were to die and they were at loggerheads? It had never been easy to love her; Abbie had wondered at times if she really did, and now she felt remorseful. After all it was her mother, the woman who had given birth to her, so it was only natural she should feel something. And her mother had been far kinder to her recently.

The letter went on to say, however, that there was no cause for alarm and on no account was Abbie to come rushing over to Blackpool. Moreover, reading between the lines, she felt that her father was sceptical about the diagnosis of the doctors at Victoria Hospital and that her mother could be suffering, rather, from severe nervous tension.

Abbie nodded sagely to herself. Yes, that was more likely to be the case and, what was more, she could guess the reason. Herself and Peter. She made up her mind she would not give way to guilt and self-reproach. Why should she? She had not done anything wrong. She was turned twenty-one, and girls of her age and much younger were getting married nowadays, sometimes when they had only known the young man for a week or two. She wrote a nice friendly letter to her mother saying how sorry she was to hear she was ill and hoping she would be well again soon.

She was even more surprised, exactly a week after her mother's supposed heart attack to receive, not a letter, but a phone call from her father.

'Abbie, phone call for you.' The warden of the hostel knocked on her bedroom door just as she was preparing to go to meet

Peter. 'Can you come now, quickly?'

Abbie's heart was in her mouth as she hurried down to the basement. She had never received a phone call before and her immediate reaction was to think, not of her parents, but of Peter. He had been on an op and she was assuming he had returned safely or else she would have heard. Maybe this call was to tell her some bad news. Feeling sick with apprehension she picked up the phone. 'Hello, Abigail Winters here. Who is it?'

'It's me, Abbie, your father. Listen, dear, I'm afraid I may have misjudged your mother. To be quite honest I thought she was putting it on, the heart attack. Well, no, I don't mean that exactly, but I was sceptical. I thought it was just her nerves, but now it seems—'

'What is it? What has happened, Father?'

'I'm afraid she has had another attack. Her heart; there's no doubt about it this time.'

Abbie gasped; she had not believed her either. 'Oh dear, that's dreadful, Father.'

'She was still in hospital, so they were able to deal with it promptly and they think she'll make a full recovery.'

'How . . . how bad is she?'

'Fortunately it was only a slight attack. Like the first one, the one that I didn't believe was genuine . . . I feel dreadful about that, Abbie. You have no idea how bad I feel.'

'Don't reproach yourself, Father. There's no need. No one knows Mother better than you do and it was only natural that you should think . . . what you did.'

'The point is, dear, she's asking for you. And although I think – no, I'm *sure* – she's in no danger, it would do her a world of good if she could see you. I know you've only just had leave, but if it's at all possible . . ?'

'Yes, Father; I'll see what I can do. If it's on compassionate grounds they're usually quite reasonable about it. I'll ask right away and . . . and I'll be with you this weekend, if I can. It might be for only one night, but Sunday's my day off anyway.'

'Thanks, Abbie. Do try. It isn't just your mother that wants to see you. I do as well. This thing – well – it's really shaken me. To think that I—'

'Don't go upsetting yourself, Father. Nobody could have looked after Mother better than you have.'

'No, I suppose not.' He suddenly sounded like an old man. 'I'll ring off now, dear. I don't think there's anything else to say. I'll see you soon, I hope.'

'Yes, very soon. Love to Mother. Tell her not to worry. I'll come as soon as I can. And love to Aunt Bertha. Goodbye, Father . . .'

Abbie's feelings as she put down the phone were ambivalent. She had been astounded to hear that her mother, after all, really was ill. But how ironic it was that Eva Winters, by some means or another, usually managed to get her own way. And even if she didn't succeed she always had a damn good try.

'You are in the Land Army, Miss Winters, I believe?' said Dr Shepherd, the specialist who was in charge of her mother. He seemed to be a practical and perceptive sort of man. Sympathetic and understanding too, she guessed, but not the sort of person who could be easily hood-winked. He had been of the opinion all along that Eva's heart was not too good.

'Yes, that's right,' Abbie replied. 'I'm working at a farm in Norfolk at the moment. Well, more than one farm actually. I live in the hostel so I'm not tied to one particular farm. I move around, within the area, of course, wherever they need help.'

That had not been the case at first. She had worked exclusively at Heathcote Farm for the first couple of months. Then, when Mr and Mrs Heath had employed a school-leaver, a big strapping lad of fifteen, as a farm hand, she had found that her services were no longer as much in demand there. But why am I telling him all this? she asked herself. I'm sure the doctor isn't interested in listening to my life story. She had a tendency, she knew, always to explain far more than was necessary. It seemed, though, that Dr Shepherd was interested. What was more, she soon began to realise that she might have said the wrong thing.

As he looked at her across the desk in his private room, where he had asked to see her, it seemed to Abbie that his glance was searching. 'So, if you are not attached to just one farm perhaps it might be possible for you to get a transfer? To somewhere in this area, maybe?'

'No!' The alarm that Abbie felt at his words made her almost shout her reply. 'I mean . . . I don't think that would be a very good idea,' she added hastily as she saw the doctor raise his eyebrows. 'I've moved twice already, you see. There were . . . problems at the other farms, and the authorities don't take kindly to too much moving around. Besides, I'm . . . well, I'm happy there and . . .' Her voice petered away as she realised she must sound very selfish. She couldn't go on to say what was really in her mind; that her fiancé was in Norfolk, that she spent as much time as she possibly could with him and that these last few months had been the happiest time in her whole life. And that she was determined that nothing, not even her mother's illness, would bring her back; because she knew without being told that this was the reason for his question. The doctor, however, was looking at her very understandingly.

'Yes, your father has told me about your plans,' he said kindly. 'That you are engaged to a flight sergeant whose home is in Norfolk. But . . . I don't think you realise how poorly your mother is, Abigail. You don't mind me calling you Abigail, do you?'

'No, but I prefer Abbie,' she answered. She frowned slightly as she went on to say, 'I thought the heart attack was only a mild one, that she was making a good recovery? I'm due to go back later today. I'll try to come home as often as I can, but as for moving back to this area . . .' She shook her head doubtfully.

'Yes, the heart attacks were mild ones,' said Dr Shepherd, 'but she has had two already, and each time it puts more of a strain on her. But it isn't just her heart we are concerned about, more her general wellbeing. Her mental state, to be quite candid, Abigail . . . Abbie. Your mother is in a highly emotional state and anything we can do to lessen that – well – I think we should try.'

Abbie looked at him keenly. 'My mother is renowned for getting her own way, or trying to. I don't want to sound unkind or unsympathetic, but my father will tell you the same.'

'He has already told us quite a lot about her. But I feel – your father and I both feel – that perhaps, this time, we should try to humour her. If she could see you more often, and she would be able to do so if you were to transfer to the Fylde area,

298

it would do her a power of good. You are her only daughter. She thinks a lot about you and it's true to say that her health has deteriorated rapidly since you've been away from home. Her mental health is what I'm referring to, actually.'

'But this is wartime, Dr Shepherd,' cried Abbie. 'I'm not the only daughter who's living away from home. And what about the poor women whose sons have been killed? They just have to . . . to pick up the pieces and get on with their lives. It's happening all the time.'

'Very true. I agree with everything you say, Abbie, and what is more I have tried to say the same sort of thing, tactfully, to your mother. But the fact that other people may be suffering more than she is does not mean that she is not also suffering, in her own way. And I believe she is. Her mental state is . . . quite alarming at times. I certainly don't want to see her end up in an asylum. We have had to sedate her once or twice.'

Abbie was horrified. She had had no idea things were so bad. She had visited her mother twice in the hospital this weekend and had found her to be cheerful and much more kindly disposed than usual, and quite resigned to staying there. Unless . . . could they be giving her something to keep her under control?

'Maybe it's because I know your father quite well – and I respect him, too, as a highly competent doctor – maybe that is why I am regarding this as rather a special case. There is something else, too.' He leaned forward, resting his elbows on the desk. 'My home is in Marton, quite near the Moss, and my wife and I have some friends there, a Mr and Mrs Webster. They have a market garden, growing tomatoes, mainly, but all sorts of other produce as well. The thing is – and this seems to be quite a strange coincidence – they are applying for a land girl to go and work for them. I'd only just heard about this when your father mentioned you were in the Land Army, and when I met you I thought, Well, why not? It seems like an answer to both problems, to the Websters' and to your mother's as well. Very providential, I would say. What do you think? If we could arrange it, and I am sure we will be able to . . . ? Would you consider transferring to Marton Moss? Especially as you tell me you're not attached to just one farm?'

Abbie shook her head slowly, not in negation, but because she felt she was being manipulated. Did her father know about this? She had felt so sure that he was on her side, ready to support her in whatever she chose to do.

'Does that mean no, Miss Winters . . . er, Abbie?'

'No, not really. It means I'm undecided,' said Abbie. 'In fact, I'm overwhelmed. I had no idea my mother was so bad. Does my father know about this, about the job on Marton Moss, I mean?'

'Yes, I have mentioned it to him. He seems to think . . . it might be a good idea,' replied the doctor, a trifle guardedly. 'But the decision must be yours, of course.'

'And the War Ag. Committee,' said Abbie curtly. 'We can't decide things off our own bat. You'll have to let me think about it.' She rose to her feet. 'If that's all, Dr Shepherd, I will have to go now. My father is waiting to take me home before I go for my train. Goodbye . . . and thank you for looking after my mother.' She held out her hand to him, but her lips and her eyes refused to smile.

Her father appeared somewhat sheepish on the drive home. 'Yes, I know, I know,' he kept saying as Abbie told him, quite forcefully, that she most certainly did not want to move. 'I know what I said. I felt your mother was pulling a fast one. But I was wrong, wasn't I? And circumstances alter cases. I really am worried about her. What Dr Shepherd says is true. She's heading for a nervous breakdown, almost on the verge of one I would say, and anything we can do to prevent it – well – I think we should consider it. If you were nearer, if she could see you more often . . . Yes, yes, I know, dear, and of course I want you to live your own life, but . . .'

But, in the end her mother had won. 'Peter and I are getting married at the end of the year, Father,' Abbie said decidedly, 'whatever happens. Just before Christmas, we thought, and we're not going to put it off, not for . . . anything.'

'Yes, dear. Of course you must go ahead with your plans. Your mother should be much improved by then, especially if you are living nearer. You will consider it, won't you?'

'It seems as though I've no choice, doesn't it? We had thought we might live with Peter's parents after we were married, then we could be together when he had time off. But if I'm up here . . .'

'Yes, yes, I realise you are making a big sacrifice, Abbie. But don't try to look too far ahead. Just . . . take one step at a time, OK?'

'That's all I can do, isn't it, Father?'

Peter seemed to be much more philosophical about the whole thing. 'That's tough, darling,' he said, 'but it really does sound as though your mother is in a bad way. You'd better humour them. But we'll be married come December, then nothing will be able to separate us.'

'But my job will be in Blackpool – if they agree to move me – and you'll still be down here.'

'Don't fret, my darling. We'll think of something.' He kissed her gently. 'Now, we'd best get this wedding planned, hadn't we? I'll leave it to you to see the vicar at your church. My parents are quite happy for it to be in Blackpool. I think they're looking forward to going dancing at the Tower again. They once spent a holiday there, soon after they were married.' He counted on his fingers. 'Only five months and a little bit more. And then you'll be Mrs Horsfall. Cheer up, darling. It's not long.' But to Abbie it seemed like a lifetime.

There was a dance at the NAAFI soon after Abbie's return from Blackpool, an impromptu affair with gramophone records so, for once, Peter was not playing with the band.

'*I'll be looking at the moon . . .*' crooned Anne Shelton as Abbie and Peter clung together, shuffling rather than dancing round the crowded floor.

'Come on, let's go outside,' Peter whispered. They walked round the perimeter of the airfield as they had done the first night they were reunited and so many times since, their arms around one another, stopping every few yards for a lingering kiss. 'Funny how that has become "our song", isn't it?' said Peter. 'That one about looking at the moon. They were playing it when we first met in Blackpool and now we're hearing it everywhere.' 'I'll Be Seeing You' had, indeed, become one of the most poignant of the wartime songs, holding a special significance for lovers who knew that all too soon they must be parted. And with none more so than Peter and Abbie.

'Yes, whenever I hear it I'll think of you,' said Abbie, knowing that quite soon she and Peter would have to part. 'And whenever I look up at the moon, I'll think of you.'

Peter stopped to kiss her again. 'And I of you, my darling,' he whispered. There was a full moon that night, casting only a milky radiance at the moment as the sky on that midsummer evening was still quite light. Later, as the sky darkened, it would become a real 'bomber's moon', but Peter did not have an op that night.

'Oh, Peter . . .' Abbie clung to him. 'I don't want to go. I don't want to ask for a transfer to Blackpool. I want to stay here with you. You know how we've always said we belong to one another. We can't be parted. We can't!'

'It won't be for long, darling. And you know it's what you have to do . . . don't you? We've already talked about it.' She nodded glumly. 'And of course we belong to one another. A few miles won't be able to separate us. How could they? Promise me that whenever you feel lonely you'll go outside and look at the moon . . . and remember that I'll be looking at the same moon and thinking of you. Nothing can keep us apart, my darling, not for long.'

Abbie knew that was true. Her love for Peter would last for eternity . . . however long that might be.

The rows of greenhouses seemed to stretch for miles, from north to south and from east to west, although the small fertile area of land known as Marton Moss – or often just as 'the Moss' – was, in reality, only just over a mile in width and six miles from north to south. The market garden owned by Mr and Mrs Webster and their son, Jim, covered several acres of land and was, in a contradiction of terms, quite a large smallholding.

Abbie had been loath to move to the area; more than that, her whole being had rebelled against the idea, but in the end she had known that it was what she must do. So she had succumbed to the inevitable and put in a request to be moved, yet again. There had been no opposition as the transfer was on account of her mother's ill health and not on some selfish whim of her own, which was the view the authorities sometimes took of land girls' requests for a move. Also, the Websters were badly in need of help, which was a point in her favour. Or, rather, her disfavour, Abbie had thought at first, hoping against hope that her application might be refused. When she arrived at her new place of work, however, she was forced to change her mind because she could tell at once that she would be happy there, as happy as she could be, that was, so far away from Peter.

She had been in the Land Army for almost a year and a half now and she had to admit that she had never really enjoyed working with animals. Especially the cows; they had always been her greatest bugbear although she was proud of the fact that she could now milk quite competently without the animal kicking over an almost full pail, which was what had happened more than once when she was first learning the art. Here, at the market garden, it was solely arable work, and Abbie knew this would be much more to her liking. The Websters cultivated not only the famous Blackpool tomatoes, but lettuces, cucumbers, cabbages and cauliflowers, mustard and cress, carrots, onions and beetroot – ugh! Abbie still remembered the beetroot sandwiches of her early WLA days – and, to her surprise, it being wartime, carnations, chrysanthemums and spring flowering bulbs.

Mr and Mrs Webster were a kindly couple, in their mid-fifties, Abbie guessed, roughly the same age as her own parents, and their son, Jim, was an amiable fellow of about thirty whom Abbie was sure she would get along with very well.

'I dare say you're wondering why I'm not in the army, aren't you?' he asked whilst he was showing her around the grounds, soon after her arrival.

'No, not really,' replied Abbie. 'I hadn't thought about it.' That was not strictly true. Of course she had thought about it; one always did when meeting a man of call-up age who was not in uniform, but it would not be polite to say so. Anyway, Jim Webster seemed a genuine sort of man and she was sure there would be a good reason. Which there was.

He grinned at her. 'You're just being polite. As a matter of fact, I was in the army; the Lancashire Fusiliers, I volunteered right at the start. But I caught a bullet in my leg in the Dunkirk fiasco, so that was that. They wouldn't let me go back. I'd be more of a hindrance than a help, so they say, though I can't help feeling guilty. It didn't stop Douglas Bader, did it, and he's in a far worse shape than me.'

'He's a flier, though, isn't he?' said Abbie. 'He's not on his feet all the time. I expect it makes a difference. Don't run yourself down, Mr Webster. You've done your bit. You volunteered and that is what's important.'

'Call me, Jim, won't you?' he said, smiling at her. He had a friendly smile and thoughtful blue-grey eyes in a thin-featured face. She noticed now that he did walk with a slight limp although he was trying to disguise it.

'All right, Jim,' she replied. 'And I'm Abbie. I prefer it to Abigail.' That was what his parents had called her.

'OK, I'll tell Mam and Dad. I'm glad you've come, Abbie. We're badly in need of some help. We've had a few assistants, but they've left for one reason or another. The last girl decided she wanted to go and work at the aircraft factory. It's difficult getting someone permanent. The youngsters who live on the Moss usually work for their own parents once they leave school. Most folks round here have their own bit of land, even if it's only a small piece. And it's good that you can live in with us. Mam was pleased about that – a bit of feminine company for her, you see. We thought that you might want to live at home, with you being so near.'

'No, I much prefer to live in,' replied Abbie. 'It's not all that near to my home, well over a mile. I ride a bike, of course,' although she had not yet acquired one of her own. 'But there's no danger of me being late, is there, if I'm right on the spot?' And that reason was good enough for Jim Webster. She didn't know him well enough yet to tell him that on no account would she go back to live at home, that she had, in fact, flatly refused to do so.

That had been Eva's intention once she knew that Abigail had managed – with the help of a timely word from Dr Shepherd – to get a transfer to the Fylde Coast. Marton Moss was an ideal placement in Eva's opinion, and she took little heed of the suggestion that 'live-in' accommodation was available, that Mr and Mrs Webster would prefer their land girl to lodge with them if possible. No, Abigail must live at home. That was what she, Eva, had decided and it was what would happen. That was the whole idea of securing a transfer for Abigail, to get her back again under the family roof.

When Abbie had arrived home at the end of July to take up her new position she found that her mother's health was much improved. She was out of hospital, but was still 'taking things easy', as the doctor had insisted she must do for the time being. Abbie had never known her mother to do anything else. Aunt Bertha, as usual, was rushed off her feet, tackling not only the housework and the cooking but dealing with the copious demands of her cousin. But Abbie chided herself for being uncharitable. She really was pleased to find her mother so much improved. Her unhealthy pallor had quite disappeared and her eyes had assumed their former pale blue brightness . . . and sharpness. Eva had relinquished her position as doctor's receptionist, the job she had done somewhat unwillingly for the last couple of years, to Mrs Cuthbert, the woman from church who helped out twice a week with the housework. Mrs Cuthbert was grateful for the extra money that this convenient little job gave her and Abbie was relieved that this extra chore had not fallen to Aunt Bertha, as it might well have done. Bertha had more than enough to do already, but seemed quite content with her lot. Abbie detected a glow of happiness in her aunt's eyes which was giving her face a radiance it had never had before. Could it be at seeing her, Abbie, again? It might well be; Abbie knew that her aunt thought a lot about her and would be pleased she was back in Blackpool, but she felt that there must be something more to explain Bertha's obvious contentment. Every now and again she would start smiling, for no apparent reason, as though she just could not help herself.

Abbie soon discovered that the light in her mother's eyes was one of elation because she thought she had won the day. 'It is lovely to have you home again, Abigail,' she said, 'after all this time. It will be much better for you, living here, than in some draughty uncomfortable farmhouse. I'm sure I don't know how you've put up with it for so long.' Abbie opened her mouth to protest, but her mother carried on regardless.

'Your room is all ready for you, dear. Bertha has changed the sheets and put a hot-water bottle in to air the bed. I know it's supposed to be summer, but it can still be rather chilly, especially in the mornings. You will have to get up early, won't you, to get to the Moss? I dare say they will want you to start about eight o'clock, won't they, but there is a bus that goes that way; I've been consulting the timetable, not that I ever travel on the bus if I can help it, but it can be quite handy, I suppose. And Bertha can arrange for us to have our evening meal a little later to fit in with your hours. I quite understand you may sometimes have to work late, but you must insist that you have all day Sunday off, Abigail, and perhaps Saturday as well. They will have to—'

'No, Mother.' Abbie eventually managed to break in to her mother's monologue. 'You've got the wrong idea. I won't be living here.' Her mother had got it all worked out in her own mind: the bus route, the meal arrangements, even her days off . . . everything. 'I have been told there is living accommodation there, at the Websters' place, and I'm going to live in. I did tell you, Mother, in my letter. I will be staying here tonight, of course, and going to Marton Moss tomorrow. And I will come home at the weekend as often as I can, but—'

The expression in her mother's eyes changed from one of complacency to irritation. 'I know perfectly well what you said, Abigail. I know you thought you might have to live there because it is what you have been used to doing. But it isn't necessary now. In fact it is quite out of the question. I want you here. You have come home and that is where you are going to stay. That was the whole idea of you coming back to Blackpool.'

'It may have been your idea, Mother, but it certainly wasn't mine.' Abbie was aware of her father giving her an imploring look which seemed to be saying, Don't upset her; you know what she's like. So she tempered the sharpness in her tone, even going so far as to cross the room and sit at her mother's side on the settee, taking hold of her hand. 'Listen . . . Mum. I've come back to Blackpool, haven't I, like you wanted me to and I'll be able to see you much more often. But it will be much easier if I live on the premises. I haven't met them yet, the Websters, but

306

I wouldn't be surprised if they want me to start work at seven o'clock, or even earlier. That's quite usual with country folk. They're always up with the lark. And it will be much more convenient for me to have my evening meal with them.'

'They'll charge you for it,' said Eva. 'They're not going to keep you for nothing; it stands to reason. You'd be far better off living here. Less trouble for them as well, though I dare say they're trying to make as much out of you as they can.'

Abbie sighed inwardly. 'It doesn't make much difference, Mother. They adjust our pay accordingly.' As far as Abbie was concerned the question of money did not enter into it. Land girls were not well paid, but there was little enough to spend their wages on anyway. Here in Blackpool, of course, there were more 'bright lights' – though considerably dimmed by the blackout – than there were in Norfolk, but as a young woman engaged to be married she would not be taking advantage of them. 'Don't worry; you're going to be seeing quite a lot of me, much more than you have done lately. You'll probably be glad to see the back of me, I'll be here so often.' Abbie smiled, but her mother did not respond. 'I'm pretty sure I'll have every Sunday off, so I'll be here every weekend, I promise.'

Eva snatched her hand away from her daughter's grasp. 'Just make sure that you are,' she retorted. 'It seems as though you don't even want to live here with your own mother and father. After all we've done for you ... And nobody would think I'd had two heart attacks, the way people treat me ..'

Abbie sighed. Yes, she was well and truly home again. She had not realised just how much she had appreciated her freedom and she was determined she was not going to relinquish it. She would dance attendance on her mother, if that was what she wished, but only at the weekends, and only until Christmas, when she and Peter would be married. And after that ... well, she had no idea what would happen, whether she would stay here in Blackpool and continue with her work as a land girl – that was what she really ought to do, until the end of the war, unless ... unless she and Peter had a baby, a thought which filled her with the most unbelievable joy – or would she go back to live in Norfolk with Peter's parents, as they had once planned? Oh dear, everything was so unsettled, so unsure, but that was how it was in wartime. Abbie knew that all she and Peter could do was take one step at a time, like thousands of other engaged couples, looking forward to their next meeting, counting the weeks, the days, the hours . . . and thinking of one another as they looked at the same moon. Already she was missing him more than she had thought possible. She began to feel miserable, wishing she had stuck to her guns and stayed in Norfolk. But she put on a brave face and went off with her aunt to help prepare the evening meal.

'I've got something to tell you,' said Aunt Bertha, as soon as they entered the kitchen. 'You'd never guess what's happened, Abbie, not in a hundred years.' But Abbie thought that she might guess. Surely there was only one thing that could make her aunt so bubbling over with happiness, even though it seemed too incredible to be true.

But she went along with the pretence. 'No, I can't guess, Aunt Bertha,' she said, 'but I know you're dying to tell me. Go on . . . What is it?'

Chapter 20

Bertha's visitor had come to see her towards the end of July, just a few days before Eva came out of hospital. Bertha could not help feeling relieved that her cousin was not at home to witness the reunion. She knew she would have to break the news to her sooner rather than later, but Bertha wanted that to be in her own good time. She would have to choose her moment, a time when Eva was having one of her better days, or else her cousin was likely either to go into a rage or retreat into a sulky mood. This, alas, seemed to be the way she reacted to other people's good news. Hearing that her daughter had got engaged had resulted in a fit of anger and then sullen moodiness that had lasted for ages. She had been polite enough, admittedly, to that nice young man Peter Horsfall, although she had carried on about him alarmingly when the couple had departed.

Bertha found she was trembling as she waited in her little room, from very early on Saturday morning, for the knock on the front door which would tell her that William J. Armstrong – which was how he signed himself – had arrived. Her trepidation was due partly to excitement and partly to fear. What would he be like? Would she take to him, and, which was just as important, would he take to her? Or it might well be that he wasn't who he said he was; it could all be a dreadful mistake, or he might be an impostor, or, as Cedric had hinted, but not said outright, he might just be trying to get friendly with her, an unattached elderly spinster, who would have to leave her money to someone. Bertha had, in the end, emboldened by Eva's absence, told Cedric the truth, that the visitor might be her long-lost son, Johnnie. Far-fetched ideas, maybe, but then this whole incident smacked of unreality. It was like something you read about in a romance – a lovely story, but something that was not likely to happen in real life.

As soon as she opened the door, however, all her doubts and fears and uneasiness vanished. For the sight of the young man standing there had transported her back almost thirty years. He was the spitting image of young Johnnie Tennant as she had last seen him, just before he went off to the war. The same fair curly hair, finely chiselled features – such an aristocratic face he had – and eyes of that unusual greeny-blue that she had never seen the like of before or since. Even the uniform, although this young man was dressed in the rough battledress of an ordinary soldier, the stripes on his sleeve denoting that he was a sergeant, whereas Johnnie had worn the finer cloth of an officer.

Bertha felt a smile break out all over her face. She just could not help it and she had to bite back the cry of 'Johnnie . . .' that came to her lips. Instead she held out her hand, relieved that she was no longer trembling, and said very politely, 'How do you do? You must be Mr Armstrong; Sergeant Armstrong, I see. I'm Bertha Shorrock. I'm very pleased to meet you.'

The young man did not stand on so much ceremony. 'Hello there,' he said, taking her hand. 'Yes, I'm Sergeant Armstrong, or Bill, or John.' He gave an easy laugh. 'I've been called a few things in my time. And I'm delighted to meet you too . . . Miss Shorrock.'

She invited him into her little parlour, seating him in the most comfortable chair by the fireside. She always kept a low fire, even in summer, because it was from this back boiler that the water was heated. Then she, too, sat down and they looked at one another in an emotive silence. It was Bertha who broke it, although the young man appeared to be quite at ease, just looking at her intently.

'Well, there's no doubt about who you are, lad,' she said, almost in a whisper. 'The likeness is staggering. You're the image of your father, you are that. It's . . . it's unbelievable, just how much like him you are. And did you say you were called John?'

'Yes, sometimes,' he replied. 'I was christened William John. When I was a little lad my mother and dad called me Billy. Then when I was growing up I had this whim to be called John. I thought it sounded more . . . well, more mature, I suppose. So that's what most of my friends call me. I was always Billy to my parents, though. And to my wife; she's known me since I was a little lad, you see.'

'Tell me about them, about your parents,' said Bertha. 'I often wondered, in fact I never really stopped wondering where you'd gone, and what they were like.' She felt her eyes were moist with tears of happiness, but she quickly brushed them away. 'You see . . . there's no doubt about it. I know now that you're the little lad that I lost. I'm . . . your mother. At least, I'm the person who gave birth to you. I know it must be very hard for you to think of me . . .'

Bill – or John – smiled very understandingly. 'Let's just take it slowly, shall we?' he said. 'We've both got an awful lot to get used to. My parents were wonderful people. No one could have wished for a better mum and dad. That was why it was such a shock to me to find out . . . They never told me, you see. I had no idea until I came across my birth certificate – I told you about that, didn't I? – with your name on. And I must admit I felt very hurt at first, very resentful. It was bad enough losing them both in the air raid, but then with this coming on top of it . . . Why couldn't they have told me? I kept asking myself. And asking my wife as well – I must have nearly driven her crackers – but she said that they don't always. Some adoptive parents can't find the words to tell the child, and so it just gets left until it's too late. That's what happened to me.'

'Yes, I know. It often happens, lad. You're not the only one it's happened to, believe me.' Bertha knew of other cases where the self-same thing had happened. There was a couple at chapel who had adopted a baby, and everyone seemed to know about it except the little girl who was concerned. 'I can't get over you being called John. That was . . . his name, you see. And it was what I called the baby – you, I mean – to myself. Johnnie . . .' She smiled reminiscently. 'I dare say his friends called him John, but I never heard anyone call him anything but Johnnie, or Master Johnnie. Do you mind if I call you John?'

'No, of course I don't,' he replied. 'You can't go on calling me Sergeant Armstrong. What did you say, though? Master Johnnie? Who . . . who was he?'

'No, of course you don't know, do you?' mumbled Bertha.

'His name wasn't on the birth certificate; only mine. It was "father unknown", 'cause I never let on, not to anybody. But I'd best tell you, hadn't I? Your father was Johnnie Tennant, younger son of Sir Reginald and Lady Tennant of Tennant Hall in West Yorkshire. Don't know whether you've ever heard of 'em? Those two may be dead by now, of course. I don't know who's inherited the title; I've never bothered to find out, but I dare say young Master Reginald'll still be alive – that's Johnnie's brother.'

'Good God! That's incredible. I can't believe it.' To her surprise he burst out laughing. 'Just wait till my wife hears this. She's always telling me I've got big ideas, too big for my station in life. It's not true, of course. She's only teasing – I'm a socialist through and through – but I've always had good taste, though I say it myself. I enjoy music and books, and I like looking at paintings, though I can't afford to buy them, of course.'

'What did you do ... John? I mean, what was your job before you joined the army?' asked Bertha.

'I was a teacher, and it's what I'll be going back to when this lot's over ... God willing. I taught English at a senior school on the outskirts of Bradford, but I joined up soon after the war started. We'll soon put paid to Hitler and his cronies, that's what I thought, but I was wrong, wasn't I? I'd never have believed it could take so long. Still, things are looking up now. It's all over in the African desert and it shouldn't be long before Italy surrenders. And once we get our marching orders, well, that should be the beginning of the end. Victory next year, that's what we're all hoping for.'

'You'll be involved in it, then ... whenever it is?' asked Bertha fearfully. She had only just found him; please God she wouldn't lose him again.

'Yes, that's what we're training for.' He stopped talking suddenly. Bertha knew that plans for the Second Front were strictly hush-hush although the general public were aware that preparations for the enterprise were well under way. 'But we won't worry about all that now, eh? You and me, we've more important things to think about, haven't we?'

'Yes, yes, indeed we have, lad,' replied Bertha. 'I still can't get over it. I keep thinking I'll wake up and find I've been dreaming.'

'I'm real enough, believe me,' John laughed. 'Although it's been a bit of a facer for me as well. As I was telling you, I felt resentful at first, very angry with my parents for deceiving me, and I must admit I was not all that curious about . . . about you. It was my wife, Dorothy, who persuaded me to try and find you. I had grave doubts myself. I thought . . . well, to be quite honest I thought you might be dead, or you might have disappeared without trace, and – I'm going to be very straight with you – finding out where I was born was one hell of a shock. Now I've met you, of course, I know differently, but I was so afraid.'

'You thought I might be a barm-pot, you mean?' Bertha tapped significantly at her temple. 'Only eleven pence in the shilling?' She smiled ruefully. 'Yes, I don't blame you for thinking that. But I hope you can see I've got all me faculties. I was ill, I don't mind telling you, when you were born. That's one reason why I was in that place. I'd had a sort of breakdown. My relations didn't want to know, so that's where I ended up – for much longer than I should have done, but that's what used to happen to girls who were unlucky enough to find themselves pregnant.'

'Yes, I know,' said John. 'It was my wife who explained to me that this sort of thing used to happen, far more frequently than anyone realised. She knew of other cases. I'd never given it much thought, to be honest, never needed to. Dorothy said you were most likely to have been an ordinary sort of girl who just couldn't cope with having a baby. The amazing part was that it was so easy to find you. I'd never dreamed that I would.'

'You went to . . . that place then?' Even now Bertha could not say the name of the institution where she had spent long, long years of incarceration.

'Yes, I did. The records were still there from the time I was born. They were a bit reluctant to let me see them, but I can be quite charming and it's amazing what the odd back-hander will achieve. I think the uniform helped as well. So, I got this address and I must admit I thought I would reach a dead end. I could hardly believe it when you answered my letter. You've been happy here, have you, with your . . . you said she was a cousin, didn't you? Well, you must have been happy or you wouldn't have stayed so long.'

'Yes, I've been very contented on the whole. Much more so, recently, since I've managed to put the bad memories behind me. Eva and Cedric have been very good to me. I'll take you to meet Cedric – that is Dr Winters – in a little while. Eva – she's my second cousin, actually – she's in hospital at the moment, and their daughter, Abigail, is in the Land Army. I've become . . . one of the family. Yes, they've been very good to me.' Almost one of the family was what she had been about to say, when Eva permitted her to be, but now was not the time to be telling this young man whom she had only just met that things were sometimes less than perfect. She changed the subject, wanting to know more about John and his family.

'You say you were a teacher in Bradford?' she asked. She had been quietly impressed by this. 'I thought you said your home was in Southampton, that that was where your parents lived?'

'So they did,' he replied, 'and so did I for several years while I was in my teens. My father was in the navy, you see, and they decided to move down there to be near his ship. I had to go as well, of course – I had no choice in the matter – but my heart was always in Yorkshire. That was where we lived at first and where I grew up. Our home was in Halifax and that's where I met my wife, Dorothy. We were childhood sweethearts – corny, isn't it, but that's the way it was. We lost touch, but when I went back to Yorkshire to do my teacher training we met up again and – well – that was that. It was as though we'd never been apart. We live in Bingley now. Do you know it?'

'I'll say I do. I was brought up not all that far from there, although I've not been back to Yorkshire for a long time. Once I left I tried not to look back. There were a lot of bad memories.'

'I can well imagine.' John looked at her sympathetically. 'Forgive me asking, but . . . you were employed at Tennant Hall, were you? It was the usual story, was it, of the wealthy young upstart taking advantage of a servant girl? And I suppose, afterwards, he didn't want to know?'

'Not exactly.' Bertha smiled a little sadly as she shook her head. 'As a matter of fact, he never knew. He was killed, you see. I wouldn't want you to think badly of him. I was very fond of Johnnie, and I like to think he was of me. I wasn't a young

314

kid, you know. I probably should've known better and it was as much my fault as his . . .' She told him the story that she had told only to Abbie, while he listened in silence.

'And I've never let on to anybody, not then, not since, about who your father was. Only to my niece, Abbie, and now to you. Oh yes . . . and to Daisy, the lass that was a parlour maid along with me, but she's dead now. The Tennant family never had any idea.' She laughed. 'So it's no use you going knocking on their door, Johnnie, and telling 'em you're a long-lost relative. I dare say the title'll have gone to young Master Reginald. He came back from the war – the first one, I mean – all in one piece, so I heard. And I expect he's got a few sons. They usually have.'

'Don't you worry.' John gave a somewhat cynical laugh. 'I'm not much of a believer in inherited wealth so I won't be troubling them. I told you, I'm a socialist, for what it's worth, and I think this country is ready for a change, once this lot is over. It's ironic that I should have aristocratic blood in my veins. No, it's not the Tennants I'm concerned about. It's you. I'm so glad I've found you . . . But I don't know what to call you.'

'Bertha will do,' she replied simply. 'It's what most folk call me, apart from my niece and she calls me Aunt Bertha, but you can't do that. And Mother wouldn't be right. You've had a mother, haven't you? And one that's brought you up to be a credit to her. So . . . I'll be Bertha. And you're John. Although you won't have to mind if I forget and say Johnnie now and again. And your wife is Dorothy, you said? And have you any children?'

She learned, to her joy, that they had one of each: Andrew, aged three, and Angela, aged two. What was more, John was going to make arrangements with his wife for Bertha to go and visit them in Yorkshire as soon as it could be arranged.

'There, what do you think about that, then?' said Bertha, smiling with a delight that could not be contained, when she came to the end of her story. 'I'm a grandmother – would you believe it? – and I never knew.'

'I think it's wonderful, Aunt Bertha,' said Abbie. 'It's a fantastic story, almost too incredible to believe. I'm so glad for

315

you, but it's no more than you deserve. Do you know, when you first told me your story – you remember, when you were ill that time? – I had a wild idea that perhaps I could try to find him for you. And then when I went to work in Yorkshire I thought about it again, especially with me being so near to Tennant Hall. But I dismissed it as impossible. They'd never have told me anything; at any rate, the Tennant family had no idea, had they? They'd have just thought I was a mad woman. Anyway, let's face it, it would have taken a lot more courage than I've got, in spite of my best intentions. And you'd not told me the name of the place where . . . where he was born, so that was no good either.'

'No, I tried to put that place right out of my mind. It's amazing what you can keep hidden away when you have to. I'd never let on to anyone who the father was neither, except to you, and now, of course, I've told him . . . John.' She smiled as she said his name. 'Oh, and I've told your father as well. I thought he'd the right to know. He's been very good about it all, has Cedric. John stayed here on the Saturday night, you see, and the pair of them got on like a house on fire. He'd booked into a boarding house – John, I mean – and he'd stayed there on Friday, but Cedric told him to cancel it and stop here. Just the one night, then he went to Yorkshire on Sunday to see his family before he went back to camp.'

'And what about my mother?' asked Abbie. 'She was still in hospital, wasn't she, when all this happened? I suppose you've told her your good news?'

'Yes, I've told her, for what it's worth,' replied Bertha, sighing quietly. 'She was very – what shall I say? – noncommittal, almost as though she wasn't listening. Mind you, I think Eva only listens to what she wants to hear, or am I being unkind? I try to remember she's been poorly, poor lady, and that if it hadn't been for her taking pity on me all those years ago, goodness knows where I would be now.'

'That's a long time ago, Aunt Bertha,' said Abbie. 'You've repaid your debt of gratitude, if that's how you see it, a thousand times over. Mother can be very difficult and it's affecting us all. I know we have to try to be tolerant. The doctor at the hospital told me what a state her nerves are in, but she still can't have everything her own way. I'm in her bad books now, refusing to live here, but I can't do it. I just can't, Aunt Bertha! I've come back to Blackpool when I really didn't want to, but it isn't a good idea for me to live at home. I'm just hoping she'll get over it. I'll be here as often as I can.'

'Yes, you're right to stick to your guns, Abbie, although nobody is more pleased than me that you're back home again; well, in your home town at any rate. It must have been a wrench for you, though, leaving Peter. Are you going to be able to see him, with him so far away?'

'I certainly hope so. He gets quite a lot of time off, being a flier. He may be able to manage the odd weekend up here; we'll have to see. Anyway, it won't be all that long before we're married. I'm going to see the vicar very soon and set a date, then there'll be all sorts of arrangements to make. The time will just race by.'

'And your mother'll get used to the idea in time,' said Bertha. 'Don't you worry.'

'What, of me getting married?' said Abbie. 'I'm not too sure. I can't help feeling that's why she wanted me back in Blackpool, to get me away from Peter. But it won't work. Peter thought she was OK when he was here, quite nice and friendly towards him. He didn't think she was half as bad as I'd made out, but he doesn't know her like I do. I always have the feeling that she's . . . plotting something.'

'She's not got enough to think about at the moment. But your father's very good with her. He seems to be able to talk some sense into her now and again. Then there's that medicine she takes; it helps to calm her down. Yes, your father's a saint, Abigail, the way he's looked after her just lately. He's got the patience of Job. He's going to try to persuade her to take up her whist drives and meetings again soon, and happen some of her charity work, all in good time, of course. That should help to take her mind off things . . . Come on, we'd best get these spuds peeled and the chops in t'oven. Standing here gossiping won't buy the baby a new bonnet, will it? Happen you could scrape the carrots, eh, if you want to help?'

Abbie tied an apron round her waist, ready to start on her task. 'So you'll be off to Yorkshire soon, Aunt Bertha, to see your new family?'

'Yes, I had such a lovely letter from his wife. Dorothy, they call her; I told you that, didn't I? Yes, in a couple of weeks, I'm hoping. Mrs Cuthbert says she doesn't mind staying longer and helping out with the meals, but I thought I'd best wait until your mother's on the better side.'

If she ever is, thought Abbie. Medicine was all very well and she knew her father was doing his best, but she did not like the frenzied, almost maniacal light in her mother's eyes which she had perceived once or twice.

Abbie found the work on Marton Moss to be to her liking, as she had guessed after her first appraisal of the place. Most of her time during the late summer was spent in the greenhouse, tending the tomatoes: watering the thousands of plants, feeding them with superphosphate and fertiliser, spraying them with a solution called Bouisol to keep the green and white fly and leaf mould at bay, and nipping off the side shoots to make the plants grow stronger. The job she had looked forward to most of all was picking the tomatoes, that famous Blackpool product that she had eaten so many times and with such enjoyment ever since she was a little girl. She was gratified to think that she was now playing her part in the growing of them, but the gathering of the crop did not prove quite as delightful as she had expected. By the end of a morning spent trudging up and down between the rows of plants carrying heavy boxes of tomatoes, her neck, shoulders and back were aching as they had seldom ached before, even when she had been beet pulling or potato picking. Another job which was not very congenial was picking up all the rotten tomatoes that had fallen to the ground. The smell of fresh tomatoes, especially when thousands of them were growing together, had a characteristic aroma, sweet, yet pungent and earthy, whereas the stench of the rotten ones was something else altogether, their decaying putridity reminding her of the smell of dead mice. (There had once been one in the pantry at home and she had never forgotten it.)

But Abbie was young and strong, and the work was, on the whole, agreeable. She did many other jobs besides tending the tomatoes. Outside in the large vegetable patch she helped with pruning, hoeing, thinning, watering, planting out and

318

gathering all kinds of vegetables, in particular what seemed like millions of lettuces. Very much to her liking, and a pleasant change from the more arduous outdoor work, was cutting the greenhouse-grown chrysanthemums and carnations. The colours of the chrysanthemums – gold, russet, mauve and an almost pure white, the tips of the petals tinged with pale lemon – were a delight to the eye, and their musky aroma almost overpowering in the enclosed space. Abbie preferred the smaller clusters of flowers, several growing from the one main stem, to the huge single blooms which reminded her of mop heads. A funeral flower, she always thought, not particularly to her liking, but she had to admit that Mr Webster and Jim had perfected their growing.

Carnations, however, had always been one of her favourite flowers. She loved the myriad colours of the blooms – the delicate white and pink, the deeper reds, shading from rose to a dark magenta, and the variegated flowers, yellow veined with red, or white edged with purple. Their peppery fragrance was unique and, like that of the chrysanthemums, gave her a heady, almost giddy, sensation as she breathed in the scent. Flowers were possibly an extravagance, but a much-needed and well-deserved luxury, in Mrs Webster's view, in those bleak days of wartime austerities and deprivation, and they were dispatched in their thousands to the markets and shops of the Fylde and further afield.

Once a week Mrs Webster drove their own little van, laden with their produce – flowers, tomatoes, vegetables, and even jars of home-made marmalade and pickles, for she was a most industrious woman – to Preston where she 'stood' the market. Occasionally, possibly as a reward for her hard work, she guessed, she asked Abbie to accompany her, and this was a welcome change and a time of great delight to the young woman. She took her turn at serving on the stall, but she had her time off as well, when she could wander around between the various other stalls, not buying very much apart from the odd quarter of boiled sweets, but savouring the atmosphere, all the sights and smells and sounds of a busy market.

She remembered that when she was a little girl Aunt Bertha had – very occasionally – taken her on a red Ribble bus for a visit to Preston market. She had been enthralled then, as she was now, by the huge canopied roof, supported by massive iron pillars decorated with intricate wrought-iron work, which covered the open-air market. There were stalls with pots and pans and crockery, the more extrovert of the stallholders sometimes drawing a crowd around them by banging the pan lids together and starting a mock auction. Stalls with rolls of brightly coloured cotton material, many of them seconds or off-cuts from the local mills; several more fruit and vegetable stalls like their own; potted shrimps from Southport and freshly caught fish from the port of Fleetwood; stalls with handbags and shopping baskets and gas-mask cases (not much needed in this area, thank goodness, but still obligatory); and stalls with cheap dolls and cars, marbles and painting books, bats and balls, where children could spend their Saturday pennies. The memories flooded back as Abbie wandered around, memories of dear Aunt Bertha, making her think again how glad she was that her aunt was finding such joy in the discovery of her new family.

Abbie could not say that she, herself, was happy, not unreservedly so. How could she be when she was parted from the person she loved so much? But she had to admit she was contented and was experiencing a feeling of serenity in the congenial surroundings of the market garden on Marton Moss. She still missed Peter dreadfully, and looked forward to his frequent letters. He wrote almost every day, when he was not on an op, as she did. She cherished the memory of their last evening together, and the secret thought, known only to her and Peter, that she now truly belonged to him in a very real way. They had made love that last time, giving full rein to their feelings in a way they had never allowed themselves to do before, and Abbie had felt no guilt and no regret. Peter's parents had gone out for the evening and they were on their own, as they had been on several occasions before; but this time there was an urgency and an inevitability about their lovemaking which had surprised and then enchanted them both.

All the same Abbie had been relieved, during her first week in her new job, to discover that she was not pregnant. She realised now how easily this could happen. They had done

320

nothing to prevent it. So must it have been, and always would be, she guessed, for countless thousands of girls. Girls like Aunt Bertha . . . She understood now. She also remembered her aunt telling her she should wait until she was married. But she was sure Aunt Bertha would understand. Her mother wouldn't, however, that much was certain, so it was as well that nothing had gone wrong. In spite of the nagging pain at the pit of her stomach Abbie breathed a sigh of relief and got on with her hoeing.

Jim Webster was a cheerful and agreeable companion in her day-to-day work. She began to look forward to his merry whistling of 'Run Rabbit Run', or his somewhat off-key rendering of 'A Nightingale Sang in Berkeley Square' or some other such song. She enjoyed his light-hearted chatter on the occasions when they were involved in the same job; in the evenings, too, when she sat with the family in their snug little sitting room. Jim seemed to be a home bird, only going out occasionally to the local, either with his father or a couple of mates – older men from neighbouring market gardens. They were gradually becoming very good friends; only friends, of course, because there could never be anything else between them, so they did not even think about it. She had told him about Peter, and Jim sometimes asked how he was going on, smiling and nodding in a sympathetic way when she reported that he had been on another mission. There could only be a few more, she surmised, then the tour would be ended. Peter had not told her how many ops there were remaining and she had not asked him, neither had she mentioned it to Jim. There was a superstitious feeling about it all and her secret fears were best kept to herself.

Jim Webster knew, to his deep concern, that with every day that passed he was growing more and more fond of Abbie Winters. He had tried to stifle his feelings and he knew, at least as far as Abbie was concerned, that he had managed to hide them very well. She regarded him as a good friend, which he was, of course, and she obviously thought that that was how he regarded her. He had known right from the start that she was spoken for. She wore an engagement ring and she had told him, somewhat hesitantly at first, but now much more openly, about her fiancé, the young flight sergeant Peter Horsfall, whom she was planning to marry in December. And once they were married that would be that. Even if she stayed here in the Fylde and continued with her present job Jim knew there would be no point in harbouring false hopes. Indeed, there was no point in it now, but Jim couldn't help the way he felt.

Love was a funny old thing, wrapping its tentacles around you and causing you, against your better judgement at times, to have feelings you knew jolly well would never be reciprocated. If only he could feel the same way about Sylvia, his friend Alec's sister, as he did about Abbie. Sylvia was a very nice girl, quite attractive, intelligent and fun to be with. She sometimes accompanied Alec to the Welcome Inn of an evening, although she was not the sort of girl who would ever enter a pub without a male companion. Jim enjoyed her company and he could tell by the way she looked at him – he was sure he had not imagined it – that she liked him more than a little. But she did not set his pulse racing the way that Abbie did, and he did not think about her when he was away from her, not in the way he thought about Abbie.

He was surprised when, one evening in early September as the three of them, himself, Sylvia and Alec, sat drinking their shandies, Sylvia said there was a film she would like to see at the Oxford Cinema: *The Road to Morocco* starring Bing Crosby, Bob Hope and Dorothy Lamour. She had missed it the first time, but it had come round again. She looked straight at Jim, half-smiling, a quizzical gleam in her eyes, and nobody was more surprised than himself when he offered to take her. After all, why not? Dorothy Lamour was worth a few hours of anybody's time.

Eva paused by the surgery door, standing back so they would not see her. There they were again, heads close together, giggling away like a couple of naughty schoolchildren: her husband and that nurse Faith Summers. Cedric seemed to think that the sun shone out of her . . . her backside! Eva allowed the lewd thought to linger in her mind, although she would never have uttered such a vulgar word out loud. It wasn't the first time she had seen them laughing in that immoderate way. There were no patients in the surgery, admittedly; from what she could see she thought they were looking at the record cards prior to beginning the tea-time clinic that Cedric ran for all the rag, tag and bobtail of the neighbourhood. (Not their immediate neighbourhood, of course; more the area where that awful Miller family lived.) She thought their behaviour was most unseemly. She had also seen him helping that nurse on with her coat at the end of the afternoon, even, on one occasion, pumping up her bicycle tyre, of all things! Cedric had no idea at all of the proprieties, and mixing with these rough folk was only making him worse.

She crept away without them seeing her, the resentment she was feeling against him festering away in her mind. She stole upstairs, making no sound, but once in her bedroom her self-control snapped. She flung herself on to the pink eiderdown, pummelling it with her fists, biting at the lace edge of the pillow-slip and feeling the scalding hot tears of fury and bitterness well out of her eyes and run down her cheeks. There was not one of them who cared about her or what happened to her. They were all against her. Her husband and that . . . that hussy Faith Summers! She wouldn't be a bit surprised if the two of them were up to no good . . . Like that other time; Eva had never forgotten that. It was written all over them, but she would show them. Oh yes, they would soon find out they couldn't get the better of her.

And Bertha, too. Eva felt hot with anger every time she thought about Bertha and that ridiculous family she had just taken up with. She had been like a dog with two tails, silly woman, ever since she had started getting letters from that Dorothy person. It was 'Dorothy this and Dorothy that' all the time, and Cedric had no more sense than to listen to her with a stupid grin on his face. She, Eva, had walked out of the room more than once when Bertha had started on another boring tale.

And as for Abigail . . . Eva tried to push all thoughts of her daughter to the back of her mind, as she always did. But the memory of what the girl had done could not be submerged. After refusing to live at home, after all they had done to get her back to Blackpool, she was actually going ahead with plans for her wedding. Her mother had been at death's door, and still the selfish girl was planning to get married. The church was booked for the Saturday after Christmas, and now she was looking for somewhere to have the reception, Jenkinson's in Talbot Square or some such place. Eva had taken no part in the discussions, but she couldn't help overhearing them talking, Abigail and her doting father. And Bertha, too. Oh yes, Bertha always had to be part of it. They had made a big mistake when they started treating that woman as one of the family and not just a housekeeper.

Well, they would get a shock when the wedding day arrived – if it ever did, which she very much doubted – because she, Eva, would not be there. She would flatly refuse to go, just as Abigail had flatly refused to live at home. That would show her. It would show all of them.

Eva was not thinking rationally, though she was unaware of just how much she was losing touch with reality. Her thoughts ran off at a tangent these days and she seemed unable to control them . . .

'Eva, Eva, my dear. Come on now, wake up.' Eva gave a startled gasp as she opened her eyes. Cedric was gently shaking her shoulder. 'Bertha's just about to put the meal out. We thought you were in the sitting room, and we were worried when we couldn't find you. How long have you been up here?'

'Oh . . . I don't know. How should I know? You were busy in the surgery, weren't you . . . with Nurse Summers? So I came up here to have a rest.' Cedric did not seem to notice the emphasis she put on that woman's name. He was studying, rather, the half-empty bottle of medicine on her bedside table.

'It's not like you to rest during the day; well, not to fall asleep, at any rate.' He gave a slight frown. 'Have you taken some of your medicine? More than you should have done, I mean?'

'I might have done.' Eva sat up now, patting her hair into place. She shrugged impatiently. 'What does it matter? I may have taken two spoonfuls instead of one. Would you go now, Cedric, and let me tidy myself up before dinner? Tell Bertha not to serve it out until I come. Go along, what are you waiting for?' He knew how she hated him watching her. She didn't even like him in the same room when she was getting dressed. Not that she was undressed now. She had fallen asleep fully clothed, but she needed to tidy her hair and repair her make-up. It was so important not to allow one's standards to slip. Why was he still standing there watching her, the silly man?

'You must not take more than the stated dose of this medicine, my dear,' he said, just as though he were talking to a child. 'It says quite clearly on the bottle how much you must take. It's pretty powerful stuff. Well, that's obvious, isn't it? It's sent you off to sleep and that is not the intention, not in the middle of the day. It's supposed to just . . . calm you down.'

'Well, it has done,' snapped Eva. 'I feel fine. Please don't lecture me, Cedric. I am perfectly capable of taking care of myself. Now, if you don't mind.' She looked pointedly towards the door. 'I would like some time to myself.'

'Very well, Eva. Just remember what I've said, that's all. It could have been . . . quite dangerous.' His voice was curt and he looked aggrieved now, rather than worried, as he went out, closing the door quietly behind him.

It served him right if he was hurt. She had meant to hurt him; carrying on in that shameless way with that good-for-nothing nurse. She would hurt him even more before she had finished with him. She would make him suffer for the way he had humiliated her . . . A plan was beginning to form in her mind. He would be consumed with guilt. So would Bertha. So would Abigail . . .

Chapter 21

Three spoonfuls should be sufficient; no, maybe four, just to make sure. It might be a good idea to take what she thought was enough and then pour the rest down the sink. An empty bottle would show that she had really meant to do it, although she would, of course, make sure that Cedric found her in good time.

Saturday afternoon, she thought. Bertha was going to Yorkshire for the weekend to stay with that precious family of hers, so she would be well out of the way. Abigail never came on a Saturday, although Eva suspected she had the half-day off. It was as much as the girl could do to visit them on a Sunday. And Cedric would be at Bloomfield Road. Blackpool was playing at home so he would be sure to go to the football match. A common sort of hobby, she always thought, and she couldn't understand why a well-bred gentleman like Cedric should take such an interest in the sport. He even did the pools, checking his coupon every Saturday evening, just as though he belonged to the working class. He was always back, however, by five o'clock at the latest on a Saturday afternoon, the football ground being within walking distance of their home.

She would write a note, too. That would make it look as though she had meant business. She would mention them all: Cedric, Bertha, Abigail, even that flighty nurse, Faith Summers. Yes, her more than anyone. She was the cause of Eva's unhappiness. Oh yes, none of them was going to escape. She would have Cedric crawling to her before long. He would be on his knees, begging her to forgive him. She loved him so much. She had always loved him, though he might not have realised it, and she could not bear the thought of losing him now, especially to . . . her.

'Are you going out this afternoon, my dear?' he asked after

the two of them had finished their Saturday lunch. It had been cooked, quite ably, by Mrs Cuthbert, as Bertha had gone gadding off to Yorkshire. But once Mrs Cuthbert had done the washing up she would have finished for the day. She would not be coming back to make the evening meal. Eva had said they could manage for once with something on toast, which she would be able to prepare herself. By that time, of course, her plan would have worked and it would be Cedric who would be making the meal. He would be falling over himself to make amends.

'I might go into town and look round the shops,' she answered now, in a casual voice. 'I haven't decided yet. What about you? You will be going to the match, I suppose?'

'Yes . . . yes, I thought I would. It's a first team match so I would like to see it . . . if you don't mind?'

'Why should I mind?' Eva raised her eyebrows. 'You don't usually bother to ask, do you? No . . . I don't mind.' She could not resist giving a martyred sigh. 'So long as you are back at your usual time. You will be back by five o'clock, won't you?'

'Of course. Why do you ask?'

'No reason, except that Bertha is away and I shall have to make the meal myself. I would be glad of a little help. I thought Abigail might have offered to come round, seeing as I'm on my own, but that would be too much to expect of her.'

'She'll be here tomorrow,' said Cedric brightly. 'So there'll be just the two of us for tea today. That's nice. And of course I'll give you a hand. I'm not much good in the kitchen, as you know, but we'll manage between us. It will be . . . quite like old times.' He smiled at her, a contemplative look in his eyes, but she could not tell what he was thinking. What did he mean by old times? The time before Abigail arrived? Or even before Bertha came to live with them? It had been a long time since there were just the two of them. She supposed they had been happy in the beginning . . . before he went and spoiled everything. Perhaps they could be happy again. She looked at him musingly for several seconds. But she was determined to go ahead with her plan. Maybe, then, he would realise what she had meant to him all along.

'What's the matter, dear?' He was looking at her curiously. 'You've gone all broody.'

'Nothing . . . nothing at all.'

'I don't have to go to the match. I can stay here if you like, perhaps come into town with you?'

'No,' Eva answered quickly and a shade too loudly. 'No . . . of course you mustn't, Cedric. You know that town bores you, and you enjoy the football match. No, off you go. I'll see you at five o'clock.'

'All right then, if you're sure,' he replied hastily. She knew he had not meant it about staying with her. He stooped and kissed her cheek. 'Goodbye, dear. Enjoy your afternoon. Take care now and don't go walking too far in town. I'll see you later.'

She had never had any intention of going into Blackpool. As soon as she heard the door close behind him she went into the dining room where she kept her writing bureau. She opened the lid and took out her Basildon Bond notepaper and her Parker pen. It took her a long time to compose the letter, almost an hour. She knew it might have been more effectual if the letter appeared to have been written in a frenzy, the writing untidy and blotchy and the phrases all disjointed. But not once in her life had Eva done anything in a slipshod manner and she would certainly not do so now. When she had finished she put the single sheet of paper in an envelope, writing 'Cedric' on the front in neat block capitals. She closed her bureau and, going upstairs, she propped the letter up against a china figurine on her bedroom mantelpiece. He could not miss it there.

She had just started a new bottle of the greeny-yellow syrupy medicine. She was not sure what was in it, but it was quite pleasant-tasting. She could tell by the effect it had on her, making her a little light-headed and woozy, that it was not what Cedric called a placebo; something that made you feel better because you believed it would, but which was, in fact, useless. People must be fools to be taken in by such a ploy, she always thought; she never would be, as Cedric well knew. No, this medicine was genuine enough – it had been the doctor at the hospital who had prescribed it in the first place, not her husband – but she was quite sure it was not dangerous. Cedric had just been making a silly fuss, telling her to be careful. She had thought he might have taken the precaution of measuring out the medicine for her into single doses, but after that first admonition he seemed to have forgotten about the matter; and she had been careful, ever since, only to take one spoonful at a time.

After Mrs Cuthbert departed Eva idly flicked through the pages of a magazine, but *The Lady* did not seem to be holding her attention this afternoon. She picked up *Ideal Home*, but that was not much better. Even that high-class magazine had started lecturing about how one could economise or 'make do and mend'. A ghastly phrase! Eva hated scrimping and saving. Goodness, the afternoon was dragging. She wondered about making herself a cup of tea, but she could not be bothered. She would have to wash the things up afterwards. Someone who intended killing herself would not be likely to sit drinking a leisurely cup of tea.

At four o'clock she went upstairs again and, as she had planned, swallowed four – no, better make it five – spoonfuls of the thick liquid. Then she poured the rest of the bottle into the wash basin in the bathroom, making sure that all traces of it had gone. She grimaced. It was rather sickly taken in such a large quantity. She drank half a tumbler of water, then noticing a packet of Aspro on the bathroom shelf she decided, for good measure, to take a few of those as well. She was feeling reckless by this time, not absolutely sure of what she was doing or even of why she was doing it. She swallowed three, then another three, of the little white tablets. After all, what did it matter? She was not caring much about anything now, but she knew she would have to lie down and have a rest. She was very tired. But Cedric would be here soon . . .

Pictures of the handsome young doctor she had fallen in love with drifted across her mind as she closed her eyes. Years and years and years ago they had danced together at the Palace Ballroom. He had held her close . . . He had told her that he loved her . . . But it was all so very, very long ago. Gradually the images began to fade . . .

'Hello there, Dr Winters. Do you mind if I walk home with

330

you? We're going the same way.' Cedric turned round on hearing the voice. It sounded a little breathless, as though with walking quickly, as, indeed, the owner of it had been. It was Mr Smedley, one of his patients – a private, not a panel patient – a man in his early seventies who lived in an avenue off Whitegate Drive, quite near to the doctor's house.

'Hello there, Mr Smedley. Yes, of course; I will be pleased to have your company. Been to the match, have you?'

'Yes, for what it's worth. They didn't make much of a showing today, did they? If you ask me they didn't deserve to win. Yes, I saw you in front of me when I came through the gate and I've been trying to catch up with you. By heck! You can't half walk fast.'

Cedric smiled. 'I'll slow down a bit then.' He looked somewhat anxiously at his companion, who still appeared to be gasping a little. 'Do you always walk home, Mr Smedley? It's a fair stretch there and back, and I suppose you walked there, too?'

'I did that! It's what keeps me fit, all the walking I do. The wife was making a fuss today, though. I had this bit of a pain, you see, in my chest and she said I should take the car. But I said, "Get on with yer bother. I'll be as right as ninepence once I get some fresh air into my lungs. It's only indigestion." Besides, the petrol allowance doesn't go far, does it, and I need it for taking her shopping. She forgets that.'

'And . . . did it go? That pain you had? You must take care, you know. If I remember rightly you had a scare, not all that long ago.'

'Oh, that. Aye, it was my heart that time, but it was something and nothing. Don't worry, Doctor; I'm not doing too badly for an old 'un.' He sounded, however, as though it was becoming more of an effort to speak. 'Well, I don't consider myself old. I'll bet I'm not all that much older than you, am I? Not much more than ten years, anyway.'

'Something like that.' Cedric smiled. George Smedley was quite well known for his plain speaking. 'I'm not so far off sixty, although I don't broadcast the fact. You didn't answer my question, George. Have you still got that pain?'

'Aye, well, I suppose I have, a bit. That's why I said . . . could

I walk home with you. Hang on a minute, Doctor, I'll have to stop and have a rest.' He stopped, leaning against the brick wall of one of the houses in Park Road. His breathing was very uneven by now, coming in short gasping pants as he clutched at his chest. 'It's getting . . . Oh, dear God, I can hardly breathe. I'm . . . I'm in the right company though, aren't I?' He managed a feeble smile before he slumped down on to the pavement.

There was no shortage of passers-by, men who were, likewise, walking home from the match, and there was soon a little crowd about the recumbent figure.

'Hey, what's up?'

'Oh dear . . . Poor old chap.'

'We'd best ring for an ambulance. No phone box here though. Wouldn't you know it? Never one near when you want one.'

Cedric at once took charge of the proceedings. What a mercy it was, he thought, that he was here. 'I'm a doctor. As a matter of fact this gentleman is one of my patients. Yes, we do need an ambulance. I wonder if one of you could ask if we could use the phone? No, that house. See the telephone wires? They must be on the phone . . . Very well, I'll make the call. Could you just stay with him, please? No, we'd better not try to move him too much. The ambulance shouldn't be long. Yes, it's his heart, I suspect . . .'

The woman at the nearby house from where the phone call was made offered to take him inside, but Cedric thought it was better to leave George Smedley just where he was. They covered him with a blanket and when, in about ten minutes, the ambulance arrived, Cedric volunteered to go with George to the hospital. There was no way they could contact George's wife, not yet. The Smedleys were not on the phone, but Cedric decided he would go round personally and tell Mrs Smedley what had happened once George had been admitted into hospital, as Cedric was sure he would be. The poor fellow seemed to be in a bad way although Cedric, from what experience he had, did not think he would die. He had made things worse, though, by over-exerting himself and not taking notice of the warning signals.

One thing Cedric had not done, however, and which he remembered in the ambulance, was to ring his own wife and tell her he would be late home. He glanced at his watch. Five o'clock. Oh dear, he was late already. Never mind, it couldn't be helped, and Eva would understand once he told her what had happened. He would ring her from the hospital. She should be sympathetic considering she had herself recently suffered from heart trouble; and the fact that George Smedley was a private patient – he smiled wryly to himself, thinking of Eva's reaction – and not a panel one should help to mollify her.

But where on earth was she? The phone rang and rang, but there was no answer. It was quite obvious that she was not at home, but Cedric did not feel worried, probably because he had other concerns at the moment. George was waiting on a trolley-bed in an annexe and Cedric had promised to stay with him until he was admitted to a main ward. It was six o'clock before this happened, hardly any length of time at all to wait, in reality, but long enough for Cedric to know he would be well and truly in the doghouse by the time he arrived home. Ah well, might as well be hanged for a sheep as a lamb, as the saying went, he thought philosophically as he left the hospital, after making sure that Mr Smedley was settled and as comfortable as possible in the ward. The danger had passed, but they were keeping him in for a while for observation.

Cedric caught a bus, which dropped him near the avenue where the Smedleys lived. He had decided not to phone home again. What would be the point? He would only be subjected to a tirade of complaining before Eva stopped, if she ever did, to listen to his explanation. He had come to the conclusion that she must have still been in town when he rang. Most probably she had met one of her whist drive friends as she sometimes did and they had lingered longer than usual over a cup of tea. At all events, he was in no hurry to be at the receiving end of her grievances, and Mrs Smedley was the one who was more in need of his attention now. The poor woman must be frantic, wondering what had happened to her husband.

She thought the worst when she saw the doctor on her doorstep, but he was soon able to pacify her. It had been only a mild heart attack, he assured her, and George should make a full recovery provided he heeded the advice to take things more easily. What a miracle it was that the doctor had been right there on the spot, she kept saying and she was effusive in her thanks for all he had done. He told her that his own wife had recently had two such attacks, but she was doing very nicely now.

He would soon find out, in truth, how she was doing, he thought as, with more than a few misgivings, he opened his front door. He expected her to be there in the hallway, greeting him with a torrent of recriminations, but the house was silent, uncannily so, it seemed.

'Eva, Eva, where are you? I'm so sorry I'm late, my dear. I know you must have been worried, but I can explain . . .' he called out as he looked in the downstairs rooms – the sitting room, the dining room and the kitchen – before going upstairs.

He could not comprehend at first the sight that greeted him in the bedroom. His wife was lying motionless on the bed, on top of the pink billowing eiderdown, one arm hanging lifelessly over the edge; there was an empty medicine bottle on the bedside table and, at the side of it, an opened packet of Aspro tablets. He rushed to her side, feeling the coldness of her flesh as he lifted her arm, the clamminess of her forehead as he gently rested his hand there. Frantically he kneeled at her side feeling for a pulse . . . Yes, there was one – thank God – but it was very faint. He patted her cheeks, calling out her name. 'Eva, Eva, come along, love.' He put both arms round her. 'Eva, oh, Eva! Come along . . . please wake up!' But she felt like a dead weight and there was no waking her.

In a daze, still hardly believing what was happening, he lifted the receiver of the telephone on the bedside table and, for the second time that day, rang for an ambulance. It was while he was making the call that he noticed the letter propped up on the mantelshelf. 'Oh no . . .' he murmured as he read it, feeling an unbelievable sadness. How could she have thought that? How could she have believed for one moment he would be unfaithful to her? For that was what she was saying, wasn't it?

Dear Cedric, *the letter read*,
I can't go on any longer living such a useless life. It is quite obvious that nobody needs me or wants me any more. Bertha has a new family who already mean far

more to her than the family who has cared for her all these years. Abigail is determined to go her own way in spite of all I have done for her. You will agree that I have always done my best for the girl, as I promised I would. I have been a good mother to her, but I know that she never really loved me.

And I know that you, Cedric, are already finding happiness elsewhere. I am aware of your close friendship with Nurse Summers and I wish you joy of her, if that is really what you want.

Your loving wife, Eva.

Tears were blurring his vision, but he felt suddenly angry as well as very, very sad. Fiercely he screwed the letter up into a ball, clenching it tightly in his fist. This would be seen by no other eyes. Abbie would be shocked and dismayed beyond belief to read such words; not just the ones about himself, although they were not true, but about her as well. She had been such a dutiful, considerate daughter; maybe not all that loving, he realised now, but when had she ever been given any encouragement to be so? And Bertha, poor downtrodden Bertha, always so willing, always, until recently, so subservient – she would be dreadfully hurt. Cedric had been so pleased that she was finding some true happiness at last. Her happiness, previously, had all been centred around Abigail, but how wonderful, now that Abbie was getting married, that Bertha had something else to celebrate. He was damned if he was going to let her be upset by the last words of a sad, disillusioned woman.

But were they truly meant to be her last words? He was not at all sure. Furious though he may have been with his wife at times, and fed up with all her moods and erratic behaviour, he had never, even when she had suffered her heart attacks, wished she were dead. It was the last thing he would have wanted to happen and he prayed now that she would live. He could see that she was hanging on to life by a thread and if it were in his power he would get her back. It was his duty to do so, and besides, it was what he wanted. He knew, however tiresome she might be, he did not want to lose Eva. But what had been in her mind, the silly deluded woman? Had she really wanted to die or was it an extreme cry for help, for sympathy and attention? Yes, that is what it must have been. He remembered now how she had insisted he must be home at five o'clock . . . and he had let her down. That knowledge was very hard to bear even though he knew it was not his fault.

He looked sadly at his wife, sighing and shaking his head. How could she have believed that about him and Faith? As far as he knew he had never given Eva any cause to doubt him. He enjoyed Nurse Summers' company and they did have a laugh together from time to time – and, God knows, that was more than he was able to do with Eva. Nurse Summers was efficient, too, capable and caring, and the patients all liked her immensely; in fact Cedric could not imagine how he had ever managed without her. But as for anything else . . . the thought had never entered his mind.

Resolutely now he picked up the envelope from the floor and tore it in two. Then, after a quick glance at the motionless figure of his wife – she was not likely to come to any more harm if he left her for a moment – he took the incriminating letter downstairs. There was a low fire burning, as always, in Bertha's little room and Cedric threw the paper on to it, pushing it beneath the glowing coals with a few furious digs of the poker. There! No one would ever know about that except himself . . . and Eva, if she recovered. But he would face that problem when it arose.

The ambulance soon arrived. There was a feeling of unreality about the journey there, the second time that day that Cedric had found himself being driven along East Park Drive in the back of an ambulance en route for Victoria Hospital. The doctor and nurse dealt with the emergency quickly and efficiently. Eva, still as deeply unconscious, was wheeled along the endless hospital corridors, Cedric walking at her side. But even though he was a doctor he was allowed to go only so far and no further. He was left in a waiting room while they took Eva into the theatre. He knew they would be using a stomach pump. Poor Eva. How she would hate the indignity of that. They would do all in their power to revive her.

The waiting seemed endless although, in reality, it could not have been much more than half an hour. There were a few other people in the room, none of them speaking, one or two idly flicking over the pages of a magazine. Cedric guessed they were not reading, just as he would not be able to concentrate on the written word, so he did not try. He stared blankly ahead at the shiny pale green wall, his eyes resting momentarily on the notice board with its plethora of notices and posters, many of them still dealing with matters of propaganda. It was four years, almost to the day, since war had been declared, but the people of Britain were still being warned that 'Careless Talk Costs Lives', depicted by two women gossiping on a bus. 'Let us Go Forward Together,' proclaimed a bowler-hatted Winston Churchill against a background of Spitfires and anti-aircraft guns, while, on a lighter note, Dr Carrot announced he was 'the children's best friend'.

Cedric closed his eyes to shut out all the images around him and concentrate more fully on willing that his wife would live. He had not ceased to do this since he had found her. He was not exactly praying, not in definite words, but he was sure that God, were He tuned in to Cedric's mind – as one had to believe that He was, to everyone's mind – would hear and understand . . . and answer. The trouble was that you did not always get the answer you wanted.

'Dr Winters . . .' He opened his eyes at the sound of the nurse's voice. She was not smiling at him and he guessed at once from the sorrowful look in her eyes and her regretful tone of voice what he was about to hear. 'Would you come this way, please? Dr Gilchrist will have a word with you.'

Dr Gilchrist was known to Cedric only by sight. He had never before had any direct dealings with him, but he held him in the same high esteem as he held all other members of his own profession. 'I am sorry, Dr Winters, but I am afraid your wife has died. We did all we could for her.' Cedric nodded as he heard the meaningless words, the words that were always spoken as a consolation to the bereaved one. They went without saying, really. All doctors and nurses worthy of the name would do all they could.

'We managed to bring her round. She regained consciousness, but I'm afraid it all proved too much for her. She suffered another heart attack and there was nothing we could do to prevent it. Nothing at all. I really am terribly sorry.'

'Thank you ... I know you have done your best,' replied Cedric. He shook his head numbly. 'I can't understand why she ... did what she did. I know you will have heard all this before. I've heard people say the same sort of thing myself, but there was no reason for it. She had a good life, she was well looked after. I know, of course, she had been ill recently with her nerves ...'

'Maybe more ill than we realised,' said Dr Gilchrist. 'How can we tell what goes on in another person's mind? I looked at your wife's case notes, of course. It is a pity that Dr Shepherd who had care of her is not on duty today.'

'It wouldn't have made any difference if he had been,' replied Cedric. 'Believe me, I know you did all you could. The balance of her mind was disturbed. That's the official phrase and I know that's the one that will be used. What we will never know is if she really meant to do it, or if she just wanted ... what, sympathy?'

Dr Gilchrist nodded gravely. 'Strictly speaking she died of a heart attack. That is what happened, so that is what I shall put on the death certificate.'

'Thank you for that,' said Cedric.

There were certain formalities to attend to. There would be many more in the next few days, but the first, most important thing he had to do was to tell Abbie. He walked the mile or so to his home in an endeavour to clear his head, but partly, he admitted to himself, to put off the evil moment. He thought Abbie would be at home on a Saturday night; well, not at home exactly, but he knew that the Websters' place on Marton Moss was almost like home to her. He was glad she was so contented there. Poor lass; she was missing Peter dreadfully although she did not talk about it very much. He knew she was disappointed that they had not yet managed to spend a weekend together since she came back to Blackpool. It was ironic really. Abbie had come back, against her better judgement, to be near her mother, and now Eva was dead. Cedric forced himself to say the word in his mind. She had not 'passed away', nor was she 'no longer with us', euphemisms which were often used to evade the stark reality. Eva was dead and that was what he would have to tell Abbie.

It was Mrs Webster who answered the phone and she went to fetch Abbie. 'Hello, Father.' She sounded surprised. 'I didn't expect to hear from you. I'm coming home tomorrow. Is there . . . some problem?'

'Yes, I'm afraid so, my dear. More than a problem. I have some very bad news for you. I'm afraid your mother has . . .' In spite of his best intentions he could not say the word. 'Your mother has . . . gone.'

'What do you mean, gone? Do you mean she's . . . left?' When he did not answer Abbie gave a gasp. 'Oh no, you don't mean . . . ? She can't be . . . dead?'

'Yes, I'm sorry, my dear. That is what I mean, but it's so difficult to say. She had another heart attack and she . . . she died. Could you come home, Abbie, tonight? I know it's late and I know you would be coming tomorrow anyway, but I would appreciate it, dear. Bertha is away and . . . well, I would be glad of your company.' Abbie could hear the break in her father's voice and tears sprang to her eyes.

'Of course, Father. I'll come at once. I'll be with you as soon as I can.'

Mr and Mrs Webster were very sympathetic. Mr Webster offered to run her home in his little van right away. She was to stay as long as she was needed at home, they told her. They had recently employed a fifteen-year-old girl, a school-leaver, to help with the glut of tomatoes and the autumn flowers and produce so they would manage all right. Jim was not at home that evening. Abbie had been pleased for him when she learned that he was taking Sylvia Cardwell to the pictures. Sylvia worked at the aircraft factory and although Abbie had met her only a couple of times she could tell the girl was more than a little smitten with Jim. But he seemed to be unaware of her fondness for him. Now was not the time, however, to be thinking of Jim and his love life, or lack of it. What a dreadful shock it had been to hear about her mother. She could not take it in at all, not yet.

Neither, it appeared, could her father. He still seemed to be in a state of shock. He clung to her in a way he had never done before, as though in desperation, and she could see the bewilderment as well as the sadness in his grey eyes. He looked, suddenly, much much older, his face ashen and his tall figure stooped with the burden of his grief.

Abbie knew then that he must have loved her mother more than she, Abbie, had realised, maybe more than Eva had realised, too, although at times she had seemed unworthy of that love. She felt tears of sadness – of guilt, as well, that she had not loved her mother as she should – spring to her eyes. And she found herself remembering, not the times when her mother had been difficult, but the fact that she had so wanted her to come back home. Whatever the reason, her mother had wanted her near, and she, Abbie, had been unwilling. Now she had gone and it was too late to make amends.

For several minutes they held each other and cried. Eventually, Cedric produced a large, immaculate handkerchief from his pocket and they shared it to mop their tears.

Then Abbie looked a little apprehensively around the hallway, glancing at the closed sitting-room door. 'Where is she? Mother, she's not . . . ?'

'No, she's not here,' said her father. 'She was in hospital. That is where it happened, you see.' He gave a deep shuddering sigh. 'Come along and sit down and I'll tell you about it. There's a lot you don't know . . . A lot you will have to know.'

It was an even greater shock to hear that her mother had tried to commit suicide. Even if it were only a plea for help, as her father seemed to think, that was bad enough.

'But why?' she cried. 'There was no reason for her to do that. You have been so good to her, Father, especially since she has been ill with her nerves, and then the heart attacks. You've been marvellous with her. Aunt Bertha said so, but I could see it for myself. Couldn't it just have been a mistake, that she took an overdose without meaning to? Besides, wouldn't she have left a note if she had meant to . . . to kill herself?'

Her father did not answer. A closed look came over his face and he stared down at the carpet. 'You . . . would have thought so,' he said in a strangled sort of voice, 'but there wasn't . . .'

'I know she has been angry with me,' Abbie went on, 'but I have tried, I really have, to understand her, and I've come home whenever I could. Perhaps it wasn't enough . . .'. The guilt she had been feeling resurged. 'Oh, Father, I do hope it wasn't anything I've done that made her . . . But whatever I did, I didn't seem to be able to please her. Oh, it's so terribly sad. I can't believe she's not here any more. And if it was my fault . . .'

'Don't reproach yourself, Abigail. Nothing we can say or do will make any difference now,' said her father, sadly. 'We will never know exactly what happened. Let's just try to think that her mind was disturbed, and in the end it was just a heart attack. It's so good to have you home, Abbie.' His glance, though not quite a smile, was as warm as she had ever seen.

'Aunt Bertha won't be home until this evening, then?' said Abbie the following morning. She was surprised that her father had agreed readily when she had offered to cook bacon and eggs for his breakfast. He did not appear so haggard this morning and he had lost some of that awful haunted look that had worried her. He was after all, a practical man who had seen death many times albeit at more of a distance.

'That's right. She'll be home tonight. There didn't seem to be any point in phoning her with such bad news; that is, if I could have found the number. I dare say she's got it in her address book, but I thought it best to leave it and let her enjoy her weekend. She will know soon enough. Dearie me, Abbie, it still feels dreadfully unreal. I keep expecting her to walk through the door.' He glanced uneasily in that direction. 'Silly, isn't it?'

'Not really, Father. I'm finding it just the same. Do you want to go to church this morning? I know you and Mother usually attended, but under the circumstances, perhaps you may not want to?'

'All the more reason to go, I would say. Yes, I would like to, if you will come with me. We had better have a word with the vicar, then he can make an announcement. A lot of people knew your mother. She was a very . . . popular woman.'

Abbie nodded, although she was not sure it was true. Eva was well known at the church, certainly. Whether she had been popular or not was debatable, but the congregation would be surprised and shocked to hear of her death.

After the service Abbie and her father did, indeed, receive many expressions of condolence. 'We will miss her at the

Mothers' Union meetings,' said Mrs Ferguson, who was the enrolling member for that organisation. 'A most dependable lady. She was our hard-working secretary, you know; that is until recently when she became rather unwell. As a matter of fact, dear,' she said confidingly to Abbie, 'she had a list of names and addresses to give me – suggestions for speakers, you know, for next year's meetings – but with her being so poorly I didn't like to remind her. In fact, I haven't seen her for several weeks. I wonder, when you are looking through her papers, if you come across it, could you let me have it? I don't like troubling you at such a sad time, but it would be helpful if you could?'

'Of course I will,' replied Abbie. 'It shouldn't be too hard to find. Mother was a very meticulous person . . . and thank you for the kind things you have said about her.'

Abbie grilled the lamb chops she found in the larder for their Sunday lunch. Her father told her it was to have been a simple, easily prepared meal as Bertha was away. I would probably have ended up cooking it anyway, she thought, as she put two chops on her father's plate and one on her own, together with the mashed potatoes, gravy and carrots. Her mother, no doubt, would have insisted on putting the vegetables into serving dishes, but Mother was no longer here.

Her father ate most of his meal, the chop that had been intended for Eva as well as his own, but he was very quiet. He had a lot on his mind, Abbie guessed, and tomorrow they would have to start making arrangements for the funeral.

'Mrs Ferguson has asked me to find a list for her, Father,' she told him, after they had finished their lunch and she had cleared everything away and washed up. 'Something Mother should have given her, but has overlooked. I expect it will be in her bureau. Do you think I could have the key, please?'

'Oh, no, I don't think so, Abigail.' Her father sounded alarmed at her question. He looked alarmed, too – almost frightened. 'She always kept it locked, but I . . . I don't know where the key is. Besides, I don't think it would be right to interfere with her private papers, not so soon after . . .'

'I know, Father. I know how you must feel, but . . . but Mother has gone now, hasn't she?' said Abbie gently. 'We will have to sort her things out eventually, but it's just that list I want at the moment. She kept the key in her handbag.' As her father knew very well.

He did not answer for several seconds, then: 'All right,' he said, shaking his head resignedly. 'I don't suppose it will make any difference . . . not now. I'll see if I can find the key.' He was back in a few moments. 'It's no use me trying to hide things any longer,' he said as he handed her the tiny key. She did not understand his words, nor could she fathom the look in his eyes, as loving as before, but full of apprehension and more than a little fear.

Chapter 22

Everything was in apple-pie order in her mother's bureau, as Abbie had expected. She soon found the list that Mrs Ferguson had requested, but as it was of no particular interest to her she did not peruse it. She put it in one of the Basildon Bond envelopes that were in her mother's leather writing case and wrote the woman's name on it. She could see that a lot of the documents tidily arranged in the pigeon holes, insurance policies and the like, maybe even her mother's will, would have to be dealt with by her father. Perhaps that was why he had been so reluctant to let her have the key; maybe he thought it was entirely his own business, his and his late wife's, and had nothing to do with Abbie. Certainly it was the first time she had ever seen inside the bureau apart from a quick glance when her mother had been writing there.

She was just about to close the roll-top lid and lock it up again when she noticed a brown envelope with the words 'Birth Certificate' written on the front. Her own, she guessed. The envelope did not look old enough for it to be either her mother's or her father's. And that, most assuredly, was her business. Strange that she had never seen it before, she thought, as she pulled out the document with the red printed words and the black spidery writing of the registrar, with his signature over the penny stamp; but then she had never needed it, not even to join the Land Army.

'Abigail Maud,' she read, wincing again at the old-fashioned names. Not content with choosing one antiquated name like Abigail they had to go and saddle her with Maud as well, which was even more out-dated. It had, apparently, been her paternal grandmother's name, but the woman had died before she was born. She did not recognise the address on the document; Reads

Avenue. How very odd. She had always thought she was born on Whitegate Drive. That was the only home she remembered, but maybe her mother and father had lived in a different house when they were first married.

'Father, Cedric Charles Winters, Doctor of Medicine,' she read, and then . . . her heart skipped a beat as the next words seemed to jump out at her from the paper, 'Mother, Sadie Elizabeth Jones.'

She stared in disbelief at the words for a few moments. Maybe it was not her own birth certificate she was looking at; it must be somebody else's. But there was her name in the second column and the date of birth in the first column was definitely hers. Her fingers were trembling with agitation as she took hold of the paper and went to find her father. He was in the sitting room, ostensibly reading the Sunday newspaper, but it was lying unopened on his lap and he was staring into space.

'Father . . .' She thrust the incriminating document towards him. 'Who is Sadie Jones?'

He did not seem surprised at her question. The look he gave her was one of resignation, the self-same look she had seen in his eyes before when she had first asked for the key to her mother's bureau. 'I would have told you,' he said. 'I was going to tell you . . . very soon, but when you said you were going to look in your mother's things I thought this might happen. I'm so sorry, Abigail, that you should find out like this, but we thought it was for the best, your mother and I, that you should not be told at first, and then—'

'You keep saying my mother,' cried Abbie, 'but she wasn't, was she? Eva . . . was not my mother. And you let me go on thinking she was, all those years, both of you.'

Cedric sighed. 'We thought it was for the best,' he repeated. 'And she was a mother to you. A good mother, I would like to think, in her own way. She did her best. You never wanted for anything, Abbie.'

'Except love,' said Abbie quietly. 'She never loved me, did she? Not really. Not as much as . . . she might have done. And now I understand why. She never wanted me. I wasn't her child. That's why she was so critical and so demanding of me. I could

346

never do right for her. I can see it all now. Oh, why didn't you tell me? Then . . . I might have understood.'

'It would have been just the same, I should imagine, if you really had been her own flesh and blood. You know what a stickler your mother . . . Eva . . . was for correct behaviour and keeping up one's standards. But the very fact that she was so possessive of you, and I know she was, must have been love of a kind. She didn't want to lose you. She wanted you near her, and she wouldn't have done that if she hadn't loved you.'

'She wanted to own me, I know that,' said Abbie. 'She didn't want to let me go. Was that really because she . . . loved me? But you didn't answer my question, Father.' She looked at him quite unsympathetically. 'Who is Sadie Jones?' Another thought suddenly struck her. 'You are my father, aren't you? I'm not just . . . some waif or stray you've adopted? I suppose I was adopted, anyway, wasn't I? If . . . Eva . . . wasn't my mother?'

'No, no, of course not,' said her father gently. 'There was no need for any adoption because I was – *am* – your father, and it was quite in order for my wife, Eva, to become your mother.'

'So who was she?'

'Sadie Jones?' Her father smiled sadly, reminiscently, she thought. 'She was a patient of mine, my dear. A young woman with whom I became friendly. Too friendly, I know. I'm not excusing myself, except to say that I did care for her very much, as she did for me . . . Sit down, Abbie. I can't talk to you while you're standing there hovering over me like . . . like some avenging angel; and you do have the right to know, I realise that.'

'Rather late in the day, Father,' said Abbie, a trifle sadly, as she sat down in the armchair opposite him.

'Yes, I realise that, too, and I'm sorry. However . . .' She heard the story of how the doctor had befriended the younger woman who had a chest complaint. Sadie had been twenty-one, Dr Winters in his mid-thirties, and he had been married for a couple of years to a woman who was not able, or willing, to give him the love he so much craved. He did not say that in so many words, but Abbie, reading between the lines, was able to sum up the situation for herself. It had been wrong, very wrong. He could have been struck off the doctors' list if the affair had come to light, but it seemed that the two of them had been very much in love. Tragically, Sadie had died giving birth to the baby, Abigail, and Sadie's mother had threatened to expose the doctor if he did not take the child and bring her up as his own, which she assuredly was. Having lost a dearly loved daughter she did not wish to be further reminded of the tragedy by taking on the child; besides, there were several younger children in the family.

'But your name is on the birth certificate, Father,' said Abbie, perplexed. 'Surely you could have been exposed by that? It was there in black and white for everyone to see.'

'Not everyone, only those who were closely involved. And the registrar kept his own counsel. As a matter of fact, I knew him. He was a friend of mine, so nothing ever came to light. I insisted that my name should be there. I did not wish to deny that I was your father ... and never have I wanted to deny it, my dear. You have grown up into a young woman I am very proud of.' Abbie continued to regard him impassively, too stunned, as yet, to smile or show any sign of forgiveness.

'The hardest thing, of course, as you can imagine,' he continued, 'was telling your mother ... er, Eva. There were many angry words spoken and recriminations, but she agreed, after a lot of heart searching I should imagine, to take the child ... er, you, my dear. And I think it was to her credit that she did so. She was very bitter at first, and I knew that was entirely my fault. I half expected her to blurt out the truth to you, as you got older, but she never did ... and I could not help but admire her for that. She looked after you; she took on the responsibility for your upbringing. Many's the time I would like to have shown you more affection,' he sighed. 'But somehow I couldn't do it. It just used to arouse her jealousy. And so I started leaving the care of you entirely to her. It's quite usual anyway. Regrettable, but that's the way it is. In most households it's the mother who brings up the children while the father takes a back seat. And there was your Aunt Bertha, of course. What a blessing she turned out to be.'

'Yes, indeed, Father,' replied Abbie, vehemently. 'I shudder to think what sort of a life I might have had if it hadn't been for

Aunt Bertha, especially now I know the truth. Even when I was a tiny girl I used to think she was the only one who loved me. When I look back at my childhood it is always Aunt Bertha I think of. Not . . . Mother, or . . .'

'Or me.' Her father's look was anguished. 'I know, Abbie. I know, my dear. And if I could make it up to you I would. I have tried, you know, over the years. Especially since you met Peter. I tried to make Eva see how right you are for one another. It makes me very happy to know you have someone who loves you so much. The reason she didn't want to let you go must have been because she . . . loved you.'

'If you say so, Father,' replied Abbie. 'Yes, Maybe you're right. I hope you are right.'

'But did you never have any suspicion, any inkling, that Eva was not your true mother? I would have thought—'

'No, why should I?'

'Well, because of your lovely brown eyes, my dear. Eva's are . . . were blue. Mine are grey. Two such parents could never produce a brown-eyed child. Brown eyes are always dominant. It's a law of heredity.'

'That's something you know much more about than I do. Why should I question what I looked like? I just knew that I was plump and not very attractive – apart from my brown eyes – and that Mother seemed to want to make me look even more plain and old-fashioned. I did ask Aunt Bertha once, I remember, why I had brown eyes, and she told me I was a throwback. I didn't know what she meant at the time, then I realised, later, that she meant someone further back in the family must have had them. So it was . . . Sadie, then?'

'Yes, it was Sadie.' Her father nodded, again smiling a little sadly. 'She had the most beautiful warm brown eyes, like yours. You are very much like her in all sorts of ways. Your mannerisms and the way you walk, the way you hold your head. I've noticed it so much since you grew up. You took after me when you were younger, with your height and build. But since you slimmed down a bit you are much more like Sadie. Oh, Abbie, I do hope you will be able to forgive me. I know it may have been wrong to keep it from you all these years, but I honestly thought it was for the best. And I would have told you anyway, when your mother died . . . when Eva died, if you hadn't discovered it for yourself.'

And as Abbie looked at him slumped in the chair, so grey and dejected and sad-looking, she knew she could do no other than forgive him. She was amazed that her father, who had always seemed so aloof and unbending, such a very proper sort of man, should have had a passionate affair; but she realised it made him seem so much more human.

'It's all right, Father,' she said. 'It's been a shock, but I'm glad I know about it now. It makes everything so much clearer.'

When Bertha came home later that day she had two shocks to contend with: the death of her cousin and the discovery that Abbie was now aware of her true parentage.

'I thought that you, of all people, might have told me,' Abbie said to her as the two of them sat drinking cocoa after Cedric had retired to bed. Bertha had had a good cry about Eva and now was much more composed.

'How could I tell you?' she replied. 'It wasn't my place, was it? And she would have been so angry if I had. You know what she was like at times.'

'Yes, I do,' said Abbie. 'Sorry; it was a silly thing to say. Of course you couldn't have said anything. I've been thinking . . . you're not really related to me, are you, Aunt Bertha? I've just realised you're not a blood relation, and I always thought . . .'

'So what does it matter?' replied Bertha. 'Nothing has changed between you and me and it never will. I always knew, didn't I, that I wasn't a blood relation, as you put it, but I loved you as though you were my own right from the start. And the fact that I've found Johnnie again makes no difference neither. I know they say blood is thicker than water, but it's not always true, not in my book. Yes, I've got two grandchildren now and that takes some getting used to, believe me, but they'll never mean as much to me as you do. How could they when I've known you since you were a tiny baby? They're grand kiddies, though . . .'

'Are you going to tell me about them?' asked Abbie, for her aunt had stopped speaking rather abruptly. 'And about Dorothy, Johnnie's wife?'

'Are you sure you want to hear me rambling on?'

'Of course I do. I'm very pleased for you,' replied Abbie. 'I think it's grand that you've got someone of your own, just like I have. I must tell you – in Peter's last letter he said he would definitely be coming to Blackpool in a couple of weeks. Isn't that wonderful news? I'd almost forgotten with all the shock about . . . Mother. And I've heard from Doreen as well. She's full of the joys of spring – well, autumn, I suppose would be more correct – because she's just got engaged to that young man she was telling us about. You remember, Aunt Bertha? He's called Norman Jarvis and he's the son of the farm where she's working.'

'Yes, I remember,' said Bertha. 'Nice lass, that Doreen. I hope everything works out all right for her. So it's not all bad news, is it, love? Every cloud has a silver lining, as they say. We can usually find summat to be happy about. And, Abbie, try not to think badly of your mother. Yes, she was a mother to you as much as she was able to be. And I'm sure she loved you. We all have different ways of showing it. And Eva . . . well, it never came easy to her.'

'Yes, Aunt Bertha.' Abbie nodded. 'I'll try to remember . . . that she loved me.'

'I feel as though I'm a real cuckoo in the nest,' said Abbie to Jim Webster as they worked together in the largest greenhouse. They were gathering yet another crop of ripe tomatoes, large and round and glossy, not quite at their full redness, but more of an orangey yellow hue, so that they could finish the ripening process in their boxes. She had returned to Marton Moss after the funeral. It was only just over a week since her mother's death and her alarming discovery about her parentage, but to Abbie it seemed much longer. It felt natural to her to talk over her problems with her good friend Jim, who, as always, was listening to her with the utmost patience and kindliness.

She had written to Peter, of course, telling him the sad news and the startling revelations, and she had spoken with him over the phone. His support and the knowledge of his deep love for her had been a great comfort, sustaining her through the awful ordeal of the funeral, coping with her father's grief and – in spite of everything – her own. There was a deep sadness and bewilderment, still, at the heart of her that she was unable to shake off. But Peter was not here, and Jim was more than willing to listen.

'It's been a dreadful shock,' she told him now. 'All these years I've been thinking one thing, and now I find out it was all a lie. I'm not who I thought I was. I feel as though I don't know who I am at all or where I belong.'

Jim paused for a moment from his task of tomato packing, standing upright and frowning slightly as he rubbed his aching back and then his thigh. He never said much about his war wound, but Abbie guessed it was quite painful at times. 'If you don't mind me being blunt, Abbie,' he said now, 'you are talking nonsense. Listen, love.' It was the first time he had used any endearment in speaking to her, but she paid little heed to this, knowing it was just the way Lancashire people addressed one another; everyone was love, or, more colloquially, 'luv'. 'Listen. You're still the same person that you always were. Your father thinks the world of you, and he's very proud of you, too. I could see it all in his eyes when he said goodbye to you. You mean everything to him. As for your . . . mother, perhaps you can understand her a little better now, eh? Why she seemed so bitter and angry at times? That seems quite understandable to me, after what you've told me. But I'm sure she loved you. And from what you've told me of your Aunt Bertha she will always be there for you. They all love you.'

She had told Jim about them all: that Eva was not really her mother, that her father had had a clandestine relationship with a young woman – it could not harm his standing as a doctor now as it was all so long ago – and about Bertha's one-time folly with the son of a titled family and the unexpectedly happy ending to this story. 'Yes, I know,' she replied. 'I know, deep down, that they care about me, Father and Aunt Bertha, and they've tried to tell me that. Mother did, too, in her own way. It's incredible, isn't it, Jim, an ordinary – well, seemingly ordinary – family like ours and underneath there are all these secrets and skeletons in the cupboard?'

'I reckon there's a few in every family,' said Jim, 'if you dig deep enough. You mustn't underestimate yourself, Abbie, or the way people feel about you. It's not just your own family who cares about you. Everybody here, for instance, cares about you very much. We haven't known you very long, but you've become one of the family, haven't you? So look at it this way – you've got two families now instead of one. To say nothing of the one down in Norfolk. I'm sure Peter's parents will be delighted to have you as a daughter-in-law. I know mine would . . . I mean, well, you know what I mean, don't you?' He gave an embarrassed laugh and, to her surprise, Abbie noticed that his face had reddened slightly. 'I only meant . . . any fellow's parents would be pleased to welcome a grand lass like you.' He was speaking hurriedly. 'He'll be here soon, won't he, your Peter?'

'Yes, next weekend, Jim. I can hardly believe it. It seems ages since I saw him.' She glanced across at Jim, but he was no longer looking at her in a funny way, as he had been a few minutes ago. In fact he was not looking at her at all; he was concentrating hard on the next bunch of ripening tomatoes. 'He'll be here on Saturday, or possibly Friday night. I'm just waiting to hear from him.' Jim nodded, his attention focused on his task.

'What about you. Jim? Are you taking Sylvia out again? Not that it's anything to do with me,' she went on, when Jim did not answer, 'but I can't help noticing—'

'Noticing what?' He was quite his old self as he turned to grin at her.

'Well, that she thinks a lot about you. You know what you just said about seeing the look in my father's eyes? Well, it's in Sylvia's eyes, too, how she feels about you. I think she's in love with you, Jim.'

Jim's grin faded a little. 'It takes two, Abbie,' he said quietly.

'You mean . . . you don't . . . ?'

'Love her? I've not thought about it. She was my friend's kid sister, wasn't she? She's sort of grown up always knowing me. I'm quite fond of her.'

'That's a good start, Jim.'

He laughed out loud. 'You're too nosy by far, Abbie Winters, like a lot of women. As a matter of fact I am taking her out again on Saturday. We're going to a film at the Empire. Satisfied?'

'Perfectly,' Abbie replied. She wanted him to be happy. Jim was a smashing bloke and he deserved a really nice girl like Sylvia. She felt so much better now, having talked to him, and she wanted him to be as happy as she was. She had been so miserable and lost during the last week, but now a surge of joy took hold of her as she thought of meeting Peter this coming weekend.

Peter had not said so outright, but she knew from various things he had let slip that his next op would be the last one of the tour. Then he would begin his officer training and by the time he finished that, well, with a bit of luck the war might be over. She counted on her fingers. Only five more days and she would be with him again.

More than anything else on the flight Peter feared the sea, that limitless stretch of jet-black ocean that had to be crossed at the beginning and end of every raid. He dreaded, above everything, the plane coming to grief there, over the North Sea. If they were forced to bale out there would be so much less chance of rescue. He had nightmares about being swallowed up in its inky depths. The fear of this was just as great as the other nightmare he had, that of being trapped in a blazing gun turret.

It was bad enough flying over the ocean when the plane was all in one piece, which, thank the Lord, it usually was. But there were times when they had suffered a near miss and were forced to limp home 'on a wing and a prayer', as the song said. Once, when the top had been blown right off the gun turret Peter had believed for a while that it was the end of everything for him. How could he ever survive this devastating mind-blowing cold, he had thought, as he had crouched in his shattered turret with the icy wind whipping round him. The cold always got to you no matter how much clothing you wore. Three pairs of gloves (silk, woollen and leather); lambswool underwear; Shetland wool sweaters; even a thermatically heated suit with a built in 'Mae West' were not sufficient to withstand the low temperatures they suffered at high altitudes. Still, they had landed safely that night, thanks to the valiant efforts and cool head of their skipper. Peter had breathed again, giving thanks to a God he was not always convinced existed.

He had been brought up to believe in God. He had gone obediently to Sunday School and church and had even been the church organist, all without really questioning what he was doing or why he was doing it. If anyone had asked him he would always have said he was a believer, until he had joined the RAF and become a flier. He had seen sights so dreadful that he was sure a merciful God could never have allowed; until a small voice inside himself whispered that it was not the Almighty who was to blame, but Man and his inhumanity to his fellow creatures. He prayed to Him though, just in case there was somebody listening out there. He suspected that all fliers did, at the beginning of a flight, and at the end when they knew they had been safely delivered to fight another day, although it wasn't something they often talked about.

The best time of the flight was when they were returning home, free from enemy flak and almost clear of the dreaded ocean, when dawn was breaking over the land. Then they could unfasten their oxygen masks and pass around their flasks of coffee; even partake of the odd cigarette (on the q.t. of course, because this was supposed to be strictly *verboten*). On landing there was the reward of cocoa laced with rum to look forward to, then after debriefing – telling Intelligence about the weather, the flak and fighter opposition, the accuracy of the Pathfinder's markings and all that – there would be sleep, blessed sleep. Dreamless sleep if they were lucky, and for Peter the sleep he enjoyed after a raid was usually free from nightmares. It was at other times, between raids, when the waiting for the next op sapped at his courage, that the gremlins started to trouble him. Since he had met Abbie again, however, he had not been nearly so bad. It was Abbie he thought of now before he dropped off to sleep, her smiling eyes and warm lips and comforting arms, willing himself to dream about her, which he often did.

The night before the last op, however, the nightmare had surfaced again – it was the sea this time, not the fire – and he had awoken in a cold sweat which he had to try to hide from his room-mates. The anxiety had stayed with him all day, but he told himself it was because it was the last flight of the tour – number thirty. He had only to get this one over, then he would be grounded for a little while before beginning his officer training. It was only natural that he should be apprehensive over this, the big one, his ultimate triumph. He had to believe it would be a triumph, but still the niggling doubts and an inexplicable feeling of foreboding haunted him throughout the day, until he climbed into the plane and then there was no time to brood.

It had seemed at first that his fears were groundless. Everything went according to plan. They found their target without any difficulty and though the sight of the blazing German town below them filled Peter with an overwhelming sadness, as it always did, he rejoiced, knowing it was the last time he would have to witness such a sight; for the time being at least, perhaps for ever, if, by some miracle the war should come to an end before he had to fly again.

In his relief that it was nearly all over for tonight and that they had come through it safely he must have allowed his concentration to lapse. The enemy aircraft appeared out of nowhere. There was a cataclysmic explosion of sound for which Peter had been unprepared, then the plane seemed to stop dead. In an involuntary action he threw himself to the floor, then the icy blast whistling around him told him, as before, that the top had been blown off the gun turret. He pulled himself together and fired a few shots at the marauding plane, but it was too late. Peter cursed himself for being taken unawares as the enemy plane turned tail and headed for home, for he knew by this time that the damage was not only in the gun turret. Unless he was very much mistaken there had been a direct hit to the nose of the plane as well. He could tell from the way the aircraft was staggering and lurching.

As he crawled to the front of the plane he discovered that Bob, the mid-gunner who had replaced Sandy, had been injured. Blood was pouring from his arm, but it appeared to be only a flesh wound. Peter did what he could to stem the flow of blood – Bob, poor devil, was unconscious – before investigating further. It was as he feared. There was a damn great hole in the metal just ahead of the cockpit and a gale-force wind was whistling through the fuselage. Most of the windscreen had shattered and how Skip was managing to keep the wings level, surrounded as he was by the torrent of freezing air, Peter could not imagine.

'Bloody fuel gauge has gone for a Burton,' gasped Flying Officer Banks – 'Skip' to all his crew. Peter could see that the needles on the instrument panel were spinning round like whirling dervishes. It was impossible to tell how much fuel was left, but he hoped and prayed there would be enough to get them back home, that was if the plane could make it. 'The engines seem OK, thank God,' said Skip. 'We might just make it. A hell of a way to go yet though, and it's going to be bloody cold.' His words were coming in short gasps. 'Check on the others, would you, Peter?'

'They seem OK, Skip. Well, Bob's been injured, but it's not all that bad from the look of things. The others are OK.'

The other four had escaped without injury. And that was a bloody miracle, thought Peter; at least it would be if they arrived back with all seven of the crew alive. It was just the plane that had copped it, but Skip seemed to be managing magnificently.

But Skip had spoken too soon, for it soon became obvious they were in serious trouble. The plane was now dipping and diving like a switchback, and Peter realised they would not be able to reach the shores of England safely; they would not even reach the ocean. They were rapidly losing height and he glimpsed, at a crazy angle, a clump of trees, a church spire, a river, some farm buildings ... The scenes were appearing then vanishing with the see-saw motion of the plane like pictures at a magic lantern show. All at once there was a coughing, spluttering sound, then a roaring noise ... then silence, and Peter knew that at least one of the engines had packed in.

'Bale out, for Christ's sake, bale out!' cried Skip. But it was too late. The world turned upside down as the plane lurched totally out of control. The sky, the trees, the barns spun crazily round and round, there was the sound of shattering metal and the deafening roar of the remaining engine engulfing Peter. There was an almighty crash as the plane dropped to earth. The wreckage whirled around him, on top of him, burying him completely, and Peter knew it was the end of everything. He had bought it. Was he dead already, he wondered, as the deafening sounds gave way to an eerie silence. Then everything went black and he stopped hearing or seeing anything.

Chapter 23

'Letter for you, Abbie,' said Mrs Webster with an understanding smile as she handed her a familiar-looking blue envelope at the breakfast table. It was, in reality, the second breakfast of the day. Mornings started early at the market garden, with a cup of tea and a slice of bread or toast at six o'clock, followed by a much more substantial meal of bacon or sausage and eggs, mushrooms and – inevitably – fried tomatoes at around eight thirty. 'This is what you've been waiting for, isn't it, dear?'

'Yes, that's right.' Abbie smiled back at her, feeling the happiness which had been gently bubbling away inside her for the last few days at the thought of seeing Peter again, suddenly rise to the surface, causing her face to break out in an uncontrollable grin. 'Peter will be telling me when he's arriving. It could be later today or it may be tomorrow.' Today was Friday, the day she had been looking forward to for so long.

She took the envelope from Mrs Webster, glancing automatically at the name and address written there. She stopped before tearing it open, frowning slightly. How strange; this was not Peter's handwriting. It was smaller and neater with a backhand slope and the colour of the ink was different too. The smile had already faded from her face and the feeling of elation that had suffused right through her was already being replaced by one of dread as she drew the sheets of closely written words from the envelope. Mr and Mrs Webster and Jim, as though aware that something was amiss, had become silent. They were watching her, not openly, but with covert looks of quiet concern.

The address at the top, Abbie noticed briefly before she started to read the rest of the letter, was that of Peter's parents in Wymondham.

My Dear Abbie, *the letter began,*

I am afraid I have the most dreadful news for you and
there is, alas, no easy way to tell you. We received a
communication today to tell us that our beloved son, Peter,
has been killed in action. Your beloved fiancé, as well, of
course, my dear, and I'm sure you can imagine how
heartbroken we are at having to give you such distressing
news. The plane failed to return from the bombing raid
and . . .'

Abbie could read no more. The paper fell from her fingers as
she gave a cry of anguish and slumped across the breakfast
table, her half-empty cup of tea spilling and flowing in a steady
stream across the red-checked table cover.

Mrs Webster was the first one to reach her side, guessing, all
too accurately, what the letter must contain. Even before Abbie's
tormented cry of 'He's dead, he's dead . . .' the woman had
known. Abbie was not the sort of girl to burst into tears at the
news that her boyfriend's visit had been delayed or cancelled.
This confounded hellish war, thought Gladys Webster as she
put her arms round Abbie. She reached out a hand and rescued
the sheets of blue notepaper from the trickle of tea that had
splashed across them. Already the ink was beginning to run a
little and Abbie would need to read the rest of the letter as soon
as she was able to cope with it. And Gladys, rather selfishly she
knew, uttered a silent prayer of thanks to the Almighty, as she
had already done so many times, that her own son had been
spared. She and Arthur had been shocked at first on receiving
the news that Jim had been injured, but when they realised that
it was the means of keeping him out of the rest of the war they
had quietly rejoiced. How many more young men who should
have the whole of their lives ahead of them, like this lovely
young woman's fiancé, were going to pay the price before the
whole bloody conflict came to an end? They had not yet reached
the beginning of the end, this Second Front, or D-Day that
everyone seemed to be talking about.

'I know, my love, I know. What a terrible thing to happen.'
Gently she stroked the girl's hair, pillowing her head against her

breast, rocking her as one would do to a child. 'Go on, love, you have a good cry. Never mind us, you cry as much as you want.' The poor lass, thought Gladys. As if she hadn't already had enough to put up with: the death of her mother and then finding out that the woman wasn't her real mother after all. She had told Jim more about it than she had told her, Gladys, and her husband, but it was no secret. It was always said that troubles never came singly, but this young woman seemed to be having a whole barrowload recently. Gladys felt, however, that Abigail Winters was a strong girl, mentally as well as physically, and that she would cope with this sorrow. She had only known her a short time, but it seemed much longer because Abbie had settled down and endeared herself to them all by her willingness to work hard and by the warmth of her personality. Not an over-effusive warmth, more of a serene gentleness and amiability that made you feel glad to have her around.

After a few moments her sobs ceased and she raised her head, easing herself from Mrs Webster's comforting arms. She took hold of the older woman's hand. Thank you, thank you,' she said. 'I needed to cry . . . but I'd better read the rest of the letter.' She drew a khaki handkerchief from her breeches pocket, wiped her tear-stained face and blew her nose. 'How awful it must have been for Mrs Horsfall to have to write and tell me. They would let his parents know, of course, with them being next of kin. I was only his fiancée. It would have been different if we had been . . . married.' She took a deep breath to check the sob arising in her throat and started to read the letter.

It went on to say precisely what Abbie had just said to Mrs Webster; that Mr and Mrs Horsfall had automatically been informed as next of kin, but they felt that she had as much right to be told straight away as they had. They wrote how very fond they had become of her in the comparatively short time they had known her; she had made their dear son, Peter, so very happy and they hoped she would keep in touch. Perhaps, in the not too distant future, she could pay them a visit at their home in Norfolk.

Abbie was a little surprised to see that the signature on the letter was that of Frank Horsfall, Peter's father. In her own family it was always her mother . . . Eva . . . who had dealt with all the correspondence: Christmas cards, letters to relatives and all that sort of thing; but she knew that this sad letter came with the undoubted affection of both Frank and Lily Horsfall. Lily, no doubt, was too distressed to write at the moment and Abbie, in the midst of her own grief, spared a thought for both of them. How unbelievably dreadful. Peter had been their only son, their pride and joy. She had seen the quiet pride in the eyes of them both, although they had never been possessive of him since he had left home to join the RAF. They had welcomed her into their family at once and she had known their liking for her was genuine. It was less than six months since she and Peter had met again, for the second time, but it seemed more like six years to Abbie, so well had she come to know him. She had felt she was part of him, as he was of her. They had become soul mates; not only lovers, but very close friends, and now it seemed as though half of her were missing.

Silently she put the letter back into its envelope then looked up to meet the concerned eyes of Jim and his father. Mrs Webster was busying herself with clearing away the breakfast pots.

'You know how very sorry we are, don't you, Abbie?' whispered Jim.

She nodded, muttering a subdued, 'Thank you . . . Yes, I know,' but she was no longer weeping.

'Would you like to go home, luv?' asked Mr Webster. 'Back to your father's? I could run you there in a jiffy.'

But Abbie decided against it, knowing it would be far better for her to keep busy. Her father would be occupied with his patients and although Aunt Bertha would listen and sympathise – and cry along with her, too – she felt she could not cope with that just yet. She had to come to terms with her grief and heartache in her own way and she could think of no better way than that of engrossing herself wholeheartedly in her work here, at the market garden. She would phone her father this evening and go home for the weekend tomorrow, as she had planned, the difference being that she would be on her own.

On her own . . . Abbie, at that moment, felt very much alone. Her mother had gone, now Peter . . . How many more of her loved ones was she going to lose? One person she would dearly love to talk to at that moment was her good friend Doreen. But she hadn't seen her for ages, nor heard from her; Doreen was not the best of letter writers. She would write to her at once, she decided, and maybe her friend might manage to come home for a weekend leave. How good it would be to have the comfort of Doreen's matter-of-fact, but very real, friendship. But, for the moment, there was another crop of tomatoes to be gathered.

She was to find, in the days and weeks that lay ahead, that work, sheer back-breaking physical toil, was an excellent remedy for her grief and for the despondency that threatened to engulf her from time to time; although she did try, desperately, not to give in to despair. At first she could not believe what had happened. She felt as though it were all some absurd tale she had been told and that she would wake up and find she had dreamed it. There was no body to see and to mourn to make it real, no funeral to attend, and she was not sure whether this was a good thing or not. So long as there was no concrete evidence of Peter's death for her to see with her own eyes there remained a feeling of unreality about it all. But Abbie, deep down, was a sensible girl and she gradually began to acknowledge the futility of this thinking. Peter had gone and she had to pick up the pieces of her life and carry on, just as thousands of other young women, in exactly the same predicament as herself in this dreadful war, were having to do.

Self-pity, too, was something she had to contend with and fight against. The feeling she had had after her mother's death came back now and again to plague her, only now it was much worse; the feeling that she did not really belong anywhere. Her father's place no longer seemed like her home, she had been away from it for so long; her Aunt Bertha, who at one time had been all the world to Abbie, was now wrapped up, and understandably so, in her new family. And the worst thing, of course, was that Peter had gone, and with his death had gone the sense of belonging she had known, of being his entirely, body and soul.

She could not speak of all this to Jim, although she had once confided in him soon after her mother had died. It was all too complex and too personal, but his very presence was a comfort to her. He worked alongside her in a companionable silence, if that was what she wished, or he chatted with her when she was in a more talkative frame of mind. And as the weeks went by it seemed to Abbie that this was where she belonged, for the time being at least, at the Websters' market garden on Marton Moss. Here she was finding solace. It was a restful haven where her grief was gradually assuaged and where she could begin the painful process of getting on with the rest of her life.

The tomato season at last came to an end. All the greenhouses were cleared of tomato plants and weeded, then Mr Webster hired a machine known as a steamer which came and sterilised the soil. Before the steamer arrived it was all hands on deck working outside, lifting soil, filling barrows with it and wheeling them into the greenhouses. And muck spreading, too, one of the least palatable of all gardening jobs.

The autumn crops were harvested – potatoes, beetroot, carrots, turnips and onions – and it was then time for the cress season which would go on from November till March. The greenhouses which had previously held tomatoes were now prepared for the cress. Each greenhouse was dug and three or four inches of finely sifted soil was spread over the surface, which was then levelled and made firm. It was now ready for the cress seed which was soaked, scattered and well watered, then, finally wet sacks were laid on the top. The seed germinated very quickly, in about five days; the sacks were removed on the sixth day and the cress was cut on the seventh. And so it would go on throughout the winter months, a fresh crop of cress being cut every seven days or so.

Abbie remembered how, when she had been in the Infant school, the teacher had grown mustard and cress seeds on a piece of wet flannel, to teach the children something of the wonders of nature and growth. They had all been amazed at how very quickly the seeds started to put out tiny green shoots. She was amazed afresh now, but before long she was sick of the sight of cress; thousand upon thousand of small boxes being stacked into containers for dispatch to the shops and markets of Lancashire and even further afield.

But it was her job, the job she had chosen just over a year and a half ago when she and Doreen had decided to join the Women's Land Army. She now had three red half-diamonds stitched on the sleeve of her greatcoat; and what a lot had happened to her in those eighteen months. The training hostel, then those awful weeks at the Rawnsleys' farm; her parting from Doreen; her meeting with Carlo at Daisy Bank Farm, and her unceremonious dismissal from that place. How strange; she hadn't given a thought to Carlo for ages, but she realised now that if it hadn't been for her friendship with him she might never have left Yorkshire. She might never have met up with Peter again. Life was full of ifs. Cause and effect, chance or mischance. But was life just a game of chance, or was there some purpose behind it all, some plan worked out beforehand by a power much greater than our own? Abbie was not sure, but the times when she worked quietly by herself and not in the company of Jim or the other helpers gave her plenty of time for reflection.

She knew that even though she had had to face heartache and loss and anguish she would not have had it any other way. She was thankful she had spent those few months with Peter. She had known, for a short time, what it was like to love someone completely and unreservedly, and though she had lost him she would not wish to have foregone the experience. She felt it had made her stronger and wiser and more understanding of others.

Christmas of 1943 was, inevitably, a quiet, sad sort of time in the Winters' family home. There were just the three of them, Cedric, Bertha and Abbie, gathered round the table for the festive meal. It was their first Christmas without Eva, and though she had caused friction at times the house seemed lost without her. And there was the thought in all their minds, though it remined unspoken, that Abbie should, at this time, have been preparing for her wedding day. Bertha, as always, had prepared an excellent meal in spite of the shortages. There was the usual chicken, ordered weeks in advance at the local butcher, and Mr Harding had come up trumps with a small quantity of dried fruit for the Christmas pudding, although the mixture was not quite so rich and dark as in previous years.

Abbie knew her aunt's mind was only partly with her and her father. She was already looking ahead to New Year, which she had been invited to spend with her son, John, and his family.

John had a few days' leave and Bertha was, naturally, overjoyed at the thought of seeing him again, though she was trying to temper her elation in respect for Abbie's unhappiness.

Something which cheered Abbie considerably was meeting with Doreen again. She had seen her friend, briefly, soon after Peter's fatal crash, but Doreen was now home for a week's leave and, as Abbie, also, was at home for several days, they agreed to meet as soon as the shops opened after the holiday period.

'Great to see you, luv.' Doreen greeted her warmly when they met at their usual place on the corner of Park Road and Church Street. She kissed her friend on the cheek, then put her arms round her in an affectionate hug which spoke volumes. Behind the irrepressible grin there was a touch of sadness and more sympathy in her eyes than she could find words to express. But their thoughts of Peter remained unspoken. 'It really is grand to see you. I've missed you so much, kid, you've no idea.'

They fell quickly and easily into their old camaraderie. They mooched around the shops, not buying much apart from essentials like hairgrips and Pond's vanishing cream and a bottle of Amami shampoo, then they decided to treat themselves to a cup of tea and a toasted teacake at Robinson's café in Clifton Street.

Abbie was anxious to hear all the news of Doreen's large family. Mrs Miller, unfortunately, was not at all well, her recurring bronchitis having been more troublesome than usual this winter. Abbie's father had already told her of this, saying he had visited her a few times. She had spent a few days in bed before Christmas, which was most unusual for her, but she was up and about now.

'It will have done her a world of good to see you again,' said Abbie. 'I'm sure she misses you a lot, and I know it's not easy for you to get home, being up in the wilds of Yorkshire.'

'No, I noticed a big change in Mam,' said Doreen. 'She's certainly a lot frailer and she coughs a lot more. It's made it harder for her, of course, with our Vera being away as well.' Vera, the second oldest girl in the Miller family, had joined the ATS as soon as she was eighteen and was now stationed in the south of England. She had had a forty-eight-hour pass at Christmas, but had gone back that morning. Abbie got the impression, one she had long held, that Vera did not consider the needs of her family in the way Doreen did.

'You must call in and see Mam before you go back to work,' said Doreen, 'if you have time, that is. That would cheer her up as much as it did seeing me. She always thought a lot about you.'

'Yes . . . yes, I will,' Abbie promised. She felt a pang of guilt that she hadn't called to see Nancy Miller before now. After all, she was working in Blackpool, not hundreds of miles away, and the nice little woman had always been very kind to her. 'And what about the rest of them?' she asked. 'Your Billy and the other two girls?'

'Our Billy's seventeen now. He can't wait to join up, but he's promised Mam and Dad he won't go till he's eighteen. They're hoping, of course, it'll all be over by then and he's hoping it won't. Well . . . no, I don't suppose he hopes that really; he wants to see the end of it as much as the rest of us do, but he would like to feel he's done his bit. He's still at Harding's, but he's rather more than an errand boy now. I gather he's taken my job over, behind the counter; Mr Harding's right-hand man now, in fact. He's a good lad, our Billy.

'But as for our Janey, well, I've never seen anyone change so much as our Janey has. Grown up over night, she has. Honestly, you should see her! Bright red lipstick and nail varnish and tight jumpers that show all her bust. I said to her, "You look like a tart, our Janey, in that skimpy thing. I can see yer nipples through it." But she told me to shut up and mind me own business.'

Abbie smiled. 'Let me see – Janey, she's the dark one, isn't she? The one who looks more like your dad?' She remembered the two younger girls, Janey and Peggy, from her first visit to the house. Quiet, well-behaved girls, busy with their homework, but she had always got their names mixed up.

'Yes, that's right. Peggy's little and blonde, more like me mam and me. Not like me in any other way, though. She's real brainy, our Peggy, and Mam and Dad've said she can stay on at school till she's sixteen to take her exams an' all that. But it was our Janey I was telling you about. She's discovered lads, y'see, and not half! She's at the Tower or Winter Gardens nearly every night, an' a different bloke nearly every night an' all, according to her at any rate.'

'I'm surprised she can afford it,' remarked Abbie, knowing that the Miller family had never had much money to splash around.

'Oh, she's got all her chairs at home, has our Janey,' laughed Doreen. 'She gets them to pay, all these RAF lads she gets to know. There's no meeting 'em inside for her.' It was a well-known fact that if you met a fellow inside the dance hall then it meant you had to pay for yourself.

'How old is she?' asked Abbie.

'Just turned sixteen. She's been left school well over a year now. She's working at a rock factory in Marton.'

'And what do your mother and dad say about all her . . . her carryings-on? They used to be rather strict with you, didn't they? Well, not as strict as my mother was, of course, but I remember you telling me that your mum wanted you to behave yourself, and that you always tried to. I know you've had a good upbringing . . . and a loving one, too. You all have, Janey as well. So what are they doing about her?'

Doreen gave a slight shrug. 'There's not much they can do, is there? They've got three daughters who've all toed the line, more or less, and now they've got one who won't. It takes all sorts and I suppose three good 'uns out of four is all you can expect. Not that I'm saying our Janey is all bad, you know. She's just . . . silly, and Mam doesn't want to be too heavy-handed in case she makes her worse. And Dad won't upset Mam so he doesn't say anything. Happen she'll settle down when she's had her fling.'

'It's to be hoped so,' said Abbie. 'Now, tell me about you and Norman.' She had already admired the small solitaire diamond ring. 'Any wedding plans?'

'No, we haven't made any definite plans yet,' said Doreen. 'I'll be twenty-one in March, so we thought we'd wait till then and see how things work out.'

'With the war, you mean?'

'Partly, but I feel I don't want to get married until I can see Mam is quite well again. She wants the wedding to be here, y'see, in Blackpool, and I don't think she could cope with all the excitement yet. Perhaps by summer we'll know definitely. One blessing is that Norman's a Catholic, like me – I told you that, didn't I? – so there'll be no problem there.'

'Why? Would there have been a problem? I'm not a Catholic, but it hasn't stopped you and me being friends, has it?'

'Ah, but it's different when you want to marry somebody that isn't. Even now, when we're supposed to be, y'know, a bit more broad-minded, like, it can still cause problems. And I do want Mam and Dad to approve of him.'

'But what about you, Doreen? Are you sure how you feel about him? You do love him, don't you? At one time you didn't seem too sure.'

'I am now,' replied Doreen. 'Yes, I'm sure, Abbie. Norman's the one for me, even though he's not the sort of bloke I thought I'd marry at all . . . I haven't wanted to go on about it too much though, luv,' she added, with a wary glance at her friend. 'I didn't want to upset you.'

'Don't worry about me,' said Abbie quietly. 'I'm . . . all right.' But she lowered her head, unable to meet the look of sympathy, yet one of delight in her own happiness, in Doreen's eyes.

When she saw Nancy Miller a couple of days later she knew exactly what Doreen meant. This frail little woman did not look as though she could cope with very much at the moment, certainly not with a wedding or a wayward daughter. Her overbright eyes, flushed cheeks and the painful thinness of her face and figure did not augur well for the future at all.

The birds that frequented the garden when she was working quietly on her own were a surprising solace to Abbie's grief. Often in the half-light of an early winter's morning she would hear a cheery whistle, and there was a lively blackbird perched on a clump of earth, his head cocked up at her and his bright beady eye seeming to beg her to help him find his breakfast. She would willingly oblige by unearthing a worm and was then rewarded by his song from the nearby hedge, a cheering sound in those dark dismal days.

There were thrushes, too, and an occasional robin, the sight of his glowing red breast never failing to bring a lift to her dejected spirit. And always there were the starlings: noisy, greedy, somewhat ugly, birds, appearing as if from nowhere, scores of them at a time, hopping and flapping and chattering away on the patch of grass that was the Websters' private garden area. As dusk fell, early on those short days after Christmas, they would gather in their hundreds on the rooftops, then, as though at a signal from their leader, off they would fly in formation across the darkening sky – sometimes, chillingly and heartrendingly reminding her of a bomber squadron – to their roosting place for the night. Under one of the piers, Abbie had been told, South Pier, more than likely, from this part of the town. And the visiting seagulls, always to be found in Blackpool gardens, especially when there was stormy weather at sea, reminded her of warm sunny days on the sands. Times when, as a little girl, she had been so happy in the company of her Aunt Bertha. And she hoped, she had to make herself believe, there would come a time when she would be happy again.

One February morning she noticed a clump of snowdrops pushing their way through the dull brown earth.

> 'Little ladies, white and green,
> With your spears about you,
> Will you tell us where you've been
> Since we lived without you?'

She found herself muttering the words of a poem she had learned at school, rather a mawkish oversentimental poem, she realised now, but she had loved it as a little girl. She couldn't remember the rest of it, but it was something about the joy that these delicate little flowers, the harbingers of spring, brought in the midst of winter. And she began to believe that spring would one day return to her own cold and empty life.

The area known as Marton Moss was unique, a few square miles of countryside, farming land and rural homesteads on the fringe of the busy, brash, often bawdy, resort of Blackpool. So unsophisticated was the Moss, and its people, that it might have been hundreds of miles away and a hundred years removed in time from the worldly cosmopolitan town on its doorstep. At least that had been true in the last century and in the early years of this one, but now the pattern was changing. As Blackpool rose to greater importance as a leading seaside resort, so did Marton Moss begin to develop. Better roads and forms of transport had resulted in the rapid expansion of the market garden industry. Countless acres of land were put under glass, and more and more of the horticultural produce was exported to the big towns of north and central England. For many years Marton had been ruled by a Parish Council and the Fylde Rural Council, with somewhat limited powers. But since 1934, Marton had been amalgamated with Blackpool, and the old ways and old places were gradually changing.

There were, however, several of the old cottages still remaining, and in one of these lived Will Webster, Jim's grandfather. He had been a widower for ten years and was now in his mid-eighties, but he still, stubbornly and independently, insisted on living alone. Abbie had heard a lot about him, but had never met him as he usually visited his son and family on a Sunday afternoon and had always gone home, driven there by either Jim or his father, before she returned. It was one evening in the February of 1944 when Jim suggested to Abbie that the two of them might have a walk round to see his grandfather. Jim chose to walk rather than drive because, although Will's cottage was a good mile or so away, the last half-mile was along a rutted country lane which was much easier to negotiate on foot than in the van. As it was a dry evening, frosty and cold, but with no sign of either rain or snow, Abbie readily agreed.

The cottage was one of a row of four, low and whitewashed with an overhanging thatched roof. Jim told her they were relieved that his grandfather was not completely isolated in this homestead, which dated from the late eighteenth century, as he had good neighbours on whom he could call should it be necessary. Not that he often did so; Will's self-sufficiency, amounting almost to pig-headedness, was legendary among the Mossites.

'Granddad, this is Abbie,' said Jim, ushering her through the low doorway. She had to bend her head a little on entering, and Jim, a few inches taller, had to stoop even more. 'You've heard me mention her, haven't you? She's our land girl.' He turned to grin at her. 'But she's more like one of the family now, aren't you, Abbie?'

' 'Ow d'yer do, miss?' Will reached out his hand, gnarled and sinewy and brown-spotted, but Abbie discovered he had a very firm grasp. 'Ah'm very pleased to meet yer.' He turned to his grandson. ''Ave I 'eard of 'er, y' say? I've 'eard nowt else for t'last six months and moower. It's been Abbie this and Abbie that all t'time, I tell thee.' He smiled at her, a roguish twinkle in his blue-grey eyes. They were not faded, nor did they have the milky opaqueness that the eyes of the elderly often had, but were clear and undimmed, very like those of Jim, in fact. There was a striking family likeness between Jim, his father and grandfather; the same slim build, thin-featured face and ruddy cheeks, and a good head of wiry hair which was inclined to curl. Will's, of course, was not dark any longer, like Jim's, but entirely white although he did not appear to have lost any of it. That and his cheerful face and upright stance made him seem much younger than his eighty-odd years. Abbie was not surprised at his fiercely independent spirit.

'How do you do, Mr Webster?' she said, rather embarrassed, but making no comment about his outspoken remarks. 'I am very pleased to meet you, too, at last.'

'Aye, well then, coom on in, the pair on yer.'

The door opened straight into the living room which had its original flagged floor, though almost entirely covered over with a faded carpet square and a large rag rug. There was a huge black range in which a well-built-up fire burned brightly, and in the light from the gaslamp Abbie could see that this was a comfortable and well-lived-in sort of room. The old oak furniture was glossy with the patina of age, and the plants on the windowsill and the tops of the surfaces – geraniums, spider plants, begonias and cyclamen; there must have been twenty or more – were not droopy and brown-leaved, but obviously tended with loving care. The room, however, was not overly tidy. Piles of newspapers and periodicals, mostly gardening magazines, Abbie guessed, stood knee-high in the corners. You could hardly put a pin between the clutter on the mantelpiece. There were letters shoved not only in a tarnished brass letter rack, but behind ornaments and vases; coloured spills in a holder; a pipe rack and ashtray; several commemorative mugs, one dating from the old queen's Diamond Jubilee; and a plethora of family photographs. Neither was it spotlessly clean. There was a film of dust on the sideboard between the saucers holding the plant pots, and the brass fire irons looked as though they could do with a polish, but Abbie guessed that old Mr Webster did for himself pretty well and would not take kindly to any interference.

He insisted on making them a cup of tea, and it was well presented, too: on a tin tray, but in delicate rose-patterned china cups and saucers which, Abbie thought, had most likely been a wedding present some sixty years or more ago.

His country accent, more pronounced than any Abbie had ever heard, was difficult to follow at times, as was his tendency to lapse into the dialect which was unique to the Moss, but she found his stories, that first evening, fascinating.

'Foower childer we brought up here, me and t'missis,' he told her with pride. 'Two lads and two lasses, and they're all in t'same line of business.' His two daughters had married lads from the Moss and lived not far away. His eldest son, Bob, had 'emigrated', as he put it, to try his luck in the wilds of Worcestershire, but Arthur, Jim's father, was 'noan doin' too badly for himself on t'Moss.'

There was no place like it, in Will's opinion. He had never been further afield than Preston all his life, until he went to visit Bob at his market garden near Worcester. He had been born on the Moss and there he would die; but not for ages yet, Abbie found herself hoping. He was a grand old fellow and she knew she could grow to like him immensely.

She learned from Will, that evening, how Blackpool first got its name. The place at that time, in the early eighteenth century, had been little more than a smattering of cobble and clay huts perched on the cliffs overlooking the Irish Sea. A sluggish dark-coloured stream emptied out into the sea at that point, bringing drainage water from Marton Moss, the peaty soil of which had stained the waters to this chocolatey-brown, almost black, colour. And so Blackpool got its name. It was a source of pride to the Moss folk that Marton, or 'Meretun' as it then was, had been on the map long before Blackpool. It had even been mentioned in the Domesday Book.

The Moss had developed over the ages through a long, long process of decomposition. In some far-off century, even before Roman times, the Fylde coastline had been a wild and marshy woodland. When the sea rose up and, driven by hurricane winds, swept over the low-lying land, gigantic oak trees were felled in its path. And there they lay, the bark and foliage slowly rotting down into peat and becoming, eventually, the rich fertile soil that characterised the area. Even to this day, so old Will said, a farmer's plough would occasionally hit an obstruction and another bog oak had to be prised from its prehistoric bed.

Abbie heard, too, about the old country customs that had prevailed on Marton Moss when Will was a lad. Pace-egging at Easter, which meant that the boys and girls went singing at farmhouse doors in the hope of being given an egg; and 'Jolly-ladding', again at Easter, when the young men of the village entered households about to retire for the night, to sing their traditional songs with actions, in the hope of some monetary reward.

Will's parents, unlike many, had always insisted that he and his brothers and sisters, all six of them, should attend school. This was originally a cottage provided by the bountiful Lady Clifton of Lytham Hall, but in later years, after the building had been replaced by a larger one and then extended, it was to be the place of learning of both Arthur and then Jim Webster. They wore clogs in his day, Will said, both young and old, because they were comfortable and practical and, above all, cheap. Sometimes, on his way home from school, he would need to call at the clogger's cottage to have his clogs fitted with new irons. There he would sit in his stockinged feet, along with his pals, waiting for their clogs to be 'fettled' on the spot. And watching, while they waited, the blacksmith reshoeing horses in the yard next door, or hammering a new iron wheel on to a cart. The blacksmith was also the wheelwright and did both jobs expertly.

It sounded like a different world to Abbie as she sat there listening, forgetting for the moment her worries and the sadness of the last few months. A much more peaceful stable sort of world it sounded, although Will had lived through four wars –

the Crimean, the Boer War, and two World Wars – though not as an active participant. It was incredible to think that in 1914 he had already been too old to enlist. Both his sons had joined up, but, thankfully, both had returned unscathed.

'Aye, I reckon you could do a lot worse than this 'un, Jim,' said his grandfather towards the end of the evening. 'In fact, I doubt if you'd ever do any better.' Abbie noticed the old man close his eye in a wink as he looked at Jim, before turning to smile at her. 'She's a grand lass, this Abbie of yourn.'

She felt herself blushing and was so covered with confusion she was quite unable to reply. It was left to Jim to explain to his grandfather that he and Abbie were just friends, that they had worked together for several months and that was why they were such good mates.

'But that's all we are,' added Abbie eventually, not daring to look at Jim.

'Aye well, if that's what tha wants to think,' replied Will, nodding sagely. 'Anyroad, tha'll coom and see me again, won't tha, lass?' And Abbie promised that she would.

It was a still night with not a breath of wind to stir the trees. A full moon, round and golden, hung low in the sky making the frost-tinged branches of the trees and bushes, and the grass in the fields shine like silver.

They walked in silence for several moments, then Jim, somewhat tentatively, took hold of Abbie's arm. 'I'm sorry if my grandfather embarrassed you,' he said. 'He's so outspoken at times it beggars belief. But we know him and we've got used to it. Take no notice; it's just his way.'

'It's all right; I understand,' replied Abbie. 'I think he's a grand old man. You must be very proud of him.'

'So we are . . . And I suppose it was only natural he should think . . .' Jim drew closer to her, putting his arm very lightly around her shoulders, as they walked along the country lane which led up to the main road. 'Abbie . . . I know it's early days yet, for you, but I would like to get to know you a little better . . . if you know what I mean.'

Abbie looked at the moon, thinking about Peter. She remembered the promise they had made, to think of one another every time they looked at the moon. She would never forget

375

Peter and she would always love him; or the memory of him, she reminded herself, because Peter was no longer here. But life had to go on and Jim was such a very good friend to her. 'Yes . . .' she replied. 'As you say, it's early days, Jim. Maybe . . . in a little while. But give me time . . . please.'

Jim stopped, then very gently he took hold of her shoulders and turned her towards him. He bent and kissed her lips, just once, almost reverently and without passion. 'I won't rush you, Abbie,' he whispered. 'I promise. But . . . I'll always be here. I think you know that, don't you?'

Abbie nodded. She thought she had known that for quite a while.

Chapter 24

Nancy Miller died at the beginning of May, and Abbie, sitting in the middle of the church with her father, was experiencing just as much emotion at the death of this nice little woman as she had at her own mother's death. It was very sad and regrettable and the knowledge of this fact made her feel guilty, but it was, nevertheless, true. She had grieved for Eva, of course, but then the news of Peter's loss, coming so soon afterwards, had driven all other considerations out of her mind. Had she not given herself the chance, she wondered now, to grieve properly for the woman she had always thought to be her mother?

At all events, she knew that Nancy Miller would be mourned far more sincerely and by far more people than Eva Winters, doctor's wife and prominent church worker and committee member though she might have been. And that was what made her sad. Poor Eva. And yet she had meant so well. The Miller family, all six of them, Harold and his son, Billy, and the four girls, Doreen, Vera, Janey and Peggy, all dressed in deepest black, occupied the front pews. There were other relations, too: brothers and sisters of both Nancy and Harold, Abbie guessed, although she had never met any of them. There was a goodly number of friends and neighbours sitting behind the family; more than thirty, Abbie estimated at a quick head count, and it was amongst this number that she and her father were sitting.

They had both been invited to sit with the family, but they had graciously declined, mainly because they were not of the same faith as the Millers and the service was to end with the customary Requiem Mass. The first hymn, 'The King of Love my Shepherd is', was familiar to Abbie as it was a favourite amongst C of E folk, too, but she did not know the second one with its refrain of Ave Marias. All the family, even some quite small children who had come with near relatives, went up to the altar rail to receive the bread and wine from the hands of the priest, filing past the tiny coffin which was completely covered by wreaths and sprays of spring flowers; daffodils, narcissi, tulips, irises and fragrant freesias, an all too poignant reminder of spring amidst the sadness and gloom of the dark cavernous church. Several of the friends who had gathered there partook of the sacrament, but there were just as many who did not.

Abbie and her father once more stayed near the back of the group as they gathered round the grave. Doreen, holding on to her father's arm, looked more wretched than Abbie had ever seen her although she, like her brother and two of her sisters, appeared to be dry-eyed. Janey, the dark vivacious girl of whom Abbie had heard quite a lot when she was at home at Christmas, was the one who was showing her grief most openly. She had been weeping copiously in the church, her sobs punctuating the periods of silence and she was still crying. Her face was deathly pale and blotchy and her eyes were red-rimmed with dark shadows beneath them. She looked far from her usual attractive sparkling self today and Abbie felt sorry for her.

Abbie had agreed to go back to the Millers' home afterwards for a 'cup of tea and a bite to eat', as Doreen had insisted she should. She and her father had gone to the cemetery in the doctor's car and he dropped her off at the house before going on to continue his home visits. A couple of helpful neighbours had been working away in the absence of the family, preparing a simple spread of sandwiches, sausage rolls, cakes and trifles, making sure a cheerful fire was burning in the hearth and that the curtains, which had been drawn at all the windows for several days as a mark of respect, were now pulled back again.

It was a tight squeeze in the little house and the scores of people overflowed from the living room into the kitchen and also into the tiny parlour which was very rarely used, except at Christmas and, recently, as a final resting place for Nancy. It had been the first time Abbie had ever seen a dead person – she had not wanted to see her mother – when Doreen had persuaded her, a couple of days ago, to 'come and have a look at Mam; she looks so peaceful.' Indeed she had, but to Abbie not a bit like the cheerful kindly and very lively little person of her memory.

But now the sunshine flooded once more into the small room, a rather corpulent aunt and uncle filled the two shabby armchairs with children perching on the arms and crouching on the fireside rug; and everywhere there was the sound of chatter and, at times, laughter. Abbie, leaning against the door jamb trying to balance her cup of tea and a plate holding sandwiches and a sausage roll, thought it was all very incongruous. It was supposed to be a funeral, for goodness' sake, not a jolly tea party, but she knew this was always the way of it. Once the weeping was over there had to be an attempt to get back to normal living. Janey had now stopped crying and seemed to be deep in conversation with a middle-aged woman, an aunt, Abbie assumed, both of them sitting at the foot of the stairs.

Doreen came and rescued her in a few moments. 'Hi there. Sorry I've neglected you, Abbie. Goodness, it's like feeding the five thousand with this lot, but we asked 'em all to come back if they wanted to and a lot of 'em did. Anyroad, me Aunt Edna and Mrs Askew from next door seem to be coping OK . . . You can't balance that lot with only two hands. Look here, grab a cake an'a trifle if you want one, then we'll go and sit upstairs in the girls' bedroom. It's a bit more peaceful up there.'

Abbie followed her friend first of all into the main room where there was still an ample spread on the table. 'No trifle, thanks, but I'd love a cake. Those almond tarts look delicious.'

'Made 'em myself, didn't I?' Doreen grinned, looking much more like her old self. 'You can't say I'm just a pretty face now, can you? . . . 'Scuse, please, Janey, Aunt Miriam.' She squeezed her way past her sister and aunt, still sitting on the bottom step, and Abbie did the same. 'Abbie and me are going to have a bit of a chin-wag upstairs. I don't see her very often and she'll be going back tonight, I 'spect.

'You will, won't you?' she asked, flinging open the door of the room where Janey and Peggy slept, Vera and Doreen, also, when they were home on leave.

'Yes, I'll go back to the Moss tonight,' replied Abbie. 'It was good of the Websters to give me the day off, but I mustn't take advantage.' Even though they were regarding her more and more these days as one of the family, she thought, but did not say. 'How about you? When are you going back to Yorkshire?'

Doreen had been home for nearly two weeks already on extended compassionate leave. She had come at once when it was feared her mother would not last very long, and Abbie guessed she would be stopping another couple of days now to see to her father's needs before she returned.

Doreen flopped down on to the bed, causing the springs to creak. She buried her face in her hands for a moment, not speaking, then, as she raised her head and looked at Abbie her friend could see the despair in her eyes. 'I'm not,' she replied flatly.

'You're not what?'

'I'm not going back to Yorkshire. I've written to tell the authorities and I'd already written to . . . to Norman and his parents. It's not like being in one of the armed services, you know, the Land Army. You can leave any time you like.'

'But . . . why? I know your father's on his own now, but he can manage, can't he? There's your Peggy and Janey . . .'

'Yes, Janey,' repeated Doreen. 'That's why. It's our Janey. She's pregnant.'

'She's what?' Abbie had heard perfectly well, but her mind couldn't grasp it at first. 'She's . . . having a baby?'

'Yes, that's what being pregnant means, doesn't it?' said Doreen drily.

'Oh goodness, how awful!'

'Hadn't you noticed? I was sure everyone must've done. She's about five months gone, and showing an' all.'

'No, I can't say I had noticed. I knew she was very upset, but I thought that was because of your mother, naturally.'

'Aye, she's upset all right. Just realising all the trouble she's caused, the little trollop. But what's done's done an' I keep telling her it's no use crying over spilt milk. She's just got to get on with it an' I'll be here to help her. It's the least I can do,' she added as Abbie gave her a quizzical look.

'Why? Can't she get married? I know she's only sixteen, but . . . Who is it? One of the RAF lads she was friendly with?'

'On no, nothing so simple as that, not our Janey.' Doreen gave a bitter snort of laughter. 'An American GI, that's who it was . . . so she says. And he's done a bunk now; she doesn't know where he is. Well, I suppose it isn't fair to say he's done a bunk. He's been posted. It's wartime, isn't it? It happens all the time.'

'And you're left holding the baby? Quite literally. Oh, I say, poor you.' Abbie's plate of sandwiches and cake lay untouched on the dressing-table top and she put her cup of tea, now cold and stewed, to join it. She linked her arm through Doreen's. 'Was there nothing else you could do? Is there ... nothing else?'

Doreen looked at her sharply. 'If you're meaning could she get rid of it, then you can forget it. We're Catholics, y'know.' She sounded quite angry.

'No ... no, of course not,' faltered Abbie. 'I didn't mean that.' Of course she hadn't meant that. She wasn't sure what she *did* mean, except that there were plenty of them in the family and it didn't seem fair that the burden of it all should fall on Doreen. 'But ... what about Vera? And there's Peggy...'

Doreen gave an exasperated sigh. 'Our Peggy's still a child, isn't she? Oh yes, I know she's going on fifteen, but she's quite immature and she's her schooling to do. I promised Mam that I'd make sure she stayed on at school and took her exams, and college an' all, if she wants to. Our Vera's in the ATS; she can't just up and out – she won't, anyroad. And our Billy and me dad can't manage on their own. Hopeless they are when it comes to what they call "women's work". There has to be somebody to stay and look after the house an' all of them, and that somebody has to be me. There's no way round it.'

'But ... what about Norman? You're engaged, aren't you? You've not broken it off?'

'We're supposed to be engaged.' Doreen's voice was expressionless. 'But we'd made no plans. We couldn't with Mam being ill.'

'Did your mother know about Janey?'

'Oh yes, she knew. Our Janey couldn't hide it. She'll be as big as a house side soon. That's another thing that's upsetting her. She thinks it may have made Mam worse, made her go quicker.'

'And do you think it did?'

'I doubt it. Mam was very poorly. She'd have died anyway – your dad will tell you. But I was so mad with our Janey I felt like telling her it was all her fault. And then I couldn't. It wouldn't be fair to her, poor kid, to saddle her with the blame for that on top of everything else.'

'So ... what about you and Norman? Will you be getting married ... sometime?'

Doreen shrugged. 'This year, next year, sometime, never, I suppose. I don't know. I've written to tell him I've to stay here, but I haven't called it off. He might, though, when he hears about it. I can't expect him to wait for ever. Don't worry about me, kid.' Doreen tried to smile, but her eyes were bleak. 'It'll all sort out in the wash, as me mam used to say. Come on, eat yer butties and yer cake. And I'll go and get you some fresh tea.'

Abbie sneaked a look at Janey before she went home. Yes, her condition was quite noticeable when you knew about it. It must have been concealed earlier by her loose-fitting swagger coat. She shook hands with Harold Miller, offering her condolences and wishing him well without making any reference to Janey's predicament or the fact that Doreen had decided to stay at home. The man had gone down more than a little in her estimation. He had always seemed such a capable go-ahead fellow, very much the 'bread winner', seeing to the needs of his family and caring so solicitously for his wife in her illnesses. Now that Nancy had been taken from him he appeared lost and helpless, and Abbie guessed it had been the wife, all along, who had been the driving force behind that family. And now it would be Doreen.

She felt angry on Doreen's behalf and that it was all very unfair. She recalled as she walked back home how, at Christmastime, Doreen had been so full of delight and pride at the thought of one day marrying her Norman, but how she had not said too much for fear of upsetting her friend. Abbie had still been trying to recover from the shock of Peter's death.

Now the boot was on the other foot. Abbie had not told Doreen about her own developing friendship with Jim Webster. They were not yet engaged; after all it was less than a year since Peter was killed, but she was growing to like the young market gardener more and more. It was a liking which she knew could very easily develop into love. A different sort of love than the one she had felt – and still felt – for Peter, but deep friendship such as she and Jim shared was love of a kind . . . wasn't it?

'D-Day has come. Early this morning the Allies began the assault on the north-western face of Hitler's European fortress . . .' Abbie, together with Jim and Mr and Mrs Webster, heard John Snagge's announcement on the radio on the morning of Tuesday, 6 June 1944.

'Thank God for that,' breathed Mr Webster, echoing the thoughts of them all. Preparations for the great day, though they were supposed to be very hush-hush, had been impossible to hide from the general public. Everyone knew that a ten-mile-deep strip of coast, from the Wash to Land's End, had been closed to visitors since April, and all over the south of the country there were tanks and army vehicles and tented camps near the coast. Tension had been running high amongst civilians as well as soldiers. And now, at last, it was here; the beginning of the end was what everyone hoped.

'I should've been there,' remarked Jim. 'I can't tell you how I feel. All those young lads – and not so young 'uns, too – taking part in the biggest venture of the war. And here's me . . .' he slapped impatiently at his wounded leg, 'too bloody useless to be of any help.'

'Nowt o' t'sort!' retorted his mother. 'That's not true, is it, Arthur? Is it, Abbie? You've done your bit. You can't help what happened to you and there's nobody that's blaming you or thinks any the worse of you. So just be thankful and let's have no more of yer daft talk.'

'OK, Mam, OK.' Jim held up an admonitory hand before grinning at Abbie. 'I was only saying . . . but I know how you feel.'

Abbie agreed with Gladys Webster. She was relieved that Jim was not taking part. If he had been, it would mean, of course, that she had never met him, but setting all that aside she was glad he was safely out of it all. She had already lost one young man and she would not wish to go through that trauma again. Her feeling for Jim, steadily growing as the weeks went by, was not the all-consuming passion, the knowledge that she belonged to him completely, that her love for Peter had been. But it was love of a kind, she often told herself, a warm and natural feeling, an enjoyment of his company and the recognition that he was honest and caring and would be entirely faithful to her.

One thing, however, which had upset her quite a lot was knowing that his friendship with Sylvia Cardwell, a friendship Abbie had thought was so promising, had come to nothing; and she felt that she, Abbie, was responsible. Sylvia had, in fact, disappeared from the scene before Abbie and Jim started to go out together quite openly. As long ago as last March she had suddenly decided to join the WAAF and was now stationed in Scotland, only coming home on rare occasions. So there was no need, really, for Abbie to be experiencing any guilt about the break-up. Jim, all along, had assured her that he and Sylvia were just good friends; and she knew he was beginning to care for her, Abbie, very deeply.

Now, on D-Day, Abbie spared a thought for her Aunt Bertha whose son, John, would be taking part in the operation. She prayed he would come through it all safely. Bertha continued to be thrilled with her new-found family. There was even some talk of her going to make her home with them in Bingley when the war came to an end. But, as Bertha kept saying, it was early days yet and there were a lot of things to consider.

Abbie knew that her father was one of these considerations. Bertha had continued to keep house for him after Eva died just as she had before. There was nothing inappropriate about the widower and the elderly spinster living under the same roof. Bertha, in a sense, was like an old family retainer though she was increasingly acquiring her own pattern of life. And Abbie had a suspicion that her father, too, was developing interests of his own. She had noticed that the nurse, Faith Summers, was spending more and more time at the doctor's house, and not just in the surgery and dispensary. She came round occasionally for Sunday tea. Abbie knew also – from Aunt Bertha – that her father had, though only once, taken Faith to see a play at the Grand Theatre; and if the fond way she looked at him and he returned that look were anything to go by ... Aunt Bertha did not need to feel she would be neglecting Cedric Winters should she decide to embark on a new life.

Abbie knew she would have her father's blessing should she agree to marry Jim Webster, as she had almost decided to do. She could not explain what it was that was holding her back, but Jim had promised he would not rush her and he was, indeed, being very patient with her. They had planned, tentatively, to get officially engaged at Christmas – by then it would be well over a year since Peter's death – and then they would marry . . . as soon as the war was over. Unless Jim persuaded her, in the meantime, that there was no point in waiting.

It was an abysmal summer, the one of 1944, with continual cloud and rain, relieved only by the good news from the battle fronts. On 25 August Paris was liberated, followed by Brussels, on 3 September. But the Germans were making a last-ditch attempt to bring the war-weary Britons to their knees. 'Hitler's secret weapon' had been regarded as a joke ever since it was first mentioned in 1939. Now, as the V-1s – nicknamed doodlebugs – began to fall on the southern counties it was soon seen that this was no joke at all. A fresh evacuation of children began, followed by even more when the V-2s began to fall.

Abbie knew, from reading her Land Army magazines, that her WLA comrades in the south of England were, daily and nightly, having to endure this new and insidious danger falling from the skies, whereas up here, on the Fylde Coast, all was peaceful and quiet, and it was difficult to imagine the country was still at war.

As the year drew on, the news, on a personal level, was cheerful. Aunt Bertha's son was safe. They were not sure of his exact whereabouts at the moment, but he had survived Operation Overlord without injury.

And Doreen Miller was, after all, going to be able to marry her Norman. Janey had given birth to a healthy baby boy in September and her Aunt Miriam, coming over from Blackburn to be of assistance at the time of the birth, had decided to stay and keep house for her brother, Harold, and his family.

'I don't know why we didn't think of it before,' said Doreen, when Abbie met her in Jenkinson's café at the end of September.

'Well, to be honest, we did think of it, but the suggestion had to come from her. We didn't like to ask, and she didn't want to push in, but all's well that ends well, as they say. She's a widow and all her kids are off her hands so she's going to move in with us. Couldn't be better, eh, luv?'

'I'm very pleased for you,' said Abbie. 'You must be relieved. But . . . is there room – you know – for your aunt and the new baby as well?' She didn't want to dwell on the fact that the house was very small – Doreen could still be a mite touchy at times – but she imagined the place would be bursting at the seams.

'Oh, they'll manage,' said Doreen cheerfully. 'We've never had much privacy, y'know, not like some I could mention.' Her wry grin tempered the waspish remark. 'I doubt if our Vera'll ever live at home again, same with Billy once he gets away. But Dad does say he'll try for a slightly bigger place; he's got his name down. And I won't be there much longer, of course, if all goes according to plan.'

'So . . . when's the wedding?' asked Abbie. Norman had vowed he would wait for Doreen, however long it took for her to sort things out, and Abbie was delighted for her friend. She deserved all the happiness she could get.

'Early next year, we hope,' said Doreen. 'It'll be here in Blackpool, of course. Aunt Miriam's dying to get going on the arrangements. I say, Abbie, you will be a bridesmaid, won't you?'

'I'd love to be,' replied Abbie. It was something she had always wanted to be as a little girl, but no one had ever asked her. 'But what about your sisters?'

'Oh, I dare say I'll have to have them an' all, some of 'em. But you're special, aren't you? Oh . . . silly me!' Doreen put her hand to her mouth. 'You may not be able to be the chief bridesmaid, with you not being a Catholic, like. But you're still special, aren't you?' There was no mistaking the warmth in Doreen's blue eyes, and Abbie was touched. Yes, their friendship had been special. 'I wouldn't've asked you,' Doreen continued, 'if I didn't know that things are working out for you as well. I didn't want to remind you . . . y'know.' Of Peter, Abbie knew she meant. 'But I 'spect you'll be engaged yourself before long, won't you?'

'Yes . . . at Christmas,' replied Abbie.

If she sounded less than whole-hearted, Doreen did not appear to notice, preoccupied as she was with her own wedding arrangements. Abbie was thinking of the conversation she had had with Jim only the previous night. They had been to the Welcome Inn for a drink and a chat with the friends Jim still kept in touch with, then strolled back, arm in arm, along the country lanes of the Moss. It was a bright moonlit night, the sort that always made Abbie thoughtful and a little melancholy.

Jim, very attuned to her feelings, could not help but notice. 'Penny for them, love,' he said, when she had not spoken for several moments. He stopped in his tracks, taking hold of her arms and looking deeply into her eyes. 'Come on, Abbie, what is it? What's the matter?'

'Nothing,' she replied. Then, realising she was not being completely honest, she went on, 'It's just . . . the moon. Moonlit nights always make me feel sad. Oh, Jim, I'm so sorry, but they always remind me . . .'

'Of Peter?' he said gently.

'Yes, of Peter.' She gave a quiet sigh. 'Oh, Jim, I don't want to hurt you. You've been so good to me and I know how much you care about me. And I care for you, too, I really do. I love you, Jim. But . . . I loved Peter so very much. I really thought he would be the only person I could ever love. And now . . . at times I feel so confused. I feel almost as though I'm betraying his memory. And yet I want to marry you, Jim, please believe me.'

'I do believe you, Abbie,' said Jim, gravely. 'But I also know that you are still in love with Peter and maybe you always will be. I don't mind that . . . so long as you face up to the fact that he is no longer here, my dear. It's just a memory that you are loving. And I'm real. I'm here, Abbie. And I love you so very much.'

'I know you do, Jim. And I'm grateful.'

'It's your love that I want, Abbie, not just your gratitude.' Jim sounded a little hurt and Abbie at once felt sorry. She must not do anything to hurt Jim.

'And you have it, Jim,' she said. 'I can assure you, I do love you.'

387

'Very well, my darling. I believe you.' Jim smiled at her then stooped and kissed her very tenderly. He knew that this girl he cared for so deeply would continue to be in love with the ghost of Peter Horsfall, but that was something he would have to learn to accept. He felt sure, however, that in time the memories would fade and she would grow to love him, Jim, just as much. That was what he had to make himself believe.

And so they were engaged on Christmas Day 1944. Abbie wore the ruby and pearl ring, a family heirloom, which Mrs Webster insisted she should have, with a quiet pride and she began to look forward to the future. She must not look back, she told herself. On no account must she look back. Jim loved her, she loved him, and they were going to be married. Next year. Everyone knew the war would be over next year.

Chapter 25

On the night of 13 February 1945, Bomber Command delivered its most devastating attack ever against the German city of Dresden. Abbie, reading of it in the newspaper, felt unbelievably sad, her thoughts being mainly with the thousands of innocent civilians who must have lost their lives. Peter had been killed after such a raid and though she felt bitter, naturally, against the German pilot who had been instrumental in causing the plane crash, her anger, then as now, was directed mainly against all the machinations of war, its futility and senselessness. Peter, she knew from the rare occasions he had talked about it, had felt the same. He had hated the idea that he was responsible for the death of one innocent – or even not so innocent – German. How sad he would have felt about this vicious bombing raid, though it may have been done with the idea of bringing the war to a more rapid conclusion.

It was the very next day that the letter arrived from Norfolk. Abbie recognised Mrs Horsfall's writing on the envelope so she did not read it at the breakfast table. She decided she would read it in the privacy of her room before she recommenced her morning's work. Lily Horsfall and Abbie wrote to one another occasionally and they had exchanged Christmas cards, but Abbie had not been down to Norfolk to see them since Peter's death, as Lily and Frank had suggested she might. Neither had she told them of her friendship with Jim and their subsequent engagement. It was not that the Horsfalls would not wish her well – she was sure they would – but she had not wanted to upset them.

She took the envelope from her breeches pocket and slit it open. There appeared to be two letters inside, one in a strange handwriting and one in Mrs Horsfall's writing, which she read first. And what she read there, even the first few words, made her gasp out loud in shock. If she had not been sitting on the bed she was sure she would have fallen to the floor. As it was her hands were trembling, her legs felt like jelly and her heart, after giving a jolt – it was a wonder it hadn't stopped altogether – was thumping wildly. And her eyes had filled with tears which she hastily dashed away so as to be able to read the incredible words that faced her.

'My Dear Abbie,' she read. 'I have the most wonderful, unbelievable news for you. Peter is alive ...' And that was where she had, for the moment, stopped reading. No, it was just not possible! He had been reported dead, not just missing in action. Admittedly there had been no body to see, no funeral to attend. It was this that had made Abbie so unwilling to believe, at first, that Peter could really be dead; but there had seemed to be no doubt about the authenticity of the bulletin. But now ... now the news that he was alive was even more impossible to take in than the news of his death had been. She went on reading.

We received a letter recently from someone who is working for the Swiss Red Cross. I have enclosed it for you to read, but I would like you to return it as I have not made a copy, only noted the address to which I have replied. I have sent a photo of Peter as they requested and confirmed the details he gave them about himself, to prove that the young man in the hospital really is our son.

I would like to be able to say, of course, that he is alive and well, but I am afraid that is not the case. Reading between the lines I guess he is still rather poorly and for a long time after the crash he had lost his memory, which is why we heard nothing about him. Anyway, you will see for yourself, dear, when you read the enclosed letter. And Frank and I firmly believe that while there's life there's hope and that our dear son will get well again in time.

The most wonderful news of all is that he is being sent home. I know you will be longing to see him again just as much as we are. As soon as we know any further details I will write to you again. Then you must come down and stay with us and we can perhaps go and visit him together. We are hoping he will be sent to a hospital quite near to our home. I am so excited I can hardly contain myself.

All for now, dear, with love and best wishes from your friend (and future mother-in-law!),

Lily Horsfall.

Feeling more bemused about this than anything she had ever heard in her life, she picked up the second letter. It was from a Swiss Red Cross worker who signed himself Johann Grunder. As the Swiss had maintained their neutrality they were able to work both in German hospitals and in those of the Allies. Abbie knew, in some cases, that they arranged for an interchange of patients, British prisoners held in German hospitals being exchanged for German prisoners who were in hospitals in England. This, it seemed, was what they were trying to arrange now, but first of all they wanted confirmation that the young man in the hospital near Munich really was Peter Horsfall.

The letter was written in faultless, though rather stilted, English. Abbie read that the young man in question had been the only survivor of the plane crash. His identification papers and his disc, too, presumably, had been lost and for a long time they had not known who he was. It did not say, though Abbie guessed, that the plane might have caught fire. She felt herself turn cold at the thought. Goodness knows what horrific injuries Peter might have suffered . . . if, indeed, it was Peter. Could it possibly be? His parents seemed sure, but Abbie was doubtful. She dared not ask herself why she was having doubts; to do so would be to complicate matters even further.

Apart from concussion and the initial loss of memory he had sustained severe injuries, though it did not say exactly what they were. He had told them he was Peter Horsfall, he had served with 102 Squadron based in Norfolk and his home was in Wymondham. Subject to confirmation of this it was possible he would be flown home to England before very long.

He was, virtually, a prisoner of war, being nursed by the Germans under the terms of the Geneva Convention. Abbie knew – which, quite possibly, Lily and Frank Horsfall did not know, or did not choose to know – that prisoners were only exchanged when there was little likelihood of their making a full recovery.

Holding both letters she went out into the grounds to find Jim. He was in the large greenhouse stacking the boxes of cress, a job Abbie knew she should have been helping with. Goodness knew how long she had been in her room, stunned beyond belief at the news she had just read.

'Abbie love, whatever's the matter? You look as though you've seen a ghost.' Jim was full of concern. He put his arms around her, trying to look into her eyes, but she found she could not meet his gaze. A silly, hackneyed expression, that, about seeing a ghost, but it was what people often said when someone looked as though they'd had a shock. But I have seen a ghost, thought Abbie. That's exactly what I've done.

Silently, still without looking at him properly, she handed him the letter. 'Read this, Jim. I'd like you to . . . read it. I'm sorry, but I'm feeling a bit strange. I'll have to go and sit down for a little while.'

She left him and went back into the kitchen. She was on her own. Mr Webster was working at the far end of the garden and she could hear the Hoover whirring away in the upstairs bedrooms and, above its noise, the voice of Mrs Webster raised in song. She sat on a kitchen stool, staring into space, unable to collect her muddled thoughts, not knowing how she felt or, indeed, how she ought to feel about anything. Jim came to find her some ten minutes later and still she had not moved. At the sight of him, his blue-grey eyes so full of concern and tenderness, she felt an upsurge of the affection she had for him coursing right through her. She burst into tears.

'Oh, Jim, whatever am I going to do?' In an instant he was kneeling at her side, his arms about her, cradling her head against his chest, and she felt her arms going round him, too. He was such a comfort to her; always he had been such a good friend and she was so glad now of the reassurance of his loving presence. 'Jim, what shall I do?' She lifted a tear-stained face to him. 'What on earth am I going to do?'

Gently he placed a finger beneath her chin, looking straight into her eyes. 'You must go to him,' he said. 'He will be wanting to see you, Abbie. You must . . . go and see him.'

* * *

Mr and Mrs Webster, of course, had to be told what had happened. They agreed that the least Abbie could do was to go and visit the young man who was – or had been – her fiancé. Abbie noticed, however, that Gladys Webster spoke as though that was now all in the past. She did not say, though it was implied, that Abbie was now engaged to Jim. Arthur Webster said very little but she was aware of his genuine concern, and Jim's anxiety, though he did not speak of it openly, was very apparent. A restraint was developing between them, and Abbie knew that, surprisingly, this was more of Jim's doing than hers. Since that first time when he had taken her in his arms and comforted her he had hardly come near to her at all, not to kiss her or embrace her, not even to hold her hand. Often she had felt like going to him in an attempt to resume the loving relationship they had previously been enjoying, but she had not done so. She knew he cared for her just as much as before, but she knew, also, that he was leaving her alone to make up her own mind about how she felt; about him, about Peter, about . . . everything, and for the life of her she did not know.

If it *is* Peter, she kept saying to herself at first. It might not be . . . But in her heart of hearts she knew that it was, and about two weeks later she received confirmation of the fact. The young man was, indeed, Peter Horsfall, and he was being transferred to a military hospital near Norwich the following week.

'Eeh, it's just like a fairy story,' Aunt Bertha had enthused on hearing about it. 'What a lovely happy ending, just like what happened to me with my Johnnie.'

'It's quite possible that he's very poorly, Aunt Bertha,' Abbie tried to tell her. 'Besides, there's Jim, isn't there? I'm . . . well . . . I got engaged to Jim, didn't I?'

'Oh, he'll let you go,' replied Bertha. 'You don't want to go worrying about that. He's a decent chap, that Jim Webster. He'll not want to stand in your way. He knew all about Peter when you first went to work there, didn't he? Well then . . .'

Abbie's father, though, was much more circumspect, seeming to comprehend all too well the dilemma she was in. 'I can't tell you what to do,' he said to her, 'indeed I would never presume

393

to do so, but I think I can understand a little of what you must be feeling. You're a fair-minded girl and I dare say you're worried that you'll have to let somebody down, aren't you? One or the other of them?' Abbie nodded; that was exactly how she felt. 'But I know you're a compassionate girl as well, capable of very deep feelings, and I could tell when I saw you and Peter together that you loved him very much, as he loved you.'

'Yes, I did . . . I still do,' replied Abbie. 'And I'm so happy, overjoyed, that it really is Peter. I still can't quite believe it. I'm so glad for his parents. But I love Jim as well. He's been very good to me. I know he loves me and I've come to rely on him so much . . . and I'm very fond of him, too. It would be such a blow to him if I had to let him down, although I know he's trying to be fair.'

'So it's a question of what is going to rule, your heart or your head?' Her father smiled a little sadly. 'I would say, when it comes to affairs of the heart, then it's the heart, obviously, that must decide. But I feel I must point out to you something that you may already be aware of.' He paused for a moment. 'That is . . . that Peter may be very seriously ill. I wouldn't want you to build your hopes up, my dear, and then have them shattered. To survive a crash like that, and memory loss . . . well, he may not be in very good shape.'

'I know.' Abbie nodded soberly. 'That is what I have to keep reminding myself. But I have to keep on hoping and praying, Father, that he will make a full recovery. Anyway, it won't be long before I see him for myself . . .'

This conversation took place around mid-March. Abbie had arranged to travel down to Norfolk the following weekend to stay with Mr and Mrs Horsfall and, with them, to go and visit Peter in hospital. This was a requisitioned manor house, similar to the one the WLA had used as a hostel and where Abbie had last been billeted. The hospital was, in fact, not very far from there and about the same distance from the Horsfalls' home.

The pair of them greeted Abbie warmly, but she could tell from their rather less than enthusiastic response when she enquired about Peter that they were not completely happy about his progress. She knew, however, that they were trying to convince themselves, and her, that in the end all would be well.

Abbie realised as they told her of the extent of his injuries that he was, indeed, lucky to be alive. He had sustained both a broken leg and a broken arm which had been set and had healed successfully. He had suffered from burns, too, something Abbie had been dreading to hear.

'We must warn you,' Lily Horsfall told her, 'he looks a bit ... different. They've had to patch up his face, just down the one side, but it's not too bad, is it, Arthur? And it's still our Peter. He was ... he was quite badly burned, you see.' Lily's voice caught in her throat and tears came into her eyes. 'It was mainly his hands and arms that caught it. His poor hands ... I doubt if he'll ever be able to play the organ again. His face was only a little bit burned, thank God, and we can only assume that somebody managed to pull him away from the wreckage before it was a lot worse. It would be one of them, I suppose – a German, I mean – that rescued him. But I've got to admit they took care of him and he's had another operation on his hands since he came home.'

There had been other injuries too. Various small pieces of shrapnel had been removed from his body and his cracked ribs had healed, but he had also suffered severe internal bleeding. He was still complaining of chest pains and though he was allowed to get up for a few hours each day he was always relieved to go back to bed, so the doctor had reported to his parents. He was listless, they said, rather than actively depressed, tending to fall asleep when they were talking to him and not showing any of the vitality or awareness that had been characteristic of the son they had known in former times.

'But it could have been much worse, Lily,' Abbie heard Frank tell his wife, as she was sure he must have told her many times before. 'What about that poor chap in the next bed? Lost his sight,' he explained to Abbie. 'They thought they might've been able to save one eye, his mother was telling us, but in the end it was no use. But there again, like us, she's glad he's alive.'

'He'll pull through, though, Abbie.' Lily nodded emphatically, but there were tears in her eyes and a slight tremor in her voice. 'Frank and me, we're both sure he'll pull through, aren't we, Frank? It stands to reason he's still poorly. He's only been home ten days or so. And he'll buck up no end when he sees you, Abbie love. We told him you were coming and you should've seen the way his eyes lit up, didn't they, Frank?'

'Aye, they did; that's right,' replied Frank. 'It was the only time he showed any spark of interest, when we told him you were coming.'

'But I'm sure he was pleased to see you as well, wasn't he?' said Abbie, feeling a trifle embarrassed. Frank and Lily were such lovely people, not the slightest bit jealous of her, nor had they ever been. All they were concerned about was that their beloved son should be well again.

'Oh yes, he was pleased to see us,' said Lily. 'Of course he was, but like we were saying, he soon gets tired. Anyway, you'll see for yourself tomorrow. I'm expecting no end of an improvement in him when he sees you.'

It was not true to say that she would not have recognised Peter, but he was very different, in outward appearance at least, from the young man she had known and loved so much. It was eighteen months since she had last seen him, when she had moved back to Blackpool, and the time in between had played havoc with his looks. He could never have been called handsome, but loving him as she did she had found his very ordinary features immensely appealing; his rather long nose, his wide mouth with its crooked teeth and his slightly hooded eyes. Now the leanness of his face exaggerated his angular features; his nose looked longer, his mouth wider and his eyes, sunk in deep shadows, more hooded. His left eye was pulled down slightly as that was the side of his face that had required plastic surgery. The skin was red and shiny. But as he gazed at her she was struck again by the bright blueness of his eyes. They glowed now like twin stars, lighting up and transforming his whole face as he smiled at her, and she realised, with a surge of relief, that he was glad to see her. She had feared that he might not be. And she realised, too, in that first moment, that she loved him just as much as ever. All other considerations were swept aside in an instant as she acknowledged, possibly for the first time, that Peter really was alive; he had, by some miracle, been given back to her and they would never need to be apart again.

'Abbie . . . oh, Abbie.' As he spoke her name, opening wide his arms, she noticed that he had lost one, if not two, teeth at the left side. And his left hand was swathed in bandages. Poor Peter. How would he feel if he could never play the piano again? His mother and father stood back as she went over to him, crouching on the floor beside his chair as his arms encircled her. Then he kissed her on the lips, very gently and without passion. 'Oh, Abbie . . . it's wonderful to see you. I thought I'd never . . .' She could hear the slight tremor in his voice and knew he was very close to tears, as she was. His eyes were moist as he held her now at arm's length, looking at her as though he could not believe what he was seeing. 'I thought I'd never see you again. When I came round . . . in that place . . .' He shook his head confusedly.

'Never mind, Peter,' she said. 'I'm here now, aren't I? And you're back home again.' She stood up and pulled a wooden-armed easy chair, like the one Peter was sitting in, towards him. His parents, likewise, drew up chairs so that they were in a sort of semicircle. This room was the day room, with french windows looking out on a garden area. Crocuses and early daffodils were in bloom in the flowerbeds near the window and a line of trees, leafless as yet, round the perimeter of the garden partially obscured the view of the house from the country lane that wound round the estate.

'Not home,' said Peter, shaking his head. 'They won't let me go home. Not yet. They don't say much, though. They won't tell me what's wrong with me, but I know there's something else, apart from this.' He touched his face, then pressed his hands to his chest. 'It still hurts, quite a lot at times.'

'I should jolly well think it does, lad,' said his father. 'After all you've been through. A broken arm and leg and cracked ribs and God knows what else. You're sure to have a few aches and pains, it stands to reason. But you're doing splendidly. And we'll have you back home just as soon as they say the word, don't you worry. He looks well, doesn't he? Don't you think so, Abbie?' And Abbie, lying a little, agreed that he did.

'Where's your engagement ring?' Peter suddenly asked, looking at her ringless hand. She had not known what to do. She could not, quite obviously, wear the ring Jim had given her, but she had felt she could not, in all fairness, wear Peter's ring either; not when she had since become engaged to Jim. 'I thought you'd be wearing it. We're still engaged, aren't we? You're still going to marry me?' The elation in his eyes had vanished now and he just looked confused.

'Of course.' Abbie smiled at him. 'I'm sorry, Peter. I've got used to not wearing it, you see, with working at the market garden. I can't wear it there because it would get all clogged up with soil. It's a very mucky job.' She laughed. 'And besides, I wouldn't want to risk losing it.'

'And besides, you thought I was dead.' Peter's voice was flat, emotionless.

'Well . . . yes . . . for a time I did. But you're not. Oh, Peter, I can't tell you how happy I am that you're not. I couldn't believe it when your mum wrote to me. I wouldn't believe it till I saw you for myself.' He nodded unsmilingly, still looking a trifle puzzled, all his earlier delight at seeing her again seeming to have gone.

'Come on, Lily,' said Frank Horsfall, getting to his feet. 'We'll take a turn round the garden, shall we, and let Peter and Abbie have a bit of time on their own.' He nodded meaningfully at Abbie, touching her arm in a reassuring manner as he passed her chair. 'See you later, love.'

They stopped on their way out to have a word with one of the other patients. Abbie guessed from the unfocused look in his eyes that this was the young man they had told her about, the one who had lost the sight of both his eyes. An older man and woman sitting with him looked like his parents. She did not want to stare, but she was aware that all around them were young men who, like Peter, were casualties of war. The worst cases would be confined to the wards; the ones in here were those who were able to get up for a little while each day, though there was much evidence, even here, of broken limbs, badly scarred faces, some of them much worse than Peter's, and bandaged heads.

'I'd forgotten about the market garden,' Peter said now. 'Let me see . . . you went back to Blackpool, didn't you? Your mother, she was ill . . .'

'She died, Peter,' said Abbie quietly. 'She had a heart attack. Don't you remember?' she added gently.

'I think so. I think I remember now.' He frowned. 'But you

stayed there. Why did you stay? You didn't come back to Norfolk?'

'I couldn't really. I'd done so much chopping and changing, one way and another, I think the WLA might have taken a dim view of it if I'd asked to be moved back again. And then, of course . . .' She stopped, realising she must not go on to say that then she had had news of his death and there would have been no point in moving. 'And then . . . well, I settled down again in Blackpool. My father was very pleased to have me back home, and so I stayed there.'

'But you could come back now, to be near me.' His voice was demanding and a little querulous.

'I don't know, Peter. I'll have to see. Maybe . . .'

'Try, Abbie. You must try. I want you here. I've got to be able to see you.' He leaned towards her, reaching out to grasp her hand; then he gave a sudden wince and she knew that a spasm of pain had gripped him. He crouched forward, clutching at his chest as if in agony.

She went over to him and took hold of his arm. 'Peter . . . what is it? Can I do anything? Go and fetch a nurse?'

'No . . . thanks. I'll be all right in a minute.' Slowly he eased himself back in his chair and she could see that the pain had made his face more ashen. 'It just hits me sometimes. I'm not sure . . . what it is.' She imagined it could still be the pain from his cracked ribs.

'Take it easy, Peter,' she said, squeezing his hand before she sat down again. 'And try not to worry about anything. I'll come down and see you as often as I can, and I'll ask about a transfer.' She could even leave the Land Army, she supposed. Doreen had done so without any difficulty. In an attempt to change the subject she mentioned her friend now.

'You remember Doreen, Peter?' He gave a slight frown. 'You know, my friend, Doreen? The girl who was with me at the Palace when I first met you?'

He looked vacant for a moment, then gave a slow smile. 'Oh yes, I think so. Doreen . . . what about her?'

'Well, she was in the Land Army, like me, but she left. Her mother died and she went back to Blackpool to see to her family. She's working at the aircraft factory now, but she's getting married soon to a young man she met in Yorkshire. The wedding's in a few weeks, at the end of April.' Being Catholics they had to wait till the season of Lent, and then Easter, had passed. 'She's asked me to be a bridesmaid.'

Peter had been staring vacantly into space. Then he closed his eyes and Abbie soon realised she was talking to herself.

'Yes, that's what often happens,' said his mother when they returned a few minutes later. 'We've got used to it, haven't we, Frank?'

Peter opened his eyes on hearing their voices and the four of them chatted for a while, but after fifteen minutes or so he dropped off again. 'We'd better go, I think,' said Lily. 'I'll have a word with the nurse and she can get him back to the ward. He very soon gets tired, poor lad. I'll ask her to tell him we'll be here again tomorrow.'

That was Saturday, and they went to see him again on the Sunday before Abbie started her long journey back to Blackpool. Her mind was in a turmoil. At her first sight of Peter she had known she still loved him as much as ever, changed though he might be in appearance. After visiting him a second time she realised even more that it was not only in outward appearance that he was changed. It had not been apparent at first. She recalled the glow of pure joy in his eyes when he had first seen her, but that initial look of delight had soon passed. Peter, she feared, had become fretful and rather difficult to please and it had been hard to imagine at times that this was the same kind and considerate and so loving person she remembered.

She could not condemn him, though, for his irritability and complaining because she knew he was still in a good deal of pain. At her second visit she had realised he was still very poorly and quite possibly not yet off the danger list. It was almost a year and a half since the crash and he was still in hospital. That very fact spoke for itself. Broken limbs healed fairly quickly and the burns had been dealt with, but there must be other injuries that were keeping him here. Internal damage, maybe, that was taking much longer to heal, and she knew, also, that he was still suffering the aftereffects of concussion and his loss of memory. It was quite possible, even now, that he would not pull through. Lily and Frank had not admitted this; all the time they were trying to remain cheerfully optimistic. Neither had the doctors given such a gloomy prognosis, but Abbie knew that it was so. Her work as a doctor's assistant, though she had never been totally committed to it, had given her some insight into patients' illnesses and their chances of recovery, or otherwise, and she was very disturbed at what she could read in Peter's face. And, though she had tried to push the fact to the back of her mind, she could not overlook that it was very unlikely the German hospital would have released him if they had expected him to recover. She loved him, though. She loved him so very much. But there was Jim, too. What was she going to say to Jim? Oh, dear God, whatever was she to do?

It was late when she arrived back in Blackpool. Her father, as arranged, met her at the station and she stayed with him that night before going back to the market garden the following morning. Cedric said very little, certainly nothing to help her to come to any decision. He nodded gravely and said it was just as he had thought it might be when she told him of the very real doubts she had about Peter's recovery.

'But you must not give up hope,' he assured her. 'He's in very good hands. They will do all they possibly can, and at least he's back in England. They're sure to try harder for one of their own. No . . . I know it's not supposed to make any difference, but it's only human nature, isn't it? Feelings run high in wartime and they'll not want to lose a brave young airman. I can't tell you what to do, though, Abbie, my dear. You know that, don't you?'

Neither did Abbie know what to say to Jim; not yet. He asked her how she had found Peter and she told him she feared he was still quite poorly; that she had not thought so at first, but after the Sunday visit she had not liked the way he looked at all. 'I'm sorry, Jim,' she said. 'I realise that maybe it's not fair to you, but I've promised I'll go and see him again. Next weekend, or the weekend after.'

'It's all right, Abbie. I understand.' He gave her arm a quick squeeze then turned away to continue with his task of cress cutting. But not before the look of compassion and deep understanding – and sadness, too – in his eyes brought the tears

401

to her own. She, too, turned away and went to work in another part of the greenhouse.

Mr and Mrs Webster were as kind and polite to her as ever, though no longer as chatty. There was a constraint between them, between all four of them, that Abbie found impossible to ignore. As soon as she had finished her evening meal on Monday she told them she was going to see her friend, Doreen. In fact she could not wait to get away from there.

It was staying light longer in the evening now and she pedalled furiously, on the second-hand bicycle she had acquired, along the lanes of the Moss towards the Central Drive area. It would be dark by the time she rode back, but she had lights on her bike. The total blackout that had been in force for five years, ever since the start of the war, had been replaced by a 'dim-out' last September; and there was talk that even that would be abolished soon, a sign that the war really was coming to an end.

Doreen and her family were still in the same house; Mr Miller, Aunt Miriam, Janey and baby Michael, Peggy, and Doreen. Billy had now joined the army, determined to 'get some service in' before the war ended, though everyone knew it would not be long. Abbie did not enquire where everyone slept. She guessed Mr Miller slept on a camp bed downstairs, but as Doreen would be moving back to Yorkshire when she married and Janey had her name down for a place of her own it was not necessary now for the family to move.

At all events the two friends found a quiet corner in the small parlour, though it felt chilly with disuse – in all probability it had not been used since Christmas – away from the crying baby and the wireless and Aunt Miriam's ceaseless chatter. Peggy, in need of quietness, too, for the serious studying she was doing, had retreated upstairs.

'How's Peter?' asked Doreen, inevitably.

Abbie told her, as she had told her father and Jim, that he was quite poorly. But she told her friend much, much more. She was worried about him, very worried. She feared he would not get better, that he might, in fact, die. She loved him so much; she could not bear to think that she might lose him again after he had, so miraculously, been given back to her. But she knew that Jim still loved her. And she loved him, too, if fondness and caring and companionship amounted to love. She still had Jim's ring, though she was not, at the moment, wearing either of them. She couldn't possibly tell Peter about Jim ... but how could she possibly think of letting Jim down?

'Oh, Doreen, what on earth am I going to do?' Her cry, at the end of the long story of all her problems and fears, was from the heart.

'You are asking me?' Doreen looked incredulous.

'Well ... sort of, I suppose. I've thought and thought, and I still don't know what to do. What would you do, Doreen?'

'I don't know, luv. I honestly don't know. But then it's not my problem, is it? I've not had to choose between two fellows. I've only got the one, an' I know that I love him an' I'm going to marry him. We've had a few ups and downs, but it's all turned out OK now. He waited for me while I sorted things out down here ... and Peter's waiting for you, isn't he?'

'So is Jim.'

'I know, luv, I know. I can see the problem, really I can, but it's up to you to decide, isn't it? Nobody can make up your mind for you, can they?' There was a few seconds' silence before Doreen spoke again. 'There is one way of looking at it, though, Abbie.' She paused. 'This is hard to say, but you've already said it yourself. Peter ... well, he might not get better. And if he didn't ... well, you'd still have Jim, wouldn't you? He'd still be waiting for you.'

'You mean let Peter think we're going to get married, and then, if he doesn't get better ... Jim will still be there?'

'Something like that. Oh, Abbie luv, I don't know.' Doreen was thoughtful for a moment. Then she said, 'Then look at it this way. Which of 'em would you most want to be with in ten years' time, Peter or Jim? That is, if Peter gets better, and I pray to God he will. I really do remember him in my prayers, Abbie; I've been doing that ever since I heard about it. Which one of 'em is really the love of your life, eh? Peter or Jim? It's up to you to decide, you know. I can't really help you at all.'

Abbie nodded slowly. 'You already have,' she said quietly. 'You've helped me quite a lot ... Now, let's talk about something else, shall we? Tell me about your Janey and baby Michael. And

Peggy. And how's your Billy liking army life?'

Cycling back through the dark lanes Abbie knew exactly what she must do. It had come to her in a flash when she heard Doreen say that Jim would still be waiting for her. She knew Jim would wait . . . as long as it took. She looked up at the moon lighting her path, and she knew that the path of her life was clear to her now.

The next morning she took hold of the ruby and pearl ring in its tiny velvet box and went to find Jim in the large greenhouse. 'I'm sorry, Jim,' she said, handing it to him. 'I can't marry you. I should have told you straight away, when I heard that Peter was still alive, that I couldn't marry you. He needs me, you see. He wants me to go down there to be near him . . . and I've decided it's what I must do. Besides, I know I still love him,' she added quietly, 'and I always will. I'm sorry, Jim. I love you, too, but . . . well, Peter is waiting for me.'

She had known, in an instant, as she listened to Doreen's words that she could not allow Jim to go on waiting for her until he knew she was not going to marry Peter, because Peter was . . . She closed her mind against the final word. She must not give up hope. Peter was going to live. It would not be fair to Jim to keep him waiting. It would, indeed, be very wrong. It would be making him out to be second best whereas Jim deserved so much more than that. He deserved the love and loyalty of a woman who would put him first. And Abbie knew someone who would do just that, if only Jim could come to realise it. As for her, Abbie, it was Peter who deserved her loyalty and devotion. She had fallen in love with him and given herself to him wholly before she ever met Jim. She knew that her love for him was as deep as ever. And of course it was Peter, only Peter that she would want to be with in ten years' time. Not only for ten years, but for ever. She was so glad Doreen had asked her that question. She would go to Peter wearing his ring. She would tell him they would soon be married. Maybe that was the stimulus he needed to make him well again. Or if it should be that they had only a short time together . . . then for that short time she would be his and his alone.

'Thank you, Abbie,' Jim said now. 'Thank you for being

honest with me.' His eyes were sorrowful, but resigned, and she realised it was what he had been waiting to hear her say. 'I knew you would come to that decision in the end. But it had to be your decision, you understand, not mine? I could have said I would let you go – although God knows I don't want to – but that would not have been right. You had to decide for yourself.' He leaned forward and gently kissed her cheek. 'I wish you well, love, you and Peter. I hope you will be very happy together . . . for a long, long time.'

There was no point in hanging around any longer. Abbie wrote a letter of resignation to the War Ag. Committee, then she wrote to Peter and to Mr and Mrs Horsfall to say she would be coming to Norfolk at the end of the week. For good. She had already had an invitation from Peter's parents to make her home with them, but she had been undecided. Now she knew it was what she must do. Peter loved her. Peter needed her.

It was a sombre-looking Mr Horsfall who met her from the train at Norwich station on Saturday afternoon. As she looked at his anxious face and the smile that did not reach his eyes she began to fear the worst.

'What is it?' she asked as he put his arms round her in greeting. 'What's the matter, Mr Horsfall? Peter's . . . not worse, is he?'

He nodded his head. 'He was taken bad last night with severe chest pains and they sent for us. I'm sorry; there wasn't time to let you know.' Abbie hardly dared to listen, so afraid of what she might hear. She breathed again, however, as Mr Horsfall continued. 'They moved him to the local hospital and he's having an emergency operation; in fact, he's in the theatre now. They've discovered there's a piece of shrapnel, see, near to his heart and they're operating to remove it. I think it's serious, Abbie love. They haven't said so. They never do, but I think it could be touch and . . . go.' The words caught in his throat. 'I daren't say that to Lily, though. She's at the hospital now, waiting . . . She won't leave.'

'Come on then,' said Abbie. 'Let's go and find her.'

It was early evening before they were admitted to the side ward where Peter was lying. His eyes were closed and below the white hospital gown Abbie could see his chest was swathed in bandages. He was pale, deathly pale, and seemed to be scarcely breathing.

'Peter . . . ' The nurse touched his arm. 'You've got some visitors. Just a few moments,' she whispered to his parents and Abbie. 'We mustn't tire him. You can come and see him again tomorrow.'

'He's going to be all right, isn't he?' asked Lily fearfully.

'We hope so, Mrs Horsfall,' replied the nurse. 'We . . . think so.'

Slowly Peter opened his eyes. 'Hello, Mum . . . Dad,' he murmured, but his eyes were searching for someone else. Abbie had been hanging back, but now she stepped forward. 'Hello, Peter,' she said softly.

'Abbie . . . Abbie, it's you.' His voice was a little stronger and he tried to lift his head.

'Of course it's me. But you must lie still, Peter.' She reached out a hand to restrain him. 'Don't try to sit up. The nurse will be cross if we disturb you.'

'You're wearing my ring.' Peter's eyes were shining and he raised his hand to take hold of hers.

'Yes . . . that's right. And you have to hurry up and get better. Do you know why?' She smiled at him. 'We've a wedding to plan.'

He grinned back at her and she could see, at that moment, the old Peter, the gauche, somewhat shy AC1 who had first asked her to dance at the Palace ballroom.

'You bet!' he said, and Abbie's heart was so full she felt it might burst with happiness.

There's a Silver Lining

Margaret Thornton

It's 1918, the war is finally over, and Sarah Donnelly and her cousin Nancy are filled with hope for the future. In particular, Sarah eagerly awaits the safe return of her cousin Zachary, whom she has adored since childhood. But when Zachary returns to Blackpool, shattered by the horrors of war, he can barely face his family, let alone reciprocate Sarah's affections.

Refusing to be thwarted by rejection, Sarah throws herself into her job at Donnelly's tea rooms, where her father, the owner of Blackpool's most popular department store, has allowed her to work. Then Sarah spies a run-down building to let near North Shore, and decides to set up in business, running her *own* tea rooms.

Meanwhile, Nancy, forever a dreamer, has chosen to follow in her mother's footsteps on to the stage. But it is not long before her youthful naivety lands her in trouble.

There's a Silver Lining is an evocative saga, steeped in warmth and nostalgia, in which heartache, happiness, tragedy and triumph lie in store for a close-knit Blackpool community.

0 7472 4875 3

HEADLINE

Wishes and Tears

Dee Williams

When a naive encounter at a Coronation party leaves sixteen-year-old Janet Slater pregnant there's no question in her scandalised parents' mind of keeping the baby. Bundled off to a home for unmarried mothers in South London, Janet is about to face the hardest moment of her sheltered life alone. Forced to give her tiny daughter up for adoption, Janet promises her that one day, come what may, she'll find her . . .

In the years that follow it seems, however hard Janet tries, it is a promise that will be impossible to keep. Nonetheless, she builds her life around her secret and Paula, her lost daughter, is never far from her thoughts. And one day, her searching pays off – the road to their longed-for reunion seems clear. But then a new shadow falls across the fragile happiness of both their lives . . .

'A brilliant story, full of surprises' *Woman's Realm*

'Very readable' *Woman's Weekly*

0 7472 6108 3

HEADLINE